IMMORTAL RED

KEITH HUMMEL

Immortal Red

Published by Wheatmark®
2030 East Speedway Boulevard, Suite 106
Tucson, Arizona 85719 USA
www.wheatmark.com

Cover photo: *Turritopsis rubra* 10893102.jpg by Tony Wills is licensed under CC BY-SA 4.0.

ISBN: 979-8-88747-019-1 (paperback)
ISBN: 979-8-88747-020-7 (hardcover)
ISBN: 979-8-88747-021-4 (ebook)
LCCN: 2022922444

Bulk ordering discounts are available through Wheatmark, Inc.
For more information, email orders@wheatmark.com
or call 1-888-934-0888.

2023rev01

"What you seek you shall never find.
For when the gods made man,
They kept immortality for themselves."

—*The Epic of Gilgamesh*

Journal Entry—12 June 2000

Turritopsis dohrnii is one of many species of catalogued yet unstudied Medusozoan jellyfish that inhabit the world's temperate coastal areas. *T. dohrnii*, however, has a unique trait that sets it apart from others of its species: immortality.

When faced with starvation, life-ending trauma, or impending demise due to old-age senescence, *T. dohrnii* can repair itself and emerge a healthy young adult. Unless struck down by a catastrophe sufficient to cause total obliteration, it can undergo this transformation a seemingly endless number of times.

It accomplishes this through transdifferentiation, a process by which one mature cell type becomes a different mature cell type. *T. dohrnii* is capable of near-instantaneous morphing of adult cells of one type into precise clones of irreparably damaged adult cells of another type.

This leads to the obvious question: Might there be human applications?

The specific chemical reactions, enzymes, and coenzymes necessary to initiate this change are complex. While it is true that *T. dohrnii* is many orders removed from an organism as complex as a human being, it is also a fact that even the most complex of living creatures is a composite of organ systems built from a single cell.

PROLOGUE

THE CLIFFSNOTES FOR IMMORTALITY

Friday, 23 April 2004—10:55 p.m.
Coastal North Carolina

The young woman who calls herself Lucy checked the rearview mirror again.

Still there.

The car had been her companion for twenty miles. Despite her ancient Land Rover's slow cruise at forty-five, it did not pass. Never closer than ten car lengths, it vanished on the gentle turns only to reappear on the rare straightaways.

Lucy relaxed her grip on the steering wheel and slowed to take in the nighttime view. To her left, the rising moon painted the shore an iridescent blue, while the strand of low dunes and marsh seemed to radiate rather than reflect the opalescent light. The beach was a luminous smudge separating marsh and ocean. The narrow tarmac road, an accidental pencil line in the sand, ran straight for a quarter mile then darted inland, swallowed by a vast pine forest. Lucy closed her eyes for an instant and savored the sea smells and the gentle kiss of salt air.

Another perfect night in paradise. I could live here forever—if it didn't mean certain death. One mistake in two years—one stupid mistake, and now I have to leave the closest thing I've had to a real home since—

She glanced at the ocean and touched the backpack containing her mother's research papers.

The CliffsNotes for Immortality?

To her right, an onrushing blackness punctuated by occasional flashes of light had swallowed the stars. Too far away for thunder, but it was coming fast. Soon, the approaching cold front would collide with the gentle moisture of the sea breeze, and everything would change. Storms this big—natural or personal—tended to be game changers, brief spasms of cleansing or destruction, or both. By this time tomorrow, her storms would be over.

The car was still dogging her.

Probably just an elderly driver, but enough is enough.

Lucy slowed to thirty-five. The car dipped its lights and pulled out to pass. It drew even and for a moment matched her speed. She caught a glimpse of broad shoulders and short gray hair as the driver slowed and glanced toward the ocean. A second later, the Ford sedan accelerated hard, extinguished its lights, and raced for the forest turn.

What the—

A flash drew her gaze to the strand. Halfway between the road and the ocean, a line of a dozen flashlight beams swung back and forth probing the dune and scrub, their arcs precise and barely intersecting so as not to blind each other.

Lucy lifted her right foot, and the Rover slowed as if braked. Faint tongues of light erupted from the line of flashlights.

They can't be looking for me . . . not yet . . . not out there.

She listened for the telltale pop of gunshot but heard only waves crashing in the distance.

Flash suppressors and silencers—serious stuff. Professionals, running some poor bastard to the ground, firing blind in grid patterns, hoping for a hit.

She glanced at the backpack.

They would kill me for this.

A sudden movement drew her eyes to the road. Fifty feet in front of her, a man, clothes covered in blood, staggered into her path. He stopped, turned an expressionless face toward the headlights, and raised a hand to shield his eyes.

She stabbed the brake pedal. The Rover 88 groaned in protest and pitched forward, its tires searching for grip on the uneven tarmac.

Oh, shit. He's toast.

Lucy's eyes locked on her unwanted prey. Too late, she recalled Tommie Whitefeather's defensive driving instructions.

Avoid target fixation. If you stare at the rock, you will hit the rock. Look where you want to go, not where you don't want to go.

She struck him with a dull thud. He went up and over the hood-mounted spare tire, smacking the windshield like some giant bug.

Oh, God, oh God, oh God . . .

A front brake locked, the Rover dipped, swerved, and stopped, tossing the motionless victim back across the hood and onto the pavement.

Great save, Chloe. Why not just shoot him?

"No," she said, correcting herself aloud. "There is no Chloe. I'm Lucy now."

She doused the headlights but left the engine running.

Standard operating procedure: hide the ride, but don't trust your starter. Half-moon—I can see well enough.

Lucy jumped from the vehicle and approached the motionless figure; his arms and legs were splayed like some giant crushed spider. Blood soaked his clothing.

He's probably dead. Just get in the car and go, or you'll be dead too.

Out on the strand, the flashlights still stabbed the darkness but were angling away from her position.

I can't just leave him. What if he's alive? What if it were me lying there?

She knelt by the crumpled figure.

Remember the survival training, A-B-C: airway, breathing, circulation.

Initial assessment. Blood, lots of blood and unresponsive.

Ignore that. Remember the training, stupid.

The crumpled figure gasped and moaned.

Airway. Thank God. I hate mouth-to-mouth.

Lucy palpated his carotid artery. The pulse was weak and thready but strengthened to a rapid bound in seconds.

Airway, breathing, circulation—at least he's alive. Secondary assessment—gunshot wound in right shoulder, gunshot wound in left thigh, fair amount of ooze, couple of small pumpers.

A few hundred yards away, the shots had stopped. The line of flashlights was stationary, their formerly choreographed beams flicking in all directions.

They haven't spotted us yet, but if they get much closer, the surf won't hide the diesel clatter. I've got to get him in the truck. Grab and go; grab and go.

Elbows locked in the man's armpits, she walked backward, staring at his face as she dragged him to the Rover.

Male, early thirties, athletic build. He might live if we get out of here. Remember your training, Lucy.

Struggling to open the rear cargo door, she placed his arm around her neck and boosted him to a semistanding position facing the vehicle and flopped his upper torso inside. In a squat, she put her shoulder between his legs, came to a standing position, and slid him inside.

Textbook one-man load.

She grabbed two surgical pads and some Bloodstopper from her trauma kit, but the bleeding had stopped. There was no entry or exit track, only the "fresh ground-beef" look of a healing wound.

Damn, no GSW? If those weren't gunshot wounds, where did all the blood come from? And what happened to those pumpers?

Lucy dressed the wounds, placed the Bloodstopper back in the kit, and leaned against the door until the latch made a near-silent click.

What's the plan? The gas station . . . no . . . it's closed. I can put him around back and call 911 on the pay phone. That's anonymous.

Her hand lingered on the door latch.

No, that's like putting out the trash. Tommie will know what to do with him.

Back in the driver's seat, Lucy depressed the clutch, urged the truck into first gear, and stole a look at the wandering flashlights.

Still clueless, so, no headlights. Moonlight only. A quarter-mile dash to the forest. If we're not dead by then . . . piece of cake.

Her leg shaking, she popped the clutch. The Rover bucked once and died.

Damn. Stalled it.

Lucy cranked the starter and pumped the accelerator. The heavy smell of diesel filled the truck.

It's diesel, not gas, stupid.

"Over there, a Jeep or something." A shout from the scrub.

Don't panic. Foot off the accelerator. Hand off the starter. Glow plug— count to twenty.

Cold sweat stung her eyes. She held her breath and listened.

There's no shouting now.

A rustle in the sea grass. The tentative crunch of a boot on gravel.

They're coming.

Lucy punched the starter; the engine coughed once and clattered to life.

More accelerator—less clutch. Don't stall.

She wiped the sweat from her forehead.

Something struck her hard on the left ear. She shook her head and turned to look. A young man with a crew cut, jeans, and a dark T-shirt pressed a pistol to her neck. His mouth was moving, but the roaring in her head made hearing impossible. She struggled to read his lips.

"You have something that belongs to us."

"I don't know what you're talking about." The backpack weighed heavy on her thigh.

The barrel poked harder. "Don't be stupid." He jerked his head toward the motionless figure in the rear of the Rover. "Shut it off. Put both hands on the wheel."

Lucy hesitated. She could just make out the words through the ringing in her ear.

If I pop the clutch—his shot will go wild. Or I could give him the guy and be on my way.

"Don't even think about it." The barrel moved to her temple.

The ringing faded. She heard the click as he thumbed back the hammer followed by the unmistakable cough of two silenced rounds. The pressure on her neck eased. His limp body slid down the door; his pistol clattered to the tarmac. Across the road, a familiar figure, broad shoulders, short-cropped gray hair, camo pants, black T-shirt, and military-style boots cradled a silenced assault rifle. He nodded once and raised his right hand in a two-fingered salute.

"How did you—?" She glanced from the puddled figure on the tarmac to her rescuer. "You were following me." He was the Ukrainian from the coffee shop.

She followed his gaze to the figure in the back of the Rover.

"No. It's him—you were looking for him." She shook her head. "Why?"

There were more shouts and crunches of gravel. A beam of light played across the Rover.

"Get him out of here." He fired several shots toward the advancing flashlights, ran across the road, and disappeared into the trees. Lucy slipped the clutch and accelerated as fast as the aging diesel would allow. Gunfire erupted as she raced for the curve and the safety of the woods. Bullets thudded against the iron bumper and tinked as they penetrated the aluminum body panels. Small bits of asphalt exploded on the road in front and to her left.

Semiautomatic and pistol fire, mostly wild shots.

She glanced at the speedometer.

Forty miles per hour and nearly to the turn. We might live.

Lucy braked for the corner. A brilliant red dot lit up her rearview mirror.

Laser sights.

She jinked right and the glass of her left-side mirror exploded. The thuds and tinks continued as more rounds found the bumper and body.

I'm not hit. The tires aren't hit—still moving. No paralysis-analysis— just drive.

She rounded the corner and the shots stopped. The adrenaline rush faded, and her thoughts turned to Nick, the Prince Charming she'd met on the road only two days ago. What was his place in all this?

Forget Nick. Stick to the plan. Stash the documents. Get back to the house. Talk to Tommie. Grab your stuff, ditch this unwanted passenger, and get out of Dodge.

PART ONE

TICKET TO RIDE

1

I HAD A SHORT LIST. YOU WEREN'T ON IT

Friday, 22 February 1985—5:03 p.m.
Peshawar, Pakistan

It was Nick's first time in Pakistan. It was, in fact, his first solo field assignment—period. At twenty-nine, Nicholas Caedwallan was the youngest operative in the country. His station chief had made it clear—Nick was too new to be sent to an area as sensitive as Afghanistan.

"Why me?" he had asked the station chief in Peshawar. "I've only been here six weeks."

"Can't say—I had a short list. *You* weren't on it."

"So, I wasn't your first choice?"

"Christ, no, Caedwallan, this is way above your skill level."

"Then who—"

The station chief held up a hand to silence him.

"You're flying in with United Nations credentials—a "Save the Antiquities" deal. Some of the more extreme factions in the Afghan government would like to destroy all traces of religious imagery. You are ostensibly there to negotiate on behalf of the UN—that is, to proffer development projects in exchange for preserving historic sites."

"When do I leave?"

"Tonight. Your contact will be Kasra Wahidi. He runs a local tourist operation. Done a lot for us in the last few months—very helpful to your predecessor." The station chief handed him a photograph.

The weathered face smiled back at Nick.

"What happened to my predecessor?"

"Gone missing." The station chief allowed a grin. "Anyway, Kasra will meet you at the airport."

2

WELCOME TO AFGHANISTAN

Friday, 22 February 1985—7:19 p.m.
Russian passenger plane
En route from Peshawar, Pakistan, to Fayzabad, Afghanistan

The beginning of the Fayzabad flight was unremarkable. Nick took his seat and fastened the dry-rotted canvas seat belt as the engines of the aged An-2 Anuschka transport coughed to life. The heater blew cold air and the six passengers faced one another on two rows of what looked like lawn chairs that pulled down from the sides of the fuselage. The balance of available space was filled with boxes and bags of unsecured cargo. An old man sat across from Nick. Multiple layers of bulky wool clothing rounded his thin frame. He wore a threadbare *karakul* cap with earflaps. Head down, he contemplated the frayed ends of his seat belt. There were no buckles.

"*Komakam kan,* help me." His deep-set eyes were a brilliant blue and his weather-tanned face lined with wrinkles that could hide a pencil. The other passengers ignored his pleas. He stared at Nick and held out the two ends. "*Komakam kan?*" His eyes darted from Nick to the naked ends and back again. The plane rolled down the runway, bounced once, and became airborne. The man's body jerked, and he shook the belts at Nick. "*Komakam, komakam, komakam.*"

"*Bashe.*" Nick loosened his belt, leaned forward, and patted the terrified man's shoulder. He repeated one of the few words he knew in Farsi. "It's okay, *bashe.*" The belt was too short to tie around the man's girth but would be fine for Nick's thin frame. They exchanged seats. Nick fastened the frayed seat belt for the man and placed the small cloth suitcase on his lap. The old man smiled and closed his eyes.

Nick stared through the frosty port-side window and shivered.

Who had tapped him for this mission and why?

He knew a bit about the Afghan culture but less than a dozen words in Farsi. Almost anyone in the Peshawar station would be better qualified. The plane banked for final approach into Fayzabad. The old man slept, his head lolling from side to side while the aircraft pitched in the updrafts and downdrafts. Pieces of loose cargo fell around him.

The pilot throttled back the engines and the plane lost altitude. Nick caught a glimpse of the snow-capped Afghan Mountains towering above the transport. As it descended the plane was hit by a violent updraft, followed by an even stronger downward microburst.

The elderly Afghani did not have time to wake up. The updraft compressed him into a short stack of woolen garments. The downdraft lifted him from his seat, breaking the feeble seat belt and propelling him into the solid metal of the unpadded overhead rack. His head was forced onto his right shoulder with a sickening crunch. He tumbled into the aisle and lay motionless. Nick struggled with the knot in his seat belt. The plane smacked the tarmac, gave a savage bounce, and careened side-to-side as the pilot stabbed the foot controls to avoid the worst of the numerous runway craters. Nick freed himself from the belt just as the plane taxied to a halt. He felt for the old man's pulse, although the sightless blue eyes told him all he needed to know. He stood as the other passengers rummaged through the dead man's cloth bag for cash or valuables.

Nick glanced forward. A young Soviet pilot, headphones still in place, stared through the open cockpit door. Their eyes met. The pilot shook his head. Keeping his eyes on Nick, he touched a button on his microphone. The intercom's tinny speaker crackled broken English:

"Welcome to Afghanistan."

3

TRAVELER'S ASSISTANCE

Friday, 22 February 1985—10:23 p.m.
Fayzabad Airport, Afghanistan

The civilian terminal was little more than an unheated barn. Two uni-formed Afghan soldiers watched in silence while a Russian in civilian clothes dumped the contents of Nick's two duffle bags on the floor. After chasing a few items about with his foot, he walked away, leaving Nick to repack his bags.

Nick recognized Kasra immediately from his dossier photo. He gathered his belongings while Kasra pretended not to notice him.

When all other passengers had departed, Kasra approached and with a flourish handed him a card.

Nick took the card and read the inscription.

Fayzabad Tours and Travelers' Assistance
Marco Polo Hotel
Fayzabad, Badakhshan, Afghanistan
Kasra Wahidi, Proprietor

"I see that you are without transportation. May I be of assistance?" Kasra touched first his head and then his chest with his fingertips. This dance was an affectation they would repeat many times over the next few weeks, with Kasra pretending to be the most casual of acquaintances, while serving as Nick's eyes and ears.

Within a month of their first meeting, Kasra provided Nick with his most valuable information to date. The Agency knew the Afghan War was taking a toll on the occupying Russian troops. "The Bear Trap" had become the Soviet equivalent of Viet Nam. Intelligence chatter suggested that maybe "Ivan" had bled enough and might pull out. The Russian's mission was ill-defined, the local populace extremely hostile, and the loss of Soviet life enormous. Against this backdrop, most of the occupying troops just soldiered on. Some, however, carried out bitter reprisals for the deaths of their comrades, while lesser numbers simply walked away. Most of these deserters were common soldiers with little to offer the West. A very few, however, were officers with a working knowledge of Soviet capabilities and intentions.

Local chatter suggested that a special operations Spetsnaz Alpha Group lieutenant colonel had been missing for seventy-two hours. He was both a Signal Corps and a helo pilot. The local *mujahideen* grabbed Russian soldiers whenever possible. The officers were immediately ransomed, while the enlisted were generally beheaded and hung from utility poles. Thus far, there had been no ransom request and no utility pole decorating. Nick's mission was to locate this disaffected officer, and if possible, turn him.

4

COM-PART-MEN-TAL-IZE

Saturday, 23 March 1985—3:17 p.m.
Fayzabad, Afghanistan

Nick picked his way through the maze of street-side vendors. He'd just finished coffee and pastry with a local intermediary who tried to explain why the Taliban had blown up an ancient statue of Buddha after accepting a large cash payment from his UN account. Overhead, a few clouds gathered, while a damp breeze promised an evening storm. Kasra told him it had been one of the wettest winters in memory. Nick had paused to buy a pack of black-market cigarettes when the frantic beeping of a car horn caused him to turn. A taxi, double parked and door open, choked out a rough idle—its driver, breathless, arms flailing, ran toward him.

"Dr. Caedwallan! Where—have—you—been?" Kasra's translation divided the short question into rapid gasps.

The driver of the black Mercedes Kasra had blocked in gave a shrill whistle and gestured to be let out.

Kasra dismissed the driver with a wave and turned back to Nick. "I have been driving the streets for hours looking for you."

"*Eajalu hal 'ant assamm?*" A young Afghan in western garb shouted at Kasra to hurry and asked if he was deaf.

"*Khuk.*" Kasra half-whispered, half-spat the word as he clenched and unclenched his fists.

"Calm down." Nick was astounded to see Kasra so agitated. His usual persona was the epitome of the well-known Afghan penchant for composure and public decorum. "Did you just call that man a pig?" The horn sounded again. Nick glanced toward the driver who tapped his watch with his index finger. Nick started toward the car. "Let me take care of this."

"No." Kasra blocked his path. "Wait." He took a deep breath and exhaled slowly. *"Aeudh bialllah min alshshaytan."* He rubbed his hands together and wiped them over his face. Kasra smiled and ignored the cursing driver long enough to translate for Nick. "I seek refuge with Allah from Satan." His smile broadened. He turned his hands palms up. "The fire is out."

Kasra padded up to the shaking driver. He placed his hand on the man's arm and they exchanged a few words. The driver's expression softened. He nodded once and got into his car. Kasra backed his taxi and signaled the driver with a polite hand gesture. He took the man's parking place.

"What was all that?" Nick stared at his now stone-calm asset. "I was waiting for sparks to fly."

"Anger comes from the devil." Kasra eyed the departing Mercedes. "The devil was created from fire, and fire is extinguished only with water." He presented his palms up as if he had stated the obvious. "So, when you become angry, you make *wudu*." He smiled. "You wash away the fire of your anger."

"I don't see any water."

"Tayammum." Kasra rubbed his hands together as if washing. "Better a dry ablution with dust than to submit to the anger of Satan." He glanced at the lengthening shadows of the buildings. "We can discuss theology later, but now—"

"Ah, yes." Nick grinned. "So what *jinn* was riding your back in the first place."

"A man came to my house late last night." Kasra lowered his voice as two women carrying sacks of groceries passed. "He said he needed immediate travel assistance."

"So, assist him."

He grabbed Nick's shoulder and pulled him into an alley. "He asked me to arrange a meeting," Kasra said. "The man said he must travel tonight. He asked me to bring you. He knew your name, Dr. Caedwallan."

"So?" Nick turned to leave. "Lots of people know my name."

"He was Russian."

"Where?" He took Kasra's forearm and pulled him deeper into the alley. "Where and when?"

"Your associates have set the location. They called me at the hotel. They told me where to take you."

"Where?"

"They told me you would ask, and they told me not to tell you."

"I'm not going anywhere unless—"

"They told me to say one word to you." Kasra wrinkled his face.

"And?"

Kasra pulled a scrap of paper from his pocket and read a single word, "Com-part-men-tal-ize." His pronunciation was slow and deliberate. He tore the paper into small pieces and repeated the word from memory. "Com-part-men-tal-ize," he said, smiling.

That *was* the word—the current authentication code. It had originated minimally at station chief level. Nick received the codes buried in key phrases of fake UN communiqués. It meant follow this instruction precisely and don't ask questions. The code words were changed weekly. This one was fresh yesterday.

"Where do I meet you?" Nick said.

"Our alley spot, by the river," Kasra said. "Just before dark."

He watched Kasra's silhouette shrink, trading the gloom and darkness of the alley for the light and bustle of the marketplace. Nick waited until the wheezing and popping of the car faded into the late afternoon.

He pulled a pack of Murads from his pocket and lit up, coughing at the first inhale. Nick had never smoked a cigarette before his arrival in Fayzabad. Now, he smoked two packs a day of the foul, unfiltered Turkish ovals. He stood in the shadows silently mouthing the words to his favorite Beatles song to measure elapsed time.

And when at last I find you,
your song will fill the air—

"Fat chance." Nick finished the song in his head. "A minute and fifty-six seconds should be long enough." He dropped the cigarette, ground it underfoot, strode to his apartment, and spent the next two hours smoking and reviewing the Russian's dossier.

5

THE THINGS I DO FOR LANGLEY

Saturday, 23 March 1985—7:32 p.m.
Warehouse District, Fayzabad, Afghanistan

They met just before dark in an alley by the Kowcheh River near the bridge to Regional Hospital.

Kasra opened the trunk and gestured to Nick.

"Forget it," Nick said. "I'm not riding in the trunk."

"My friend," Kasra said. "I am taking you to one of the few places near Fayzabad where we can enjoy a drink without scrutiny. If I am seen chauffeuring a westerner to a bar, my use to the resistance will be finished. It will be the end of me."

"Who is going to see us at night in the rain?" Nick said. "I could lie down in the back seat."

Kasra threw up his hands. "I am tired. Maybe I should just go home." He turned and walked toward the driver's door.

Nick examined the dilapidated Toyota Corolla, its trunk held shut by a bungee cord. Kasra could be frustrating at times, but he was a patriot and had proven his worth on many occasions.

Oh, well, one good kick and I could be out of the trunk anyway. The things I do for Langley.

Nick climbed into the trunk. "Okay, but you buy the first round."

"May the Prophet smile on you," Kasra said. "Let's go hunt the bear."

It was cold in the trunk and the right fender well was half-filled with chilled rainwater. The lid flapped against the feeble bungee as Kasra hit every pothole. The worn-out shock absorbers tossed Nick around the trunk like a pea in a can. He used the skills the Agency had taught him to plot the direction of their travel.

Five minutes and no metal joints. We did not cross the bridge. That means either west or south.

The high rate of speed meant they were heading away from city center on the NH-28.

The siren of a slow-moving ambulance confirmed they were heading west on the main road past the Assad Azizi Curative Hospital. The slow push of a long high-speed right turn meant they were now northbound. Ten minutes later, a low-flying jet passed overhead.

Russian AN-72 STOL going to full flaps and increasing engine speed. He's about a mile out and the winds are southerly. That puts us about a mile north of the airport—still on the main road.

The car picked up speed for about five minutes, then braked hard, pitching Nick to the right fender well and soaking his left leg to the knee.

He swore under his breath.

The car bounced along for about thirty seconds and came to a full stop. Another minute passed. The only sound was the ticking of the cooling engine and the rain pattering on the trunk-lid. Nick's wet clothing clung to his leg. The car door opened and closed. He heard the mud suck at Kasra's shoes as he approached.

A blast of cold damp air pummeled him when the trunk lid opened.

Kasra had backed the car into a grove of trees to hide Nick's presence. Kasra made another scan of the empty cars in the parking lot, then extended his hand to help Nick sit up. He looked from Nick's wet clothing to the substantial puddle of water in the fender well. "I am sorry for your discomfort, my friend. Let us drink and find our Russian."

Nick followed Kasra, his wet socks squishing in his shoes.

6

A MUSLIM WITHOUT A BEARD

Saturday, 23 March 1985—8:03 p.m.
Roadhouse just north of Fayzabad

The bar was a two-story concrete-block structure about twenty-four-by-twenty-four feet. Louvered shutters trapped the light behind small windows. An aging Corolla and a nondescript brand-x pick-up truck were parked near the building. In a nearby stand of cedar trees, a jeep-like vehicle, a Russian UAZ 469, wore desert camouflage. A heavy drizzle with a light fog was settling in. The parking area, more dirt than gravel, was a maze of water-filled potholes. A deep one swallowed Nick's foot as they ran for the door.

Nick scanned the room as they stepped inside. The bar, nothing special, was one of a number of unsanctioned, but ignored, establishments catering mostly to foreigners in a country where alcohol was forbidden. For a small fee, government officials turned a blind eye while infidels pickled their livers and much-needed foreign currency flowed into the local economy. Eight opaque wall sconces, most inoperable, cast piteous pools of light. The occasional bare bulb hung from the ceiling. Sparse furnishings included three simple round tables with chairs, a small booth in one corner by a fireplace, and a bar with four stools. The wall behind the bar had two shelves lined with liquor bottles in various states of fill, glasses, and a few plates. A basket of naan bread and two slow cookers offered a hypnotic aroma. The block walls and concrete floors were softened by patterned carpets and tapestries. A small fire struggled in the simple fireplace. Two men with short, well-trimmed beards sat at the bar. They wore the traditional *perahun* shirt, *tunban* pants with wool jackets, and sandals with heavy woolen socks. Their *karakul* caps lay on the bar. The bartender was similarly dressed but had no facial hair and was wearing his *karakul*.

Kasra frowned and mumbled something about "western ways." He turned to Nick. "No offense to you, my friend, but a Muslim without a beard is an insult to the Prophet."

"None taken."

Kasra chose a table in the center of the room. In the booth next to the fireplace, a third patron was sleeping. A thick blanket obscured his face and covered him to his knees. He wore the same *tunban* pants and thick socks with sandals as the men at the bar. His feet dangled over the edge of the bench. He snored loudly. A bottle, a half-empty glass, and a plate of curry sat on the table. From this vantage point, Nick could just see the bare foot of another figure lying under the table on a thick woolen rug. He was mostly covered by a heavy *kaftan*. Next to him, a muddy pair of black boots sat in a small puddle of water.

"Why don't they take a room upstairs?"

"For the price of a bottle and a plate of food, the man on the bench can sleep there," Kasra said.

"And his friend on the floor?" Nick asked.

Kasra craned his neck to see the just visible figure behind the booth's nearly floor-length table covering.

"Ah, he sleeps for free—and in the best spot in the house." Kasra was like a patient schoolmaster. "The fire warms the floor and the table covering keeps the breeze away. Do not worry. He is quite comfortable." Kasra stared with concern as Nick sat shivering and wet.

Let's sit by the fire. Take off your shoes and socks and warm your feet." Kasra pointed to a table near the fire. "Good for the body. Good for the soul."

"Just a beer and some warm food," Nick said.

"Very well." Kasra shrugged and stood. "I will get us a curry with *naan* and a couple of beers, a Kingfisher for you and a Bavaria malt for me." Kasra, a devout Sufi Muslim, sat down again and looked at Nick. "My friend, have I told you about this Bavaria drink and how it differs from so-called non-alcoholic beer?"

"Yes, several times."

"Yes, well," Kasra continued, undeterred. "Nonalcoholic beer is regular beer with *almost* all of the alcohol removed."

Kasra had been helping the Agency for nearly two years. Nick knew he had struggled with his decision. The Russians had come as liberators, but time had proven them to be oppressors. Once more the Afghanis found themselves tyrannized by foreigners. To most Afghanis, the Americans were just another in a long line of infidels waiting for their chance to exploit the country. Most felt that help could only come from fellow Muslims. Chief among them was a Saudi millionaire who used his family fortune to construct tunnels for the insurgency. He cautioned his followers to use, but not trust, the Americans. Kasra had accepted Agency money to feed his family. Because of that, he felt a constant need to prove that he was not just a mercenary but also a true *mujahideen*. Nick understood his feelings. He had been working with Kasra for over a month and was genuinely fond of him. As such, he indulged Kasra's proclamations of faith and patriotism.

"Yes, *doostam*," Nick said. "Continue."

Kasra smiled at being called "my friend" in Farsi. "Nonalcoholic beer still has some alcohol and so it is bad. It is *haram*. Something that starts bad does not become good just because you remove most of the bad. The bad is still there, *doostam*. It just takes longer to come out." Kasra looked directly at Nick. "The Bavaria—it has the same ingredients but is made differently. It has no alcohol, it is *halal*. The brewer started over, he took the same ingredients, but he removed all the bad and kept only the good."

"Are we still talking about beer?" Nick asked.

"I think, *doostam*, Nick, people are not so different. If they are bad, they cannot be good unless they are made over." Kasra stood and stared down at Nick. "You do bad things for what you think are good reasons, and so you are *haram*. You are mostly good, but the bad will grow until it consumes you, *doostam*, body and soul."

"Not a very uplifting prediction," Nick said.

"On the contrary, my friend. I think you are destined for goodness. At your lowest point, the good will come out. The bad will go, and the good Nick will move on. I am sure of it."

"Okay, but how about a little less Sufi mysticism and a little more beer."

"As you wish," Kasra said. "I hope the bartender knows his kitchen better than he knows the *Koran*." He pushed in his chair and headed for the bar.

Nick heard Kasra berating the bartender. He pulled at his beard and pointed at the bartender's hat. The bartender said nothing. The two patrons at the bar stopped their conversation and watched with arms crossed. The stranger in the booth had stopped snoring but did not move.

Kasra leaned in close to the bartender. "Who are you? Where is Mustafa?"

"He is Mustafa's cousin, from Shabar," one of the men at the bar answered.

"Is he mute? Can he not speak? Who is he that he has no beard and will not speak?"

"Mind your tongue, *kufar*. It is *you* who sleeps with dogs." The second man jerked his head toward Nick.

Nick saw Kasra straining to look past the two men. He was staring at something in the storeroom. He stiffened, then turned, and made his way back to the table.

"We must go—*now*. Mustafa is lying on the floor in the storeroom, and he is not sleeping."

The bartender reached under the bar, produced a Tokarev TT-33, and fired a shot that struck Kasra in the back. Kasra's neck arched as he stared wide-eyed at Nick. The bartender fired twice more. The final shot produced an explosion of blood and tissue as it struck the back of Kasra's head. The flimsy table collapsed as Kasra fell across it. Nick dove for the floor, reaching for the ASP-9mm he kept in his shoulder holster. Kasra and the table fell on him, pinning his arm and sending his pistol spinning across the floor. Two more shots cracked against the table. The two patrons moved toward the door, drew revolvers, and fired wildly, missing Nick and the table.

Nick heard the rapid clicking of a silenced automatic weapon from behind him. Bottles shattered. The bar splintered. The bartender seemed to dance before falling to the floor.

The two customers ceased firing and escaped to the parking lot.

"*Predatel, svin'ya,*" the bartender said as he fell.

A Russian—Kasra's instincts had been spot-on.

Nick jerked his head in the direction of the booth.

7

TRUST EACH OTHER OR DIE

Saturday, 23 March 1985—10:23 p.m.
A small café north of Fayzabad

The previously snoring man was on his feet. The barrel of his still-smoking Kiparis OTS-02 submachine gun was pointed at the floor, but his gaze was fixed on Nick. The sleeping man under the table remained motionless. Nick and the gunman stared at each other. Neither spoke.

Nick noted the incongruity. The height of over six feet, clean-shaven face, close-cropped blonde hair, camouflage tunic, and machine gun stood in stark contrast to the baggy *tunban* pants and sandals with socks.

Also, not from around here.

Nick eyed the gunman, rolled Kasra's body, and freed his arm. Kasra's lifeless eyes were fixed on something only he could see.

The gunman watched without speaking as Nick closed Kasra's eyes.

Nick glanced at his pistol less than two feet away.

"*Nyet.*" The gunman's gaze moved to the pistol and then back to Nick. He took four steps and picked up the pistol. "I am sorry for your loss," he said in accented English. "You may see to your comrade, but no sudden moves."

The gunman returned to the booth, sat down, and placed his weapon on the table within easy reach. He pointed two fingers at his eyes and then at Nick to indicate "I'm lookin' at you."

He's been shown a few American movies.

"I saved your life, but I can just as easily take it." Still watching Nick, he reached under the table and retrieved his boots. The Russian stood and removed the baggy *tunban* revealing the camo pants he wore underneath. He sat down, smiled at Nick, and patted the machine gun lying on the table. Eyes on Nick, he removed his sandals, and put on the boots.

"Your friend did not wake up." Nick pointed to the figure under the booth.

"No, sadly, his sleep is permanent. I had to take his life as well as his sandals."

"And stuff him under the table?"

"Yes, while the others were extracting information from Mustafa in the storeroom. He was here to kill us both. I saved your life twice. I think you owe me double."

In the parking lot, a vehicle started, and gravel crunched as it sped away.

"But now, Nick Caedwallan, CIA, we must go." He smiled and continued in English. "I'm afraid the legendary Afghan hospitality is about to grow thin."

Nick shot back. "Okay, Vasily Konovalov, Spetsnaz Alpha Group, you have the gun, you set the rules."

I have a dossier on you, as well.

Nick and Vasily stepped into darkness. The fleeing patrons had shot out the single pole lamp. The cold drizzle had been replaced by an even colder mist. The waxing quarter moon did little to help visibility. The pickup truck was gone.

"*Chyort.* Shit." Vasily pointed to the open hood of the Toyota. "They have taken the spark plug wires. We are screwed."

"Maybe not." Nick sprinted toward the clump of cedars concealing the Russian 4WD.

"What?" Vasily followed, squinting into the opaque mist.

When they reached the UAZ, the hood was shut, covered with undisturbed condensation.

"They missed the bartender's *bobik*." Vasily used the Russian nickname for the small vehicle. He opened the door and placed the submachine gun in the passenger footwell.

Vasily reached inside his jacket and retrieved Nick's pistol and examined it without speaking.

This is it. Nick thought for the second time tonight.

"Just do it," Nick said.

"Relax, CIA." Vasily flipped the pistol and presented it to Nick, grip-first, the barrel pointing toward himself. "I think, from this point forward, we must trust each other or die." He pulled the choke, reached behind the dash, and fumbled with a few wires. The engine sprang to life, popping and spitting.

"Universal key," Vasily said with a smile. The engine smoothed as he eased the choke in. "Let's go." He sped down the gravel drive, sliding to a halt just short of the main highway.

"Turn south into town," Nick said. "There's a safe house. I can get us to Peshawar tomorrow."

Vasily shook his head. "There is no safe house." He released the clutch and pulled forward, looking north and south for traffic. "They knew we were coming. You have a leak at best and a mole at worst. Do you not understand? That was an ambush back there."

"It could have been on your end," Nick protested

"No one on my end knew we would be here," Vasily said. "The CIA knew you would be here." He wiped the fog from the windshield with his forearm. "We have to get ourselves out."

"So, we do what—drive to Pakistan?"

"No, comrade. I have prepared for this eventuality." Vasily turned north. "I will save your ass again, and you, hopefully, will save mine."

"And exactly why did you save my life?" Nick watched through the rear window as the mist swallowed a passing car.

"He was going to shoot you while you ate," Vasily said. "It offended my sense of decency." He shrugged. "Besides, now you owe me, and you will get me to the West."

"What makes you think that?"

"Because you Americans are very sentimental," Vasily said. "But mostly because you are CIA and I am an intelligence officer with more information, I think, than *Encyclopedia Britannica*." He offered Nick a drink from his flask.

"*Stoli*?" Nick took the flask.

"God, no. Johnny Walker Black." Vasily turned east into a dense forest of pine, cedar, and a few birches. He eased the UAZ into four-wheel-drive mode.

"Why did you do it?" Nick asked.

"Do what?" Vasily took a long drink from the flask.

"Why did you walk away? As a Spetsnaz colonel, you enjoy privileges the average Russian doesn't even—"

"Ukrainian."

"What?"

"I am not Russian—I am Ukrainian." Vasily stopped the truck and stared at Nick. "The Russians regard us as subhuman."

"Then how did you—?"

"My uncle was Rear Admiral Vladimir Konstantinovich Konovalov, the most decorated Ukrainian of the Great Patriotic War." Vasily raised his flask in salute. "Hero of the Soviet Union, Order of Lenin three times." He paused and held up three fingers. "Order of Ushakov—"

"Of course," Nick said. "I thought the name was familiar when I read your dossier. You are—"

"I am—I *was*—a Russian puppet." Vasily interrupted. "My success supported the illusion of equality. The Russians starved us. They suppressed our language and our culture." He paused for another drink. "For five years I have watched them do the same to Afghanistan."

"You can do a lot to help the Afghans," Nick said.

"The Kremlin grows weary of the Afghan struggle. It is bad for their image. Too many body bags and limbless soldiers. Perhaps if I tell what

I know, I can hasten their departure." Vasily urged the truck forward again. "My uncle did what he did for the Ukraine, not for the Russians. As bad as the Russians were, the Germans were worse. He was not a Russian lapdog, and now, neither am I."

They rode in silence until a downed tree blocked their path. "We walk from here." Vasily shut off the engine and took another drink from his flask. "Antifreeze," he said, winking. "It's a bit of a hike." He handed Nick the flask and opened the door. There was a crunch and then a sucking sound as his boots penetrated the thin crust of ice and sank in the mud.

Nick drained the small amount of remaining liquor and got out. "Now what?" He returned the flask to Vasily.

The Ukrainian shook the empty flask, sighed, and placed it in his pocket.

"This way." He nodded east. "And no talking."

After several hours of trudging through ankle-deep mud, Nick asked, "Where are we going?" He still wasn't convinced he wasn't being set up.

"Patience, CIA," Vasily said. "We have arrived."

8

UNTIL WE RUN OUT OF FUEL,
OR SOMEONE SHOOTS US DOWN

Sunday, 24 March 1985—2:16 a.m.
Several hours north of Fayzabad, Afghanistan

The towering conifers yielded to an expanse of brown grass and frozen mud. The wind in the trees muttered an unintelligible warning. The field, dotted with patches of melting snow, widened and sloped to meet the rain-swollen Kowcheh River. Near the entrance to the clearing, a camouflage net hung like a spider web. Vasily lifted the edge. Under the net, trapped like some giant fly, was an ancient Soviet Mi-1 Hare helicopter.

"How did you—?"

"A symbolic gift to the Afghan forces in 1979. It had not flown since the day it arrived." Vasily patted the fuselage. "I have been working on it for months. It flies now."

"How did you get it out here?"

"My mechanic, another Ukrainian—we fixed it. He met me here. We covered it."

"Where is he?"

"Dead, I suspect—tortured and shot by our local KGB."

"Do you think he talked?"

"Do you see any KGB?" Vasily fetched two large knives from the helicopter. He flipped one, presenting the grip to Nick. "Cut now." He slashed at the net. "Talk later."

The cloud-shrouded moon struggled against a cold mist. Visibility was a quarter mile at best. The hiding place was well chosen. The Hare sat at the tip of the field, its nose facing the river for an easy lift-off. The helo wore a fresh seasonally adjusted paint scheme—olive drab mingled with dark khaki for the fallow fields, a little spruce green for the occasional clump of conifers, and a smattering of white for the patches of snow still dotting the mountain passes. Nick shivered in his wet clothes as they finished removing the camouflage netting.

"I'm no Picasso, but it should do," Vasily said.

"What's the plan?"

"Strap in, put your helmet on, and plug in." Vasily manipulated a few switches and the Ivchenko radial engine sprang to life. He scanned the gauges and ran up the engine. Satisfied, he returned the engine to a fast idle and engaged the transmission. The rotors swung slowly at first, the tips gradually rising. The helo rocked from side to side as Vasily made his final fuel and blade-pitch adjustments.

A flip of the com-switch and Vasily's voice was in his head. "We go now?"

Nick gave a thumbs up. The Hare lifted a few feet and moved forward in a slight nose-down attitude. Vasily applied power. They arced above the river and headed due east at five hundred feet above ground level. Even at a modest seventy knots, the pitching of the helo made Nick ill. He held his hand over his mouth and swallowed hard.

"First helo flight?" Vasily's eyes narrowed as he watched Nick.

"Of course not." Nick had flown three times at "The Farm," as the Agency called its Williamsburg, Virginia, training center. He had puked in his gloves every time.

"Then don't squeeze so hard," Vasily said, smiling. "You'll break the seat."

"Screw you!" Nick kept his grip on the seat.

"Staying below five hundred AGL should avoid radar contact," Vasily said, his voice calm. "We'll pass north of Fayzabad, swing south, and find the road to Zebak. We stay clear of the road but follow the pass to here." He held out a map. "Navigate. It will give you something to do." A pencil line ran from their initial location to a red X south of Zebak.

Nick released his grip and took the map. "What's here?" He pointed to the X.

"Fuel and hydraulic fluid I placed last week. It's one hundred twenty-five kilometers by air to Zebak. Fifteen kilometers south, the road ends. I have placed some supplies just south of there. No roads, no eyes. We stop just long enough to top off the fuel and the hydraulics."

"Hydraulics?"

"The seals leak a bit." Vasily glanced aft and overhead.

Nick followed Vasily's gaze to a steady drip of hydraulic fluid from the transmission housing. "Ah, yes," he said. "And then?"

"Five kilometers south, the road picks up again. Roughly a hundred kilometers southwest we'll spot the Sanglich River on our left. Twelve kilometers east is Pakistan."

"And *then*?" Nick pressed.

"And then, comrade, we fly until we run out of fuel, or someone shoots us down."

"Good plan."

9

SO, CIA, TELL ME—HOW DID YOU GET TO BE A JAMES BOND KILLER SPY?

Sunday, 24 March 1985—4:47 a.m.
Helicopter, sixteen kilometers north of Zebak, Afghanistan

At five hundred feet, the scenery flashed by at a dizzying pace, a blur of dark green trees and the occasional patch of snow.

I'm going to die.

Nick fought an intense wave of vertigo as the helicopter bobbed and weaved with the changing terrain. On the right side, about five kilometers to the west, a small unnamed settlement lit up the inky darkness. He scanned the map with a red-beam penlight to preserve his night vision.

"Watch for lights—any lights," Vasily said. "The only electricity out here is from generators."

"So?"

"The only people with generators are drug lords, Russian military, and *mujahideen*. Any of whom can shoot us down."

"Nice neighborhood."

"*Da,*" Vasily said. "But I hear the school system is not so good." He adjusted the trim on the rotor blades and dropped the nose for better visibility. "So, CIA, tell me—how did you get to be a James Bond killer spy?"

10

IT'S THE SURNAME THAT SET THE TONE

Sunday, 24 March 1985—4:51 a.m.
Helicopter, thirteen kilometers north of Zebek, Afghanistan

Nick took a deep breath. They were going to die. This might be his last chance to be honest with himself.

"First, I never wanted to be a spy. I have a PhD in ancient history and archaeology. I just want my life back." Nick blew out his breath.

"*Da.*" Vasily fiddled with the altimeter. "But to do that you must understand how you got here."

"I know how I got here. I plan to be out in twelve months."

"*Da.*" Vasily swept the cockpit with his hand. "But this is our reality. Let us make a map so you can find your way back."

Nick hesitated.

Vasily glanced at him and nodded encouragement.

"When I was eighteen months old, the nuns found me wandering in the courtyard of St. Joseph's Convent in Milwaukee," Nick said. "I grew up in a dozen foster homes—a new one every few months."

"Why so many?"

"I was a difficult child." Nick felt himself relaxing. "The nuns marked me as bad from day one."

"Why that?" Vasily asked.

"The nun who found me was Sister Hildegard," Nick said.

"As in Hildegard, the Seer?"

Nick nodded. "Mother Superior and the other nuns felt she had the gift of prophesy. They gave her a lot of latitude." Nick's chest tightened. "She saw something that scared her, and she named me accordingly."

"Nicholas?"

"After Nicholas of Myra, the patron saint of scholars," Nick said.

"And he's Father Christmas," Vasily said. "That sounds pretty benign."

"It's the surname that set the tone," Nick said.

11

AND SO, ARE YOU REMORSEFUL?

Sunday, 24 March 1985—4:55 a.m.
Helicopter, ten kilometers north of Zebek, Afghanistan

Nick scanned the inky blackness for a hint of light.

"She named me Caedwallan, after St. Caedwallan of Wessex."

"Who the hell is St. Caedwallan?" Vasily asked.

"You got the hell part right." Nick grabbed the seat as Vasily corrected for a downdraft. "He's the patron saint of serial killers."

"There's a patron saint for serial killers?"

"Yes. Caedwallan was a king who expanded his influence by murdering his way across Saxony in the seventh century, eventually becoming king of Wales. After being wounded in battle, he became very remorseful and abdicated his throne. He went to Rome and was baptized by the pope. He died ten days later, still wearing his white baptismal robes."

"And that made him a saint?"

"The Church said the wounds were mortal and should have killed him. He survived to abdicate his throne and become a new man. The bar was low."

"And so, are you remorseful?" Vasily asked.

"Not at this time," Nick said. "I'm still in the 'extending my influence' phase."

"So, why the foster home problem?"

"For the same reason the Agency recruited me," Nick said. "I adapt. I make things up."

"You mean you lie?" Vasily snorted.

"I prefer to call it reality augmentation. As an orphan, I grew up with no identity, and so I would make one up—sometimes two or three a week—a new name, a new address, a new story. The foster parents would get tired of it and send me back to the nuns."

"How did that make you feel?"

"People handle loneliness in different ways. I read books—books on everything, two or three books a week from the time I was six until I graduated from high school," Nick said. "And I studied people—on the street, in malls, at the home until I could predict how any person would react in a given scenario. I learned situation management."

"What's that?"

"At the outset of any situation or relationship, there are many possible outcomes. I determine which one best serves my interest and make it happen with no regard for collateral damage."

"That must make friendships difficult."

"I have no friends, only assets," Nick said. "The closest thing I had to a friend is back at that bar with his head blown off."

"Again, I am sorry for your loss. I, too, have lost a friend."

"An asset—Kasra was an asset," Nick said. "You have friends. I have assets. It's much cleaner."

"And the CIA?"

"I had just finished my doctoral studies in ancient history and archaeology at the University of Leicester," Nick said. "I was flying home from the U.K. to D.C." He paused. "Do you really want to hear this crap?"

"What else is there to do?"

Nick paused, pretending to scan for lights.

"Come on, let's have it," Vasily said.

"See? You're being manipulated already," Nick said. "Anyway, I had convinced the flight attendant that I was gay. I told her that I was receiving an unwanted sermon on the evils of homosexuality from the Jesuit priest sitting next to me, resulting in my relocation to the only open seat, which I had already noted was in first class—and a miserable seven hours for the priest while the stewardess berated him for his intolerance."

"Cold."

"Just situation management." Nick smiled. "More?"

"Da."

"As you wish." Nick took a deep breath. "I had just convinced my new seat mate that I was a neurosurgeon returning home to Iowa City after teaching a new laser technique to surgical residents at the Royal College.

"Impressive."

"Yes, considering he was a fellow in neurology from Georgetown. The passenger across the aisle took great interest in my presentation. She flashed an ID for the flight attendant and switched seats with the neurologist. She explained that she had observed my performance with the flight attendant and had overheard me in the departure lounge describing in German my career as the chief pipe organist at St. Hedwig's Cathedral on the Bebelplatz in Berlin."

Vasily laughed out loud. "How will I know if you're telling the truth?"

"I'll tell you I'm speaking *ex cathedra.*" Nick flashed a half grin.

"Flimsy."

"Anyway," Nick continued. "To cut to the chase."

"What?"

"Sorry. To shorten it up. She was CIA."

"And your psychopathic tendencies made you a perfect fit?"

"No, I think they saw my archaeology creds as my passport to anywhere. The Agency shrinks concluded my 'adaptive' abilities were a result of nurture not nature and just icing on the cake."

"Ah, there were no openings for a politician, so they made you a spy?"

"Something like that. Anyway, three months, eight interviews, and four polygraphs later, the Agency offered to repay my six-figure education loan in exchange for a two-year commitment. Four months later, I was training at The Farm in Virginia. Now, I'm here with you, about to die."

12

AT LEAST WE DIE ON A FIRST-NAME BASIS

Sunday, 24 March 1985—5:02 a.m.
Helicopter, five kilometers north of Zebak, Afghanistan

"Zebak, ahead and portside," Vasily said. "A few scattered lights—should be okay."

"How about you, any regrets about leaving?" Nick said.

"No regrets, only concerns." Vasily scanned the gauges. "I have family. I fear repercussions. I am hoping for some measure of protection for them."

A blinding light illuminated the windscreen.

The helo flashed by the light at 110 knots and five hundred feet of altitude.

"Searchlight on a truck." Nick banged his helmet on the side window as he strained to look back. "And muzzle flashes."

"*Govno,*" Vasily swore. "We've been made. The fuel is okay, but the hydraulics are low. If we don't stop, we crash in thirty minutes. If we do stop . . . well, what do you think, Nick?"

"Your call, Vasily." Nick was surprised that he was no longer scared.

"We go for it." Vasily lowered the nose a few degrees and increased the forward airspeed. "At least we die on a first-name basis." A low-pitched hum was now audible from the transmission.

"The dripping has slowed." Nick gave a thumbs-up.

Vasily shook his head. "That's because it's going dry, CIA genius."

The road ended, a narrow mountain pass made a sweeping left turn, gaining altitude. The ground was now totally snow-covered—the river below frozen. The humming of the transmission grew louder, and the dripping had totally ceased.

Vasily pitched the helo hard right and a broad snowfield opened in front of them. The mountain peak loomed ahead, jutting above the limited field of vision afforded by the windscreen.

"First the bad news," Vasily said. "The service altitude of this bird is one thousand feet less than the ridge we must clear."

"The good news?"

"We have a thirty-knot tail wind. We will approach at maximum speed, close to the surface. The windward updraft should carry us up and over."

"On the leeward side?" Nick gripped the seat again.

"The downdraft will most certainly cause us to crash, especially with the failing transmission."

A tongue of fire flashed by the passenger-side windscreen and struck the mountainside. An explosion of ice and rock pummeled the helicopter.

"A missile," Vasily shouted in the com. "There must be a Hind on our tail."

The helo's transmission was roaring now, but Vasily kept full power, skimming the snowpack and climbing at a forty-five-degree angle. The airspeed dropped:

Ninety knots.

Eighty.

Seventy.

Nick could see the navigation lights of the Hind attack helo standing off about a quarter mile. They weren't wasting another missile. They were waiting for the mountain to make the kill for them.

Sixty knots—the transmission was roaring and flopping in the housing now. The helo was approaching stall speed, bucking violently. The craft shot over the crest and continued upward for another fifty feet.

"We made it!" Nick shouted. "Pakistan!"

The transmission seized and the helo plunged in the downdraft. Vasily auto rotated the craft in an attempt to slow the descent. With the rotor seized, the helo spun like a tilt-o-whirl carnival ride. Nick was stunned by the slow-motion quality of the impact. The fresh snow puffed in a silent explosion, muffling the sound of the crash. But the absence of sound was deceptive. The impact crumpled the helo's floor and forward bulkhead, showering debris and tossing him about the cabin as his seat was ripped from its anchor points. The Hare came to rest on a large flat plain, its fuselage canted to the pilot's side at a forty-five-degree angle. There was silence except for the ticking of the cooling engine and transmission.

Nick tested his limbs one by one. His helmet was off, blood from a cut on his forehead trickled into his right eye. He couldn't feel his left arm, but his fingers seemed to move okay. He wiggled the toes of both feet. His right arm functioned without difficulty.

Well, at least everything is still hooked up.

The crash had been a painful experience, but there was no fire.

"We're alive," Nick said, still checking out his body parts.

"I'm stuck," Vasily said.

Nick glanced to his left. Vasily was still in his seat, a section of forward bulkhead pinned him against the fuselage.

"Hang on, I'll find something to wedge it back."

"Wait—listen." Vasily held up a finger.

Rotors beat the frigid mountain air. The pitch changed as they grew closer.

"Out, out, out." Vasily pushed Nick toward the door. There was an explosion thirty yards ahead. Bullets ripped the fuselage, shattering the remnants of the Plexiglas wind screen. The Hind roared overhead. Smoke began to fill the cockpit.

"Go, go," Vasily shouted. "I'm trapped. They will be making another pass to finish us. Get out."

"Not without you." Nick lay on his back and kicked at the soft aluminum of the bulkhead with his heel. After several kicks, it yielded, and Vasily pulled free. They climbed through the hatch and tumbled into the snowpack. Snow-blind, they half-ran, half-rolled away from the smoking craft.

The Hind approached again. Nick squinted scanning left and right—a few rocks, too small to provide cover, no trees, and no place to run.

I should have taken the teaching job.

13

CAN YOU DRIVE A CAR?

Sunday, 24 March 1985—6:07 a.m.
Mountaintop snowfield, Pakistan

Nick and Vasily dove into a drift and waited for the inevitable strafing. The Hind broke off short of firing range, veered west, and climbed to clear the ridge separating them from Afghanistan. An explosion erupted just below the peak. Looking east, Nick saw two Apache gunships in hover mode near their position. A third helo had fired on the Hind and was closing in on their position.

The three settled in a plume of snow. A half-dozen figures in white parkas fanned out and approached, MP-5 machine guns pointed at the ground. A short figure with no weapon led the way.

Nick and Vasily got to their feet.

"We thought that was you." The unarmed man lowered his parka hood. "AWACS picked you up halfway between Fayzabad and Zebak, but we weren't sure until all hell broke loose. We were biting our nails waiting for you to clear the ridge."

"We could have used a little help back there." Nick jerked his head in the direction of the ridge and Afghanistan. "You could have taken out the Hind."

The little man's eyes narrowed. "We had to wait until you cleared the border."

"We do cross-border interventions all the time," Nick said.

"You've exceeded my expectations, Caedwallan." The short man clenched his jaw. "Don't make me regret my choice."

"*Your* choice." Nick raised his jaw. "So, *you're* the reason I got this assignment?"

"I'm the reason you're in Afghanistan, period." The short man dismissed him with a wave and turned to Vasily. "Vasily Konovalov, Lt. Col. Spetsnaz Alpha Group." He glanced at Nick. "And Nick Caedwallan, field operative, *formerly* of Fayzabad station, I welcome you to Pakistan." He pulled off his glove and extended his hand. "I am Basiliskoi Orlov, CIA station chief, Karachi."

"You are Russian." Vasily kept his hand by his side.

"Yes, and you are Ukrainian." His smile faded. "But I can find a use for you anyway." He lowered his hand. "Can you drive a car?"

PART TWO

DO YOU WANT TO KNOW A SECRET?

PROLOGUE

PART TWO

Thursday, 11 June 2000—5:11 p.m.
Coastal Shallows, Cape Fear, North Carolina

Chloe Spencer stared through her fogged facemask and listened to the gentle whooshing of breath in her snorkel. Her arms moved back and forth in small arcs; an occasional kick of the flippers maintained her position in the nearly imperceptible tide.

Two weeks earlier, her mother, Dr. Karen Spencer, a marine biologist, had been drawn to a rippling veil of color just beyond the breakers. Last night, her mother had promised her the "discovery of a lifetime."

At five feet, the "discovery" was a rhythmically undulating pink cloud. Close in, the cloud became a colony of dime-sized creatures with bright red stomachs. But it was not the red stomachs that caught her attention.

Chloe watched as a few of the jellyfish sank to the seabed. Some had shattered domes and missing tentacles, some were shrunken and malnourished, and still others—their coats dull and stomachs pale—simply looked old and tired. All had one thing in common; they were obviously dying. As these unfortunates descended, an equal number—their coats shiny and stomachs crimson—raced for the surface to join the colony's gentle dance.

They paddled closer. Karen removed a small glass-collecting device from her belt and collected some samples. She tapped Chloe's shoulder and pointed upward. They broke the surface, spat out their snorkels, and treaded water.

"Mom, what did I just see—?" Chloe slid her face mask to her forehead.

"The impossible?" Karen raised the small collecting vessel above her head. "Probably—but I can't be sure until I test my hypothesis in the lab and discuss it with—"

"Whoa, slow down. You should consider limiting those discussions, Mom."

"Why?" Karen repositioned her face mask. "This could be earth-shaking! Wound healing. Organ regeneration. Maybe even—"

"Exactly why you need to be smart about this. Not everyone shakes the world in a positive way."

Karen mouthed the snorkel and made for the beach.

Chloe had a bad feeling. Her mother had a Pollyanna-like tendency to see the best in everyone and an unshakable belief that science could right the world if just given a chance.

Chloe, on the other hand, as a cultural anthropologist, was all too familiar with the historical precedent of man's penchant to use scientific discoveries to wreak havoc on the planet or its residents. Sometimes both. The sound of an ambulance keening in the distance only heightened her anxiety. Swimming in her mother's wake, she had chills despite the warm waters.

14

FOR YOU OR FOR ME?

Thursday, 19 April 2000—10:25 a.m.
Georgetown University campus, Washington, D.C.

Dr. Ted Spencer, breve latte in hand, deftly navigated the between-class throng of Georgetown undergrads while replaying Basil Orlov's brief but hopefully life-changing, invitation in his mind for the umpteenth time.

"Dr. Spencer—Ted—how are you?" Basil's tone had seemed friendly, collegial even. A good sign.

"Fine, sir, and you?"

"Up to one's ears." The timbre became more direct. "To the point then. You think yourself competent to transition from screening recruits to working in Spec Ops?"

"Yes, sir, I feel certain I could."

"Thursday, 14:30, the Predator Cat Exhibit at the Smithsonian then." The tone defaulted completely to Basil's usual asperity. "I'll need some convincing." Basil clicked off.

Ted Spencer held a PsyD and had taught at Georgetown for fifteen years, but his real love was the intelligence game. He'd been fascinated by the CIA since grade school. While other kids played outside, Ted had sat, glued to the TV, watching *The Man from UNCLE*, his Napoleon

Solo ID in his pocket and his official UNCLE plastic convertible rifle-pistol on his lap.

The infatuation continued through college. Ted had applied to the Agency as a graduate student. He had gotten as far as the interview and personality inventory, only to be dropped after his lie-detector test, with no explanation or response to his inquiries.

Undeterred, Ted had concentrated his studies on the psychology of intelligence and his doctoral dissertation, "The Superiority of Nonchemically Enhanced Interrogation," was published in toto in a well-respected intelligence journal.

Two years earlier, his brother-in-law, Don Bel Castro, a CIA employee, had gotten him an interview with the Agency's office of medical services. Six months later, after a background and reference check, Ted was onboard as a part-time independent contractor helping to screen applicants to the clandestine service program.

Now, at last, he had a chance to join The Game, as the insiders called it. To make a difference, to be his wife's equal, to have her respect.

Ted imagined the pride in his wife Karen's voice as she spoke to her friends at a cocktail party, intimating but not disclosing that he worked at the Agency.

"Ted is so busy. He drives into Langley at the oddest times. Some kind of government job . . ." She would look at him with adulation from across the room. "He doesn't tell—I don't ask."

The ring of Ted's cellphone interrupted his fantasy.

"The Financial Oversight Committee went thumbs down on my funding." Karen's voice quivered in his ear. "They're reassigning my research assistants and refitting the lab to study herbicide runoff and seagrass."

"Any other avenues for funding?"

The lump grew in Ted's throat.

Wait for it.

Ted was more than a little envious of his wife, who had provided scientific consulting services to the Agency on a dolphin-related project and was now their unofficial liaison to the Marine Science Institute. His emotions ran more toward self-scrutiny than jealousy. Karen had reached the pinnacle of her chosen profession and was now a valuable cog in the machine that had been his obsession since childhood.

"Could you mention my research to Mr. Orlov?" Karen asked.

Basil Orlov was director of special operations—jokingly referred to as the PDD or Plausible Deniability Department—a little-known, and even less discussed, "black" department charged with resolving problems the rest of the Agency's clandestine service found too hot to handle.

Ted had previously given a lecture on his doctoral dissertation to a small group of the department's operatives and, as a result, was being considered for permanent part-time status with the office of medical services. It was Basil's policy that anyone involved in any aspect of psyops must pass his muster.

Ted hesitated. He wanted to be the sole focus of Basil's attention.

"Please." Her voice quivered in uncharacteristic desperation.

A picture of his wife smiled hopefully from the corner of Ted's desk.

"I'll try." He put his hand on the frame.

This interview is about my future—not some jellyfish.

"Thanks," Karen said. "Tell him it may have some field applications in rapid wound-healing."

"I don't know a lot about it," Ted said, hoping to decrease her expectations.

"Mention the rebirths, the immortality." Her speech was rapid, her enthusiasm palpable. "I'll fax you a half-page synopsis of the research."

"Sure." He frowned at the photo. "I'll take care of it."

"Bonne chance. I'm sure it will all work out." Karen hung up.

"For you or for me?" Ted said to the dial tone.

His office fax whined. Ted tore the fax from the tractor feed and stared down at it.

And the Dr. Karen Spencer Show rolls over another dream.

15

TENDS TO VIOLENCE WHEN ANGRY

Thursday, 19 April 2000—3:55 p.m.
Predator Cat Exhibit
Smithsonian Museum of Natural History, Washington, D.C.

Ted stared at the array of taxidermized predators and pondered Basil's choice of location for their interview.

"Spencer." Ted recognized Basil's signature accent at once—clipped BBC with a dash russkiy yazyk thrown in for authoritarian menace. "Over here." The voiced brimmed with impatience.

The short, gray-haired man and his thirty-something female associate stood near the base of a raised platform. At the top of the twenty-foot monolith, a well-preserved African lion seemed to survey his kingdom.

Ted felt suddenly small in the presence of his hero. He thought it appropriate that the angle of the afternoon sun streaming in the museum windows gave the CIA legend's five-foot-seven frame a golden glow and cast a ten-foot shadow.

Talk about bigger than life. If only half the stories were only half true.

"Time is short, Spencer." Basil tapped his watch and motioned Ted forward. He shooed his companion away. She walked a few feet and paused beneath a tree where a contented leopard guarded a bloody antelope draped over a branch.

"I read your doctoral dissertation on the superiority of physical augmentation in nonchemically enhanced interrogation."

Ted held his breath and nodded.

"Well thought out. I like your approach—kind of the Reid Technique on steroids. You've done a good job in your part-time role with the Agency. Breathe, son, I'm not going to eat you."

Ted exhaled a bit too forcefully.

"That said, the Agency is a bit fat with psychologists right now. Any new hires would need to bring something significant to the table." Basil caught the attention of the young woman standing under the leopard. He tapped his watch and held up five fingers.

So, that's it. A pat on the head and a punch in the gut.

Ted decided he might as well keep his promise to Karen.

"My wife, Doctor Karen Spencer, sends her regards." Ted emphasized her title.

"Ah, yes, the dolphin consultant." Basil smiled. "How's she doing?"

"Not so well." Ted saw Basil's interest as a way to keep the interview alive. "She just lost funding for her pet project."

"What's she working on?" Basil's tone and blank expression suggested the question was perfunctory.

Ted launched into a brief discussion of the research and handed Basil Karen's half-page synopsis. Ted stressed the study's currently nonexistent field applications for rapid wound-healing. Basil stood, his face sagging and eyes glazed, until Ted got to the part about the repeated rebirths and mentioned the word immortality.

"Immortality?" Basil's face brightened. He stared through rather than at Ted for a few seconds. "I believe that I, or rather, the Agency, could be convinced to provide some preliminary funding for a project that might . . . enhance battlefield survival or something."

Ted sighed and stared at the paper in Basil's hand.

Predictable. Karen wins. I lose.

Basil reread the synopsis. He started to speak, then paused and focused his gaze on Ted.

Ted could tell the old man was calculating the possibilities. He crossed his fingers in his pocket.

Basil cleared his throat. "I think it would be in everyone's best interest if we worked toward bringing you on full time." He glanced again at the synopsis. "Providing that I can count on you to be a good facilitator." He summoned his assistant, gave her the paper, and returned his gaze to Ted. "Are you a good facilitator?"

"Sir?"

"In addition to your other duties, could you liaison between your wife and my department?"

"Yes, sir. I could do that." Ted stuck out his hand. "But I had rather hoped to make it on my own merit."

"Think Nechayev." Basil ignored Ted's outstretched hand. "If a goal is important enough, any method of getting it is acceptable."

"Sergey Nechayev was a terrorist—the worst kind—a murderer, and a blackmailer."

"One man's terrorist, another's patriot." Basil motioned to his assistant.

"This is the CIA, Ted. We are in a never-ending war. Check your morals at the gate."

Ted dropped his hand to his side.

"We'll be in touch." Basil extended his arm to the young woman.

"That's *Panthera pardus*." Basil pointed to the leopard as they strolled away. "He purrs like a kitten when contented." Basil glanced over his shoulder at Ted. "But he tends to violence when angered."

Ted took one last look at *Panthera* Leo on his monolith, half expecting the long-dead lion to dip his chin in deference to the real king of the jungle.

16

ALL THE QUALITIES OF A DOG, EXCEPT LOYALTY

Friday, 13 July 2001—3:55 p.m.
Dr. Karen Spencer's office
Virginia Institute of Marine Science (VIMS), Gloucester Point, Virginia

Karen Spencer looked up from the microscope and rubbed her eyes. She watched the red second hand on the wall clock chip away at the time remaining on her CIA research grant. In five minutes, she would be receiving a call from Dr. Zane Strenke, director of the Agency's Science and Technology Division. Strenke, a mediocre researcher-turned-bureaucrat, had been reassessing the Agency's funding of her research.

He had promised—or threatened—a final decision by 4 p.m. today.

A buzzer drew her attention to the lab's glass security door.

A young woman in a white lab coat stood outside the door. "I've got the latest test results." She held up a computer printout.

Karen toggled the security door release and scrutinized the approaching research assistant's face for clues.

Please let these numbers be good.

The wide eyes, big smile, and perfect head tilt revealed nothing. They were permanent accessories that Elaine Cochran, PhD candidate, never left home without. Elaine, like Karen's Airedale terrier, Henry, was ingratiating. Both were always upbeat and eager to please. Henry would lick your hand and hold out a paw. Elaine could be counted on to bring you your favorite latté and compliment your appearance on what you knew was a wretched hair day. Both wanted to be everyone's best friend. The difference was you could trust Henry.

Karen took the printouts and scanned the summary sections. "How do they look?"

"I don't know." Elaine's smile faded as she glanced first at the phone and then at the exit. "If you don't need me." Another glance, this time from the clock to the phone and back. Elaine's demeanor reminded Karen of a criminal anxious to flee the scene of the crime.

"Why don't you stick around and check some slides?" Karen made a head gesture toward the microscope. "Depending on the outcome of this phone call, we may need to alter your schedule." The rapid blinking and ear pulling told Karen she had guessed correctly.

Elaine opened her mouth, but the telephone sounded before she could speak.

Karen held up one finger and answered on the first ring.

"Dr. Spencer." Strenke's voice was impossible to read. "Is this a good time?"

"That depends." Karen did her best to sound confident. "Am I still your favorite researcher?"

Several seconds passed.

"Well…" Strenke hesitated. "You're still our governmental liaison."

"Why?"

"Dr. Spencer." He let out a long breath. "We've been over this before."

Karen Spencer knew what was coming.

"The CIA has an interest in research, but, unlike academia, our grants are driven by results. Practical results." Strenke droned on about how the Agency's interest in *Turritopsis* was limited to its use as a battlefield wound-healing enhancer and how the purpose of funding her research had been to demonstrate the possibility of mammalian applications. "Quite frankly, your research has shown us nothing."

"So that's it?" Karen bit her lip. "The Agency has no further interest?"

"Not exactly." Strenke hesitated. "The Agency intends to take over the research and begin immediate canine and primate studies on the use of the serum as a diaphragm sparing—"

"You mean a weapon." Karen's despair turned to anger. "That violates the terms of our agreement."

"Easy, doctor." Strenke seemed alarmed. "I pulled a few strings. As a professional courtesy, we will provide finite funding for you to continue a constrained evaluation to determine if the transdifferentiation-rejuvenating abilities of your jellyfish have the potential to enhance mammalian wound healing."

"Limited funding. Constrained evaluation." Karen felt her face flush. "You mean you're buying my complicity."

"Call it what you will." Strenke's voice was calm. "I need your decision now."

"How long?" Karen hated herself right now, but this was her research. She wasn't going to just give it up.

"Thirty-day increments." She could feel Strenke relax. He knew he had her. "Continuation based on results."

"I just received some research results that might change your mind."

"Do you mean the salamander and mouse studies?" Strenke laughed. "Nothing new there."

"How did you know?"

"Your lab assistant faxed them to me an hour ago. They helped make up my mind."

Karen heard the click of the security door and turned to see Elaine striding down the hall.

All the qualities of a dog except loyalty.

"In or out?" Strenke sounded like he was about to hang up.

"In." Karen placed the receiver in its cradle.

17

I'M THE LINE YOU DON'T WANT TO CROSS

Friday, 29 August 2001—11:32 a.m.
CIA conference room, Langley, Virginia

Nick couldn't decide which he hated most—the weekly Science and Technology acquisition meetings or Basil for making him attend them. A half dozen victims and a secretary gathered around an imitation oak table.

Three unbroken hours of bad coffee and no cigarettes.

The HVAC system, anemic at best, was made even worse by the Agency-mandated seventy-five-degree thermostat setting. In two hours, the fan had come on only twice, providing a scant thirty seconds of noise before shutting down again. The only bright spot was that this meeting was attended by current CIA director Michael Collins, the only person in the room fidgeting and staring at his watch more than Nick.

Dr. Zane Strenke, the director of Science and Technology, was doing what he did best—waiting for retirement while he eschewed every new project that didn't originate in his department. On the block for humiliation today was a junior field operative who dared to ask for a research grant to study the feasibility of deploying miniature reconnaissance drones during covert operations.

"Playthings." Strenke gave a dismissive wave. "My ten-year-old son has one." He leaned forward and pulled his wallet from his pocket. "Here." He slid a twenty-dollar bill toward the chastened petitioner. "Run down to Toys 'R' Us and save the Agency a hundred grand." He scanned the audience for laughs or smiles. Seeing none, he turned to the director for approval.

"We're going to table this for now, Chip," Collins said to the disappointed young operative. "Prepare a formal request." Still talking to Chip, he looked at Strenke. "And drop it off with my secretary."

"Yes, sir." The operative raised his head and smiled. "Thank you, sir." Chip closed his folder, stood, nodded, and left the room.

"Next on the agenda," Strenke said, frowning, "Dr. Karen Spencer's research."

Nick stared at his watch and rolled a pencil back and forth.

"We're up." Basil pulled the pencil from Nick's fingers.

"Ah, yes," Strenke said. "The jellyfish project." He scanned his yellow legal pad. "To date, we have disbursed—some would say wasted—three hundred and sixty-two thousand dollars on this scientific novelty, with zero concrete evidence that the unique healing abilities of *Turritopsis* has any mammalian applications. The Science and Technology Division sees no benefit in Dr. Spencer's research approach. I know that some in Special Operations have championed this research." Strenke glanced at Basil. "I suggest that we allocate twenty-five thousand to Dr. Spencer and VIMS for secure shutdown and end the Gloucester research in thirty days. We can ramp up canine and primate testing in-house to determine whether the jellyfish venom could be the basis of a diaphragm-sparing paralytic."

DCIA Collins ran his finger down the spreadsheet, then looked up.

"Absent any compelling counterarguments, I'm inclined to side with Zane on this one." Collins turned to Nick's boss. "Basil?"

Basil nodded at Nick.

Nick stood and scanned the faces, settling on Collins. "Spec Ops," he said, pausing to lend weight to the Agency's code name for Basil, "has no objection to in-house evaluation of the paralytic effects." He nodded at the smiling Strenke. "He does, however, request continued parallel funding of Dr. Spencer's wound-healing research."

Strenke's smile disappeared.

"Further, Spec Ops requests an immediate sample for field testing." Nick returned his gaze to Collins and sat down.

"That's absurd!" Strenke leaned forward and grasped the table edge with both hands. "That implies human application." He turned to Collins. "We need detailed primate testing."

Basil touched Nick's arm.

Nick stood again. "Spec Ops requests a private five-minute audience with DCIA."

Collins nodded. He and Basil stood and left the room. Nick followed, leaving the door ajar. Basil and Collins moved ten feet down the hall and began talking. Strenke squeezed through and started toward the pair.

"Spec Ops requested a private audience," Nick said, as he blocked Strenke's path.

"Who do you think you are?" Strenke pushed against Nick.

"I'm the line you don't want to cross." Nick placed his hand on Strenke's left shoulder and squeezed the man's trapezius muscle between his thumb and forefinger.

Strenke sank to his knees.

"Just go back in and sit down." Nick released his hold, assisted Strenke to his feet, and guided him toward the conference-room door.

"There will be a day of reckoning, Caedwallan." Strenke rubbed his shoulder. "For you and for him." He jerked his head toward Basil.

Nick turned his back on Strenke and watched Basil lay out his case to Collins. He had no idea what Basil was saying, but the DCIA's concerned expression suggested it was having the desired effect.

Returning to the room, Collins cleared everyone except Basil, Nick, and Strenke. "Zane," Collins said, "funding will continue at its present level."

Strenke opened his mouth.

The DCIA shook his head. "The research director will report directly to Mr. Orlov under eyes-only protocol."

"You can't cut me out," Strenke stammered. "Orlov's not a scientist."

"This isn't a discussion." Collins stood to emphasize that the meeting was over. "It's a directive."

"Michael—"

"And please see that Spec Ops receives sufficient quantity for field testing immediately."

All stood except Strenke.

Nick fixed his gaze on the humbled director of Science and Technology. "Spec Ops thanks you for your cooperation."

18

THE MORNING OR THE EVENING COMMUTE?

Thursday, 11 December 1919—2:23 a.m.
Alexandra Hospital, Kiev, Soviet Russia

His name wasn't really Basil. That was just a nickname, short for Basilis-koi. A premature delivery, he had weighed a mere four pounds at birth. The doctor and Basil's father, Radislov, watched as he lay in his hospital crib, blue and gasping for air.

"See how he lies there, comrade," the doctor said, his voice devoid of emotion. "Like a plucked bird." He turned to Radislov. "He is done. A sick capon drawing its final breaths."

Basil's father had been a humanities professor during the tsar's regime. In the new Soviet Union, he cleaned hospital toilets. "Da, com-rade doctor, he is a bird." Radislov raised his chin. "But not a chicken. A Basiliskoi."

In Eastern European mythology, the Basiliskoi is a diminutive ser-pent-tailed bird that kills by touch, sight, or breath. It is sometimes referred to as "the little king." The name fit Basil well. Eighty-two years later, the little Russian, who stood only five-foot-seven-inches tall, had survived to become the undisputed king of black ops. A fix-ture within the CIA for as long as there had been a CIA, Basil was the go-to guy for difficult assassinations, foreign or domestic. He planned and orchestrated killings, kidnappings, plane crashes, and bombings all over the world. His specialty was arranging accidents. A plane crash in Madrid? No problem. A bridge collapse in Minneapolis? Would you prefer the morning or evening commute? The wrong drug administered during surgery? Do you want IV or IM?

19

THERE'S ALWAYS THE CHANCE OF BLOWBACK IN OUR PROFESSION

Friday, 24 August 2001—10:14 a.m.
Basil Orlov's office, CIA, Langley, Virginia

The secretary's voice crackled over the intercom. "Vice-Admiral Fletcher to—"

"Never mind, sweetie, he's expecting me." The slow drawl sounded like it should be accompanied by twenty units of insulin.

Basil's office door banged against the stop and Vice-Admiral Robert Fletcher's six-foot-four-inch frame filled the entry. Fletch, as he preferred to be called, was on the fast-track to the CIA's deputy directorship. In his early fifties and graying, he was developing a paunch from too much of the good life, but his posture remained ramrod straight. Overall, he still looked like a naval officer.

"Can I come in?" Fletcher strode across the room and towered over Basil.

"Can I stop you?" Basil crossed his arms and took a step back. Fletcher loved to play the naval hero, but Basil knew the truth—Fletcher had lived on his family's influence since high school. His father, a genuine war hero, had twisted arms to get Fletcher into Annapolis, where he graduated 1,133 in a class of 1,135.

"When was this room last swept for bugs?"

"Three times a day." Basil's eyes narrowed. "And after every questionable visitor."

In an ideal world, someone would offer Basil a contract on the good admiral.

"What's the hold-up on the Moretti deal?" Fletcher fiddled with the pencil can on Basil's desk. "She's making noises about a Senate investigation."

"Don't you read the papers?" Basil gestured to the newspaper lying on his desk. Fletcher picked it up. The photo of a well-dressed, sixty-something female smiled at Fletcher from below a banner headline:

SENATOR MORETTI TO INAUGURATE
HIGH-SPEED RAIL TOMORROW

"Slut!" Fletcher dropped the newspaper. "Have we gotten paid for this yet?"

"The wire cleared the Cayman account yesterday."

"How much?"

"Enough. Campbell wants to be a senator." Basil walked to his sidebar and poured a scotch without looking at Fletcher.

"Not that it matters." Fletcher tapped the senator's picture with his index finger. "I'd do that bitch for free. She's a real pain in the ass."

"And I think she's in with Bel Castro," Basil said.

"You think everyone's in with Bel Castro. Pour me two fingers while you're at it."

"Pour your own." Basil added some ice to his glass. "Twenty-three emails between the two of them this week."

"Easy." Fletcher poured a drink. "We're on the same side, remember?"

"Yeah, well. It doesn't matter. Ten minutes into Moretti's inaugural ride, a computer glitch opens the throttle. Ninety seconds later, a wheel bearing fails." His hands moved up and out, simulating an explosion. "The spectacle should be fantastic."

"Spare me the details." Fletcher finished his scotch and poured another.

"Anyway," Basil took the decanter from him, "Campbell will be appointed to fill the vacancy, and he is very Agency-friendly. Plus, we have a record of payment to ensure his friendship." He opened his desk drawer and produced a wire receipt.

"All this says is Windward Island Resources, Ltd." Fletcher's tone was uncertain.

"Dumb-ass is the sole owner."

"How do we know the governor will appoint him?" Fletcher asked.

"Already taken care of, I—"

"Stop," Fletcher said. "I don't want to know. Christ, how do you do it?" He placed his glass on the desk and put his hands in his pockets. "What's the deal with field-testing this unproven jellyfish drug?" He began to pace. "Why don't you just snatch and grab this guy?"

"You don't want to know details, remember? I have it covered."

"Why risk something going wrong and drawing attention to you—and, ultimately, me?" Fletcher rubbed the back of his neck. "Look, we've both profited from these side deals. I don't want this coming between me and the directorship."

"I said I have it covered," Basil snapped back. "There are two of us in this partnership."

He touched the shoulder holster under his jacket and thought how nice it would be to just do Fletcher now.

20

WELCOME TO BLACK OPS

Wednesday, 02 September 2001—11:53 a.m.
Seventeenth-floor conference room, across the Hudson River from Lower
Manhattan

Nick put down his fork and looked around the table. He knew almost everyone in the room: Basil and Vasily; Martin Schwartz, the new guy; and Max Hegel, a former Navy flight surgeon and graduate of The Farm, Basil's first choice for any covert operation requiring medical expertise.

Why are we having lunch on the seventeenth floor of an office building in New Jersey?

The only person in attendance Nick didn't know was the man sitting alone in the back. When he and Vasily arrived, the man was sweeping the room for listening devices. While everyone else had lunch, he retrieved photos and documents from a briefcase and placed them in four stacks. Now he sat in the back, typing on a laptop computer

Basil stood, cleared his throat, and tapped his water glass with a fork. Satisfied with the response, he pressed a button at the head of the table. The curtains opened on a wall of windows, revealing a panoramic view of lower Manhattan.

"That," Vasily said, "is what it's all about."

Beyond the floor-to-ceiling windows, the twin towers of the World

Trade Center, seeming close enough to touch, stood in stark relief against the cloudless blue September sky.

"Appreciate it." Basil swept the vista with his arm. "If our friend from the FBI is correct—" he gestured toward the man in the dark suit, "this may be your last chance."

All eyes turned to the man with the laptop. He held up an index finger, made a few more keystrokes, and gave each man two large-format photographs.

Nick studied the photos. The first was of an olive-skinned, Middle Eastern man in his early thirties, who seemed familiar. The second, was someone new, a sixty-something male with icteric sclera, a hint of jaundice, and numerous pale-brown spots on his face.

"Gentlemen." Basil pulled out a chair for the dark suit. "Meet FBI special agent Daniel Fine." Fine nodded once and took the proffered seat.

"Daniel is here unofficially and at great professional risk." Basil walked to the window. He stood silent, back to the table as an airliner passed over the skyline of lower Manhattan.

Nick watched the shrinking aircraft until it was a dot in the blue sky.

When the speck vanished, Basil turned to face the group. His face sagged. There were dark crescents under his eyes. Nick wondered how long it had been since he'd slept. He thought of all the crises he had been through with Basil. The man was a rock. Nothing shook him. Nick looked at the view across the river and then at Basil's face. He felt the hair stand up on the back of his neck.

If it's enough to rattle Basil…

"What I'm about to tell you cannot leave this room." Basil trudged back to the table. "And this man," he pointed to Fine, "was never here." He waited until the four nodded their affirmation. "On 6 August, I attended a presidential briefing." Basil took a seat and continued. "The NSA intercepted communications in which Osama bin Laden, the architect of the USS *Cole* bombing, made it clear his intention to strike at the United States 'with something big' in September. Further—"

"Why haven't—" Marty interrupted.

Basil silenced him with a look. "Numerous airlines have complained about the FAA dictate that detaining more than two Arab male travelers simultaneously constituted harassment. After being threatened with fines and sanctions, they had relaxed their screening to what they considered an ineffective and dangerous level."

Nick thought of all the terrorist threats that never materialized. Still, bin Laden was well-financed and had delivered on numerous occasions.

"I was extremely disappointed at the lack of interest or response to this information and mined my street-level contacts in the various intelligence agencies." Basil looked at Fine. "Daniel was my last stop. We pooled notes and prepared a one-page report. It was the information in that report," Basil explained, "that convinced the DCIA to release a quantity of the unproven jellyfish serum for field use. Daniel?"

"A Saudi American living in coastal Jersey City opposite Manhattan reported that he and other members of the Muslim community had been told to keep watch on the Manhattan skyline for a good show. Details to follow." Fine glanced at his notes. "Several flight schools have called the bureau to voice concern over Middle Eastern students paying huge sums of money for a few hours flight-time in jumbo jets. They had no interest in takeoffs, landings, or ground school, only the rudimentary mastery of flight controls."

"What happens to these reports?" Vasily asked.

"Sometimes a note, rarely a follow-up interview. Ultimately? Nothing." Fine looked at Basil. "In 1996, one of these students, Abdul Hakim Murad, was convicted of conspiracy to blow up a dozen commercial aircraft and then crash one into CIA headquarters at Langley."

The litany of ignored warnings to various agencies continued until Vasily interrupted.

"For God's sake, aren't any of these agencies talking to each other about this?"

"No." Fine's speech was measured. "And they've been encouraged not to—at the highest levels."

"Why?" Vasily asked, slack-jawed.

Fine looked at Basil and received a quick nod.

"Because it might piss off the Saudis." Basil took a drink from the Styrofoam cup he was holding.

"Who gives a crap what they think?" Vasily said.

"The administration." Basil crushed his cup and threw it toward a trash can. "Oil companies, strategic interests, personal ties." He filled another cup. "They won't move without hard proof, and they don't want to see hard proof."

"You brought us here for a reason," Nick said. Basil was a man of action and, failing that, opportunity. If he did not think there was a way to avert this disaster, he would have waited for it to occur, issued his "I told you so," and profited from the result.

"Danny?" Basil signaled Fine.

"This memo may be their wake-up call." Fine passed the document around the room.

Nick read the single FBI paragraph.

On 30 August 2001 @ 00:23 hours, NSA intercepted a cellphone call setting up a meeting between Mahaz Abadi, a known planner of the 1998 Dar es Salaam embassy bombing, and Arthur Hunt, an employee in airport security at LaGuardia Airport. Furthermore, Hunt was to fly to Detroit, Michigan, and meet with Abadi in George S. Patton Park in Dearborn on the afternoon of 03 September 2001.

"When his Agency took no action," Fine continued, "the NSA analyst, at considerable personal risk, hand-delivered a copy to Basil. A detailed background check revealed Hunt to be a sixty-year-old habitual gambler with severe alcoholic pancreatitis, chronic liver failure, and massive debt. Hunt's job in airport security includes the sensitivity calibration of airport metal detectors."

Fine smiled for the first time. "Based on this information, Spec Ops has devised a plan to ameliorate this cluster-fuck of inactivity." Fine pushed back his chair. "I am going to leave you now." He scanned the faces of the four men. "No offense," he paused for another smile, "but I think I'll live longer if I'm not seen in your company."

The five men applauded.

Fine walked to the door and gave a two-finger salute.

Basil returned to the window and again stared at three departing planes until they became pencil-points and vanished. He retrieved a briefcase from the floor.

"Tomorrow morning the four of you will fly into Custer Airport in Monroe, Michigan, in a medevac-equipped Beech King Air." He produced four bundles of papers and handed one to each operative. "The airport is about forty-five minutes from Dearborn."

The top document of each stack was a map of Wayne and Monroe counties, with red and green lines indicating alternate ingress and egress routes between Custer Airport and Patton Park.

"Why the medevac plane?" Nick shuffled through the papers, which included pictures of the King Air, a rescue-squad truck, some medical equipment, and printouts of medical resuscitation protocols.

"There are two missions here." Basil pulled a small device that looked like a joke handshake buzzer from the briefcase and placed it on the table.

"I take it that's not a party favor?" Nick used a pencil to pick up the object by its nylon web strap.

"Careful. It's preloaded with a reasonable facsimile of Dr. Spencer's jellyfish serum," Basil said.

"Reasonable facsimile?" Nick looked across the table at Max Hegel's frowning face and lowered the device to the table.

"That idiot Strenke pissed Spencer off," Basil said. "The serum is reconstructed from her research notes."

Hegel stared at the device. "I saw those notes. Maybe we should just snatch and—"

"Vasily," Basil said, ignoring Hegel. "When Abadi and Hunt finish talking and separate, you will keep Hunt from leaving."

Vasily nodded.

Basil shifted in his chair. "Nick, you will use this to administer the serum to Hunt, who will collapse, paralyzed, but breathing, due to the selective—"

"If this stuff works." Nick could not believe they were going to administer an unproven drug to a high-value target. "Can't we just snatch and go?"

Basil held up a hand. "No. You and Vasily will take him to the ambulance, where Hegel and Schwartz will be waiting."

"Ambulance?" Hegel said. "So, you already know this serum is bad news?"

Basil gave a dismissive wave of his hand. "The ambulance is just for cover. You are only to monitor him."

"Yeah." Hegel looked at Nick and rolled his eyes. "Purely precautionary."

Basil ran his finger over the red egress route and leaned back in his chair. "Then you return to Custer Airport and fly back to Andrews for transport to Langley, where Hunt will sing like a bird."

Marty examined the terrorist's photograph. "What about Abadi?"

"He's booked on the red-eye into Dulles Thursday night," Basil said. "Fine will shadow him from there."

"Why aren't we interrogating Abadi?" Marty asked.

Basil turned to face Marty. "Because, genius, if Abadi disappears, they will change their plans and we will be nowhere."

The look on Marty's face told Nick that the new guy still didn't get it. Nick sensed Basil's irritation with the newbie's inability to connect the dots. "Later, Marty," Nick said.

But Marty went double or nothing. "Won't they do the same thing when they see Hunt again?"

Basil scrubbed his hand over his face. "Nick?"

"They're not going to see Hunt again," Nick said. "No one's going to see Hunt again."

Marty glanced from Nick to Basil.

"Christ, Schwartz," Basil said. "The man's an alcoholic and a traitor.

He's plotting to kill innocent, noncombatant Americans." He waved his arm toward the window. "We need the specifics—the where and when—and we need them now. We question him, fill him with IV alcohol, and the archaeologist here," he said, pointing at Nick, "will see that he has a very public, very fatal accident Friday morning on his way to work."

Nick glanced from Marty to his boss. "He's got it, Basil. We'll bring him up to speed en route."

"This is not a teaching moment."

Nick scanned the room for help taking the heat off Marty.

Vasily avoided eye contact by staring at his info packet, but Hegel jumped in.

"Has Collins signed off on this?"

"Unofficially." Basil leaned forward. "The director is flabbergasted by the administration's lack of response and endorses the mission."

"And officially?" Marty asked.

Basil scowled at Marty. "Officially, he has no knowledge whatsoever and has authorized nothing." He directed his open palm toward Nick. "And—"

"And, if this goes south and becomes public—" Nick drew a finger across his throat.

"We are declared rogue and prosecuted in civilian court." Vasily said, looking up from the maps and photographs scattered across the table.

"Welcome to black ops." Hegel pumped Marty's hand.

Basil picked up his briefcase and stood. "You leave for Dearborn Thursday morning." He pointed at Marty. "Except for you."

21

WHAT'S A FEW DEAD MONKEYS?

Thursday, 03 September 2001—09:22 a.m.
Cafeteria, CIA headquarters, Langley, Virginia

Basil looked around the cafeteria. It was empty except for a single female staffer drawing coffee from an urn on the other side of the room. Basil watched her add cream and sugar, place a lid on the cup, and leave the room. He took a sip of cold coffee and inspected his chastened tablemate.

"Schwartz," Basil paused, "do you know why I held you back?"

Marty didn't raise his eyes. "Yes, sir."

"I brought you in because the instructors at The Farm told me you were aggressive, loyal, and trustworthy."

Actually, they said you were an ass-kissing sociopath who should be kept in a cage when not in use.

The café door banged open before Basil could continue, "Uh-oh, trouble." Marty picked up his half-eaten bagel and cream cheese. "Strenke approaching on your six."

"Basil!" Strenke waited for a greeting. When there was none, he continued. "Your secretary said I might find you here."

"I'll fire her after lunch." Basil looked up. "What do you want?"

"When I found out you were planning a field test for today, I accelerated the primate trials."

"And?"

"All ten are dead." Strenke tossed a computer printout on the table.

"My God." Basil picked up the printout. "You were right all along."

Across the table, Marty choked on his bagel.

"I tried to caution you." Strenke's tone softened in response to Basil's acknowledgment. "Shall we go to the DCIA?"

"No," Basil said. "He's in London. I'll call Caedwallan immediately. This changes everything."

"Excellent." Strenke's face was aglow with victory. He reclaimed the computer printout and left.

"Should I call Nick?" Marty glanced at his watch.

"Of course not." Basil pushed back his chair. "What's a few dead monkeys?"

22

GAME ON

Thursday, 03 September 2001 — 6:08 p.m.
Custer Airport, Monroe, Michigan

The flight from Andrews AFB to Monroe, Michigan, took just under two hours. Max, Vasily, and Nick re-examined the contents of their information packets. Nick noted that Max, an experienced combat physician, had insisted on no fewer than three in-flight reviews of the Advanced Life Support Protocols.

The plan called for the three operatives to board a waiting ambulance at Custer Airport, drive to the pond in Patton Park, and take up station on a gravel path within eyesight of the Abadi-Hunt meeting site. Upon positive ID of the two conspirators, Nick and Vasily would disembark under the guise of prepositioning medical supplies for a weekend ten-kilometer race scheduled to pass by the pond.

Vasily would verify Abadi's departure, while Nick would approach Hunt and administer the serum. When Hunt collapsed, Nick and Vasily would signal Max to bring the ambulance with lights flashing and collect Hunt. If observed or questioned, they would be a contract paramedic crew who just happened to be on location when the jaundiced and ill-looking middle-aged man collapsed and required a transfer. Once in the ambulance, they would proceed to Custer Airport by the egress route marked in red. The sedated Hunt would be loaded onto the King Air, flown to Andrews, then transferred to Langley.

The afternoon was cloudless, a dry sixty-three degrees, with a slight breeze from the northwest. The ambulance in the photos had been replaced by a white crash truck with green striping and an array of antennae. The lettering on the side of the ambulance looked authentic:

MEDILINK PARAMEDIC SERVICES
CONTRACT ALS
PRIVATE CONTRACT ONLY

A red stripe underlined the lettering and morphed into an exaggerated QRS electrocardiogram complex.

Nick laughed. "An Agency special. No phone number, no address."

"No," said Vasily, pointing to the truck's roof. "But it comes fully equipped with the latest lifesaving listening devices."

"Did you know anything about this?" Max stepped in front of Nick.

"Relax," Nick said. "It's probably from another operation."

"This serum thing stinks." Max waved the resuscitation protocols at Nick. "Why make something that should be simple so complex?" He gave a long exhale. "Hunt might be the one getting the jellyfish-serum injection, but I can't shake the feeling that we're the ones who'll get stung."

~

Nick, Vasily, and Max donned the black, military-style boots, dark blue pants, and white shirts with "Medilink Paramedic" and an EKG waveform emblazoned across the pocket.

"You look very professional—" Vasily read the name on Nick's pocket. "Harold."

"Thank you—" Nick lifted the fold of fabric on the too-large uniform obscuring Vasily's name tag. "Leroy."

Nick's cellphone rang. "Basil," he said, holding up an index finger.

Max swiveled in the driver's seat to face Nick.

"Yes, the ambulance was here," Nick said. "The uniforms all fit. Yeah, we saw the listening gear."

"Here it comes," Max said.

"Yeah, Basil. We can try for a recording," Nick said. "Sure, I understand. Just precautionary."

"Give Basil a message for me." The flight surgeon extended his middle finger.

"Yeah, I understand." Nick shrugged his shoulders, looking first at Vasily and then at Max. "Why don't we forget the serum? Okay." Nick ended the call.

"I told you," Max said.

"Easy. It's good news." Nick turned to Vasily. "He wants us to record their conversation. It may give us what we need."

"And why has Basil just now come to this conclusion?" Vasily glanced at Max.

"Because he's afraid this crap is going to kill Hunt," Max said. "And this is his only chance to get the info he wants."

"Stow it." Nick's tone was sharp. He regretted it immediately as Max flushed, turned to face forward, and started the truck. "Hey, Max, I didn't mean anything."

Max gave a dismissive wave of his hand, put the ambulance in gear, and pulled forward. He did not speak for the balance of the trip to Dearborn.

They entered the park, drove along the greenway, and parked near the pond.

"Ready to talk now?" Nick thumped the back of Max's seat. He shared the flight surgeon's concerns but felt certain Basil would not risk using an unvetted serum on such a high-value target.

"No." Max crawled between the two seats, sat cross-legged before the console, and powered up the audio system. "But I can listen."

"Heads up." Vasily nodded toward the side window. "Here comes the town drunk."

A solitary figure shuffled along the gravel path and sat on a wooden bench by the algae-covered pond. A hundred feet away, two workmen knelt by an electric junction box. One made frequent trips to and from a van marked Detroit Parks and Recreation.

"Terrorist at six o'clock." Nick recognized Abadi from Fine's photo.

Abadi, briefcase in hand, skulked along the walkway, scanning the area. He slowed his pace, staring at the two workmen, but continued when he saw Hunt sitting on the bench.

"On it." Max slipped on the headphones and adjusted the knobs on the listening unit.

Nick was relieved but not surprised by his colleague's instant transition from pissed-off to mission mode. The flight surgeon wrinkled his forehead and squinted as he fine-tuned the surveillance unit. He grinned, flipped a switch, and the overhead speaker gave a slight hum.

"Do you have the money?" Hunt's voice sounded like a rake scratching through gravel.

"Yes." The answer was calm, the accent heavy but understandable. "Let's go over the details one more time." Across the pond, Abadi patted the briefcase and smiled for the first time.

"Cha-ching." Vasily elbowed Nick in the ribs. "Jackpot."

"For Christ's sake. I have it memorized." Hunt reached for the bag.

"Indulge me." Abadi moved the case further away. "Start with the sensitivity threshold." A high-pitched squeal filled the ambulance.

"Damn." Max ripped the headphones off and cranked the volume down.

In the middle of the pond, an enormous jet of water shot skyward. The two Parks and Recreation workers stood up. One pointed at the geyser coming from the aerator while the other picked up his bag and walked toward the repair truck.

Max twisted numerous dials and flipped switches in an attempt to filter the noise. The squeal changed pitch with each maneuver but was unabated.

"We're done." Max turned to Nick. "Sixty-cycle interference from that unshielded pump." He shut down the set.

"Back to the poison pen." Nick slipped the device onto his right hand.

"You can try these, but I think we're flying silent on this one." Max handed Nick and Vasily the in-ear com devices. "Put them in but keep the volume low until we see if they work."

"Abadi's standing up," Nick said. "Let's roll."

Vasily opened the ambulance load door. He and Nick jumped out, canvas bags in hand.

"Any changes?" Vasily glanced at Nick. Nick shook his head, and they moved off in different directions. The Parks and Recreation van pulled onto the greenway and drove north. The fountain continued spewing its twenty-five-foot plume of water.

"Vasily. Can you hear me?" Nick said in a low voice. The answer was a continuous hum. Nick watched Vasily make a show of dropping waterproof bags along the path as he tailed Abadi.

Nick looked down at the device strapped to his hand and placed a bright yellow waterproof pouch next to the bench where Hunt sat clutching the briefcase and smiling.

The aerating sprinkler sounded like a gentle rainstorm.

"Supplies for the weekend's ten-K," Nick said to Hunt as he walked by.

Hunt nodded and stood but said nothing. Something caught Nick's attention. Silence. The artificial shower had ceased.

"Vasily?" Nick stole a glance at the dead sprinkler.

Vasily's response was loud and clear. "Abadi's out of here. The Parks and Recreation van picked him up."

"Damn!" Nick was amazed at the terrorists' level of tradecraft. "They planned the interference."

"So?" Vasily said.

"Game on." Nick grabbed the unsuspecting Hunt by the neck and jabbed the needle into his external jugular vein.

"What the—" Hunt's two words were followed by a single forceful inhalation.

Nick was surprised at the man's strength as he twisted from side to side.

"Calm down." He grasped Hunt's writhing shoulders and held him at arm's length. Hunt's eyes had rolled back, exposing only the yellow-white sclerae. Nick realized that what appeared to be an attempt to escape was instead a violent tonic-clonic seizure. Nick lowered the bucking man to the ground and pinned his shoulders

"Holy crap." Vasily panted in his earwig mic as he ran down the path. "Is that normal?"

"No, but it's predictable." Max's matter-of-fact tone answered Vasily in the earpiece.

"Thank God." Nick released Hunt's shoulders. "He's stopped seizing."

"But he's blue!" Vasily knelt beside Hunt. "Is he breathing?"

"No." Nick watched for the rise and fall of the man's chest. He palpated Hunt's carotid artery. "And no pulse. Shit. Max?"

"On my way." The flight surgeon's voice lacked any element of surprise, but Nick could hear the truck's engine fire up and the gravel crunch. The ambulance was backing up, reverse klaxon blaring.

Max jumped out, stethoscope in hand, and ran to where Nick and Vasily crouched beside Hunt. Vasily opened the back door of the ambulance.

"Asshole, Basil!" Max felt for a pulse and listened with the stethoscope. "Nothing." He looked at Vasily. "Get me the automatic defibrillator. I can use its scope for a quick look."

Vasily ran to the truck.

"No." Nick glanced around the park. "We can't risk getting caught." He yelled to Vasily. "Get the gurney. We'll work on him in the truck."

"Seconds count, man." Max was pumping on Hunt's chest. "It's getting dark and the park's deserted."

Nick knew Hunt's best shot was to allow Max to attempt the

resuscitation here. He watched the traffic cruise along Dix Avenue. A City of Detroit police cruiser slowed, then accelerated, but did not turn on its lights.

"I'm sorry." Nick motioned for the gurney. "We're too exposed here. Our cover won't hold up."

"It doesn't look good, anyway." Max looked up from Hunt's purple face.

They lifted Hunt onto the stretcher. Vasily retrieved Abadi's briefcase. Max walked alongside, continuing chest compressions as they loaded Hunt.

Nick climbed into the back and shouted orders. "Max, keep pumping. Vasily, drive. Lights and siren for show 'til we pass the nearest hospital."

Vasily nodded and pushed the door shut.

Nick handled supplies, while Max gave a running commentary of the resuscitation. The flight surgeon ripped open Hunt's shirt revealing a chest wet with sweat.

Nick dried it with a towel to get the defibrillator leads to stick.

"Fine V-Fib or asystole." Max stared at the monitor, and flipped a switch, "but I'll override. He defibrillated three times. Each time Hunt's body jumped, but the monitor remained flatline. "Pass me an endotracheal tube," he ordered.

"What size?" Nick pulled out four tubes.

"Eight point five. Now. Take over compressions." Max lubed the ET tube and checked the light on the laryngoscope.

"How fast?" Nick had never used the CPR he learned in his Agency course. His job was stopping hearts, not starting them.

"Think 'Stayin' Alive' by the Bee Gees."

Nick pumped Hunt's chest at a rate of one hundred times a minute.

Max moved to the head of the gurney. "Stop compressions."

Max secured the airway on his first try, attached a bag-valve, and began squeezing air into Hunt's lungs at regular intervals. "Resume compressions."

Nick marveled at the flight surgeon's coolness as he watched the now blue and cold Hunt's chest rise and fall with each squeeze of the bag.

Max injected epinephrine three times in an attempt to coerce Hunt's heart into contracting. The resuscitation attempts continued until the ambulance stopped on the tarmac next to the waiting King Air at Custer Airport.

Vasily jumped from the ambulance and ran to open the back door. "No go?" He looked from Nick to Max

"Get me the BD-4," the flight surgeon said, referring to the heavy black body bags used to transport servicemen killed in action.

They slipped the bag under Hunt and rolled him into it.

"What do we tell Basil?" Nick looked down at the black rubberized bag.

Max jerked the bag shut. "Tell Spec Ops his jellyfish cluster is officially zipped-in."

Nick knew the term: A dead body ready for transport.

23

ONE MAN'S EXECUTION IS ANOTHER'S BROKEN ROPE

Friday, 11 September 2001—08:49 a.m.
The hallway outside Basil's CIA office, Langley, Virginia

It had been a bad week. Basil's reputation had taken quite a hit. Strenke had forced an internal investigation, and the "long knives" were out.

His pager buzzed like an angry bee. "Collins" flashed in the display.

Christ. Every hour, on the hour for the last eight days. Give it a fucking rest.

He switched off the pager and walked toward his office. Basil was surprised that his secretary was not at her desk. As his hand cupped the doorknob to his office, the pager buzzed again. Basil walked into his office before reading the display:

"Collins Emergency."

The direct line. A secretarial bypass. Okay, I'll bite.

Basil dialed the DCIA's phone number and waited for the shit to hit the fan.

Basil could hear Collins chewing on a cigar.

Give it a fucking rest. "Do you have your television on?"

"No," Basil said. "I'm working."

"Turn it on," Collins ordered. The chewing got louder. "We've got a situation."

Basil turned on the television. A picture of lower Manhattan filled the screen. Black smoke boiled from one of the World Trade Center towers. Basil's hand, still holding the phone, dropped to his side.

"At eight forty-five this morning, an aircraft struck the North Tower." The anxious announcer continued. "Authorities have not ruled out terrorism."

Basil watched for a few moments until he became aware of the telephone shouting his name. He lifted the receiver to his ear.

"Get up here now. This could be what you were talking about." Collins disconnected.

The elevator stopped on the DCIA's floor. Basil stared at his shoes and waited for the door to open. He felt guilty. He knew there was an opportunity here. He wasn't sure of the extent yet, but he knew it was there. He looked at his watch: five past nine.

The elevator door slid open. The DCIA stood looking at him, his face gray.

"A second plane just hit the South Tower." Collins sighed and looked up at the ceiling. "The president is in Sarasota, on his way to the airport." The DCIA looked off to the side. "He wants to talk to you."

~

By noon, WTC One and Two had collapsed with a loss of over two thousand civilians. One hundred twenty-five died when the Pentagon was struck, and a fourth airliner had crashed in a field in rural Pennsylvania. The flights originated from JFK, Logan, and Dulles International Airports.

Authorities were puzzled why LaGuardia Airport, less than five minutes' flight time from WTC, was not involved in the attack.

By three o'clock, Basil had gone from goat to hero. Someone said the president had suggested that Basil's takedown of Hunt, for all its warts, had probably saved the White House or the Capitol Building. At four o'clock, Basil was summoned to the DCIA's office.

Collins stared out the window, his back to Basil. "Congratulations, you are now almost untouchable, and your budget has been nearly doubled." He turned toward Basil but avoided eye contact. "One thing." He shifted his tie.

"Yes?"

"It never happened." Collins pushed a stack of papers and a pen across the desk. "Sign this."

"What's that?" Basil reached down.

"That is the most stringent nondisclosure agreement I have ever seen." Collins threw his wet cigar in the waste can. "Just sign it. Reap the benefits and move on."

"I'm not the only one who knows about Hunt." Basil thumbed through the papers. "What about the others?"

"Caedwallan, Konovalov, and Schwartz have already signed their agreements." Collins gave a dismissive wave. "Besides, you have enough dirt on all of them to ensure their loyalty."

"What about Hegel?"

"The flight surgeon?" Collins executed a sloppy salute. "He doesn't know it yet, but he's on a six-year loan to a very grateful New Zealand Navy."

"And Strenke?" Basil knew the director of Science and Technology was furious and desperate for revenge.

"Dr. Strenke has been convinced to take a one-year research sabbatical," Collins said, his face tightening. "He and his lovely wife will be visiting some fascinating but hazardous locations." Collins picked at some imaginary lint on his sleeve. "I doubt that we will ever see them again." He paused. "As for the research, the Agency is done with it unless you decide to keep it going in the black."

"You seem to have thought of everything, except Agent Fine." Basil knew there was no way they could buy Fine off.

"I handled it. I had to." Collins's stare was cold. "You fucked up a lot of lives, came out smelling like a rose, and left me to clean up the mess."

Basil said nothing, took a seat across the desk from Collins, and scanned the document again. Satisfied, he scrawled his name on all three copies and pushed them across the table.

Collins placed the documents in a wall safe, closed the door, spun the knob, and turned back to Basil. "How does it feel? You knew that the serum was unsafe."

Basil shrugged. "Hunt was a traitor."

"You fucked up, killed a guy, and profited from it." Collins's gaze was ice, his jaw stiff.

"One man's execution is another's broken rope," Basil said, raising his eyebrows. "You, Michael, should know that better than anyone."

24

IT LOOKS LIKE HIS LIVER MISSED THE MEMO

Friday, 11 September 2001—4:21 p.m.
Elevator, CIA headquarters, Langley

Basil stood before the closed elevator doors. He had just been given a reprieve and should feel pretty good.

But he didn't.

He stared at his reflection in the polished stainless steel of the door. *I'm still old.*

The elevator chimed and the door opened. Max Hegel stared at him.

"I've been looking for you." Hegel held out his hand. "Congratulations."

"Thanks." Basil shook the outstretched hand. "You were looking for me?" He stepped on the elevator and stabbed the button for his floor.

Hegel held out a brown folder. "Hunt's autopsy report."

"Just give me the highlights." Basil held up his hands to block the folder. "It's been a very long day."

"It's pretty straightforward. Cause of death was cardiac arrest secondary to ventricular fibrillation. But there is something curious." The elevator arrived at Basil's floor, and the door opened. "Hunt's medical record said he had end-stage hepatic failure and advanced alcoholic pancreatitis."

"So?" Basil waved him off and started to exit. "That's all in his file."

"Yeah, well, it looks like his liver didn't get the memo." Hegel pressed the "door open" button.

"What?"

"The pathologist said Hunt had the liver and pancreas of a healthy thirty-year-old."

25

ALL THE MORE REASON TO NOT STIMULATE THEIR CURIOSITY

Monday, 18 September 2001—11:01 a.m.
Psychology classroom, Georgetown University

It was the second week of classes at Georgetown, and D.C. was clawing its way back to normal. Ted Spencer watched the students file into the room. Same faces, different year. He was teaching the same undergraduate course he'd taught for the past five fall semesters: the Psychology of Aging. The familiar eight-page syllabus lay on his desk.

He didn't need a semester to cover this topic. Bob Dylan had already summed it up in one line, "Twenty years of schooling and they put you on the day shift."

It wasn't fair. Just seven miles away in McLean, people with far less talent were doing things that impacted national security. He, on the other hand, sat here year after year, pouring the same mush into the heads of future drones. Each year his childhood dream of work in espionage seemed more and more to be just that—a dream.

He'd told the Agency often enough of his interest but could never seem to gin up any enthusiasm. He'd hoped Karen's research would make him attractive by association, but his hopes faded with her lack of a breakthrough. Basil had told him he would be participating in the interrogation of a high-value acquisition. At last, he'd thought, a chance to make himself indispensable by extracting some game-changing information. But the interrogation was canceled, and he was back on the outside, screening applicants one afternoon a week. The Pentagon and WTC incidents of 9/11 brought a surge in Agency funding, especially for Basil's black ops. If he could just get noticed, he could join the fraternity. That's what it was, the ultimate fraternity, the ultimate secret handshake.

His first class of the semester always began with the nature of aging: What caused it and how it might someday be slowed or even reversed. He briefly covered the various aging theories, both the crackpot and the credible.

"Most theories involve some programmed obsolescence."

An enthusiastic hand shot into the air.

The door at the back of the room opened, and Basil Orlov entered. He scanned the room, nodded a brief greeting to Ted, and took a seat in the back.

The student's hand flapped like a signal flag in a gale-force wind.

"Yes?" Ted acknowledged the student. "A question?"

"Which theory do you favor?"

"Well, the deteriorating telomere theory has many proponents." Ted launched into a cogent description of what was, by now, a rather tired theory. "These protective end caps preserve the integrity of the chromosomes." This was not his favorite spiel, but he'd learned it from Karen. "After many repetitions, these caps are rubbed away like pencil erasers." This analogy was also borrowed from his wife. "The chromosome ceases to function, and the cell dies. Repeat this often enough, and the organism dies." The student was impressed, and he thought he saw a nod and the hint of a smile from Basil.

Another student raised a hand. "Any theories on how to possibly reduce the telomere fragmentation?"

"Telomerase enzymes." Ted described how, under controlled

conditions, the enzyme could repair the telomeres, slowing the aging process.

"What about out-and-out reversal of the aging process?"

Ted glanced at Basil. He was leaning back in his seat, arms crossed, looking bored.

"A study of the jellyfish *Turritopsis dohrnii* and regeneration by transdifferentiation holds some promise," Ted said.

Basil uncrossed his arms and leaned forward.

I thought that would wake up the old fossil.

"Some researchers have claimed limited success in the restoration of internal organs, particularly heart, liver, and pancreas of amphibians."

Basil frowned and shook his head back and forth.

"Who's doing this research?" The student picked up a pen and turned her notebook to a blank page.

"The intensely deleterious effects on the nervous system have, to this point, discouraged testing on higher mammals."

Ted waited for Basil's reaction. Basil was leaning back in the chair, staring at Ted.

"But who are the researchers?" the student pressed.

Basil drew his finger across his throat.

Ted hesitated. "Mainly small, foreign research centers. No truly reputable researcher has yet duplicated this data."

Basil smiled and nodded.

"But—" the student began.

"That's it for today," Ted said. "Class dismissed." He followed the surge of students as they exited the classroom.

Basil remained seated until Ted reached his chair at the back of the hall. "Impressive lecture. There may indeed be a place for you on my team."

"Doing what?" Ted could almost feel the secret handshake.

"Tonight, come by my place in Georgetown for celebratory cock-tails." Basil placed his hand on Ted's shoulder. "And bring that lovely bride of yours."

"What time?"

"About eight." Basil started to leave but stopped and turned back. "That student with all the questions," he said, squeezing Ted's forearm.

"Yes?" Ted felt the grip tighten.

"The less said about *Turritopsis*, the better."

"They're just students." Ted tried to shake Basil's grip on his arm. "They're interested in anything new."

Basil gave a final hard squeeze and released Ted's arm. "All the more reason not to stimulate their curiosity."

26

UNFORTUNATELY, IT ALSO KILLED HIM

Monday, 18 September 2001 — 10:29 p.m.
Basil's townhouse, Washington, D.C.

Basil's cocktail parties were a diverse stew of major players from the intelligence world: a senator; members of the House; flag-rank Pentagon officers; and, of course, wall-to-wall CIA, NSA, and DIA operatives and analysts.

Ted was ecstatic.

Karen, on the other hand, was not so impressed. She remained the agnostic observer of Ted's worship of the intelligence apparatus. Further, she was astounded and disgusted by the fact that those entrusted with the nation's secrets would drink so much and talk so freely. They'd arrived at seven o'clock and had been introduced around to the generally disinterested guests. By ten-thirty, she had tired of the alcohol, smoking, and loud conversation. She asked Ted several times to take her home, but he demurred. Karen was embarrassed as Ted circulated among the various cliques, trying without success to insinuate himself into their drunken tête-à-têtes. She was about to tell him she'd had enough when Basil, also approaching a state of profound inebriation, took her arm and gathered in Ted. He guided them to a study off the dining room. Three of the walls had floor-to-ceiling bookshelves with sliding ladders. There were several small oak library tables and a matching bar. In one corner, two dark-brown leather chairs faced each other across a small table. Floor lamps and wall sconces with dark green shades cast intersecting shadows while providing just the right amount of light. A dark green carpet with buff-colored flecks completed the effect—a well-thought-out power room, meant to show visitors that they were in the company of someone special.

Basil slid the pocket doors shut. "I want to discuss something privately with both of you."

"Great party." Ted glanced at his wife and then at Basil.

"Thanks." Basil paused. "Anyway." He glanced at Karen and made a clucking sound before continuing. "The 9/11 attacks have made the civilian government see the need for, shall we say, more diverse interrogation techniques."

Ted's eyes brightened as Basil told him that he envisioned a significant role for him going forward.

"I think you would be perfect for the job," Basil added, reeling Ted in. "The position would involve travel and fieldwork." He turned to Karen and smiled. "Do you think he might be interested?"

"Careful." Karen was stoic. "If you jerk any harder, the hook will pull through."

Basil ignored the comment and opened the pocket doors.

"Walter." Basil beckoned one of the two-stars. "Show Ted around." The admiral nodded and led Ted to one of the previously impenetrable knots of people.

Basil closed the doors and turned his attention to Karen. With his back against the door, he told her how impressed he was with her *Turritopsis* research. He walked to the portable bar and continued. "In fact, I find your work so compelling that I have instructed my division to continue funding your independent research for another year." He retrieved a bottle of port and poured two glasses. "But the research reports now come directly to me."

"Not to Science and Technology?" Karen was shocked but hesitant to say anything that might jeopardize funding. "What about Dr. Strenke?"

Basil took a sip of port. "The good doctor has, uh, retired. Besides, I envision a higher purpose for your research." He held out a glass.

"None for me." Karen held up her hand. "I should eat."

"A taste." Basil pressed the glass into her hand. "It's twenty-one years old." He stopped short. "How old do you think I am?"

"I don't know." Karen decided that a low-ball number was her best option. "Sixty-ish."

"Don't patronize me." Basil took a generous gulp of his port and winced at the burn. "I'm eighty-two years old and feeling every day of it."

"I'm sorry, I didn't mean to—" Karen felt the heat in her face and turned to leave. "I should find Ted."

"Don't go." Basil blocked the door. "What I meant is . . . I don't plan on getting any older."

"I don't understand." Karen shook her head. "Are you ill?"

"No, I'm talking about research," Basil said. "Organ repair, telomere regeneration, transdifferentiation, and such."

"Honestly." Karen looked for a place to sit. "There's been little progress to date."

"But there have been some interesting developments," Basil said.

Karen sipped the port. "I thought the research was directed toward developing a neuro-muscular paralytic to rest acute injuries."

Basil refilled her glass.

"Transdifferentiation in mammals. It's just not—" Karen had skipped dinner and could feel the effects of the alcohol.

"Let's stop dancing and lay it out." Basil took her empty glass and placed it on the bar. "Immortality is achievable, and *Turritopsis* could be the key to achieving it."

"Perhaps accelerated wound healing." Karen could sense her vision blurring. "But immortality?"

Basil put his right hand on her shoulder and steered her to one of the overstuffed leather chairs. He dropped into the opposite chair and leaned forward. "What if I told you that your serum had repaired and rejuvenated the liver and pancreas of a subject with hepatic failure and end-stage pancreatitis?"

"Where is he?" Karen asked, her head cleared by Basil's revelation. "Can I examine him?"

"I'm afraid not." Basil looked at the floor. "Unfortunately, it also killed him. But we have tissue samples."

"I don't know." Things were getting fuzzy again.

"You know you want to be part of this." He paused. "Besides, Ted's success at the Agency is tied to your participation."

Karen shivered as she contemplated the strings attached to the funding.

"But that's small potatoes compared to the concept of immortality," Basil said. "Think of a new world, a better world."

"A new world?" Karen's head was swimming.

"I have occupied a spot on this planet for nearly a century." He leaned closer and lowered his voice. "I have observed—and made—history. And I think—hell, I know—the world is better because of it."

"It's late. I need to go."

"Wait." His speech was slurred. "I need—the world needs—for me and people like me to stick around."

"What are you trying to say?"

"That the problems of the world would be well-served by a plutocracy of immortals who could rule with the accumulated wisdom of centuries of life."

"Immortality?" Karen forced a laugh. "It would get pretty crowded."

"The number of people should be drastically reduced. But that's another issue." He straightened. "Immortality should be a privilege doled out to a select, deserving few."

"Doled out?" She had to be hearing him wrong.

Basil took her hand. "As the discoverer of this brave new world—you, and of course, Ted, and your daughter, Chloe, is it?—would all be participants."

"So, who takes charge of this project?" Karen could feel the hair standing up on her arms. "Who extends the invitations to this exclusive club?"

Basil patted her hand and led her to the door. "Enough shop talk for tonight."

27

HERE'S SOMETHING NEW

Tuesday, 09 April 2002—3:07 p.m.
Karen Spencer's lab, Gloucester Point, Virginia

"How does that compare to the amphibian survival rate from the week of March twenty-ninth?" Karen Spencer swiveled her desk chair, waiting for a reply, while Elaine Cochran, her research assistant, ate a cup of yogurt and checked her flight reservations online.

Karen cleared her throat, watching Elaine quickly change screens.

"Looks like maybe a nine-percent improvement." Elaine sounded bored.

"I need the breakdown by class for any DECO [DECreasing Oxygenation] hormone effect." Karen rubbed her hand over her face. She was exhausted and had consumed all the coffee she could stand. "Just give me those three categories, and then you can go." Elaine, who was flying to Cleveland that night to visit her boyfriend, had already mentally left the lab.

Elaine put down the yogurt cup and increased her speed. "Starvation specimens, three-percent improvement. Senescent specimens, thirty-two percent. Double-pithed trauma specimens—uh, hello!" Her voice went up an octave. "Here's something new." She changed screens twice and tapped on the keyboard. The printer rattled off several pages. "A sixty-nine-percent increase." She handed the report to Karen.

"Okay, take off." Karen said, taking the report. "Have a good time. Fly safe."

Within thirty seconds, Elaine hit the buzzer for the security door and disappeared.

They had been crunching numbers for over three hours without a break. Although Karen appreciated the continuous flow of money from Basil, his demand for a weekly report—progress or no—was time-consuming.

She scribbled the data in her leather research journal and spent the next thirty minutes cobbling together a second report for Basil. She always felt a little guilty when she cooked the books, but there was no way she was going to provide Basil with research that might someday allow him to carry out his plans. Ted might think Basil's revelations at the cocktail party were inebriated musings, but Karen didn't trust him.

The hepatic and pancreatic samples Basil had provided from the Agency's test subject were of no value. Karen had concluded that, while they were indeed sections from the organs of a thirty-year-old, it was probably a specimen mix-up. Given today's findings, however, she was not so sure. Karen slid Basil's report into a manila envelope.

Ted was at his northern Virginia apartment until Friday. She felt in her pocket for the keys to the old Volvo, activated lab security, and walked to her car.

Time to go home and eat alone again.

28

THAT'S ONE LUCKY DOG

Tuesday, 09 April 2002—7:15 p.m.
The Spencer home, Gloucester Point

Karen and Ted's secluded home was in rural Gloucester County on the York River, across from the Naval Weapons Station. Ted's teaching position at Georgetown required that he stay in the city through the week, coming home only on weekends.

Another dinner alone.

Henry, their ancient and arthritic Airedale, met Karen at the kitchen door.

Well, not entirely alone.

She let Henry out to conduct his business, then dropped her jacket, journal, and bag on a chair.

It had drizzled all day. With the evening's cooling temperatures came a dense fog. Karen stood in the kitchen, pondering the research data showing improved survival rate for the mortally traumatized frogs. She opened the refrigerator door, then closed it. She hated cooking for one. She picked up the phone and called into nearby Gloucester for Chinese takeout. She slipped on her jacket, ran to the Volvo, and backed out of the driveway.

There was a yelp and a sickening thump. Henry, who had been under the car to avoid the rain, lay on his side. He whimpered but did not move when Karen touched him.

~

"Henry has massive internal injuries." The vet put his hand on Karen's shoulder. "Given his age and health issues, maybe we should—."

"No," Karen interrupted. She couldn't bear the thought of putting Henry down. "I'll take him home and sit with him to the end."

But as she headed home, Karen recalled the new research data: The subjects with the best survival rate had severe trauma—mortal wounds to be precise.

Karen turned the car around and drove to the institute. She struggled to lift the forty-five-pound dog from the backseat. She was shaking, partly from the cold, early-April rain, and partly from the thought of what she was contemplating. She was about to drop Henry when two hands reached in to steady the dog.

"Dr. Spencer." Larry, one of the security guards, took Henry's full weight. "What happened?"

"I backed over him in the driveway." Karen was drenched. Her shaking increased. "The vet says he probably won't survive the night."

"I'm sorry." He carried the dog to the building and placed him on one of the stainless-steel tables in Karen's lab. "Can I get a blanket or something?"

"No, thank you." Karen blotted Henry dry with lab towels. "I'll just sit with him and hope for the best." She buzzed him out.

"Let me know if there's anything I can do." He nodded and pushed through the lab door.

Karen shaved a three-by-six-inch spot on Henry's neck over the right jugular vein, inserted a venous catheter, and hung a bag of normal saline fluid at a wide-open rate. She shaved two four-inch-square spots on the dog's chest and applied cardiac-monitor leads. The heart rate was much too fast. Over two hundred beats per minute with normal being around 130.

A tense and swollen abdomen indicated significant internal bleeding. Henry was panting, his shallow respirations of fifty per minute were twice normal.

Karen palpated Henry's chest. At least four ribs were broken in two or more places, meaning probable pulmonary contusions. A rectal temp of ninety-eight—three degrees below normal—supported her diagnosis of shock.

"I'm so sorry," Karen whispered. She retrieved a vial of the *Turritopsis* serum from the lab fridge, drew up ten milliliters, and waited.

Henry's heart rate reached 250 before beginning a steady descent. His respirations began to alternate between rapid bursts and periods of nonbreathing. Karen suppressed a sob as the dog's heart rate fell to fifty and then thirty. His breathing came in agonal gasps.

"It won't be long now." She stroked Henry's head.

The dog's breathing stopped. The monitor chirped softly, showed a heart rate of thirty, and then flatlined. Henry was clinically dead. Karen silenced the monitor.

It's now or never.

She inserted the needle of the syringe into the IV port, injected the serum, and removed the IV.

Nothing to do but wait.

For thirty seconds, nothing happened. At sixty seconds, Henry had a seizure. He lay still for a few seconds and then gasped. His heart rate jumped to forty, and he began to breathe.

By four a.m., Henry's vital signs had returned to normal. He whimpered.

At five a.m., he opened his eyes and licked Karen's hand.

At six a.m., he was walking around the room, wanting to be taken outside.

At six thirty-five, Larry saw Karen outside with her dog. "What happened?" He bent down to pet Henry. "I thought he was a goner."

"Temporary spinal shock." Karen had already concocted her story. "Seventy-five milligrams of IV Solu-Cortef and he's as good as new."

"That's one lucky dog."

29

THERE'S BEEN A DEVELOPMENT

Wednesday, 10 April 2002—7:35 a.m.
Ted Spencer's Georgetown apartment, Northwest Washington, D.C.

Karen's call woke Ted from a deep sleep. His first class wasn't until noon.

"It's incredible!" Karen was almost shouting. "The cataracts are gone—and the arthritis—he keeps jumping from the chair to the floor and back again."

"He's like the jellyfish," Ted whispered, even though he was alone in his apartment.

"This is big, Ted," Karen said. "It changes everything."

"We are set now," Ted said. "Basil will be ecstatic."

"I don't think this discovery should be in the hands of the CIA."

"I thought that maybe Basil could—"

"No. Remember what he said."

"Forget the cocktail party." Ted stared at Karen's photo on his desk. "He was enthusiastic about your research, and more than a bit tipsy. That's all. He's done a lot for us."

"That has to stop." Her voice cracked. "I don't want Basil to know what happened with Henry."

"Your research would be dead without his support." Ted struggled to keep the desperation out of his voice.

"I can get other funding."

"And what about me? It's not just about you."

"He can't have it."

So that's it. There would be no spy job.

"You can teach."

"Absolutely," Ted said. "Whatever you want." There was a moment of silence. "We'll discuss it over the weekend and search for alternate funding."

"Thanks, Ted," Karen said. "It's the right decision."

Ted hung up and drummed his fingers on the desk, bit his lower lip, and turned his wife's photo face down. "Sorry, babe. Not this time." He keyed the speed-dial on his cell.

"Basil—Mr. Orlov—there's been a development."

30

DO I GET A PONY?

Monday, 20 May 2002—12:23 p.m.
Lafayette Park, Washington, D.C.

After thirty minutes searching for a parking space within walking distance of Lafayette Park, Nick found Bel Castro—lunch and sodas in
hand—sitting on a bench near the General von Steuben statue. He
hadn't told Nick the reason for the meeting, only that it was top pri-
ority and time dependent. Nick assumed it was Agency business. Don
Bel Castro was the recently widowed son of a Cuban immigrant who
died in the CIA-planned invasion that introduced JFK to the CIA's penchant for interventional diplomacy. A fierce protector of the Agency's
integrity and reputation, Bel Castro was also a lawyer and former D.C.
police detective. He taught part-time in the Criminal Justice program
at Georgetown University while heading an internal-affairs investigation of corruption within the CIA. He suspected, but could not prove,
that Nick's boss, Basil Orlov, was running black ops for hire out of the
Agency.

"Von Steuben was an interesting character." Bel Castro pointed to
the statue of the Revolutionary War hero who stood—jaw firm, hand
in pocket—on a fifteen-foot-high masonry platform. "He left Prus-
sia because of suspected homosexual activity with his aide-de-camp.

Denied promotion and threatened with arrest and prosecution, he found a niche in the colonies, training our troops. He was made a citizen in 1784 by an act of Legislature, but it's taken over two hundred years to recognize him."

"Okay." Nick ground out his cigarette and turned to Bel Castro. "I appreciate the history lesson, but why are we here?"

"To discuss you and Ted," Bel Castro said. "To find out what you know and what we might do about it."

"Know and do about what?" Nick frowned. "And why we?"

Bel Castro began pacing back and forth in front of the bench. "Ted is a good guy. He's devoted to his daughter and his wife—my sister-in-law. But he's obsessed with this spy thing, always has been." Bel Castro jammed his hands into his pockets. "I told him not to get involved with Basil Orlov." He pulled his hands from his pockets, sat down on the bench, and crossed and uncrossed his arms. "Jesus Christ."

Nick listened as a mockingbird in the tree above them did its best to attract a mate. He removed his jacket and draped it over the arm of the bench. The clouds had cleared. The wind had eased. The May sun was warm. Nick felt himself beginning to sweat, although he suspected this was more from the conversation than the temperature.

He rolled up his shirtsleeves, unbuttoned his collar, and loosened his tie. "What I know is this." Nick patted his pockets and retrieved a pack of cigarettes. "Ted has gone from office joke to hot commodity." Struggling with how much info to disclose, Nick held a cigarette in his hand without lighting it. He stared at the yellow stains between his index and middle fingers. He was disgusted by the comfort that he got from holding the cigarette, just knowing it was there. "I suspect his newfound success is barter for his wife's research."

"That's what I thought." Bel Castro took a deep breath, held it for a moment, and then exhaled. "I want you to help me convince Ted to leave the Agency and return to teaching full-time."

"Basil would not appreciate his number-two man undermining him."

Bel Castro held up a hand to silence him. "You need to distance yourself from black ops and especially from Basil. You and Vasily should consider transferring to internal affairs and working for me, ASAP." He gave a quick sigh through pursed lips.

"Leaving Basil's black ops and joining the Agency's internal watchdog would be life changing, if not life shortening." Nick cleared his throat. "You and I are friends, but not that close. Why the concern for me?"

"Because—" Bel Castro started to speak but stopped when a police car rushed by, lights flashing and siren wailing. "Because to Ted, you and Vasily are heroes, the ultimate spies." He paused as if searching for words. "If you and Vasily, especially you, were to throw it all over—well, I don't know." He threw up his hands. "Something bad is coming." Bel Castro shook his head again and looked away. "I can't say more."

"So, you're looking for a quid pro quo. I jump ship and use my influence to extricate Ted."

"More or less."

"Thanks, but no thanks." Nick lit the cigarette. "As much as I would like to be doing something else, the risk-to-benefit ratio just doesn't cut it." He watched Bel Castro's face sag. "I'll give Ted a word of caution, but it's the best I can do."

Bel Castro paused to smile and wave at a toddler in a stroller. He turned back to Nick, still smiling. "Let me sweeten the pot a bit."

Nick returned the smile. "Do I get a pony?"

"Better than that." Bel Castro looked like a poker player hiding four aces. "My best friend in the world is the chairman of the history department at Georgetown."

"So?" Nick felt his pulse quicken.

"I have taken the liberty of setting up a lunch meeting for the three of us next week to discuss a tenure-track position for you in ancient history and the classics, which has opened up due to a sudden retirement secondary to some indiscretions."

The cigarette slipped from Nick's fingers.

Forget the pony, he's offering me the car.

"You were discussed at length." Bel Castro leaned in closer. His grin looked like that of the Cheshire cat. "Although you have been, shall we say, engaged in other than academic pursuits for a while, your PhD and previous writings . . ."

Nick's ears were buzzing so loud he couldn't hear the rest.

"Very receptive . . . six-month probationary period . . ."

The roar subsided.

"Sound good?" Bel Castro's voice pierced the droning in his head.

"A parking space?" Nick mumbled, searching for a cogent thought.

"Yes, I'm sure, but—" Bel Castro pointed to wisps of smoke, "your jacket is on fire."

"Damn." Nick remembered the cigarette, jumped to his feet, and began patting his jacket. He picked it up and looked at the dime-sized smoking hole. "Forget it." He dropped the jacket in a mesh trash can near the bench.

Nothing can spoil this.

"That's the tipping point." Nick patted his pockets again. "If you can get me back into academics, I'm yours." He walked to the trash can and retrieved his cigarettes. "How do we proceed?"

"I want Ted out of the Agency altogether." Bel Castro said. "I want him back at Georgetown full-time, before it's too late. If it isn't too late already. Ted's not like us. He's not mentally equipped to play this game."

"You're pretty heavily vested in this." Nick lit another cigarette.

"Karen Spencer is the younger—and only—sister of my late wife, Marie." Bel Castro stared down at his feet. "And I am Chloe's godfather."

"I'm sorry for your loss," Nick said.

"Thanks." Bel Castro raised his head and looked up. "Marie loved Ted, but she knew he was a bit of a squirrel." He turned to face Nick. "I promised her I would look after them."

"Basil doesn't give a shit about Ted," Nick said, taking a draw on the cigarette. "But he's hot on Karen's research."

"Karen needs to convince Basil the research is a dead end." Bel

Castro wrinkled his forehead. "Tell her to just give him some bogus notes and forget the jellyfish."

"Georgetown will contact Basil's dummy company for a reference on me," Nick said. "He won't be happy."

"Already taken care of." Bel Castro smiled. "They'll say you're being considered for a part-time, non-tenure, temporary slot."

Nick took one last deep pull on the cigarette. "Call Karen now and tell her I'll phone this afternoon." He dropped the cigarette to the bricks, ground it out with his foot, and exhaled slowly. "This thing with Ted is a bit trickier. He's riding high. I need to choose my time."

"You can handle it." Bel Castro grinned and extended his hand, "Professor."

31

SPY TO SPY

Monday, 20 May 2002—3:14 p.m.
Fifth floor, Edward B. Bunn Intercultural Center, Georgetown

Nick spent the early afternoon wandering the Georgetown University campus, fantasizing about his return to teaching. He had coffee and a scone at Saxbys on O Street before winding his way across campus to the Edward B. Bunn S.J. Intercultural Center or, as it was better known, ICC. Eschewing the elevator, he climbed the stairs to the fifth floor, where several medieval- and ancient-history courses were being taught. He stood, back to the wall, listening as a professor and student discussed thesis topics.

"How about whether or not the actions of Arminius at the Battle of the Teutoburg Forest made him the father of the German nation?" The student, a bookish twenty-something, pushed her glasses up on her nose and waited for an accolade. Nick stared at the wall and waited for the takedown.

"Too broad, Theresa." The professor made a clucking sound. "And beaten to death."

"I don't know where to go." She twisted a lock of hair. "Can you just sort of point me in the right direction?"

"This is graduate school, not junior college." The professor tilted his head like he was looking at a lab specimen. "You've been skating on gentleman's BS since you got here."

Nick bit his lip to keep silent.

Pompous ass.

"Take some education credits. Consider teaching high school or something." The professor glanced at his watch. "Think about it. No shame in that." He started to put his hand on her shoulder, then pulled back. "Not everyone is meant to be a PhD."

The student stood staring at the floor as the professor latched onto a passing colleague and moved down the hall.

The educator in Nick was incensed. He was astounded that a professor would humiliate a student in public.

When I'm in the department . . .

Nick eased over to where she stood. "Theresa, is it?"

She raised her head and looked at him through puffy eyes.

"I couldn't help but overhear." He kept his hands in his pockets.

"Do I know you?" She squinted as if she should recognize him.

"No, but I have a suggestion for your thesis." He started down the hall. "Walk with me."

She fell into step. "Do you teach here?"

"Soon, maybe." Nick exhaled and looked up. "Anyway, consider this."

"At this point, I'll consider anything." She wiped her eyes and smiled.

"At Teutoburg Forest, the Germanic army triumphed against a numerically superior and better trained Roman legion." Nick stopped walking and turned to face Theresa. "Your thesis might posit Arminius as a proto-führer, the genesis of the concept of German invincibility."

"Arminius justified the ambush and slaughter as a means to an end," she said, her eyes brightening. "The only way to defeat a better equipped and numerically superior foe. I could tie it all to Kant's Categorical Imperative."

"There's your thesis." Nick stopped walking and looked at his watch. "Don't forget to ask if this outcome-based philosophy and the German concept of otherness may have helped rationalize the Holocaust."

"Thank you," she said, leaning in. "Doctor . . .?"

He opened the door to the stairwell. "We'll talk again when you've chosen your dissertation topic."

Nick sat on a bench outside the Lauinger Library. He raised his paper cup and took a sip of cold coffee. A passing student smiled at him. He smiled back and took a long drag on his cigarette.

She rolled her eyes.

He looked away, dropped the cigarette into the inch of stale coffee, and made a mental note.

The day I sign the teaching contract is the day I smoke my last cigarette.

He glanced at his watch. It was nearly seven o'clock. Bel Castro said Karen was usually home by six-thirty. He pulled out his cell and punched in the number Don had given him. He was about to press send when he changed his mind. While it was unlikely that Basil had tapped the Spencers' home phone, Nick's cell was, per Basil's orders, department issued. He knew that Basil's secretary reviewed the monthly bill for interesting numbers. It would be hard to explain a call to the Spencer residence, especially if the Spencers deserted Basil. Nick jingled the coins in his pocket and located a nearby payphone.

Karen Spencer answered on the first ring. "Don told me you would be calling."

Nick was pleased to learn that she had already made the decision to sever ties with the Agency and had been submitting factitious research findings to Basil while storing her actual findings elsewhere. Over the next six weeks, she would paint an increasingly dismal scenario, culminating in a report stating that the peculiar capabilities of *T. dohrnii* had no discernible mammalian applications.

"But that's not the problem."

"Then what?" Nick held the phone between his neck and shoulder while he retrieved his cigarettes and lighter.

"Ted." Karen gave a deep sigh. "He's all in for the James Bond experience."

Nick struggled to hold the phone and light his cigarette. "Does he know you've doctored the research notes?"

"No. I was going to tell him Friday when he came home."

"Don't. It's best if he doesn't know." Nick put the cigarette pack and lighter back in his pocket and took the receiver in his left hand. "Let me handle this." He put the cigarette to his lips and inhaled deeply. "You know, spy to spy."

32

LEAVE BEFORE YOU LOSE IT ALL

Monday, 20 May 2002—8:47 p.m.
Willard Hotel, the Round Robin Bar, Washington, D.C.

Ted eagerly accepted Nick's invitation for drinks at the Willard Hotel. It was no coincidence that Nick had chosen the Willard, a watering hole and meeting place for espionage activities since the Civil War. The hostess seated them at a corner table. Ted sat facing the entrance, scrutinizing every patron who entered as if they were about to make a dead drop.

"You know, I'd gladly trade my situation for yours," Nick said.

Ted laughed.

"I'm dead serious." Nick took a sip of scotch. "I've had quite enough of this." He paused, searching for words that would have the maximum impact. *Hell, I'll just tell it like it is.* He ground out his cigarette in the ashtray.

"Twenty years ago, I was a newly minted PhD with an offer to teach at Princeton." He went on to describe poor choices, bad outcomes, and lost opportunities. "You have a wife, a daughter, and a career." He put his hands on the table. "I'm throwing it in to return to teaching." Nick leaned forward. "My advice is do the same before you lose it all." Nick thought he might be getting through to him.

Ted pointed to a couple who had just sat down three tables to their left. "She just slipped something into his hand."

"Probably a room key." Nick grabbed Ted's arm. "Did you hear what I said?"

Ted shook off Nick's grasp. "I'm sorry you're disillusioned, but I feel alive for the first time in my life." He jerked his head toward the couple. "I think it was an envelope or a small box."

$\sim$

Nick called Bel Castro at home at a little after eleven to tell him that Ted was a harder sale than he had anticipated.

Don said that he had expected as much but that he had some good news.

"I talked to Arthur this afternoon." Bel Castro paused. When Nick said nothing, he continued. "The chair of the history department."

"Oh, yeah." Nick pulled a pack of cigarettes from his pocket, thought about his earlier pledge, and put them back. "And?"

"He suggested lunch in a couple weeks to seal the deal. Contract to follow." There was another long pause. "The Basil investigation is heating up. This needs to happen soon."

"No problem." Nick could see his Lotus parked in a Georgetown University faculty spot. "Give me two weeks."

33

WE JUST NEED A BIGGER HAMMER

Tuesday, 11 June 2002—5:49 p.m.
Nick's Georgetown townhouse

Two weeks of cajoling had failed to move Ted one iota. In fact, Basil had given Ted an office of sorts at the Agency.

Nick looked at the caller ID on his secure landline and picked up.

"I have news." Bel Castro's tone was difficult to read.

"Good or bad?"

There was a hard sigh. "Both."

"And?" Nick wanted to reach through the phone and shake Bel Castro.

"I just saw your contract. You're a go for the fall semester."

"And the bad news."

"I just talked to Karen."

"And?"

It's like poking a dead animal with a stick.

"Ted shows no signs of leaving."

Nick could visualize the campus cops laughing as they scraped the faculty parking sticker off his Lotus.

Bel Castro continued. "Are you sure we can get this done?"

"Yeah." Nick pulled out his cigarettes. "We just need a bigger hammer."

34

HE DIDN'T WANT TO BE A SPY ANYMORE

Wednesday, 12 June 2002—4:17 p.m.
Ted Spencer's office, CIA annex, Langley

Ted thumbed through a journal extolling the vices and virtues of the latest neuromuscular paralytic drug. The dull polysyllabic chemical compounds began to blur on the page.

He put the journal down and squinted to clear his vision. He opened his eyes and surveyed the six-by-eight-foot room that was his office; long-neglected walls screamed for paint, linoleum squares curled on the floor. Overhead, a single bare florescent tube crackled with irregular rhythm as its contents alternated between bright white and gray. His desk and seating consisted of a plastic utility table and a metal folding chair. The smell of various cleaners, waxes, and disinfectants insulted his nose.

It looked like a broom closet, which, a month earlier, is exactly what it had been.

"Space is at a premium," Basil said, as the workman removed the brooms, mops, buckets, and plungers from the tiny room. "It's only temporary." A custodian mopped the floor with dirty water. "I'm sure something better will open up by the time your wife's research bears fruit."

"It's perfectly satisfactory." Ted would have gladly occupied a toilet stall to be in this building.

"I'm afraid there are no phone lines in here." Basil retrieved a cell-phone from his pocket. "Use this for all calls, Agency and private, from this point forward."

It had been over two months since Ted had phoned Basil with the news about the dog. Basil had been ecstatic and, as promised, brought Ted onboard as a member of the interrogation team. Ted now had crypto-clearance and played an ever-increasing role in the black division's psy-ops activities. Basil agreed to keep secret his knowledge of the event with the Spencers' dog but had grown increasingly impatient over the past several weeks, constantly pushing Ted for research updates.

Thank God that's all over now.

Ted had left their Gloucester home early that morning with two fat manila envelopes, each containing a copy of Karen's research to date. Despite her initial reluctance following the "Henry event," she now seemed willing to continue providing Basil with research updates. He had dropped one copy off at the Marine Institute's library for archiving and then he'd driven straight to Langley, where he handed the second copy to Basil's secretary.

He was jogged back to the present by the vibration of his silenced cellphone. Ted watched it jitter across his plastic desk, rotating like some stricken beetle trying to right itself. By the second ring, it had turned to the point that he could read the display. It was Basil's secretary. He reached for the phone. Anything from Basil or his secretary was urgent until proven otherwise.

"Sheila," Ted said, expecting the usual banter.

"Basil wants to see you immediately." The secretary's tone was all business.

"I'll be in his office in five minutes." Ted made a mental note to stop at the Agency canteen and bring the grumpy secretary coffee and a bagel.

"Not the office." Her speech remained clipped. "He wants to see you in the basement animal lab." Ted could hear a muffled voice in the background. "Marty Schwartz will meet you at the elevator."

"Ah, yes, Dracula's younger brother." Ted and Sheila often joked about Marty's morbid persona. I'll bring a hammer and a stake?"

"Five minutes." She hung up.

Ted could guess the reason he was being summoned. Basil was bringing him on full-time as chief psychologist overseeing the interrogation of high-value prisoners. He had just gotten back from an intensive three-week training course at The Farm, where he'd learned everything from competitive driving to dead-drops. He surprised everyone at the pistol range by qualifying as "Expert" with his Walther PPK. He was inching ever closer to real fieldwork.

His new position would be more like developing customized torture programs based on a prisoner's psychological profile, but that was fine with Ted.

An outcome-based utilitarianism had gripped the Agency and other intelligence-gathering bodies since the 9/11 attacks. The administration, stung by the public spectacle of Americans jumping to their deaths from One and Two WTC to avoid being burned alive, had fully embraced the Jeremy Bentham approach: that curious blend of hedonism and Christianity in which "the end justifies the means." Ted had never heard of waterboarding, much less seen it. He wondered to himself if it got the truth or just an answer.

Ted had been shocked when Nick told him over drinks that he hated the interrogations, missed teaching, and was contemplating a return to academia. On numerous occasions over the last few weeks, Nick had encouraged and even pressured Ted to do the same, telling him that the Agency was like drug dependency. It blurred ethical boundaries and destroyed personal relationships. Ted attributed Nick's burnout to the post-9/11 emotional and physical demands experienced by Agency personnel. Ted had interviewed and guilt-counseled numerous Agency employees who, with the benefit of hindsight, felt they had missed something crucial leading up to that horrific day.

As the elevator door opened, Ted was struck by an odor, not unlike that of a well-maintained stable, a pleasant blend of bedding, animal food, and cleanser, tainted with just a hint of animal waste.

Marty stood before him, arms crossed, wearing the flat-grin smirk he usually reserved for questioning detainees. Marty, unlike Nick, seemed to relish the interrogations—the more brutal, the better. On numerous occasions, his extremes would have killed the prisoner had Nick not reined him in.

"This way." Marty took Ted's arm and pulled, more than led, him to a door marked:

CAUTION
VENOMOUS SNAKES

Marty opened the door, pushed Ted in ahead of him, and pulled the door shut.

The room was approximately six by twelve feet, and of block construction painted a sick green. One of the twelve-foot walls consisted of one-foot high, three-foot wide drawers going from floor to ceiling, each topped by a two-inch strip of fine wire mesh. The opposite wall had a three-foot tall glass window at eye level running its entire length. In the back, a telephone receiver hung on the wall.

In contrast to the pleasant smell in the hallway, this room had a heavy, musky odor, somewhere between that of a skunk and rotten cucumbers. Basil stood in the far corner, frowning, a handkerchief held over his mouth. Next to him was an unkempt man in his early twenties wearing a lab coat over his blue jeans and red T-shirt. In his right hand was a three-foot-long pole with a trigger-operated pincher on the end. His left hand cradled a red plastic bucket.

Basil turned to face Ted but did not greet him. He was holding a blue binder Ted had dropped off that morning. For a moment, there was silence. Basil scowled. Marty just stared, his mouth the same flat grin.

Ted felt himself start to sweat. This didn't look like a venue to discuss promotions.

Basil turned to the man with the red bucket and nodded. Marty moved to a position just behind Ted.

"What's this all about?" Ted was surprised at the squeak in his voice.

Basil tapped the blue notebook with his index finger. "A lesson in what happens when you fail to meet expectations."

The lab attendant used the pincher to retrieve a mouse from the bucket, then slid open one of the drawers. The drawer was half-filled with straw and a few rocks. A dark blue head was just visible, moving back and forth as if assessing the situation. As it rose, Ted noticed that the snake's body was composed of alternating blue and gray bands. The man with the red bucket pushed the pole with the mouse inside the drawer and banged it against the side. The mouse squeaked in terror. The sound reminded Ted of his own voice a few moments before. The snake struck—first a feint at the handler, and then, secondarily, at the helpless mouse.

"Simon." Basil adopted the tone of a college instructor teaching freshmen students. "What kind of snake is that beautiful creature, and how fast do you die when one bites you?"

"It's a blue krait. The venom takes effect in twenty to thirty minutes." Simon closed the drawer.

"And the mortality rate?" Basil's glance lingered on Ted.

"Fifty percent with anti-venom, a hundred percent without."

Basil opened the blue notebook. "Show us some more."

Ted stared wide-eyed as drawers were opened and closed for the next thirty minutes: large snakes, small snakes, brown snakes, yellow snakes, snakes with hoods. The snake handler had several near misses, eliciting chuckles from Marty. Each feeding was accompanied by a flippant discussion of the relative lethality of each snake.

"That will be fine for the moment, Simon." Basil smiled at the handler. "Thank you."

He held out the blue research folder.

"What the hell is your wife trying to pull?" Basil went on to explain that the report failed to mention the dog and further stated that the serum had no mammalian applications.

"I—I'm not sure," Ted stammered. "I didn't read it. I assumed it was all there."

"I'm beginning to think you just made up the part about the dog to get this job." Basil tapped Simon on the shoulder. "Show us the good one."

Ted bolted for the door. Marty grabbed Ted from behind and moved him closer to the snake handler.

"Mr. Orlov, sir, are you sure?" Simon looked at Ted. "This guy's too close, and this one's unpredictable."

"Just do it." Basil smiled at Ted.

Simon picked up the bucket and walked to the column of drawers nearest the door.

Ted noticed that these drawers were about twice the size of the others.

Basil nodded to Marty, who then turned Ted toward the drawer just behind Simon. The handler hesitated until Marty nudged him with his foot. Then he retrieved one of the mice with the pole and slowly opened the door. Hands shaking, Simon pushed the baited pole into the drawer.

A large, dark-gray head rose from the rocks and straw. The snake ignored the mouse and remained motionless, its eyes fixed on Simon. The snake opened its mouth to reveal a jet-black interior.

"The Black Mamba," Basil said. "Paralysis in seconds, death in five minutes. You have two weeks to bring your wife around." He paused. "Or else."

"I quit," Ted said.

"I'm afraid that ship has sailed." Basil nodded, and Marty pushed Ted closer to the drawer. "Do you understand the gravity of your situation?"

"Yes, sir." Ted kept his eyes glued to the massive gray head and black mouth.

"I think he needs a little demonstration of our sincerity." Basil tipped his head.

Marty used Ted's body to push Simon against the drawer. The Mamba lunged, rotating its head ninety-degrees to bite Simon on the neck. Marty threw Ted to the side and kicked the drawer shut.

Simon slumped to the floor. No noise. No twitching.

Basil faced Ted, who stood shaking in the corner next to the door. "Think about what a dangerous world it is."

Basil gestured to Simon's motionless form on the floor and then to the Mamba's drawer. "It would be a shame if this fellow turned up in your daughter's car."

Marty pushed Ted toward the door.

Basil lifted the telephone receiver. "There's been an accident in the snake room." He paused to listen and smiled at Ted. "No, it was the Mamba. I'm afraid it's too late for that." He hung up. "Your family's counting on you, Ted." Basil tilted his head toward the body on the floor. "Don't let them down."

Marty opened the door and gave a quick bow. He made his right hand into the shape of a gun, pointed it at Ted, and then jerked his finger upward as if in recoil.

Ted was beyond embarrassment at the warmth and wetness that spread down his pant leg. He didn't want to be a spy anymore.

35

THE *NATIONAL ENQUIRER* HAS BETTER INTEL

Monday, 17 June 2002—6:01 p.m.
Basil's office, CIA headquarters

Sheila, Basil's secretary, had gone home for the day. Her desk sat in a an eight-by-twelve alcove off the main hall. Nick was surprised that an agency as secretive as the CIA did not have an enclosed space for secretaries. A gray-carpeted noise partition was all that separated her from the passing foot traffic. The wall common with Basil's office contained the obligatory framed woodland scene, while the president and the DCIA stared each other down from the other two opposing walls. Sheila had decorated the divider with an assortment of postcards, family photos, and grocery lists.

Like Sheila, it was pleasant but generic.

Nick stopped at the empty desk and pressed the button on the intercom. "It's me."

The door clicked open a few inches.

Basil stood behind the desk, his back to Nick. Marty leaned against the wall in his usual corner spot, facing Basil, who gestured in animated conversation while Marty's head bobbed in agreement. Marty caught Basil's eye and gave a small head jerk toward Nick.

Basil stopped speaking and turned to face Nick. "I was just briefing

Marty on the protocol for tomorrow's Spencer interview." He glanced first at Marty and then at Nick.

"Why brief him?" Nick nodded in Marty's direction. "It's just me and Vasily going to Gloucester."

"There's been a development." Basil glanced at Marty again and began to pace. He took out a pack of cigarettes and tapped them against the desk. "I have information that the Spencers may be attempting to market their research to the Iranians."

"That's complete bullshit," Nick said, looking at Marty who was staring at the floor. "Where did you get this?"

"Fletcher," Basil said, an unlit cigarette hanging from his lips.

"Christ, Basil." Nick shook his head. "The *National Enquirer* has better intel than Fletcher. What's his source?"

Basil patted his shirt and pants pockets, looking for his lighter. "He wouldn't say."

Marty sprang, drew his lighter, and lit Basil's cigarette.

"Down, Rover," Nick said.

Marty glared at him. Since the failed Hunt mission in Dearborn, Marty had been Basil's constant companion. When Basil held Marty back from that mission, Nick had been sure he was toast. Instead, the sycophantic Marty had become Basil's de facto valet—lighting cigarettes, fetching coffee, and eavesdropping on casual conversations for him. Bel Castro posited that Basil had big-time dirt on Marty, something so bad it guaranteed absolute loyalty.

Bel Castro had said there was a rumor describing how Marty, in a psychotic rage, had drowned his cheating ex-stripper wife and her Chinese crested pup in the family swimming pool. When the mother-in-law arrived home and found him fishing the body out, he did her, too.

"How did he get away with it?" Nick had asked.

"He called, sobbing. Basil sent the cleaners over, concocted a rock-solid backstory, and bought Marty's loyalty for life."

"Any proof?"

"I'm digging," Bel Castro had said. "But, well, you know how thorough Basil is."

Nick thought of the actor George Raft as he watched Marty creep back to his corner, turn to face Basil, and slouch against the wall.

The only thing missing is the coin flip and pinstripe suit.

"Enough." Basil acknowledged Marty's gesture with a quick nod and fixed his gaze on Nick. "This is how it's going to go down. You and Vasily will conduct the interview and ask nicely for Dr. Spencer's research notebook. It's a dark brown thing with a leather tie. The only time I saw her without it was at a cocktail party."

"And if she won't give it up?" Nick returned Basil's stare. "It is private property, after all."

"Conclude your interview and leave." Basil opened his desk drawer, took out a document, and handed it to Nick. "Marty will have this."

"A search warrant?" Nick shook his head in disbelief. "Forget that and let us take Bel Castro along. He's family, and their daughter's godfather. He can—"

"Precisely why he can't go." Basil took the warrant. "We need arm's-length credibility to clear them. We can't have their child's godfather involved."

"And Marty?"

"Marty and Blair will carry out the search and, if necessary, bring the Spencers in."

"Isn't this a bit soon for Blair?" Nick said. "She's just finished training. She's been Marty's partner for less than three weeks."

"No." Basil ground his cigarette in the ashtray. "She's perfect for this mission." He took out his cigarette pack again.

"Because?"

Basil rubbed the back of his neck. "This is a touchy one. If this goes public, things could go south fast, so I want only junior people on the spit."

"Does Rover know this?" Nick gestured to Marty.

"Marty is aware that he is expendable." Basil made eye contact and held Nick's gaze. "Besides, you and Vasily are too valuable to be put at risk."

"Then why send us at all?"

"To lend gravitas. The Agency respects both of you." Basil leaned back in his desk chair. "You and Vasily will be first team from eight until ten."

"I thought it was eleven until one." Nick interrupted.

"I don't want to risk them bolting before we arrive."

"For God's sake, don't you think—"

"We've had them under surveillance for three days." Basil picked up a sheet of paper from his desk. "Karen Spencer refilled their routine prescriptions two months early. They just bought five-hundred dollars' worth of freeze-dried food."

"So?" Nick said.

"Ted withdrew twenty-two thousand dollars in cash. He told the bank manager he was buying his daughter a car."

Nick shrugged.

"Instead," Basil said, staring at the paper, "he bought four prepaid credit cards and two prepaid phones."

Basil passed the paper to Nick. "Look at the last entry."

Nick's eyes widened. "Twenty boxes of .380 hollow-point ammunition."

Basil glanced at Marty again. "Ted owns a Walther PPK .380 mil. You know, his whole 007 thing. Anyway, he's good with it. I've seen his range records." He tapped out another cigarette. "So, we handle it this way." Marty sprang, lit it for him, and did a quick pirouette back to the corner.

"You?" Basil proffered the pack.

"No." Nick shook his head. "I quit."

"Again?" Basil laughed. "Anyway, Marty and Blair will show up a little before ten." He waved his hand. "Maybe that's all it will take. If not, they toss the place and bring them in."

"I don't like it." Nick patted his jacket pockets before pointing to

Basil's cigarettes. "Damn." He took a cigarette from Basil, put it in his mouth, and patted for a lighter.

"Predictable." Basil fished a lighter from his pocket and lit Nick up. "It's like the spy game." He snapped the lighter closed. "You'll quit when they nail your box shut."

Nick walked to the door, then turned back to Basil.

"It's taken care of," Basil said.

Nick hesitated.

Basil pushed a button under his desktop and the door clicked open. "Now, go find that dumbass Ukrainian and have a drink," Basil said. "And pull the door shut behind you."

~

Basil watched Nick leave and wondered if he was losing his edge. He had been informed that the history department at Georgetown University was considering Nick for a part-time position. Basil was not keen on having him go off the reservation, not even part-time.

Tomorrow should help Dr. Caedwallan find his compass.

"Do you think he bought that line of shit?" Marty walked over to Basil, took out a cigarette, and put it in his mouth.

"Maybe," Basil said, staring at the door. "But it doesn't matter. You know what to do." He stood and turned to Marty. "I want that journal."

"Yes, sir." Marty lit his cigarette and inhaled deeply.

"And I want that dog."

"Yes, sir."

"And Marty?" Basil pulled the cigarette from Marty's mouth and snubbed it in the ashtray. "No smoking in my office."

36

EVERYTHING SEEMS TO BE BLOOMING AT ONCE

Monday, 17 June 2002—6:27 p.m.
Spencer home, Gloucester Point

Chloe Spencer had mixed feelings about spending the summer with her parents before resuming her graduate studies in anthropology at the University of Chicago in the fall. She loved her parents but became anxious whenever she took a break from academics. Her parents had always been there for her, and she assumed that wasn't going to change. It was the same with friendships and dating. Those things could wait until her thesis was approved. Her mother and father both had doctoral degrees. They understood the demands of preparing a thesis and dissertation. As far as friends and romance, well, if you didn't form attachments, you didn't have to say no.

Still, all in all, her situation was much better than the other students in her cohort. She had a hand-me-down car that her parents maintained. And every three or four days, she had a call from home offering help with food, rent, or other living expenses. She was cautious with her credit card but never saw a bill; it went straight to her parents.

She stared in the full-length mirror and thought about what else she was deferring until after graduation. In high school, Chloe had run track and been on the swim team. No matter how much she'd eaten, she wouldn't gain an ounce. That all changed with college and grad school. Although she ate less, she devoted all her time to study. Her only exercise was walking to class. Each year her weight had gone up a few pounds, and each year she told herself the same thing: "When I finish my thesis, then I'll have a life." Her five-foot, seven-inch frame hid a lot, but summer and swimsuits, well, a one-piece would do until graduation.

She dumped the contents of her duffle bag on the bedroom floor. She didn't know why, but both her parents seemed nervous. Chloe was amused that her parents were so motivated to take this trip. They'd already started piling supplies in the living room next to the front door. It looked like they had enough stuff for a month, even though they planned to be gone for only a week. She'd watched her mom pack freeze-dried food in a duffle. At five-thirty, her father had announced that he was off to the local food mart.

"I want to hit the ATM one more time," he said. "You never know who takes credit cards."

"Gee, Dad," Chloe said. "They took my credit card in the Yucatan when I was there for my field trip last year."

When he got back, he said, "Let's pack the tent and sleeping bags, just in case."

"Is this a vacation or an expedition?" Chloe asked.

Her father ignored her.

Chloe was still marveling at the frenetic activity when the phone rang. She ran to the kitchen and picked up on the second ring. It was her uncle.

"Chloe, it's Don." Chloe thought his voice sounded strained. "How's my favorite niece?"

"Your only niece is feeling a bit bored and abandoned," she said.

"I heard the rumblings." His voice lightened. "Your mom called. She said you could use a date tomorrow."

"Tomorrow? No kidding? Are you coming down?" Chloe asked, watching in amazement as Henry danced around the room with a squeeze toy.

"I thought you might come up and spend the night," he said. "Oh, and your mom wants you to bring Henry so that he won't be in the way. We can picnic at Lafayette Park."

"Sounds great," Chloe said. "Mom and Dad are packing for the Lewis and Clark expedition."

"Is that Don?" Karen Spencer zipped a duffle shut and reached for the phone.

"If you leave soon, you'll get here before dark," Chloe heard Don say as she passed the phone.

"Don, hi. It's me." Karen looked at Chloe, blinked several times, and turned away. "Thanks for everything." She twisted the phone cord. "Okay. I'll tell her. Good-bye, and thanks again."

Chloe watched her mother stiffen as she ended the call.

"Let's get you packed and on the road," she turned around to face Chloe. "Don wants you to bring enough clothes for a couple of days." She wiped her eyes with her hands. "He's expecting a guided tour of the Smithsonian Museum of Natural History from you."

"Mom," Chloe said, touching her mother's cheek, "what's wrong with your eyes?"

"Allergies," she said. "Everything seems to be blooming at once."

"I thought we were leaving Saturday."

"Your father and I are going ahead tomorrow to get things set up." Karen looked away again. "Don's been down since Marie died. He's excited to spend a little time with you." She took a tissue from the dispenser on the counter and dabbed her eyes. "You can catch up to us on Saturday."

37

MAYBE AFTER DINNER, OR MAYBE TOMORROW

Monday, 17 June 2002—8:41 p.m.
Don Bel Castro's home, Stafford, Virginia

Chloe exited the freeway and made her way along the familiar route to her uncle's home. The drive to Stafford had been hectic but uneventful. The old Volvo's air-conditioning had failed long ago, which was fine since Henry loved the gale-force feeling of seventy miles per hour with the windows down. The dog pulled against the restraint that held him in place, trying to get his nose further out the window. The drivers on I-95 were up to their usual antics, bobbing and weaving like professional boxers. Chloe gave up on blowing her horn when they cut her off since each tap of the horn was greeted with a stab on the brakes, a quick middle-finger salute, and even worse driving. The further she drove, the more anxious she became. Something didn't add up. Chloe turned on her lights less than a mile from Don's house. He should be happy; she'd made it alive and before it was truly dark. As she turned into the driveway, she could see the shadows already creeping in between the tall boxwoods surrounding his yard.

Why couldn't I stay at home and leave with Mom and Dad on Saturday? Why was Don so insistent that I come right now and stay so long?

Don appeared at the front door the moment she pulled into the driveway.

"My two favorites!" He gave Chloe a quick peck on the cheek and released Henry from his restraint. "I'm grilling steaks out back. Drag your bag upstairs. I'll put Henry on the tie out by the patio."

Chloe shouldered her backpack and picked up her duffle. "Give me five minutes to freshen up and I'll be down." She started up the stairs but turned back. "Something is up, and I think you know what it is."

"We'll talk over dinner." Don's expression went from smile to frown to smile again. "Maybe after dinner." He shook his head. "Or maybe tomorrow."

Chloe half-carried, half-dragged her duffle upstairs. In the room, she probed the depths of the bag for her cosmetic case. Her hand jammed against something; a soft parcel tied with a leather strap.

A book? I didn't pack a book.

She shook the contents of the duffle onto the bed. Out tumbled her mother's leather-bound research journal and a large, square-top key.

38

IT'S OUT OF OUR HANDS NOW

Tuesday, 18 June 2002—8:00 a.m.
Yorktown Bridge, Gloucester Point

"Thank you and have a nice day." The attendant waved and smiled as Vasily pulled away from the Coleman Bridge tollbooth. The drawbridge crossed the York River, allowing U.S. 17 to connect Gloucester Point with the "Golden Triangle" historical attractions of Yorktown, Williamsburg, and Jamestown.

As they drove on, Vasily realized they were near where the numerous buildings of the William and Mary Marine Science Institute hugged the east bank of the York. "Since that's where Mrs. Dr. Spencer works," he said, lifting his foot from the accelerator, "do we need to check there first?"

"No." Nick waved him on. "Basil's snitch, that Cochran woman, overheard Karen Spencer say she would be out for most of this week."

It took over thirty minutes for Nick and Vasily to navigate the maze of ever-narrowing tarmac roads leading to the Spencer residence. The twenty-two-acre parcel was located on a marsh-like cove just off the York River. The house was a modest, two-story brick cottage surrounded by three well-groomed acres. It sat about a hundred feet from the road. Forty-foot-tall white pines covered the balance of the property, allowing a glimpse of the house. A crescent-shaped drive of brown pea-gravel curved from the road through the trees. Vasily stopped the car at the end of the driveway and drummed his fingers on the steering wheel.

"I hate this shit." He turned to face Nick. "Basil and his games. Bel Castro says—"

"We don't work for Bel Castro." Nick patted his empty pocket for a cigarette. "We both know Basil has an agenda. Our mission is to get that journal and spare the Spencers a meeting with Marty."

Vasily trolled up the curved driveway to the open clearing surrounding the house. The Spencer's SUV was surrounded by an assortment of duffle bags, camping gear, and grocery bags. The doors and hatch hung open. Ted Spencer was strapping something to the roof rack, while Karen was moving excess items back into the house. Nick and Vasily exchanged glances. Maybe Basil had guessed right.

"Sorry for our early arrival." Nick followed Ted around the SUV as he closed the doors and rear hatch.

Ted Spencer turned to his wife. She paled and shrugged her shoulders.

"What's this all about, Nick?" Ted closed the last of the car doors.

Before Nick could begin, Vasily put his hand on Nick's shoulder and stepped between him and Ted.

"Looks like quite the operation." Vasily glanced from pile to pile, and then back at Ted.

"It's a family tradition." Ted avoided eye contact as he adjusted a bungee cord to secure a tent and four large duffles on the SUV's roof rack. "We always kick off the summer by taking our daughter on a week-long trip."

"Where is Chloe?" Vasily asked.

"She's out of town today, with her dog, Henry," Karen said. The couple exchanged nervous glances. "Visiting friends," she added. "She missed spending time with her dog when she was off at college."

Nick considered how little he knew about the Spencer family. He had never seen Chloe. He'd met Karen at one of Basil's cocktail parties. His only other contact had been a single phone call in which they discussed prying Ted loose from the Agency. Nick's impression of Ted was that he was a brilliant psychologist and a mostly all-right guy with a terrible James Bond–wannabe complex.

Nick said nothing as he circled the Spencer vehicle, but he noted that the gray Suburban was tightly packed except for a passenger or duffle-sized space in the second-row seating. "It seems fully loaded," he said, nodding at the vehicle. "Looks like you're ready to roll."

"We thought so." Karen shuffled another load to the front door.

Another thirty minutes and we would have missed them. I don't think they planned on keeping our noon appointment.

"That is a lot of gear, even for a long weekend," Vasily said to Ted, smiling. "More like a bug-out."

Nick turned away and smiled.

Ah, good cop/bad cop. It looks like Vasily has chosen his role.

Ted's face tightened. "Three days, three weeks." He stretched the last cord and turned to face Vasily. "What difference does it make?"

Karen Spencer kept her head down as she carried things inside, pausing to catch the conversation, but avoiding interaction or eye contact.

"There's no OPM-71 leave-request form on file." Vasily narrowed his eyes and blocked Ted's path when he tried to walk away. Karen Spencer stopped short of the front door without turning around.

"I'm not an employee," Ted said, trying without success to push past Vasily. "I don't need to file any forms." He pressed his back against the car to slide by. "I'm an independent contractor, and my assignment has ended. And with shit like this," he said, shoving past Vasily, "I don't think there'll be another."

"I apologize for my friend," Nick said. "Let's take this inside, talk a bit, and get you started on your vacation." He wrinkled his forehead. "Or whatever."

Ted opened his mouth, then closed it without speaking.

Karen touched her husband's arm. "Let's just get this over and done," she said.

"You don't know these people," Ted tugged at a loose strap. "Nothing is ever over and done with them." He took a bag from Karen's hand and guided her into the house.

Nick and Vasily followed.

"Please, sit." Karen gestured to a pair of wing chairs. The Spencers sat on a loveseat on the opposite side of a coffee table, facing Nick and Vasily.

"Look…" Nick glanced first at Ted and then at Karen. "I know this is not easy."

"Just get to the point," Ted said, frowning.

"Okay. I'll be blunt." Nick hardened his tone. "The Agency has received intelligence that you and your wife may have been in contact with a hostile foreign government."

"Bullshit," Ted said, giving an abbreviated laugh. "Why would we do that?"

Nick continued as if he had not been interrupted. "Further, the source suggests that you, in particular, offered to provide a formula for a weaponized jellyfish toxin developed by your wife."

"More bullshit," Ted said, raising his hands over his head.

"The jellyfish serum hasn't been weaponized," Karen said, entering the conversation for the first time. "I was assured of that."

Nick thought about the Hunt affair but said nothing.

Tell that to the poor bastard that shit left twitching on the ground.

"We're not here to discuss specifics." Nick turned to Karen Spencer. "Not directly, anyway." He faced Ted. "But we do need to know why you cleaned out your checking account to buy prepaid credit cards and untraceable cellphones."

Vasily leaned toward Ted. "And two hundred rounds of ammunition."

"I thought I might get a chance to do some hunting." Ted shrugged his shoulders and looked at his wife, who stared at the floor.

"With a Walther PPK?" Vasily put both hands on his knees and peered into Ted's face.

"That's my business. I don't have to tell you." Ted pulled on the inside of his shirt collar with his index finger. "I have a legally obtained Virginia conceal/carry license." He glanced back and forth between Nick and Vasily.

"Ah, but sadly," Vasily said, pausing to smile, "no official decoder ring."

The insult was lost on Ted, who continued trying to stare down Vasily.

"Tell him." Karen looked at her husband and touched his wrist. "Tell him about the snakes."

"The snakes?" Nick placed his arm across Vasily's chest and slid forward to get Ted's attention. "If you have anything that can clear this up, now is the time."

Ted switched his attention from Vasily to Nick but said nothing.

Nick studied his face.

Guilty or scared?

Nick moved closer and lowered his voice. "Trust me," he paused and put his hand on Ted's quivering knee. "We're much easier to deal with than Marty Schwartz."

"Marty?" Ted's eyes opened wide, and he stared at the door like a prey animal. "Okay," he said and glanced at Karen. She nodded, and he continued. "The pistol is for self-defense." Ted jammed his hands into his armpits and rocked back and forth.

Definitely scared.

"Go on." Nick increased the pressure on Ted's bouncing knee.

Ted swallowed hard and squeezed his eyes shut for a moment. "They threatened me." He jumped to his feet and began pacing. "And my family." Beads of sweat dotted his forehead.

Nick stared at Karen. She leaned forward, head down, her long brown hair shielding her face.

Make that scared shitless. Both of them.

"Who's they?" Vasily stood and placed his right hand behind his back, where he kept his weapon holstered.

Karen looked up at Vasily and gasped.

"Easy," Nick said. "He's just scared."

"Where's the gun now?" Vasily had pasted on his tight-lipped, don't-fuck-with-me face.

"In a shoulder holster in the small green duffle by the door," Ted said quickly, having read Vasily's body language and facial expression. "Do you want to see it?"

Vasily's empty hand came back into view. He crossed the room, rummaged through the bag, and returned, holding the gun. "It's probably in your best interest if we keep this until everything is resolved." Vasily folded the shoulder strap around the holstered weapon. "You good with that?"

"Keep it." Ted squeezed his wife's hand. "I'm through with this spy shit."

"So, who threatened you, Ted?" Nick looked at Vasily and tapped the dial of his watch.

"Basil and that grinning psychopath," Ted said.

Nick looked at Ted. He was trembling and sweating. "Marty?" Nick felt his gut momentarily tighten. He and Vasily exchanged glances. Marty's mental status was a frequent topic of conversation. Many at the Agency wondered how he had passed the Agency psych qualifications and why Basil kept him on.

"Yes." Ted was visibly shaking. "We have to get away."

"Ted." Nick rubbed his eyes and looked at Ted again. "I'm sure Basil was just trying to convey the gravity of the situation." He looked at Karen. Her eyes were wide with fear. "I'm sure he just wants your help in squelching this accusation." He turned back to Ted. "That's why he sent us down here. It probably didn't help your anxiety that we showed up at eight-thirty instead of twelve."

"What do you mean?" Ted looked up, frowning.

"For our appointment."

"We had no appointment," Ted said. "We didn't know you were coming."

"I knew they were coming." Karen swallowed hard and twisted her wedding ring. "I had a call yesterday afternoon."

"Bel Castro?" Nick watched for a reaction. She said nothing, but her eyes widened for a moment.

"Why didn't you tell me?" Ted's face reddened. "We could have been gone by now."

Karen crossed her arms and leaned forward, avoiding Ted's gaze. "Because you were so upset." She turned to face him. "I was told they weren't coming until noon." She placed her face in her hands.

"Give us a moment." Nick's gut tightened again. He stood and led Vasily to the front window. They paused when they were out of earshot but could still see the Spencers. Karen Spencer had started to cry. Ted's jaw was set. Fear was turning to anger.

"What the hell's going on here?" Vasily shook his head. "What's Basil's game?"

"We'll work that out later." Nick pointed to a pair of nondescript sedans that had just pulled up and parked on the road next to the driveway. Through the pines, Nick could see that they were identical except for color: one tan, one brown. Only with studied inspection could the nearly invisible wire-reinforced glass shield between the front and rear seats be discerned.

"Marty and Blair." Vasily exhaled through pursed lips. "This is bad."

"We have one chance," Nick said. "We're going to get that journal and send those two back to Langley." He nodded at the vehicles across the street.

Marty had gotten out of his car. He leaned against it with his arms crossed and stared at the house, his lips squeezed into that tight, toothless nonsmile of anticipation he wore when he was about to hurt someone. When Marty saw Nick, he put the index finger of his right hand to his forehead and gave a quick salute that ended with his finger pointing at Nick.

"Let me know if he moves," Nick said. He left Vasily to watch Marty and returned his attention to the Spencers. Ted had his arm around his wife. She had stopped crying, but her shoulders drooped. She looked small. "There's another crew outside." Nick gave a short jerk of his head toward the window. "I have no idea what's going on here, but what I do know is that you're a lot better off dealing with me than with Marty Schwartz."

"Oh, no. Not him." Ted's fear was palpable. His pupils were dilated, and Nick could smell his sweat. It wasn't the benign eccrine sweat of heat or exertion. It was the heavy, acrid smell of fear-induced apocrine sweat— the kind of sweat that told dogs, like Marty, that their prey was ripe for the taking.

"It's going to be okay," Nick said, keeping his voice calm. "If you give me Dr. Spencer's research journal, you can be on your way and have no contact with Marty. Take Bel Castro's advice. Stick to teaching." He leaned in close to Ted and put his hand on his shoulder.

"That's my new plan." Ted managed a weak smile and placed his hand on his wife's knee. "Give him the journal."

Karen Spencer broke her silence. "It isn't here."

"Don't play games." Ted turned and grabbed his wife by both shoulders. "For Christ's sake, just give him the journal."

"Where is it, Dr. Spencer?" Nick put his hand to his forehead. "We can have someone pick it up and then you can go."

Karen stared past Nick as she mulled this over. "No." She squeezed her eyes shut and shook her head from side to side. "I can't."

"Karen. Please." Ted put his hand over his face. "He'll kill us."

"I can't," she said in a whisper. "I just can't."

"Blair's getting out of the car," Vasily said.

"Wait." Nick punched a number into his cellphone. It rang once.

"Do you have it?" Basil's tone was flat.

"No. It's not here, but I think—"

"Come back now and let team two handle it." Basil's voice showed no trace of surprise.

"Something isn't right," Nick said. "They're terrified of Marty. Let us bring them in." Nick stared at the wide-eyed couple on the loveseat. "I will have the location of the journal before we reach Langley."

"No, I want you and Vasily kept out of this. They're not terrified. They're guilty," Basil said. There was a long pause. "Did you see their dog?"

"Their dog?" Nick stared at the ceiling and shook his head. "Their daughter took the dog and went out of town. What's the dog got to do with it?" He glanced at the Spencers. Both stared at him, then leaned toward one another whispering.

"You and Vasily are done there." Basil's tone was sharp. "I will brief Marty. Come back. Now."

"Basil, I can—" Nick was interrupted as Marty and Blair came through the front door. Vasily moved to block their path. Nick thought he heard Ted whimper. Marty grinned and pointed his finger at Ted.

"Negative," Basil said. "Back here. Now." Basil added, "That's an order, Nick."

The phone clicked and was silent.

"Change your mind?" Nick said, looking at the Spencers.

They both shook their heads and then looked down.

Nick walked to where Vasily blocked Marty's path. Blair stood, arms folded, chin down in deference to her partner. Nick touched Vasily on the shoulder. "Let's go. It's theirs now." He turned and tapped Marty's chest once with his finger. "Remember, you're just the chauffeur. The interrogation takes place at Langley."

Blair looked out over the top of her glasses and spoke for the first time. "Dr. Karen Spencer will ride with me. Everything will be—"

Blair was silenced by a wave from Marty. "Where's the fucking dog?"

"Again with the dog," Nick said. "It's not here. Why?"

"I don't like dogs," Marty said.

Vasily and Nick walked through the open door. Vasily paused halfway to the car. "I'll be right there." He waved Nick ahead. "Got to make a quick call."

"Make it in the car."

"Give me a minute." Vasily waved Nick on. "It's personal."

Nick watched Vasily pace back and forth, alternating glances between the house and the car while making excited circles in the air with his free hand. Nick suspected the call was to Bel Castro, but he had learned over the years not to press Vasily.

Vasily put the cellphone in his pocket and glanced at the Spencers' door. He stared at Nick and jerked his head toward the house.

Nick mouthed "No" and motioned to Vasily to come. Vasily gave a last look at the house and trudged to the car. He sat in the passenger seat but left the door open.

"We have to go back," Vasily said, looking at Nick.

"We have our orders." Nick held the wheel with both hands and stared straight ahead.

"Orders?" Vasily said, closing his door.

Nick pulled away. "They made their choice." He watched the Spencers' mailbox shrink in his rearview mirror. "It's out of our hands now."

39

THEY'LL BE GONE BY THE TIME YOU GET THERE

Tuesday, 18 June 2002—9:51 a.m.
Lafayette Park, Washington, D.C.

Chloe sat on a park bench near the von Steuben statue, munching a piece of baguette while the pigeons assembled in front of her, hoping for crumbs. A short distance away, Don Bel Castro, her godfather, paced back and forth. He'd spent most of the morning jumping up from the bench to field what appeared to be Agency calls.

"You're damn right I'm pissed off," he said. The index finger of his free hand stabbed the air. "This should be my investigation." He massaged his forehead with his thumb and forefinger as he listened to the response. "My personal connection has nothing to do with it." Bel Castro glanced at Chloe but looked away when their eyes met. He snapped the flip phone shut and started for the bench. Bel Castro had taken two steps when the phone rang again. He flicked the phone open, listened for several seconds, and resumed pacing.

Chloe broke the last of her baguette into pieces and fed it to the pigeons. She could hear only snippets of her uncle's conversation.

"Keep me informed, Vasily. Call me before you leave Gloucester." There was another snap as the phone closed.

Gloucester. That's got to mean Mom and Dad.

Chloe watched her uncle frown and rub the phone as if expecting a genie to appear and solve his problem. Bel Castro turned and started for the bench. He paused to stare at the von Steuben statue, tapping the closed phone with his index finger.

Chloe told herself she was being paranoid, but she couldn't shake the feeling that she was somehow the topic of his conversations.

Get over it, Chloe. He's CIA. He has a dozen irons in the fire. It's not always about you.

But he had mentioned Gloucester. She had pressed him last night while they grilled steaks. He had revealed only that there was a minor "flap" at the Agency regarding her mother's research.

"Nothing important," he'd said, turning the steaks.

"Flap?" she'd asked.

"Nothing that can't be worked out." Don kept facing the grill as he plated the steaks. "Two men I trust are going to talk with your mom and dad in the morning." He turned around and handed her a plate. "Don't worry, it will all be over by Tuesday lunch."

Chloe kept thinking of that conversation as she sat in the park, feeding the birds. She couldn't hold back any longer. "This is more than some minor flap," Chloe said, sitting erect and jutting her chin. "I want to talk to them on your cellphone right now."

"You're like Henry," he said with a sigh. "You're going to keep this up all day until I throw you a bone, aren't you?" His thin smile showed no teeth.

"Yes." She straightened her back even more.

"If I give you the short, sanitized version, will you let it go until lunchtime?"

She gave a single nod and put her hands in her lap.

Don told her that, because of the misunderstanding, her parents had decided to take a sabbatical until things were straightened out. They didn't want the Agency to bother them until the issue was resolved and, as such, were keeping their itinerary a secret.

"Your dad will call me this afternoon." He paused to clear his throat. "He will tell me where you should meet them."

Traveling in secret sounded like more than a misunderstanding to Chloe. "I'm going home," she said.

Don shook his head. "They'll be gone by the time you get there. Hang in there. Everything should be fine."

Don's half-hearted denial did little to quell Chloe's growing anxiety. His phone jangled again. He retrieved it from his pocket and flipped it open. Chloe could hear the low tones of the speaker's voice but was unable to discern any words.

"Marty?" Don jumped to his feet. "What's that bastard doing there?" He shook his head back and forth. "No. No. No. I don't care what Basil says." He stared down at Chloe. "Go back! You can't leave them alone with him."

40

THE CLEANING CREW

Tuesday, 18 June 2002—12:03 p.m.
Interstate 95N, Occoquan, Virginia

Nick and Vasily were less than an hour from CIA headquarters in Langley. Nick drove while his partner made and received numerous phone calls. Vasily crossed and uncrossed his arms, rubbed the back of his neck, and fumbled with the door latch. Several times he glanced at Nick and opened his mouth to speak, only to close it again and rub his forehead or pull at his ears.

Their conversation was superficial and sparse, limited to Vasily's griping about Nick smoking in the car and smoking in general. Vasily's phone rang again.

"What do you mean, incident?" Vasily clenched and unclenched his fist. "Look, I don't care how you do it. Find out what's going on and call me." He jabbed the end-call button. "Shit."

"Let's have it," Nick said. "Who was that?" He glanced at Vasily. "Bel Castro again?"

"My contact at the com center." Vasily's brow wrinkled. "How did you know?"

"If you're going to have the volume on max, you may as well be on speakerphone."

"Something's going down." Vasily bit his lower lip. "Don's been trying to get transfer updates all morning."

"That should be easy for him." Nick tapped the horn and jinked right to avoid a driver who wandered into his lane. "He's the IG's fair-haired boy."

"Not today." Vasily shook his head. "The com center says they have no info. Everything is running through Basil's office." Vasily ran a hand through his hair. "Don tried calling Basil."

"And, let me guess." Nick said.

"Basil won't take his call."

"Are you surprised?" Nick said. "Bel Castro's trying to bury him."

"This is serious, Nick. We have to go back."

"No dice." Nick threw his cigarette out the lowered window. "We have our orders."

"They're not guilty, Nick."

"They were getting ready to bolt." Nick pulled out another cigarette. "What does that tell you?"

"They're scared." Vasily held out his hands. "You saw them."

"Or hiding something."

"Marty's going to kill them."

Nick recalled the look of fear on Ted's face and the wicked grin on Marty's. "Marty is clearly capable of cold-blooded murder, but not Blair. He can't go rogue with Blair along."

"Well, maybe." Vasily seemed almost convinced. "No, let's go back." He grabbed Nick's arm. "Please," he said. "For me, do it for me."

"Christ." Nick thought about all the times Vasily had pulled his chestnuts from the fire. "Basil will have us for lunch."

Nick darted across two lanes of traffic to make the Occoquan ramp. A tractor-trailer horn blared, and Nick gave the driver a one-finger salute. "Asshole." Nick turned right at the end of the ramp and parked at a convenience store.

"Thanks." Vasily released Nick's arm. "I just have this feeling."

Nick's cellphone rang. He glanced down at the number. "It's Basil."

Nick put his finger over his lips to quiet Vasily and hit the talk button. "Yes?"

"Where are you?" Basil's voice was an octave above normal.

"Occoquan," Nick said. "We're going back."

"Negative." Basil's voice cracked. "There's been an incident. Come straight to my office."

"Are we talking about the Spencers?" Nick had that squeezing in his belly again. Vasily's silenced cellphone began to buzz. Nick shook his head at Vasily, held up one finger, and mouthed, "Wait."

Vasily smacked his head with his hand and bounced like a child needing a bathroom. He held out the phone.

Nick could see the caller ID.

Don Bel Castro.

"Not on this line," Basil said. Nick could hear muffled speech as Basil covered the phone with his hand.

"It's gone to shit," Basil said to Nick. There was another pause. Then Nick heard more garbled conversation.

"We've got to prepare," Basil said.

Nick glanced at the phone screen. "Call ended," it read.

"What?" Vasily was interrupted by his phone buzzing like an angry bee. "Don—"

"Listen. Don't speak." Nick recognized Bel Castro's voice. Vasily pumped the phone's volume to the max so both he and Nick could hear. Bel Castro's voice grated like boots on gravel through the tinny speaker. "I can only say this once."

"Don, please." Nick could hear a voice he assumed to be Chloe Spencer in the background. She was pleading, her voice cracking.

"Just a second," Don said. The cries faded as Bel Castro put some distance between himself and Chloe. "This is what I've got."

Vasily heard him take a deep breath.

"There was a shooting at the Spencer house," Bel Castro said. "The Agency has sent out an incident-containment team." He paused. "Wait,

Chloe's walking over here again." There was another pause. "Coming, Chloe." His voice was a shout in comparison. Bel Castro paused again, then continued. "Okay." His whisper was a rasp on wood. "The forensics ambulance and the cleaning crew. You know what that means. One medevac by helicopter." He croaked. "I've got to get Chloe out of here."

Vasily turned to Nick. "There's been—"

"I heard it," Nick said.

Vasily's phone rattled its warning again. He stared first at the phone and then at Nick, unsure if he should take the call. After two rings, he pushed the talk button as if touching a cactus needle and put the phone to his ear. Nick could hear Bel Castro's broken voice.

"I went full CIA to get info from a local LEO." Bel Castro's voice was high-pitched and trembling.

Nick heard a long low "Nooooo" in the background.

"They're gone. Ted and Karen are gone." Bel Castro began to sob. "That fucking psychopath Marty killed them." He choked but then continued. "Blair is headshot and unresponsive. Basil sent a helo from The Farm to pick up Marty. Local LEOs say they found payoff money. It looks like Marty just walks away. They're calling him a hero." There was a pause. "They're saying he killed two terrorists."

"What about Chloe?" Vasily said.

"There's a BOLO on her," Bel Castro said, his voice just audible. "They say she's a terrorist, too, armed and dangerous." There was another long pause. "Oh, shit."

"Don—" Vasily shouted at the phone.

"No, she's fine, Officer. Just got some bad family news, that's all." Bel Castro said something unintelligible.

Vasily stared at Nick. He didn't have to say anything. Nick knew what Vasily was thinking.

"Capitol police," Nick said.

Bel Castro's voice was again a whisper in Vasily's ear. "Later," he said. "I've got to figure out someplace for Chloe to stay safe."

Vasily ended the call and put the phone in his pocket. He pointed at Nick. "We're no better than Marty, Nick." He slammed his fist on the dash. "We could've stopped this." Vasily held his head in his hands. "Basil ordered this hit, and we looked the other way. For Christ's sake, I took Ted's gun." He opened the car door and vomited in the parking lot.

PART THREE

RUN FOR YOUR LIFE

41

CHARRED BEYOND RECOGNITION

Wednesday, 23 October 2002—4:19 p.m.
Basil's office

Basil leaned back in his chair and stared out the window as the wind tugged at the last of the leaves on the trees. Only the oak managed to hold a few of its shriveled brown husks. The birch and maples had already surrendered theirs to the ever-deepening carpet of color. Occasional snow flurries bounced off the windows of his corner office. Basil wondered how much longer it would be his office. A gust of wind shook the oak tree, and it yielded a few more leaves. The triple-glazed, bullet-resistant windows insulated Basil from the howling wind, but they could not protect him from the storm that was raging in the conference room two floors above. Michael Collins, the DCIA, was giving Fletcher the results of the Agency's internal-affairs investigation. Basil had read the papers and knew heads would have to roll. And his would, no doubt, be one of them. He suddenly felt very old, but that's what had gotten him into this mess in the first place. He looked at his reflection in the window and managed something between a thin-lipped smile and a smirk. "Thank God for hard copy." He gave a small snort and patted his insurance policy: the "Eyes Only" file he maintained on selected Agency personnel. J. Edgar would be proud of him.

"Mr. Orlov?" The intercom crackled as his secretary's voice shattered the silence. "Admiral Fletcher to see you, sir."

Basil waited for Fletcher to burst into the room, but the door remained shut.

Bad news when a shitbag like Fletcher adheres to protocol.

He pushed the button on the intercom. "Send him in."

"How are you holding up?" Fletcher stopped a respectful three steps from Basil's desk and stood, a brown folder in his hand. His lower lip stuck out in mock concern as he gave a small nod to the chair facing Basil's desk.

"You tell me," Basil said. "Sit down." He pointed to the chair. "And for God's sake," he said, "stop acting like you give a damn."

"I have good news and bad news," Fletcher said.

"Cut to the chase." Basil glanced outside as a particularly violent gust of wind managed to rattle the window.

"I tried, but you're out. So are Nick, Vasily, and Marty." Fletcher opened the file. "This division is being officially . . ."—he lingered on the word and smiled—"shut down and incorporated into field operations. You might have made it." He closed the file. "But Bel Castro laid out his case."

"That son of a bitch." Basil stood, walked to the sidebar, and retrieved the decanter of scotch.

"Thank God he had no proof, but he swayed the director. It's a done deal." Fletcher stood and placed the file on his chair. "Make it two."

"And you?" Basil said, pouring two drinks.

"No mention of me, only a nebulous higher up."

"So," Basil said. "Fuck you very much for nothing." He handed Fletcher a glass.

"Do you want the good news?" Fletcher said, grinning. "The director took to heart your statement that you kept records on where the Agency—him included—buried their bones." Fletcher referred to the closed-door meeting he and Basil had with the director. "I recall how the director's face first turned red and then gray-white as you quoted from your 'Eyes Only' file."

Basil twitched.

"He also believed you when you said you had a fail-safe mechanism for release in case you met with an accident." He pointed to the file on Basil's desk. "I thought he'd shit his pants when you said, 'Well, Michael, we'll always have Abu Ghraib. Raped any fifteen-year-olds lately?' Anyway, the black-ops division is now a private operation," Fletcher said, "and you have the contract."

"What about criminal convictions for myself and the crew?" Basil took a drink.

"National Secrets Act," Fletcher said, smiling. "That was my doing." He waited for an "atta-boy" from Basil. When there was none, he frowned and continued. "Everything is sealed, permanently. And here's the best part. Bel Castro is out of the IG office. He's now the FBI liaison. His IG days are over."

"And Blair Underwood?" Basil said, studying his glass.

"Coma," Fletcher said. "Feeding tube for survival."

"Why the life support?" Basil scratched his cheek.

"Because her family's a pack of minnow-munchers, and that's what they do."

"But her parents are dead." He lifted an eyebrow.

"Yes, the plane crash was a nice touch." Fletcher saluted Basil with two fingers. "Who knew the family trust specified full life-support until natural death." He held up his hands. "Go figure."

"Can we help that along?" Basil asked without looking up.

"Forget it," Fletcher said. "It's a nonissue."

"And the Spencer girl?" Basil said. "And don't tell me that's a nonissue."

"You know as much as I do." Fletcher shrugged. "They found the old Volvo in southern Ohio, burned to a crisp, body of a young girl and a dog inside—charred beyond recognition. They found Chloe Spencer's

IDs and a few scorched fragments of a leather notebook with her fingerprints." He gave a quick exhale. "The FBI is calling it a terrorist deal gone bad. The BOLO was canceled."

"Dental records?" Basil stared at Fletcher.

"Lost. The dental clerk remembered a transfer, but there was no paper trail."

"Shit. She's alive." Basil stamped his foot. "You know it and I know it." He clenched and unclenched his fist. "That bastard, Bel Castro, used our own story to fuck us up."

"Look, she doesn't know anything." Fletcher straightened his posture. "She's a designated terrorist, remember? If she surfaces, we can prove it."

"I don't give a shit about the girl. I want that research journal."

"Then we wait. If she's alive—and she's probably not—sooner or later she'll screw up and we'll have her."

"And I still want that dog alive."

"Sure. But while we wait, we're going to be billionaires, partner." Fletcher patted Basil's shoulder.

"Partner?" Basil's eyes narrowed.

"Sure, buddy," Fletcher said. "I make sure you get the contracts, and you make sure I get a percentage and credit for the kill." He straightened his tie and smoothed his jacket. "In a couple of years, I'll be the director of this outfit. From there, who knows?" He raised his chin and smiled. "From the Agency to the White House. I wouldn't be the first."

Outside Basil's window, the oak tree gave up another leaf.

42

OFFICIALLY DEAD

Saturday, 22 February 2003—7:39 p.m.
A secondary road just west of I-93, Northern New Hampshire

The young woman checked the heater controls again to be sure they were on maximum. She turned on the penlight and played the weak yellow beam across the face of a small thermometer lying on the seat. Forty-seven, with the heater on max. She checked the outside temp on the stick-on thermometer attached to the windshield: eleven degrees. Even with a winter fuel mix, the Rover's diesel clattered like pebbles in a tin can. She wiped her eyes with her mittened hands and wondered at what temperature does saltwater freeze. She thought about her dad making ice cream. He always used a brine slurry to chill the ice cream, so she thought it unlikely her tears would freeze anytime soon. She retrieved the ice scraper and scrubbed at the patches of frost on the windshield and redirected the pitiful stream of heat from the floor to the windscreen. No need to worry, her toes would freeze long before her tears.

Eight months and five tearful rendezvous with her uncle had gone by since the loss of her parents. Each one was the same: an overnight meeting in some mom-and-pop motel in the middle of nowhere. They would have dinner in a truck stop, then go back to the motel where she would cry on his shoulder until it was time for bed. In the morning, Don would push a wad of cash and a new ID into her duffle when he thought she wasn't looking. Then she would drift again until their next meeting, her sole purpose in life to survive and remain invisible.

She thought back to the first of these meetings. It was August in West Virginia, two months after the murders—six months, ninety degrees Fahrenheit, and a lifetime ago.

She remembered the clumsy attempts at small talk.

"How's the Land Rover doing?" Her uncle had forced a smile as he gestured toward the sad-looking, thirty-year-old vehicle.

"Fine." She teased the plate of untouched food with her fork. "Classes start in two weeks."

No eye contact.

"Can I go back to school?" She remembered the desperation in her voice.

"You're thin as a rail," he'd said, avoiding the subject. "And you look like you haven't slept in days."

"Yeah." Chloe had bitten her lip to fight back the tears. "Two months on the road will do that to you." She stared out the window, put down the fork, and stared at him. "My life. I want to know when I can have— what's left of my life back."

"Wait." Bel Castro had placed his hand over his coffee cup to prevent the waitress from refilling it. He'd paused until she moved on. "There's no easy way to put this." He watched as the waitress made her way to the kitchen with the empty coffee pot. "You're officially dead." Don nodded toward Henry, who watched them through the restaurant window from the SUV's passenger seat. "Him, too."

"Dead?" Chloe's stomach roiled. A droning sound filled her head. "But what about grad school and Chicago? I've got my scholarship and a TA position!"

"Chloe." Don's tone made her name sound past tense. "You're going to have to rethink things."

His voice seemed far away, a tiny sound competing with the growing roar in her ears.

"According to the FBI, you and Henry were killed."

The roar obscured his voice.

"I'm afraid the scholarship and the teaching assistantship died with you."

His face became a distant blur in the expanding smudge of darkness creeping in from the edge of her vision. She woke to a cacophony of crashing cymbals and tympani drums, which proved to be the clatter of flatware and dishes as her face struck the table. The further insult of the contents of an overturned water glass in her lap restored full consciousness.

"What's the matter with her?" The waitress rushed to the table with several towels. "She ain't on drugs, is she?"

"No. Of course not." Don had jumped to his feet and began wiping the food from Chloe's face. "She has diabetes." He lied. "She's having an insulin reaction."

"We don't tolerate no drugs here." The unconvinced waitress leaned in across the table and stared at the stricken girl's pupils. "Here's your check." She spun on her heel and walked to the kitchen at the back of the restaurant.

"I believe they're telling us goodbye." Don nodded his head toward the lunch counter. The manager had come out of his office and joined the waitress behind the cash register. "They look like a pair of buzzards drying their wings on a barn roof while they stare at something rotten."

"That seems appropriate," Chloe sighed, "seeing as I'm officially dead."

"I know it's bad," Don said. "Let's talk outside."

She'd put one hand on the table and stood up. Her legs were like rubber. Her vision tunneled. She leaned against the booth until the sensation passed. She brushed away her uncle's hand as he tried to steady her.

"I'm fine." She straightened and lifted her chin. "Just let me go to the restroom and freshen up." She managed a tight-lipped smile. "I'll meet you at the car."

In the restroom, she washed her face and studied her reflection.

It's not a mirror. It's a window. That's someone else. Someone who is not Chloe.

The stranger stared back at her through puffy eyes, rimmed with dark circles in a lined, saggy face. Splotchy skin, drooping shoulders, and dry scarecrow-like hair completed the picture. Bad food, seedy motels, and too much time alone had caused her to drop fifteen pounds. She forced a laugh. A year ago, she would have been thrilled to lose those fifteen pounds and maybe another, but she didn't look better, just thinner. The mummies she'd studied in her archaeology class had looked more alive.

No. It's not someone else. It's Chloe. Chloe's dead and I'm staring at her corpse.

She dried her face with a rough paper towel and stared down the image in the mirror before returning to the car.

"We can't delay this conversation any longer." Don brought her up to date. "According to official records, you and your dog were shot and torched along with your car, presumably because a terrorist deal went bad."

Chloe began to mist up.

Don handed her a tissue and continued. "It was the best I could do," he'd said. "I'm sorry." He sighed and paused. "I had to call in a lot of favors to get that done."

"How did you convince them it was me in that car?" Chloe blew her nose.

"A 'Jane Doe' body from Indianapolis, a euthanized dog from an animal shelter, and a convenient disappearance of your dental records."

"I guess I should thank Jane Doe?" Chloe said, attempting a smile.

He nodded.

Her tears began to flow again.

"I was the sole survivor on your parents' beneficiary list." Don searched for some shred of information that would comfort her. "They left a substantial estate. I'll dole it out to you incrementally to avoid arousing suspicion." He held out a thick white envelope. "Oh, yeah," he said, retrieving a card from his shirt pocket. "You'll need this." He pressed it into her hand.

"What's this?" A grainy unsmiling likeness of herself stared back at her from a very official-looking driver's license.

VESPER MORGAN
143 N. LOBDELL DRIVE
OKLAHOMA CITY, OK

"It's a new ID." He pushed the envelope toward her. "We might be able to do something permanent in a year or so. For now, though, you're invisible. It's the only way to stay safe."

"Won't Vesper need her driver's license?'

"She's dead." Don said, looking away.

"Won't they cancel the license?"

"Her death went unreported." He sighed without looking up. "She wasn't the kind to have permanent friends."

"Ah, a kindred spirit." Chloe took the envelope.

"I'm sorry, Chloe," he said, taking her hand.

"Chloe's dead," she said, pulling away.

"I wish things were different," Don said, still looking down. "We'll meet again in a few weeks."

She wiped her eyes, took a deep breath, and listened while he gave the details.

A glowing splash of orange and the painful throbbing in her feet brought her thoughts back to the present. The icy fog of her breath etched patterns on the frozen windshield. The glow in the distance would be the convenience store and fast-food restaurant at the inter-state highway junction. The satin sheen of the road told her she was driving on black ice. She relaxed the pressure on the accelerator. The constant headwind slowed her speed to a manageable thirty-five mph. She wiggled her frozen toes as she eased up on the accelerator to try to regain feeling in her feet. Her legs were pins and needles to the knee.

Fumbling with her penlight, she glanced at the thermometer again. A strong gust of wind forced her vehicle to the right. She braked hard—too hard. The boxy Rover was like a sail in the wind. An invisible hand pushed her to the road's edge. She over-corrected, and the Rover began a slow counterclockwise rotation, pirouetting down the black-ice-coated, little-traveled county road—a drunken ballet dancer on an over-waxed stage. She watched as the high curtains of snowbanks lining the road revolved around her. She gripped the wheel in anticipation of the crash. Henry awoke and emitted a continuous wolf-like howl from the back seat. A utility pole arced left to right through her field of vision. It reminded her of learning the tricks of skating spins as a child.

Pick a reference point for each rotation. It will stop the dizziness and inform you when to push out and stop the spin.

As the lights of the convenience store came into view over her left shoulder, she turned her wheels to the right. When lights were just visible at the left side of her windshield, she depressed the accelerator. The spin broken, she now found herself in a slide, going straight down the road, the vehicle canted at a forty-five-degree angle with the rear left of center. She corrected the steering slightly left, by increasing pressure on the accelerator and ever-increasingly applying the brakes. As the vehicle slowed, she lifted completely from the accelerator, shifted to neutral, and feathered the brakes until the Rover came to a halt. She sat with her eyes closed, shaking from the combination of cold and adrenalin. The fog of her breath froze white on the windshield.

Traffic?

She stared over her shoulder. Nothing. No one. Empty and black. No trace of light penetrated the frost-covered window behind her. She looked forward. The defroster had made little progress on the frozen windshield. She rubbed a small circle clear with her mittened hand. No traffic—only the dark silhouette of the pine forest dressed in the icy lace on the windshield. She put the Rover in gear and drove toward the faint promise of temporary heat and safety offered by the glow of lights to the south.

43

NOT CHLOE

Saturday, 22 February 2003—8:57 p.m.
A café and truck stop, Northern New Hampshire

"Chloe," the urgent voice called out from somewhere behind her.

She wrapped her frozen hands around the rapidly cooling cup of coffee. The hair on the back of her neck stood up, partly from fear, partly from hope. Under the table, Henry shifted in response to the familiar name.

"Chloe," the voice repeated. "Stop crying and eat your food. What's wrong?"

"I'm sad," a small voice said.

"Why?" the adult voice said.

"I don't know. I just am," the young voice answered.

The young woman didn't bother to look around. She wasn't Chloe anymore. She was no one and everyone. She thought about the half dozen IDs in her duffle bag, each a passable forgery from a different state. It seemed so long ago that Don had informed her that she was no longer Chloe.

"Look how happy your sister Lucy is. I can't believe you're twins." There was shuffling behind her. A small girl of about four stood near the booth, staring at Henry.

Henry raised his head in anticipation. His tail gave a couple of tentative swishes.

"Don't bother the other diners," the same urgent voice called out.

"It's okay. You can pet her," the young woman said, shifting her thawing feet.

"Hi." The small girl looked at the young woman, then touched the top of the dog's head.

"Hi yourself," the young woman said. Another girl, a near-identical twin, ran over and stood by her sister.

"My name is Lucy," the smiling girl said. "What's yours?"

The young woman hesitated for a moment, then said, "My name is Lucy, too."

"Not Chloe?" the frowning girl asked.

"No, not Chloe," she said. "I'm Lucy."

44

I'M STAYING RURAL AND MAINTAINING A LOW PROFILE

Sunday, 13 March 2003—7:19 p.m.
Room 338, Jefferson Hotel, Richmond, Virginia

After the chance encounter in the diner, the young woman, now known as Lucy, decided to trade the cold and strange for the warm and familiar. She chanced a call to her uncle and arranged a meeting at the Jefferson Hotel. Until she left for college, her parents had taken her along each year to celebrate their wedding anniversary at the place they had gone for their honeymoon. The Jefferson was a favorite with the Spencers because, despite the five-star rating, it welcomed both children and dogs.

Lucy was disappointed that her uncle had insisted on room service out of fear that he or his niece might be recognized in the dining room. "I wanted to sit at Mom and Dad's favorite table." She looked down at Henry, who waited patiently for a treat.

"It's too risky." Don reached into his pocket. "What made you decide on the name Lucy?" He handed her a driver's license, automobile registration, and insurance card. "And why North Carolina?"

"It's where we always vacationed." Lucy ignored the first part of his question. "It's where Mom discovered the jellyfish."

"You can't go to a big city like Wilmington." Don bounced a piece of steak off the back of Henry's head. "And you can't be asking questions about jellyfish."

"Don't worry, I'm staying rural and maintaining a low profile." Lucy put her plate on the floor so that Henry could finish her half-eaten burger. "I want to visit Blair. She's in North Carolina, isn't she?"

"She's at St. Martha's in Barringer, but it's too dangerous to visit." He shook his head. "You could be discovered."

"I don't think the nuns are going to know me." Lucy picked at her chocolate cake without eating any. "I need to see her."

The next morning was the all-too-familiar tearful goodbye, an envelope of cash, and the number of his latest burner phone.

45

ASAKAN, THAT'S OUR NEW HOME

Monday, 22 March 2003—4:49 p.m.
St. Martha's Convalescent Center, Barringer, North Carolina

"Blair and I share a lot of history," Lucy said, signing the clinic's guest book. "I couldn't pass this way without stopping to sit with her for a bit. Sister . . .?" Lucy tried to read the smiling nun's name tag.

"It's Ann." She turned the tag so that Lucy could read it. "And God bless you." The nun closed the book and gestured for Lucy to follow her. The medical wing, obviously new, was a tasteful blend of polished concrete, stone accents, and indirect lighting designed to complement the convent's century-old granite facade. "There haven't been any visitors since the family's plane mishap." She stopped speaking and crossed herself. "Before that, they came every week. They were certainly friends of St. Martha's, generous when they were living, and—" Sister Ann paused, unable to continue.

Lucy put her hand on the nun's shoulder. "They were wonderful people," Lucy said, assuring herself that it had to be true.

"Yes." Sister Ann pulled a crumpled tissue from her pocket, dabbed her eyes, and continued. "Their posthumous donation paid for the renovations of this wing." Sister Ann led Lucy down the hallway past walls adorned with pictures of saints, cathedrals, and the occasional crucifix.

"The Underwood family has certainly suffered." The sister paused, her hand resting on the door latch to a patient room. She opened the door, ushered Lucy in, and pulled a chair up to the bed. "Stay as long as you like." She left the room and closed the door behind her.

Lucy sat down and looked around the room. If not for the array of medical equipment, it could have been a bedroom. Pictures of Blair and her family hung on the robin's egg-blue walls. Sunlight streamed in two large windows framed by white muslin curtains. The floor was a light oak with a braided oval rug. Blair's adjustable bed was a wooden poster covered by a parchment-colored woven cotton spread. It was at this point that the peaceful allusion ended. A boxlike, roller-feed pump with a digital display hummed as it counted the milliliters of a chalky white liquid pumped into Blair through the tube that slithered under the bedspread on its way to her abdomen. A cardiac monitor beeped with each contraction as a QRS complex raced across its face. The automatic blood pressure cuff wheezed with periodic inflations and deflations.

Lucy turned her attention to Blair. Her skin was pale but healthy. A catheter in her right upper arm had a small tag marked PICC, meaning the line was a permanent IV going all the way to her superior vena cava. A small scar on her throat marked where a tracheotomy had been performed. A special air mattress hissed as it constantly shifted to prevent pressure ulcers. Blair's face was without expression. If not for the medical paraphernalia, she could have been taking a nap. She looked as though she might wake up at any moment.

"Blair." Lucy touched her hand. "We've both lost a lot." She stopped. "But you have lost more." She touched the young woman's face. "At least I can get up and walk out of here." She bit her lower lip and watched the waveforms on the cardiac monitor. "I promise you this." She leaned in and put her lips close to Blair's ear. "I will find out who did this to us and hold them accountable—or die trying."

Lucy returned to the Rover where Henry lay sleeping on the seat. She drove south and east until she was almost to the coast. The pale beams of the Rover's headlights illuminated a green road sign with an arrow pointing left. Lucy recognized the Siouxan word on the sign from her Native American anthropology study:

Asakan 6

As the sign flashed by, Lucy thought about her mother and smiled. She made an about-face, turned at the sign, and patted Henry on the head.

"Asakan," she said. "That's our new home."

46

DO I KNOW YOU?

Friday, 16 April 2004—2:07 p.m.
Library stacks at Virginia Institute of Marine Science, Gloucester Point

Lucy knew she should leave right away. In fact, she knew she shouldn't be there at all. Tommie had warned her against the trip.

"What if someone recognizes you?"

But, after almost two years of running and too many aliases to remember, she needed some answers. So, here she was, deep in the stacks of the William & Mary Institute of Marine Science Library, holding her mother's unpublished research in her hand. She'd spent countless hours on the internet only to reach a dead end that had brought her here to thumb through the dry, dusty documents that could be reviewed in-house, but not checked out. She just knew that something in this research had been the cause of her parents' murder; she just didn't know what. She'd come to the library looking for something more than the random drawings and scribblings in her mother's battered leather journal. She had read and reread the journal countless times in the last two years. It was filled with gene maps, formulas, and drawings of little jellyfish, but no specifics or conclusions.

Her fingers were dry from hours of turning pages. She was ready to give up when something caught her eye. A handwritten note on a single page. Should she risk asking for a photocopy? She glanced around. The stacks seemed empty except for her. A gentle pull at the page's edge and the paper tore, a lion's roar in the quiet stacks. A sound caused her to stop.

Footsteps?

Lucy held her breath and listened. The book jumped in her hand with each heartbeat.

Imagination.

She sneezed loudly, tore the last three inches, and stuffed the page in her pocket.

Another sound.

Definitely a footstep.

She returned the book to its place on the shelf and pulled out another.

"You, there." Lucy recognized the voice of the librarian who had checked her in. "What do you think you're doing?"

Lucy turned. The thin fifty-something woman, hands on hips, scowled at her from the end of the long aisle.

"I'm sorry," Lucy said. "The dust is getting to me, but I'm finished now." She cleared a spot on the shelf and raised the book.

"You just wait right there," the librarian said, closing the distance between them as if on a rail. "Let me see that book." She took the book from Lucy and examined every page for signs of damage. "What else have you looked at?" she said, doing her best to block the aisle.

"Quite a few items, but I have to go now." Lucy flattened her back to the stack and slid past her.

The librarian followed her to the door, still holding the book in her hand. As the door closed, Lucy noticed through the wire-mesh glass-door insert that the librarian had paused at her desk and picked up the phone. Hurrying down the hallway, she stopped just short of her mother's old office, taking note of the nameplate on the door:

Elaine Cochran, PhD
Government Liaison

Lucy had met Elaine Cochran once—almost five years ago when dropping off some papers at her mother's office. Her mother described Cochran as a mediocre graduate student who survived by carrying coffee to her professors and sucking up to Agency contacts.

So, she brown-nosed her way to a PhD.

Lucy looked at the title on the door: "Government Liaison." She clucked and shook her head. "CIA lackey." She stood in front of the door and peered through the glass insert. The doctor was out liaising, no doubt. Lucy tried the door. It was unlocked. She opened the door and leaned in. Looking up, she saw a security camera near the ceiling. The light on top turned from green to flashing red. Lucy jumped back, pulled the door shut, and walked toward the exit.

"Can I help you?"

She turned to see a woman in a lab coat and black horn-rimmed glasses bearing down on her.

"I was looking for the government grant office." Lucy recognized the face and continued toward the exit.

"This is my office," Cochran said, following her. "The grant office is upstairs. Are you a graduate student?" Her eyes narrowed and she turned her head to one side. "Do I know you?"

"No, I'm just visiting from California. Sorry. I've got a plane to catch." Lucy dashed out the exit and walked through the parking lot, away from her vehicle. When she was sure she wasn't being followed, Lucy doubled back to her Land Rover. She sat in her SUV for a moment, waiting to see if anyone looking like security came out of the building. Seeing no one, she started the Rover and drove to a nearby fast-food restaurant. Over fries and diet soda, she examined the page she had torn from the research record. It contained five dated entries in her mother's handwriting.

05 May 2001: Stressed turritopsis with brief periods of very high water temps. Observed over one hundred "rebirths" with reversion to mature but healthy state.

11 July 2001: Turritopsis is an interesting academic exercise, but as yet I see no mammalian applications, save redundant nerve-agent technology.

10 September 2001: Took a chance. Surprising results from an unexpected source. Best friends are the best. Will observe and note.

20 September 2001: Incredible!!!!!

The final entry was a barely legible scrawl written two weeks before the murders.

04 June 2002: No beneficial mammalian applications. Strongly recommend immediate shutdown of research on turritopsis and redirection of assets to a more useful program.

K. Spencer, PhD

Vice-Chair and Govt. Liaison, W&M Inst. Marine Science

It was clear to Lucy that there was much more to her mother's research. The leather journal had made constant reference to research notes. The Institute had no records from September until June. The *Turritopsis* study had yielded something her mother did not wish to share. But where were the findings?

47

I THINK IT WAS A NORTH CAROLINA LICENSE

Friday, 16 April 2004—3:52 p.m.
Security Office, Virginia Institute of Marine Science, Gloucester Point

Back at the Institute, the librarian, the security guard, and Dr. Cochran reached the door of the security office at the same time. A brief search by the librarian had yielded the book with the torn-out page.

"I knew she was up to something," she said.

"She looked familiar." Cochran's lips were a thin line. "Something about her face." Her eyebrows shot up. "Chloe Spencer!"

"Dr. Spencer's daughter? No." The security officer shook his head. "She's dead."

"And besides," the librarian said, spreading her arms to increase her girth, "too thin." She pointed to her head. "And the hair color."

"Yeah, you're right," Dr. Cochran said. "Did you get her name?"

"I don't remember the name on her ID," the librarian said, her cheeks flushing. "But I think it was a North Carolina license."

"That's odd," Dr. Cochran said. "She told me she just flew in from California."

"Since it was your office she poked her head into," the guard said, "we'll send the security pictures from that camera to your CIA buddies." He hummed the opening of the 007 theme. "Just to be safe."

48

NO, YOU WOULDN'T

Friday, 16 April 2004—6:43 p.m.
Office of Don Bel Castro, FBI/CIA liaison, Langley, Virginia

The guard transmitted the grainy black-and-white, security-camera image with the tag "Chloe Spencer?" to The Farm at Camp Peary, where it was forwarded to Langley, landing on the desk of Don Bel Castro.

Bel Castro tapped his finger on his desk and bit his lip. He'd recognized his niece immediately. But with the poor quality, bad angle, and weight differential, he hoped no one else would.

What the hell were you thinking?

He put the photo on his desk, thanked God for the crappy security cameras at the Marine Institute, and buzzed Jerry Harwood, his administrative assistant.

"Jerry," he said over the intercom. "Come in here for a minute." Jerry was at Bel Castro's desk in less than thirty seconds.

"Yeah, boss," Jerry said.

"I've reviewed this transmission, tagged as a possible Chloe Spencer sighting," Bel Castro said, staring at the image. "It's head-down and piss-poor resolution, inconclusive for positive ID and not suitable for submission to the facial-recognition data bank." He looked at the photo on his desk. "But it's not Chloe Spencer."

"Disposition?" Jerry asked.

"Shitcan it in the dead file. Somebody just opened the wrong door. Besides—she's dead."

"Roger that." Jerry picked up the photo and left the room, closing the door behind him.

Bel Castro retrieved one of over a dozen burner phones from his wall safe and called his niece. Her voice was just audible over the Land Rover's engine and wind noise.

"What were you thinking?"

"I think I've got something," Lucy shouted over the wind noise.

"I hope it was worth it." Bel Castro fumbled with the volume control. "I'm guessing you've been made." He stared at the phone as if willing better reception. "You're going to have to hit the road again."

"Documents . . ." The earpiece hissed. "A breakthrough . . ." The hissing grew louder. "Afraid of something..."

"I'll call you in a couple of days." Bel Castro didn't know if his niece could hear him or not. "It's not all bad news. I have new intel on the murder."

When she did not reply, he pulled the phone away from his ear and stared at the flashing display:

Call Dropped.

Jerry Harwood leaned back against the heavy door and smiled. On the payroll of an independent black-ops company for over two years, he had been paid a thousand dollars a month just to watch for this name. He stared at the crude photo in his hands. He did busy work until seven, then said good night to Bel Castro. He cleared security, walked to his car, and called his contact at Conflict Resolutions, LLC.

In twenty minutes, Jerry was in the vestibule of Basil Orlov's office. He handed a folder containing the photo and transcript of events to a grinning Marty Schwartz while a stern-faced security guard stood nearby.

"Mr. Orlov appreciates your service," Schwartz said, handing him a fat, white envelope.

"That's very generous." Jerry sneaked a look at the wad of bills. "I would like to meet Mr. Orlov sometime."

"No, you wouldn't." Schwartz's grin flattened. "Goodnight." He nodded to the guard who gave a quick head jerk toward the front door and escorted Jerry outside. Marty entered Basil's office and handed the folder to his employer, who stood waiting behind the desk. Basil sat down, opened the folder, and read the brief report.

"Bel Castro," Basil said, smiling as he picked up the phone and punched in a number. In less than twenty-four hours, two dozen operatives had fanned out across North Carolina in a quiet search for the young woman.

49

DOES SHE LIVE AROUND HERE?

Monday, 19 April 2004—9:22 a.m.
Tommie's Café, Asakan, North Carolina

Tommie Whitefeather stopped wiping down the counter and rubbed his forehead. There it was again, the second time this week: pinwheel sparklers, like a migraine headache, but without the headache. He had blown off the first episode, but this was the real deal.

Okay, so it's a little earlier this time, but it's been a rougher ride than usual. You know the drill. You've got a little time. Suck it up, gunny, semper fi.

Tommie shook his head to clear the fireworks and looked out the window. He watched a greenhorn trip as he climbed out of his pickup truck. The stranger fell, landed on one knee, then sprang to his feet. He dusted off his too-new jeans, glanced around for witnesses, and gave his best imitation of a casual country stride.

That one's working at it. New boots, new jeans, new walk. Someone gave him a new look, right down to the L.L.Bean catalog pickup truck. Must have taken hours to scuff the paint and get the dirt just right.

The small bell over the café door tinkled. Tommie looked up at the stranger and smiled.

The stranger pasted on a plastic smile and casually panned the

room, feigning interest in the Native American and Marine Corps paraphernalia that adorned the café. He paused at the rear exit, the restroom
door, the couple at the corner table, and the shotgun hanging above
the kitchen pass-through behind Tommie. His gaze finally settled on
Tommie, looking him up and down. Tommie could practically read
the stranger's thoughts: Native American, late sixties, five-seven, slight
build, blind in one eye. Threat analysis—minimal to nil. The whole
thing took less than three seconds, and the smile never left the dude's
face. He sat on a stool three down from Tommie and swiveled, his back
to the corner, with Tommie, the other diners, and all doors within his
field of vision.

Tommie placed his hand on his belt, instinctively touching the
P10-45 concealed beneath his apron.

"Mornin'," the interloper said, in his best attempt at a North Carolina drawl.

"What can I do you for?" Tommie did his own five-second evaluation.

*Close-cropped expensive haircut, contact lenses, excellent build, and a
bulge in his left armpit suggesting some pretty big iron—9mm minimum,
probably a .45. Intruder alert. This is not just a city slicker playing country.
This is a shooter, a little too cocky, but definitely a professional, and not here
for the coffee.*

"Coffee, black, and a toasted bagel with cream cheese," Shooter
said, still smiling. "Nice diner."

*It's a café, not a diner, asshole. And a bagel? What part of New Jersey
are you from? Be diplomatic, Tommie. A lot of good marines from Jersey.*

"We're all out of bagels. Would you like toast?"

"Nah, coffee's fine." The smile faded for just a moment as he realized his mistake.

Shooter downed the hot coffee in a single gulp and tapped the rim
for a refill.

Wow, he's either a cokehead or a caffeine addict.

"I'm here with a group from Raleigh. We're looking for a few hundred acres to build a game preserve." Shooter extended his hand. "My name's Bobby Ray Curtis. I'm their accountant. Kind of the front guy—if you know I mean?"

Tommie took the outstretched hand. The grip was firm, with a bias to the index finger. The callous on the flexor surface of the middle phalange index finger and the ulnar surface of the thumb suggested he spent a lot of time holding something in his right hand other than an accountant's pencil.

A shooter. A hunting retreat, huh? So, tell me, Shooter, just what kind of game do you run to ground with a .45 ACP, anyway?

Shooter seemed to sense the examination. He frowned and pulled his hand back. "Word is, you might have the inside line on any available property."

"And why might that be?"

The man nodded toward his coffee cup, which Tommie filled for the third time.

"Well," Shooter said, "you run that survival school. You must know people."

"It's not a real-estate agency. How do you know about the school?"

Shooter hesitated. "A couple of guys from Raleigh mentioned taking the course."

You've stepped in it now, buddy.

"Really," Tommie pressed. "Who were they?"

Shooter saw the trap too late and stammered, unconsciously touching his shoulder holster with his right hand. "Just, uh, just some guys in a group at the club," he said. "I can't remember their names."

Okay, back off. Keep him talking. Don't spook him.

Tommie watched the pro fidget. He was getting nervous and wanted to leave, but there was something else he wanted.

"Listen, I know you own the local motel and some rental houses. I need accommodations for the team, about a dozen guys. Interested?"

Fat chance. No, wait—keep friends close, enemies closer.

"Sure," Tommie said. "How many rooms and for how long?"

"Four guys per room, three rooms, at least one with an unrestricted hardline for fax." He paused and stared at the ceiling. "Two weeks, starting Wednesday. Oh, and something deluxe for my boss, Nick Caedwallan."

"Sixty-five hundred, with a credit-card deposit." Tommie quoted high and waited for the counteroffer.

Shooter smiled and plopped a stack of hundred-dollar bills in a mustard-colored wrapper on the counter with $10,000 emblazoned on the band. Now Shooter was in his element. Money is power. "Paid in full." He tapped the cash with his index finger. "The extra thirty-five hundred is for your discretion. We don't want any publicity." He lowered his voice and looked around. "You know how steep the competition is for good hunting land."

Tommie stared at the stack of bills.

"Wow, that coffee's yearning to be free. I've got to hit the head." Shooter stood and scanned the room.

"Back there," Tommie said, gesturing toward the rear.

Shooter started for the restroom, then stopped and turned back to face Tommie.

"Oh, yeah," he said, placing his index finger to his lips as if remembering a small detail. "One of the guys wanted me to look up a cousin of his who might live here. Name's Chloe. Chloe Spencer, I think. A little chubby, mid-twenties, dark-brown hair. An anthropologist or something like that." Shooter fixed Tommie's gaze. "Do you know her?"

Jesus, he means Lucy. The shooter's looking for Lucy.

"No. Don't know her." Tommie hesitated a bit too long. "But if someone like that comes in, I'll tell her you're looking."

"Oh, don't do that," Shooter said. "He wants to surprise her. Just tell me."

Shooter headed for the restroom, pulling out his cellphone as he walked.

Tommie crept to the back and put his ear close to the door.

Shooter was talking fast, stumbling over his words. "Basil, this is

Marty . . . could have something here. . . . What? . . . Sure, if it's that important. . . . Me? . . . What about Nick?" Shooter took a deep breath and slowed down. "I'll meet the chopper here at one and beat the afternoon thunderstorms. Sure, I'll be at the lodge by three and in your office by six." There was a long pause. "Yes, sir. You know I want to be number one." Marty ended the call.

Tommie could hear Marty talking to himself as he did his business.

"Screw you, Nick. It's my turn now." The toilet flushed, and Tommie slipped to his spot behind the counter.

50

THE WAGES OF SIN

Monday, 19 April 2004—2:28 p.m.
Basil Orlov's mountain lodge, ninety miles west of Washington, D.C.
Blue Ridge Mountains of Virginia

Nick hated going to the lodge, but that's where Basil wanted to meet, and it was Basil's show. Since leaving the Agency, Basil had enhanced his reputation as the first stop for any difficult assassination, foreign or domestic. He was not only good at it; he enjoyed it. In a scant two years, Basil's firm had made tens of millions solving other people's difficult problems. His clients included not just the CIA but some of the most brutal and repressive governments in the world.

The lodge was well out in the Virginia mountains. Nick was thankful Basil had sent the chopper, converting the three-hour drive to a fifty-minute flight.

"There are people all over the pad, Nick," the pilot said through the headphones as they circled the massive redwood-and-stone structure. "I'll have to drop you at the bottom of the hill in the parking lot. Sorry."

"Forget it, Vasily." He lied. "The exercise will do me good."

"Not like the old days," Vasily said, laughing as the helo touched down. "I would have buzzed them off the pad and landed anyway."

"You've gotten too PC." Nick removed the headphones and climbed out with his head down to avoid the still-turning blades.

Once clear, he signaled by rotating his index finger above his head. Smiling, Vasily acknowledged with a crude gesture of his own. The helo rose, pivoted, and headed east.

Nick turned and looked up at the lodge. As he climbed the 152 stone steps, he mentally reviewed his pain résumé.

Stiffness, neck: February 1985: Afghanistan Mountains, helicopter crash, his first date with KGB Col. Vasily Konovalov.

Pain, left leg: September 1989: Brussels, gunshot, left thigh when I took out that finance minister.

Ache and stiffness, ribs and back: December 1994: Karachi, beaten with a lead pipe for eight hours after liquidating an uncooperative tribal chieftain. One of Vasily's many last-minute saves.

Popping and aching, right shoulder: March 1997: Kiev, fell off the roof after an evening with a Russian general's daughter—all in the interest of preserving East-West relations, of course.

Blurred vision and throbbing, right eye: August 2002: Salina, Oklahoma, stabbed in the right eye with a fork when a Texas oilman's poisoned meat tenderizer took too long to take effect.

Nick placed his foot on the top step and paused. His breath rattled in his throat. For the first time in his life, he felt every one of his fifty-one years. The dress shirt seemed to corset his chest. He stripped off his suit jacket, his knees quivered, and an uncustomary wave of panic washed over him. Nick's throat filled with blood. His vision blurred and blackened around the edges. He pulled at his shirt collar, popped the top button, and loosened his tie. The urge to cough was irrepressible. Nick stepped off the walkway into the tall grass. Struggling to maintain control, he tossed his jacket a few feet and tucked his tie into his shirt ahead of the first cough. An explosive spray of red mist painted the pampas grass as he struggled to keep his clothes clean. He backed away from the now-crimson vegetation and lowered himself to a squat, coughing up ever-smaller quantities of blood. His vision and breathing returned to normal. Nick reached for his jacket and retrieved one of the two handkerchiefs that were now his constant companions. He wiped his mouth, checked his clothing, and popped a breath mint. His legs steadied. He stood, donned his jacket, and returned to the path. Smoothing the wrinkles from his clothing, he made the final addition to his pain résumé.

Gross hemoptysis: February 2004: Georgetown University Hospital, the thoracic surgeon informed him that he had inoperable small-cell lung cancer, courtesy of a two-pack-a-day cigarette habit of twenty-years duration. No surgery, chemo, or radiation recommended. And no magazine subscriptions longer than six months.

Rita, who had been Basil's secretary since he went independent and created Conflict Resolutions, LLC, was waiting on the porch. She frowned and gave a restrained wave as Nick emerged from the tall grass. He tossed the bloody kerchief into the weeds before she could see it and waved back. Rita was a striking woman—her beauty matched only by her phobias. Nick swallowed hard. He could have had someone, maybe even Rita, and he wouldn't be facing this alone. They had been quite close after he resolved a nasty relationship problem for her. Their affair had burned white-hot before succumbing to Rita's overwhelming obsessions. A chronophobe, insecure, and obsessed with age, Rita saw the grim reaper around every corner. If Rita knew he was dying, it would only reinforce her convictions. They remained friends, but friends without benefits. Nick forced a smile as he crossed the gravel parking lot.

Suck it up and do your job, Nick. It's all you've got and all you're going to have. You made your choices. No family, no friends, and no commitments. Just pedal to the metal and to hell with the consequences. These are the wages of sin.

51

I WAS OLD THEN, AND I'M OLDER NOW

Monday, 19 April 2004—2:45 p.m.
Basil's mountain lodge, Blue Ridge Mountains, Virginia

Rita studied Nick as he approached. He paused and wiped his mouth. He looked shaky and a little pale.

Another night of wine, women, and song? Maybe it's that, or perhaps age is catching up with him.

There it was again, age, the specter that hung over everything she did. It occupied every thought, insinuated its way into every aspect of her life. Every day brought a new wrinkle, a new ache, or a name forgotten. And it was not just her; it was everyone she knew. They were failing a little every day. For twenty years, she had looked over her shoulder and seen the slow rot of senescence creeping up behind her.

Even as a young girl, Rita, stunning as she was, had feared the loss of physical beauty. Her youth and physical appearance had been her passport to success. As a child and teenager, she had seen how the other girls envied her. Rita's mother had made sure of that, pushing her to exploit her physical appearance through elementary-school beauty pageants, junior high pom-poms, and high school cheerleading.

Rita remembered the day in second grade when she had gotten off the bus and found her mother sobbing at the kitchen table. Rita's father was gone. He had left them for a younger woman. Rita began to cry. From that day forward, Rita's mother taught her that all men were bastards, concerned only with a woman's physical attributes. Her mother's sole mission in life became teaching Rita to use those attributes before they faded.

Rita had believed her mother, but then she went to college and met Doug. He'd seemed perfect, listening patiently to her every concern. Rita ignored her mother's advice and married him. He had an answer for everything.

"Wake up, Sleeping Beauty," Nick said, shaking her out of her daydream. "You look like you're on another planet. What's wrong?"

"Just thinking," Rita said.

"About me, no doubt," he said, kissing her on the forehead. He took her arm as they walked toward the lodge's front door. Rita noted with awe Nick's instantaneous recovery. A single shake of his head, and he was again the picture of confidence and proficiency—agile, mobile, and hostile. If Brooks Brothers sold professional assassins, Nick would be their poster boy. He moved with effortless grace. His hint of a limp and faint facial scar provided just the right amount of mystery—Dr. Nick Caedwallan, the hitman with the PhD.

"What were you doing in the weeds?" Rita picked at the seeds clinging to his jacket.

"Just a call of nature." Nick tugged at his zipper. "Forget that. You look fantastic."

"I look old." Rita waited for the rebuttal.

"You're as beautiful now as you were when we met."

"Yes, I was old then," Rita said, frowning, "and I'm older now."

"You're incorrigible," Nick said, smiling.

"Yes," Rita said, "and old."

As they walked, Rita remembered the night she'd met Nick.

It was at one of Basil's D.C. cocktail parties, the ones he frequently hosted to wine and dine potential clients. Basil loved to showcase Nick. On this particular evening, Basil had a bit more to drink than usual.

"This is my chief of operations, Dr. Nicholas Caedwallan, who holds a PhD in ancient history and archaeology," Basil said. "He is a man of many talents. He can bury you and, years later, dig you up and examine you. In his case, PhD does truly mean piled higher and deeper."

In the next few weeks, Nick had asked Rita out numerous times. She was resistant. She found him attractive but questioned the wisdom of an office romance. Finally, she agreed. Over the course of several dates, Nick was able to extract the bulk of her story. After each date, he invited Rita to his Georgetown home for a drink. Each invitation was met with a polite but firm refusal, which only seemed to pique his interest. On their fifth date, Rita spoke very little. She made frequent trips to the ladies' room, returning with her eyes red and puffy.

"Okay, it's none of my business," Nick said, "but you're not eating or talking, and—"

"It's a long story and kind of private."

"Just give me the short version."

"When Doug asked me to marry him, I told him about my dad leaving and what it had done to my mother."

"And?" Nick took a sip of his drink and leaned forward. "What did he say?"

"You are not your mother, and I am not your father. In forty years, we'll be sitting on our back porch watching the grandchildren play in the yard."

"And you bought it?"

"Every word. I quit college and put him through law school, working as a flight attendant. We were building a house. And now, the job is gone and so is Doug."

"You're probably better off." He put his hand on hers.

"He left me for a nineteen-year-old student clerk, a runner-up in the Miss Kansas pageant. He said she was fresh and au courant, and I was passé. The bastard loves to speak French. It makes him feel superior."

"And the house?"

"The divorce was final last week. MW and the HWW just got married, and he's taking her to Paris for their honeymoon. "Rita stared at the young couple at the next table. "To cap it off, they're going to come back and live in the house I paid for."

"MW? HWW?"

"Mr. Wonderful and the Home Wrecking Whore," she said. "I wish they were both dead."

Nick nodded. "He was a fool," he said, seeming to look through her. "He'll realize what a mistake he's made." He refocused his gaze and laughed.

The next day Nick canceled their upcoming weekend date. "Duty calls," he'd said. "Hazards of the profession. I'll wrap it up in a couple of days." He held up two fingers. "I'll bring you something from France."

"Do you know what I want?"

"Better than that." He flashed his half-smile. "I know what you need."

On Monday, Rita came to work and found a copy of the English version of *Le Monde* on her desk. The newspaper was folded to page three, on which a short article was circled in red.

"In a tragic accident, an American lawyer and his new bride were killed yesterday when a gas line exploded in the cottage they were renting in the Normandy district near the tiny town of Bayeux."

Next to the newspaper was a copy of a will in which Doug named Rita as the sole heir of his estate. It had been executed and witnessed by a French notary only twenty-four hours prior. When Nick came in, Rita stood and blocked his path.

"Are these? Did you?" Rita said, stammering as she pointed to the newspaper and will on her desk.

"I told you I'd bring you what you need."

That night, Rita said yes to drinks at Nick's apartment.

52

TONIGHT, YOU ISSUE HIS PINK SLIP

Tuesday, 20 April 2004—3:01 p.m.
Basil's mountain lodge

"Rita." Basil's voice boomed off the lobby's twenty-foot ceiling like thunder off a canyon wall. "Goddammit, where's Nick?"

"So much custard from such a small cat." Nick stepped from behind the wooden column into Basil's view. "Here I am, as per your request."

"No, what I requested," Basil said, his fists clenched, "or, rather, what I specified, was that you be here five hours ago. What would that goofy community college do if you were five hours late for that lame-ass, fairy-tale ancient history course you teach, Doctor Caedwallan?" Basil drew out the title, then hesitated, frowning.

Nick, being accustomed to Basil's crude hyperbole, ignored him, pretending to take in the framed oil paintings and art-deco motif of the lobby.

Although they called it The Lodge, the place was a three-story, sixty-room, luxury hotel, complete with steaming mineral springs. Built in the 1880s as a refuge for mining and manufacturing barons, it was now the nerve center of Basil's empire and the perfect place to shield high-profile visitors from prying eyes. Basil still maintained his McLean office but mostly as a stick-in-the-eye for the CIA.

Nick watched Basil squirm and decided to let him off the hook. "I love what you've done with the place. Is that a new coffee maker over there?"

"Okay, smart-ass, you made your point. You know you're like a son to me."

"That's reassuring," Nick said. "Considering you had your son shot for botching an assignment."

"Another Agency old-wives' tale. Anyway, consider yourself family."

"Okay, Dad. I saw the hired guns on the helipad. Who's on the menu today?"

"His Majesty, Robert Fletcher, deputy director of the CIA, will fill you in on that. We need you to clean up a mess."

"I thought you were sending me to North Carolina to end the one-woman anthropology reign of terror."

"Tomorrow, smart-ass. We have a more immediate problem."

"Such as?"

"I said, Fletcher, will brief you."

"Give me the fifty-cent version."

"Okay. You remember our old friend—you know, the one who helped boot us from the Agency?"

"Bel Castro? What about him?"

"Tonight," Basil said, "you issue his pink slip." Basil smiled and pointed to the bulge under Nick's left arm.

53

THEY'RE HERE

Tuesday, 20 April 2004—9:46 a.m.
Lucy's rented farmhouse, Rural Asakan, North Carolina

Lucy's black tactical shotgun joined the ever-growing stack of items to leave behind. She could take only so much. She was driving a Land Rover 88, not a motorhome.

She could still hear Tommie Whitefeather's survival-course instructions. "If your method of transportation is vehicular, you can have two bags. Bag number one is your true bug-out bag. It is stuffed tight with the absolute essentials from the provided list of survival supplies. It waits ever ready by your front door. It should be canvas or heavy ballistic nylon with shoulder straps." He'd paused for a moment. "I prefer fatigue green canvas, but I'm old school."

Lucy glanced at the enormous backpack.

Fatigue green canvas, stuffed to the gills, waiting by the door. Check.

"Bag number two," Tommie had instructed, "is a canvas duffle, fatigue green, of course, no more than three feet long and eighteen inches in diameter. It should have a clip-on padded shoulder strap and sewn-in handles in the middle and at both ends—sewn-in shoulder straps optional." He'd glanced around the room, smiling. "This bag is your department store. It is expendable and contains the things that are good to have, but that you can survive without. As long as your ride is operational, you live out of this bag. You do not touch your bug-out bag." He'd looked directly at Lucy. "This is a bug-out, not a vacation. If it doesn't fit in these two bags, it can't go with you. End of story."

Lucy looked back and forth between the little canvas duffle and the room full of good-to-haves. She planned to leave in two weeks. Tommie was going to inherit a lot of good stuff.

As Lucy mulled the choices of items to include, the ring of her pre-paid phone startled her. Tommie was the only one who had her phone number. They had a prearranged code. If it were something routine, Tommie would call from a hardline, let it ring three times, then hang up. This meant there was no record on his phone bill, and she could keep using the phone. If it were an emergency, he would call from the hardline or mobile and let it ring until she answered. It had never rung more than three times.

One ring.

Lucy used only prepaid phones registered to fictitious names at distant false addresses. She received no mail at her house and used a P.O. box in a city twenty miles away. Tommie always picked up her mail. All her local purchases were in cash. Her hotel stays were covered with a prepaid Visa and her identity verified with a near-perfect, forged driver's license courtesy of a guy from Raleigh known only as Vadim. She had been so careful. Until that trip to the Marine Institute last month. One stupid mistake.

Two rings.

"Lucy, there's something I've wanted to ask you," Tommie had said a month after they met.

"Well, we've only known each other for a few weeks. It's sudden, but yes, if it's a June wedding, with a zeppelin." Lucy had batted her eyes.

"Seriously," he said. "Why do you drive that old Land Rover? It's left you stranded twice since you got here. We can find you something a little newer."

"It's partly sentimental," she said. "But mostly for privacy. It's still registered in New Hampshire in my aunt's maiden name to the address of a cabin she and my uncle built up near the Canadian border. They're both dead now. We just left it in their name. My dad renewed the license every two years. Don Bel Castro, my godfather, is the executor of the estate. When the license comes due, he renews it for me, and we meet someplace. He gives me the license plate stickers and some cash from the family estate. I cry on his shoulder for a couple of hours and then disappear until the next time."

"What about proof of insurance?" Tommie had asked.

"New Hampshire doesn't require insurance. Neither does Wisconsin. I researched it."

"God, Lucy," he'd said, recoiling. "Sounds a little OCD."

"The psychiatrists call it a situational paranoid personality disorder."

"Situational?"

"It's complicated."

"How about the short version," he said.

"There is no short version," Lucy said, making eye contact. "The CIA murdered both my parents, and they—or somebody—has been hunting me for the past two years. It sounds crazy, but there's proof."

Three rings.

She'd spent the next three hours telling Tommie the story and showing him newspaper clippings and letters from friends and family. Tommie had looked at her and asked, "Why didn't you just move to the cabin?"

"I have a lot of reasons. My paranoia is part of it. I wanted to be sure that whoever killed my parents didn't know about it. I figured I'd escape and evade for five or ten years. If I lived that long, I'd move there. I went there once, a few months after the murder. I didn't see any signs of a search. I know they're good, but if they'd been there, they fell from the sky."

"So why this place?" Tommie had asked. "What brought you here?"

"My mom and dad rented a small beach house not too far from here every summer. I thought being nearby might make me feel close to them."

The next day Tommie had taken her to buy an untraceable gun through a private sale and enrolled her in his survival school.

Four rings. Maybe he miscounted.

That was almost a year ago. Lucy stared at her image in the full-length mirror. Dark brown eyes stared back at her. After the murder, she had dyed her hair red and bought green contact lenses. Last night she'd cut her shoulder-length hair into a short bob and dyed it back to her natural dark chestnut. The green contacts were stored in their case. Her only concessions to disguise were a pair of black horn-rimmed sunglasses and a headscarf. If she were "going out," it would be as herself. Lucy had dropped almost twenty pounds in the school's rigorous training program, but she had changed much more than her outward appearance. Weapons training, real-world martial arts, map reading, and street psychology had increased her situational awareness and confidence. If they came for her now, she would make the bastards work for it.

Five rings, maybe a wrong number.

Hands sweating, she checked the caller ID.

Damn, it's Tommie.

Stomach churning, she stared at the flashing number, afraid to answer.

Six rings—maybe a customer distracted him. Please.

She pushed the talk button and tried for cheerful. "So, did you forget how to count?"

"I wish. We've got to talk."

He sounds worried, almost scared.

"I'll come for lunch," she said, hands shaking.

Down, Lucy, calm down. How bad can it be?

"Not a good idea. I'll come there."

Pretty bad.

"We're going to have to advance your timetable," Tommie said.

And getting worse by the second.

Lucy hesitated. "Why?"

Tell me something else, anything but—

"They're here."

54

ANOKA, BUT HE GOES BY NOKI

Tuesday, 20 April 2004—10:01 a.m.
Tommie's Café, Asakan, North Carolina

"Is that dude gone, man?" Noki poked his head through the serving window. "He gives me the creeps."

"And he should," Tommie said.

"He's trouble," Noki said. "Cornered me at the service station, asked all kinds of questions."

Tommie pulled his apron off over his head and stared at Noki. "Questions? What kind of questions?"

"He pretended the questions were about finding a motel for his crew and buying land. But every question came back to Lucy. Except, he didn't call her Lucy. He called her Chloe, but he was asking about Lucy. He even had an old picture."

"What did you tell him?" Tommie asked in a tone that was sharper than intended.

"Nothing. I said I didn't know her." Noki's voice cracked. "But he was good, Tommie. He's like you. He reads you like a book, no matter what you say."

"It's okay," Tommie said. "I know."

"Sorry to let you down." Noki's tough-guy facade crumbled. "You know I would never do anything to hurt Lucy."

Tommie thought back to the turn of fate that had brought he and Noki together. Eighteen months earlier, he'd stood in a cold autumn drizzle to hail a cab after visiting some old friends at the Red Lake Reservation in Minnesota. He'd been delayed at the airport in Minneapolis and missed his flight. After being rebooked for a day later, he decided to look up an old Corps buddy who owned a bar on North Hennepin Avenue.

The Middle Eastern cabbie seemed incredulous. "North Hennepin? I don't do Lake Street, and I for damn sure don't do North Hennepin. Bad clientele," he said, shrugging. "You know what I mean?"

"Unfortunately," Tommie made no attempt to conceal his irritation, "I know exactly what you mean."

The cabbie's head jerked around, anger turning to embarrassment, as he took in Tommie's weathered features. "Sorry," he said, stammering. "I meant nothing by it. It's just that—I'll take fifteen dollars in advance, tip included. I stop, you jump out, and I go."

They drove to North Minneapolis without talking, the silence punctuated by the rhythmic slapping of the windshield wipers. A cold, steady drizzle created a chill that the taxi's heater couldn't erase. They drove past empty storefronts, liquor stores, and overflowing trash cans. Young men were everywhere. Some clutched bottles of cheap liquor; some huddled over grates to keep warm. One stood in the rain, begging for spare change as he offered to wipe windshields with a greasy rag.

"Stop here," Tommie shouted, as they shot past a flickering neon sign.

Last Chance, it winked with an arrow pointing to a red door with small windows on either side.

The cabbie slammed on the brakes, and Tommie stepped out and closed the door. The cab was a block away by the time he reached the curb.

His old platoon leader, Joe, stood behind the bar, staring into space. Tommie thought he looked like hell. His face brightened when he saw Tommie. "Whitefeather, *aaniin*, old friend. It's been a long time."

"Too long," Tommie said. "Friends should be closer. How are you?" He looked around the room. There were no patrons, only a teenaged boy diligently mopping the worn linoleum floor.

"Old," Joe said. "Old and tired, feeling my seventy-eight winters."

They swapped war stories for several hours. The kid straightened all the chairs and wiped all the tables before dropping to his knees to scrub furiously at one of the floor's many permanent stains.

"Now, there's an exercise in futility," Tommie said, as the kid slipped, spilling half a bucket of soapy water.

"He's a good kid, trying to make something out of nothing." Joe stared at the youth. "But he's shoveling shit against the tide here."

Tommie stared at the teen and thought about the derelicts he'd seen on the way here. Most of them probably started just like the boy, scrubbing in futility at a hopeless stain. Finally, they just gave up and gave in.

"He reminds me of you, Tommie," Joe said, reading Tommie's face. "He's keen, with a good compass, but he's got no opportunity."

"He could do what we did—join up."

"And get his legs blown off in some banker's war? No." Joe shook his head. "He deserves better. Besides, things are different now. He needs someone to guide him, someone to give a damn."

"How about you?" Tommie said. "I can't think of anybody better."

Joe held up his hand to stop him. "I'm packing it in, Tommie. I'm going to the Res. I haven't got long, and I'm tired."

Tommie felt his throat tighten. "I might be able to help with that when the time comes, Joe."

"That's not for me, Tommie. I've seen enough, lived enough. I'm ready for a few years in the porch chair and then a new adventure." He looked at the young boy. "But there is something you can do for me. The kid's name is Anoka, but he goes by Noki."

"Anything you want, Joe," Tommie said, looking at the closest thing he had to family and the only man who knew his secret. "You name it, you got it."

So, Joe went to the reservation and Tommie brought Noki home to live with him. Tommie hadn't wanted the responsibility, but he couldn't refuse Joe. He'd never regretted it. Looking at Noki was like looking at himself. Tommie had no living family and had strived to have no personal relationships, but the boy had changed that. Noki had taken Tommie's surname, Whitefeather, and was like a son to him. Now there was Lucy, who was like a daughter.

55

CROISSANTS AND FILL-DIRT

Tuesday, 20 April 2004—10:03 a.m.
Tommie's Café, Asakan, North Carolina

"Tommie?" Noki asked. "Are you okay?"

Tommie's thoughts returned to the present. "I'm fine. Just worried, that's all. You didn't do anything wrong. Just steer clear of him. I'll take care of it." Tommie tossed his apron into the laundry hamper. "Come out of the kitchen. Staff the counter. Just cold stuff and drinks 'til I get back. I'm going over to Dan's and then out to Lucy's."

Tommie walked across the street, entered the bank lobby, and climbed the ancient creaking stairs to Dan's office on the second floor. He stared briefly at the black lettering on the door's frosted glass insert.

Daniel Parker, LL.B
Parker and Associates, Real Estate Holdings, Ltd.
Parker and Associates, Investment Advisors

The glass rattled as the door stuck, then pulled free. The office smelled of old wood, old cigar smoke, and old money. Ancient Dan sat behind his ancient desk, leaning back in his ancient wooden rolling chair. Phone in his left hand, smoldering cigar in his right, stained regimental tie, rumpled white shirt, buttons straining across his abdomen.

Shirtsleeves rolled to the elbow, he rocked back and forth, struggling to land the fish he was reeling in over the phone. Seeing Tommie, he smiled and waved him in with the cigar hand, never missing a beat.

"Yes, it's swamp or, rather, wetlands now. I'll give you that. But I have it from a reliable source that I cannot reveal that the Army Corps of Engineers has—What? Yes, okay. Call me back when you can talk." He put down the phone and smiled at Tommie.

"When are you going to add 'Purveyor of Croissants and Fill-Dirt' to that sign on your door?" Tommie asked.

"Just as soon as the market declares itself, son. You can be sure of that," old Dan said. "Social call or business?"

"Business, unfortunately. I'll get right to the point," Tommie said. "You've been after my properties for some time. How would you like to buy the houses, the motel, and the survival school?"

"What about the lodge and the café?"

"Those are for Noki."

"Is something wrong? Can I help?"

"No, it's just time." Tommie looked out the window and paced back and forth.

"Well, better me than that dandy who hit town yesterday." Dan cocked his head to make eye contact. "I can't tell if he's looking for land or a girlfriend."

"So, what's it worth?" Tommie said, deflecting the question. "Are you interested?"

"Things are a bit slow, but your stuff is prime. I'll grant you that."

Tommie watched Dan pick up a pencil and scratch at a pad on his desk, pretending to calculate as if he hadn't dreamed of this moment a thousand times. He looked up at Tommie.

"Well, I don't care anything about the school, but the land it's on with the lake is worth about four hundred thousand. The motel has seen better days, but still, about three hundred and fifty. Those houses are small, but they stay rented. Another four hundred. Altogether, I'd say about a million, one hundred fifty." He scribbled something on his paper. "How about we keep it simple and say a million even and close in two weeks?" He grinned and waited for the counter at a million one.

Tommie stopped pacing and turned to face Dan. "How about five hundred thousand and we cash out in forty-eight hours?" He waited for Dan to keel over, but Dan surprised him.

"Look, I know this is all about that prick who came to town yesterday." Dan pulled the cigar from his mouth and leaned forward. "I'm all for making money, but still." He sat back and ground his cigar in the ashtray. "You need help dealing with that little shit?"

Tommie shook his head. "No, thanks. There's more to it than just him."

"I'm sure you've thought it through." Dan put out his hand. "How do you want to handle it?"

Tommie took his hand. "I want a hundred thousand in cash, nonsequential, used twenties, and the rest in a guaranteed annuity for Noki." Tommie took a deep breath and added, "I'm trusting you to be there for Noki."

"I'm a hard businessman, but you know I've never cheated anyone." Dan paused. "I'm happy to help Noki in any way I can, but you know he'll want to come with you."

"I know," Tommie said. "But he can't."

Tommie walked down the stairs, pausing in the doorway before stepping onto the sidewalk. Once again, he saw pinwheels and flashing lights. He blinked to clear his eyes. Shooter's truck rolled by, barely moving. His window was down, his arm hung out, and his fake smile was pasted on. He raised his index finger in greeting. "Mornin'," he said and accelerated away.

56

THINK OF IT AS AN ADVENTURE

Tuesday, 20 April 2004—11:16 a.m.
Lucy's rental farmhouse, rural Asakan, North Carolina

Lucy sat in the ancient rocker, resting her head in her hands.

I won't cry.

She had known this day would come, but that didn't make it any easier. In two years of running, this dilapidated farmhouse was the closest thing she'd known to a real home. Lucy looked around the room.

I love this place with its frayed carpet, peeling paint, dodgy electrics, leaky roof, and plunger-dependent plumbing. Tommie keeps it all going, all for two hundred dollars a month.

Lucy took her mother's journal from the shelf and walked to the front door. The familiar squeak of the hinges and the bang of the screen were reassuring as she stepped onto the lopsided front porch. Brown fields surrounded the green oasis of a postage-stamp yard, part of a long-abandoned tobacco farm set in the middle of a pine forest. The farm had little or no value, but Lucy loved it for its isolation and privacy. She felt safe here, sitting on the warped porch steps and hugging her mother's journal. She raised it to her face, savored the familiar smell of the leather binding, and then regarded it at arm's length. It looked so innocent.

What's your secret, jellyfish? What do you know that's worth killing for?

Lucy looked up to see Tommie's pickup truck barrel down the loose gravel driveway and slide to a halt in a massive cloud of dust. Tommie bolted from the truck, making for the porch, first at a run, then slowing to a walk. She met him halfway, placing her hand on his shoulder to calm him.

"Relax, partner." She forced a smile. "You need a drink." Lucy led him to the small kitchen table littered with papers. She cleared a space and poured two glasses of sweet tea.

His anxiety was infectious. Lucy fought the urge to panic.

Tommie took a sip of the tea. "A guy came in asking questions about you." He put the tea down and looked Lucy in the eye. "He's not the brightest bulb on the string but he's well-financed, and he's been sniffing around." Tommie recounted the morning's events, omitting his trip to Dan Parker.

"It's okay." Lucy bit her upper lip. "This isn't exactly new to me. I'm driving up to Richmond tomorrow to meet with Uncle Don and get some money from the estate." She sighed. "I'll be back by Thursday, Friday at the latest."

"Friday's a long time. That crew is moving into the hotel on Wednesday. Eventually, they're going to stumble across something."

"Maybe, but you're the only person who knows where I live. They're not likely to accidentally stumble onto this place. Anyway, if it looks bad, you can call me."

She waited for a response, but Tommie just stared at her as if deep in thought. "Well, what do you think?"

"What do I think?" Tommie said, laughing. "I think that, for a Yankee, you make the best sweet tea I've ever tasted." He leaned forward. "But seriously, Lucy, I have a proposition for you."

"Oh my," Lucy said, falling back on their standing joke. "Do you think the age difference will be a problem?

Tommie fumbled with his truck keys. "I've been thinking about pulling up stakes for a long time. I want, no, I need to get back to

Minnesota. You need help, and now's as good a time as any for me." He paused. "I want to see that you get safely away from here, and then I can go on to the Res."

Lucy wrinkled her brow.

Before she could speak, Tommie said, "Trust me, Lucy. I've got to go anyway." He tried to read her face. "Well?"

"Yes, it's yes, but we have to take the Rover."

"Oh, God, it's like a sick sheep looking for someplace to die. Why not my truck?

"The Rover's anonymous, remember?" She smiled. "Your truck has known registration."

"All right, but wear your best boots," Tommie said, holding up his hands in mock defeat. "I suspect we'll end up walking."

"Think of it as an adventure," she said. "Like Steve McQueen in *The Great Escape*."

"I seem to remember he got machine-gunned to death while trapped in a barbed-wire fence."

"Minor detail."

"Wait, "Lucy said. "What about Noki? Is he coming with you?"

"No." Tommie looked down and shook his head. "Dan Parker is buying everything but the café and the lodge. I'm giving those to Noki. Dan's setting up an endowment." He looked up. "It's bottom dollar; we're settling for cash on Wednesday."

"Okay, give it up. There's a lot more than you're telling me. Spill it." There had to be more if he was leaving Noki behind.

Tommie deflected her question. "Here's the deal." He pointed to Lucy's mountain of survival gear. "Pack your nonessential good-to-haves in that duffle with the sewn-in handle and the optional strap. Go to Richmond and meet your uncle." He paused for breath. "Meet me here for the bug-out Friday at midnight. Then I'll tell you a story you won't believe. But it's all true."

57

MAKE IT LOOK NATURAL

Tuesday, 20 April 2004—5:52 p.m.
Basil's lodge, Blue Ridge Mountains, Virginia

The drum roll and cymbals of an approaching storm covered Nick's approach. He paused outside Basil's office, a partially closed door hiding his presence. Inside, the reverberations of spirited conversation competed with the near-continuous cacophony of the advancing storm.

"Tonight, damn it. It's got to be tonight." Robert Fletcher's voice boomed. "The bastard's getting too close."

"Nick will be here any minute." Basil's was the calm voice for a change. "He and Vasily will take care of it."

"Fags and sex addicts," Fletcher said, snorting. "If that idiot Schwartz could control his zipper, we wouldn't be in this mess." Nick leaned closer to the crack in the door.

"Are you waiting for me to announce you?"

Nick turned to find Rita standing inches behind him.

"Just waiting for a break in the action." Nick straightened his tie and pushed through the opening. Rita followed, clearing her throat as they entered. The dialogue stopped as both Basil and Fletcher turned to face them.

"You could knock first," Basil said.

"I thought I was expected," Nick said.

"Ah, yes, Nick Caedwallan." Fletcher said Nick's name as if he were chewing a piece of bad meat. "The Agency's answer to Indiana Jones. It's been a while. Do you still travel the globe pawing through history's refuse?"

"You know what I'm doing. A little teaching and some consulting work for the preservation of antiquities," Nick said. He was determined not to be sucked in.

"Today's trash, tomorrow's treasure," Fletcher said, smiling. "A research PhD in ancient history and archaeology from the University of Leicester, and community college is the best you can do?"

"Well, let's see. My curriculum vitae reads: Framed and discharged by the CIA, canned by *National Geographic*, and blacklisted by every four-year institution of higher learning in the United States," Nick said. "What did you think I'd be doing?"

"Gentlemen, gentlemen," Basil said. "Let's avoid ancient history and stick with current events. We're here for a matter of mutual concern. Can we develop an action plan?"

"Yeah," Fletcher said. "You can have the good doctor here neutralize Bel Castro this evening." He flinched as a bolt of lightning struck nearby. "And your stewardess," he said, gesturing toward Rita, "can march downstairs and tell your boys that the chopper is weather-grounded, and I'll be needing a limo and driver for my trip back to Langley." He looked at Nick. "And don't give me his light-in-the-loafers partner for a driver."

Rita opened her mouth as if to protest.

"Go ahead." Basil gave a half-wave to Rita.

Rita left without comment, closing the door behind her.

"Listen, Fletcher," Basil said. "I don't appreciate you—"

"No," Fletcher said, cutting him off. "You listen." He pointed his finger at Basil. "I don't care what you appreciate. We've put up with you for too long. I don't give a damn if you do know where the bodies are buried. This time next year, I'll be the director and if you cross me, I'll shut you down."

Fletcher turned to Nick. "And you. Just do your job. Bring me that

Marine Corps ring Bel Castro wears, the one that hasn't been off his finger for twenty years." Fletcher started for the door. "You should be thrilled, Caedwallan." He turned back to Nick. "This is your chance to get even."

"I don't need you to tell me how to even a score," Nick said.

"Make it happen," Fletcher said. The door shut behind him.

Basil and Nick stared at each other. "And there he is," Basil said, "the future of U.S. intelligence."

"So now you're letting Fletcher call the shots?" Nick asked, shaking his head.

"He's right about one thing." Basil closed his eyes and rubbed his forehead. "Bel Castro has to go." He paused. "Get rid of him tonight. Make it look like a suicide." The wind-driven rain blasted the window. "Vasily will drive you back to Bel Castro's place in Stafford, and then to Fletcher's."

"But you can't just let Fletcher—" Nick said, interrupting him.

"Patience," Basil said, smiling. "Tonight, Bel Castro, tomorrow you leave for North Carolina. The Spencer girl might be in the area."

"And if I find her?"

"Another suicide," Basil said. "You know, desperate terrorist feels the law closing in." He smiled at Nick. "You're good at that shit." He sat down hard in his chair. "And find that damn leather jellyfish journal."

"Why do you care about jellyfish?" Nick glanced at the shimmering paperweight. "Why take the Spencer girl out? It's been nearly two years now."

"Since when are you so concerned about the why and wherefore of a hit?"

"I just wanted some background. I have nothing on her." Nick picked up a pencil from Basil's desk.

"Nothing on her?" Basil said. "Your team iced her parents two years ago. How much of a dossier do you need?"

"My team?" Nick snapped the pencil in half and tossed the pieces on the desk. "I interviewed those two and found nothing irregular. I told your pit bull, Marty, to transport the Spencers. Vasily and I went back to Langley. The next thing I hear, his partner, Blair, is on life-support and the Spencers are dead. A month later, I'm out on my ass without so much as a hearing."

"We were all out, Nick," Basil said. "We are fortunate Fletcher convinced oversite the Spencer couple was dirty and evoked the Secrets Act of 1911," he said. "Otherwise, we'd all be in prison."

"There should never have been a shooting in the first place," Nick said. He thought about Vasily begging him not to leave the Spencers alone with Marty.

"Look, you've seen the report," Basil said. "Marty and Blair continued questioning the suspects. The daughter was conveniently 'out' with her mother's journal. The questions got too tough, and the Spencers drew weapons."

"Where did these two science geeks get guns?" Nick asked. "We took the only gun they had."

"Where does anybody get guns?" Basil said. "They're everywhere."

"That's bull. They had no guns."

Basil waved his hand. "Anyway, the Spencers were killed, and Blair was wounded. The Spencer girl fled with the notebook. She is still out there. That's it."

"The official report lists her as deceased."

"I don't believe it," Basil said. "That report has that bastard Bel Castro's fingerprints all over it."

"Christ, Basil. You see Bel Castro's fingerprints on everything."

"And for a good reason. That death was a sophisticated fake, right down to the lost dental records. It was just too convenient, a typical Bel Castro operation."

"I saw the police photos of the Volvo burned to a crisp, along with the driver and the dog. They found Chloe Spencer's identification in the remnants of a backpack."

"With no credible trace of her mother's journal," Basil said, stabbing at the folder on his desk that contained the grainy photo. "You may be skeptical, but I view the Chloe Spencer sighting as very credible. It came through Bel Castro's office, and he tried to cover it up."

"Why do we care? It's all irrelevant."

"It was all in Marty's after-action report. She's on the run with a journal full of her mother's research notes," Basil said. "Besides, she's a loose end, and I hate loose ends."

"Marty's story stinks, and you know it," Nick said. "Ted Spencer was a clinical psychologist working under your direction, and Dr. Karen Spencer was a researcher and professor of marine biology at William & Mary. She studied jellyfish, for God's sake."

"*Turritopsis dohrnii.*" Basil pointed to the baseball-sized Lucite globe on his desk. "Like this." Inside the sphere were six perfectly preserved, dime-sized jellyfish. It sat on a black base with a light that progressed slowly through the visible spectrum, highlighting their bright red stomachs, and making them shimmer as if moving.

"That's creepy," Nick said. "Why do you keep that on your desk?"

"To remind me of why we were booted from the Agency," Basil said. "Karen Spencer found a way to weaponize the jellyfish neurotoxin. They were trying to sell it to the Iranians. The daughter was a go-between on the Iranian deal. She took the journal and ran. She was dirty, too. Fletcher proved that."

"I never saw his proof, Basil. Did you?"

"National security," Basil said. "Now, get rid of the girl and bring me that journal."

"Can I take Vasily to North Carolina?"

"No. Marty's team will back you up. I have something else in mind for Vasily. A little downtime to catch his breath." Basil picked up the jellyfish globe and swiveled his chair to face the window and the darkening sky.

"Time off? Since when do you—"

"Vasily's got a lot on his plate," Basil swung around to face Nick, "and tonight's going to be a bigger deal than you realize."

"Vasily's a professional," Nick said. "He doesn't need downtime."

"That's my decision." Basil placed the globe back on the base. "Mandatory downtime." Basil paused. "You might need a breather, too," Basil said.

"I'm fine with the Bel Castro thing." He studied Basil's face for clues. Nick wondered if Basil had discovered his illness. If so, he might be grooming Marty for his spot.

If Marty discovered the girl's whereabouts before Nick arrived—

Nick turned and walked toward the door, stopping when he heard Basil clear his throat.

"Yes?" Nick said, without turning to face Basil.

"I've thought it over, what you said, about Fletcher calling the shots."

"And?"

"When you're finished with that Bel Castro thing—"

"Yeah?" Nick continued facing the door.

"Do Fletcher, too." Basil's chair creaked as it swiveled. "Make it look natural."

Nick nodded once and closed the door behind him.

Rita sat at her desk, making notes in a document. She glanced up. Their eyes met.

"Fletcher?" she asked.

Nick nodded.

"Tonight?"

Nick nodded again.

"Good." She flashed a satisfied smile and returned to her paperwork.

Nick looked at the thin smile on Rita's face. She'd changed a lot since her husband's death. She was still obsessed with aging, but being in Basil's employ had given her a more pragmatic view on the demise of others.

"Oh, here." She pushed a small box across her desk. "Basil wanted you to have this."

58

THERE'S ONLY ONE THING I WANT

Tuesday, 20 April 2004—6:01 p.m.
Basil's lodge

Basil stared at the layered mountain vista. The third-floor window afforded an excellent view of the road leading to the lodge. He watched the black Mercedes carrying Nick make its way down the hill. The shiny, wet, black snake of a driveway seemed to swallow it whole as it disappeared into the darkening green of the forest. He looked down and shook his head. Nick had to go. He had gotten a call from his sources at Georgetown Hospital. Nick was toast, and dying men tend to develop a conscience. Then there was Vasily. In light of recent events in Dnipropetrovsk, Basil's hold on Vasily was gone.

Basil swiveled his chair to face his massive oak desk and stared at the three folders spread before him. He leaned back, massaged his temples, and reached for the jellyfish globe. Holding it tight in his hand, he polished it with a handkerchief, placed it back on the base, and focused his attention on the photographs clipped to each of the three folders.

Nick: hazel eyes, dark brown hair slipping into gray, and that look of simultaneous confidence and humility that women loved, and Basil hated, a seamless blend of truant English public schoolboy and university professor.

Vasily: head like a T-Rex, close-cropped graying blond hair, blue-gray eyes, and an amicable but intimidating "please don't make me kick your ass" expression.

Then there was Marty: short brown hair and dark soulless eyes of indeterminate color. Basil supposed some women might consider him handsome in a bad-boy kind of way. He was like the horrific car crash by the side of the road that fascinated and frightened at the same time. What had Nick called him? Oh, yes, "a psychotic pit bull gone feral."

Basil was a sociopathic bottom-liner. He had no emotional attachment to any of his associates. They were just tools to be discarded when no longer useful. It was change that he hated. Each time he eliminated a set of staffers, the youth and vitality of their replacements underscored his age and deterioration. Still, it could not be helped. Nick's condition made him unreliable. As for Vasily, well, Fletcher had given Basil the CIA's latest surveillance findings. Vasily should have stayed in the closet.

Basil considered that he would miss Nick. But the Ukrainian, not so much. They had been useful over the years, but eventually, assets become liabilities and must be taken off the books.

He turned Nick and Vasily's folders face down and sighed, not because of guilt or affection, but because they represented what he feared most: the passing of time. With great difficulty, he used his arms to raise himself from the chair. His joints cracked. His back ached. His head spun as his tired heart raced to maintain cerebral blood flow.

Shit, every bone in my body hurts. I can't eat. Can't take a crap without a pill. Can't climb stairs. Haven't known a woman in a dozen years, not properly anyway.

Basil examined the reflection of his bent frame and gray skin in the full-length window. The image stared back, a shriveled old man, eighty-three, going on ninety.

He smiled, turned to his desk, and gave the jellyfish globe another polishing swipe with his handkerchief.

Spent, he dropped hard into his chair, closed his eyes, and willed his heart rate to return to normal.

Basil pushed the button on the intercom. "Rita?"

"Yes, sir."

"Call downstairs and tell Fletcher that Caedwallan's left for D.C."

"Yes, sir. Oh, and the helicopter pilot just called. He was diverted due to the thunderstorms. Do you want to reschedule Marty's meeting?"

Marty's sardonic grin taunted Basil from the front of his folder. He contemplated the absurdity of replacing Nick with Marty.

"Have him go to our McLean office. Tell him I'll call him on the encrypted line at eight-thirty sharp." Basil sighed. "I'll need a limo back to McLean. I'll be staying in the office apartment tonight. Have a helo there at nine in the morning to bring me back to the lodge."

"Do you want Vasily for the flight tomorrow?"

Basil thumped his middle finger on Vasily's folder, which lay face down on top of Nick's.

"No. Send someone else. Vasily will be unavailable."

Basil pushed aside Marty's file and pulled a grainy security photo from his desk drawer. He had pursued Chloe Spencer and her mother's journal for a year and a half. For someone not formally trained, she had been elusive prey. Under different circumstances, he might try to recruit her rather than kill her.

Basil had bought the best scientists he could find. He'd set up a clandestine lab in Belarus and distributed millions of dollars among a dozen numbered accounts worldwide. Belarus had been extremely accommodating. He had enough U.S. secrets to keep them occupied for a decade.

The intercom buzzed. "DDCIA Fletcher to—" Rita began.

"Forget that. I'm expected." Basil could hear Fletcher on the intercom as he pushed through the door.

"Got it, Rita." Basil caught her eye as he stared past Fletcher. Rita stood feet apart, hands on hips, an icy stare fixed on the back of Fletcher's head. "That will be all for now." Basil smiled and watched Rita retreat, taking heart that this was the last time either of them would see Fletcher in an upright position.

"Make yourself at home, Fletch." Basil gestured to the decanter on his sidebar. "Drink?" The thought of Fletcher's impending demise made him feel hospitable.

"No. I've got to start back." Fletcher walked to the sidebar, eyed the decanter, and poured a drink anyway. "Do you think Caedwallan bought the show? Was I over the top?"

"The ranting was a nice touch," Basil said.

"What now?" Fletcher said.

"Nick kills the girl and destroys the notebook," Basil said, lying. "Marty will then dispose of Nick for us."

"Cold, very cold," Fletcher said, grinning. "I like it."

"Assets and liabilities, Fletch, assets and liabilities. And on your end?"

"I'll make the call this evening," Fletcher said. "Vasily Konovalov will be the victim of a hit-and-run as he leaves his favorite Starbucks tomorrow morning. I love it when people are creatures of habit—every morning, coffee with his special friends."

The intercom crackled. "Basil?" Rita said.

"Yes?"

"Marty is on the ground at the McLean office. He'll wait for your call."

"Thanks, Rita."

"She's a nice unit," Fletcher said. "You'll enjoy that."

"Rita?" Basil shifted in his chair.

"I'm sorry. Was I not supposed to know?" He raised his palms. "She may have let it slip. She's quite the asset."

"Oh? Yes. She's all that. No, that's okay," Basil said, forcing a half-smile. "I just thought it was our secret."

"Females, you know, they like to talk." Fletcher raised his glass.

Rita had handled all the administrative aspects of the fund transfers, the clinic acquisition, and the appropriate bribes and promises to the Belarus officials. Also, she had been invaluable in setting up Nick and Vasily. She knew all the secrets. Basil knew what made Rita tick and had promised to deliver. She could be a great partner. Still, Basil wondered.

"And what about Blair?" Basil asked.

"Certified unresponsive, three times. Still on life support. She's a veggie now, and she'll be a veggie until she croaks. Broccoli doesn't talk." Fletcher refilled his glass.

"All the same," Basil said. "She's a loose end."

"Forget about it." Fletcher drained his glass and placed it on Basil's desk. "We've been over all this before. She's history. Listen, I've got to get back to Langley." Fletcher turned and walked to the door. "Keep me updated."

"You'll be hearing from me." Basil clenched his teeth in pain as he rose from his chair. He followed Fletcher across the room and closed the door behind him.

Basil returned to his chair and buzzed Rita.

"Are you still here?"

"Yes. I'll be right in."

Basil admired Rita as she approached his desk. "I appreciate the time you've put into all this."

"It has definitely kept me busy."

"You know I'll make it worth your while."

"There's only one thing I want, Basil," Rita said.

"I know," Basil said, "and you shall have it."

The storm brought an early darkness to the Virginia mountains. Basil watched the forest swallow the taillights of the last car in Fletcher's entourage.

59

I'M REORDERING MY PRIORITIES

Tuesday, 20 April 2004—7:33 p.m.
A mountain road east of Basil's lodge, Blue Ridge Mountains, Virginia

The afternoon storms had forced Vasily to turn back shortly after dropping Nick at Basil's lodge heliport, making him available to drive Nick back to Georgetown. The first hour of the trip passed without their usual banter, the silence interrupted only by the driving rain and slapping wipers. A four-hour compilation of Hans Zimmer's epic soundtracks was just audible. This was Vasily's driving music, specially chosen for his transits between the lodge and Georgetown. Nick stared through the rain splattering the windshield, his focus changing from the drops on the window to the conifers flashing by at the road's edge. Vasily expertly maneuvered the large Mercedes sedan down the winding mountain road. The combination of the swaying motion, soft focus, and epic music was hypnotic. In a few moments, Nick was in a state of intellection, neither awake nor asleep. This ability to "distance in place" was a skill Nick had honed to perfection. A few minutes in this state was worth hours of conscious analysis and introspection. Today, it was just a mind game, an attempt to confine his disease to a box for a few minutes while he considered his now-truncated stay on this planet.

Nick recalled Kasra's prediction: "You do bad things for what you think are good reasons, and so you are *haram*. You are mostly good, but the bad will grow until it consumes you, *doostam*, body and soul."

In the space of ten minutes, Basil had tasked Nick with killing three people, and Nick suspected that Basil had targeted Vasily and himself, as well. Fletcher was an asshole, but the Spencer girl was innocent, and Bel Castro had only been doing his job. He recalled something else his Afghan friend said just before he was killed: "My friend. I think you are destined for goodness. At your lowest point, the good will come out. The bad will go, and the good Nick will move on. I am sure of it."

Nick had little doubt that his nadir was fast approaching. The question was how to salvage something from his train wreck of a life before he assumed room temperature.

"Ahem." Vasily cleared his throat. Nick ignored him and stifled an overwhelming urge to cough. After several more throat clearings with no reaction from Nick, Vasily could no longer contain himself.

"Okay, let's have it." Vasily averted his gaze from the road long enough to make eye contact. "What's eating you?"

Nick took a moment to reorient himself, then shifted in the seat to face Vasily. "I'm dying. I've got six months max."

Vasily's mouth dropped open. "I don't believe it. From what?"

Nick stared at the floor. "Lung cancer. Small cell, stage four, no chemo, no radiation, no future."

"Jesus Christ." Vasily shook his head. "Did you get a second opinion?"

"Yeah," Nick said with a half-smile. "And a third and a fourth."

"So, now what?"

"Let's just say I'm reordering my priorities." Nick stared out the window at nothing.

"For instance?"

"Well, for one thing, did you know that right now we're on our way to kill Don Bel Castro?"

"You don't want to do that!"

"Relax," Nick said. "We're not killing Bel Castro, though he did cost me my teaching job—my last chance to go back. He knew it was Marty taking orders from Basil, and he took us down anyway," Nick said, irritated with Vasily. "Why are you defending him? He framed you, too."

"No one framed us," Vasily said.

"I know he blames me for not saving Ted and Karen." Nick watched the rain on the windshield. "I should have turned back sooner. Hell, I should have listened to you and never left them in the first place."

"That ship has sailed." Vasily turned off the music. "What are we going to do about it now."

"So, now it's we?" Nick said.

Vasily pulled the car into the parking lot of a long-abandoned filling station and general store.

"In a way, the penny has dropped for both of us." Vasily looked down. "There are things I would like to have told you a long time ago, but I couldn't—not until now."

60

I'M NOT SO SURE HE KNOWS THAT NOW

Tuesday, 20 April 2004—7:41 p.m.
A roadside stop, somewhere between Basil's lodge and Washington D.C.

The eighteen-wheel log truck blew past on the narrow two-lane road, its shock wave of wind and water washed over the idling Mercedes. Nick heard the truck engine roar in protest as the driver downshifted for the approaching curve. The brake lights gave faint warning as the truck completed the turn, then winked out as it accelerated into the mist. The receding cacophony of light and sound was replaced by the dim glow of instrument lights and the rhythmic beating of windshield wipers.

Nick listened to the rain and waited for Vasily to continue. When Vasily remained silent, Nick said, "Go on, I've shown you mine, now show me yours."

"My older sister and my nephew." Vasily's voice cracked. "In Ukraine, in the beginning, before the Soviet breakup, they could not leave. After the breakup, my sister said her life was there. She would not leave. Now, she is, or was, old and ill. She could not leave."

"Can you shorten this up? My head is killing me."

"Your head? I thought it was lung cancer."

"Mets," Nick said, rubbing his eyes.

"Mets?"

"You know, metastases. It's in my brain."

"Your brain? Damn." Vasily took a deep breath and continued. "My nephew stayed to take care of her. They were my only family. Basil found out about this in a background check when I defected. He said he had connections in Donetsk and said he could protect them in return for absolute obedience. You know how he feels about Ukrainians in general, and he knows things about me." Vasily picked at the stitching on the leather steering wheel. "Things I never told—"

"Go on," Nick said.

"When the Soviet Union fractured, he switched from nominal protector to blackmailer. If I failed to cooperate, if I made any trouble or tried to leave, he swore he'd kill them both." Vasily looked out the window at a passing car. "I wanted to tell you everything I knew about Basil's operations, but I could not. I took a chance just sharing the letters with you."

"So, what's changed?" Nick said. "Why now?"

"Dnipropetrovsk."

"The tram bombings?"

"My sister and my nephew write every week. Two weeks passed with no word. I made inquiries. This afternoon, I got the call. That bastard Basil. He has connections. He had to know they were dead." Vasily's eyes were dry, but his voice wavered.

"I'm sorry," Nick said. Each week, Vasily had shared the contents of the letters from Ukraine. Most of Vasily's income had gone to his sister and nephew or to bribe Ukrainian officials to make their lives more bearable.

"I should have found a way to tell you," Vasily said, pulling at the frayed stitching again. "But I was afraid Basil would kill them."

"And he would have. You did the right thing," Nick said. "And stop picking at that damn steering wheel."

"With their deaths, his hold on me is gone." Vasily put his hands in his lap. "I have, in Basil's parlance, moved from asset to liability."

"I have a strong suspicion we have both passed our sell-by date with Basil. Let's drive and talk; one of Basil's toadies could be on this road. Besides, we should get back to Georgetown. Our dance card for this evening is full."

"Meaning?"

"Basil's cleaning house," Nick said. "He also wants us to do Fletcher."

"I'm not surprised."

"Because?"

"I'll keep it short," Vasily said. "Fletcher and Basil planned to let us take the fall, but Bel Castro had just enough on Basil to—"

Nick held up a finger to silence Vasily. He opened the door and stepped out into the drizzle. After a spate of non-stop coughing, Nick got back in the car. "And Blair?" He was breathing heavily and swabbing his mouth with a handkerchief.

Vasily saw the blood on the handkerchief before Nick could stuff it in his pocket. "Jesus. What can I do?"

"Forget it," Nick said. "Blair?"

"She was part of the setup. Collateral damage," Vasily said. "Only, she was supposed to be dead, not comatose."

"So, right person, right time." Nick recalled Basil's rationale for using Blair.

"Basil and Fletcher were each running their scams," Vasily continued. "Bel Castro was working Internal Affairs through the Agency's Inspector General Office. He had been monitoring communications and funds transfers for some time and knew something was rotten. He couldn't name the perps or the precise scam, but he was triangulating."

"The setup?" Nick said.

"They needed an event to take Bel Castro out of the loop," Vasily said. "The Spencers were already on Basil's radar, so they became the marks. It wouldn't have been plausible for two scientists to outgun four trained agents. They couldn't kill us there, so they brought Marty on board. You and I were sent back to the office so that Marty could set up the sting. He brought three weapons to the house. Fletcher had two of them registered to the Spencers. The third was Marty's service weapon. He shot Blair with one of the Spencer guns, the wife with Blair's gun, and the husband with his service weapon."

"The prints and powder tests?" Nick shook his head.

"He held a weapon in each victim's hand and fired a shot," Vasily explained. "One more random shot in the ceiling."

"Where do we fit in?" Nick said, trying to visualize the scene in his head.

"Officially, you were team leader," Vasily said. "Marty and I were part of the team."

"Go on."

"Basil had a reputation for being trigger-happy, and Marty was already a known nut-job," Vasily said.

Nick nodded.

"You and I were under Basil's supervision." Vasily continued. "They cooked up the story about the jellyfish neurotoxin to invoke national-security concerns. Fletcher took the whole thing to Bel Castro and muscled him into signing off on it. Fletcher and Basil wanted you and me to take the fall. Bel Castro said he wouldn't stand down if we got charged. End result, Basil is bounced out with a lucrative black-ops contract. He keeps his pit bull, Marty, and takes us along to keep an eye on us. Bel Castro is removed from the Inspector General Office and kicked upstairs, effectively ending his investigation."

"Now my head really hurts." Nick opened the car door and took several deep breaths. "How do you keep this straight?" He glanced back at Vasily.

"Bel Castro laid it out for me," Vasily said. "He's out of IGO, but he does this off the books because of his connection to the Spencers. And here's the kicker: Marty is his source."

"Marty went to Bel Castro?" Nick pulled the door shut.

"Christ, no. Bel Castro had his suspicions. Knowing Marty's penchant for call girls and pharmaceuticals, he put a female agent on him and ran the honeypot. She got him drunk and juiced him with sodium pentothal. He spilled everything, and he doesn't even remember doing it."

"So, Bel Castro is closing in?"

"Yeah, but Fletcher caught wind of the new investigation. He and Basil need an immediate hit to silence Bel Castro. They're working a frame-up to make him look dirty."

"It fits," Nick said. "They want to discredit Bel Castro. Everyone knows he's depressed about his wife's death. This makes it look like he was already unstable, couldn't face the music, and took the easy way out." Nick shook his head. "Classic Basil and Fletcher."

"So, what are we going to do about it?" Vasily asked.

"I think you and I need to have a little talk with Bel Castro."

"Both of us?" Vasily started picking at the steering wheel again.

"Well, given our past, he won't want to see me alone," Nick said. "You seem to know him pretty well. You've kept in touch."

"After a fashion." Vasily looked away. "His kids have married and moved away. One's in the Corps. The other works overseas for State. Marie dying of cancer hit him pretty hard. Two years now and he's still a mess. He's lonely and I'm a loner, so we talk."

Nick held up his hand to stop the information flow. "I don't need a dossier. Call him and tell him we're both coming by."

"Look." Vasily started to pull onto the road, stopped, put the transmission in park, and turned to face Nick. "As long as we're putting it all out there . . . there's something—"

"You mean that you're a confirmed bachelor?" Nick said. "That's old news."

"What? It's not as simple as that. I'm not some cock jock. I just happen to prefer the company of guys. Damn, if you knew, how come you never said anything?"

"Because it doesn't matter," Nick said. "Have I treated you any differently?"

"No."

"There's your answer, nothing has changed," Nick said. "You were always discreet, the best at what you do, so what difference does it make?"

"If Basil had found out, he would probably have had me killed. You know, with his old-school thinking, a 'confirmed bachelor' would be a security risk."

"Not probably," Nick said. "Definitely. And not because he's old school, but because he's old."

Vasily put the car in gear and eased it onto the rain-soaked road.

61

HE WAS GOING TO MISS NICK

Tuesday, 20 April 2004—8:30 p.m.
Basil's office at his mountain lodge, Blue Ridge Mountains, Virginia

Basil punched the number of his McLean office into the secure line. The earpiece crackled as someone picked up on the other end. Basil could hear breathing.

"Speak," Basil said after fifteen seconds of silence.

"Basil, it's me," Marty said, trying to hide his excitement.

"Yes, Marty, I called you." Basil stared at the *Turritopsis* globe as it slowly changed colors on its stand. "I need you to do something for me—two things, actually."

"Yes, sir. Anything."

Basil could envision Marty standing at attention and saluting. It was a bit refreshing after Nick's smart-ass attitude.

"After it gets dark, I need you to go to Bel Castro's house."

"And do him?" Marty said.

"No, Marty. Nick and Vasily are taking care of that. Bring me any 'eyes only' files you can find. There should only be two."

"Where are they?"

"Christ, Marty. I don't know. Use your spy skills. You worked for the CIA. Maybe in his office over the garage."

"What if Bel Castro's up there?"

"If there's no light, he won't be up there. If he's there, just wait until he goes into the house." Basil paused, waiting for affirmation.

There was only silence.

"Marty, do you understand?"

"Yes, sir. What's the second thing?"

"I'm not sure I trust Nick and Vasily."

"Should I kill them?"

"No," Basil said. "Not tonight. I just need you to wait until they leave and make sure they've taken care of Bel Castro." Basil paused to be sure Marty was getting it.

"Sir?" Marty's tone did nothing to reassure Basil.

"I may need you to help me out there, son. Call me if you don't see Bel Castro's body." Basil gave up waiting for a response. "Can I depend on you, Marty?"

"Yes, sir. You can count on me."

"This is your chance. Think of it as a changing of the guard, with you as the new number one."

Basil hung up the phone and looked out the window. He was going to miss Nick.

62

IF YOU'RE STILL ALIVE

Tuesday, 20 April 2004—9:11p.m.
Bel Castro's residence, Stafford, Virginia

"All these damn McMansions look alike." Nick strained to read house numbers in the darkness and rain. "Doesn't the GPS tell us anything?"

The night swallowed the headlights as the Mercedes crept through the fog. Every hundred feet, a streetlamp produced a decorative but useless puddle of light. Trees rendered the houses invisible, while shrubs and hedges helped hide house numbers. "I thought you'd been here before." Nick peered into the darkness. "Call him again."

"I've been here once or twice, but I wasn't driving, and it was dark then, too," Vasily said, hesitating. "Just look at the numbers on the mailboxes."

"I can't see them," Nick said. "Just call him again."

"And say what? 'I'm sorry, Don. Basil sent us to kill you, but we can't find your house. Be a good fellow and stand at the end of your driveway in the rain." Vasily sighed. "Look for a Volvo in the driveway and a light on."

"Thanks, smart-ass." Nick raised his hands in frustration. "It's Stafford; every other house has a Volvo in the driveway and the light on."

He lowered the window for a better look at the mailboxes. "Wait! There it is, 703, next driveway."

Tall boxwoods lined the narrow asphalt drive. A brick walkway cut through a small opening in the hedge and curved toward the house. Directly ahead was a white-clapboard, two-car garage with a room over it. A light burned in one of the dormers. A dark green Volvo wagon was parked in front of a barn-style garage door. Vasily parked about ten feet behind the station wagon, shut off the engine and lights, and stared in silence at the glowing garage dormer. Nick listened to the ticking of the cooling engine and noted Vasily's white-knuckle grip on the steering wheel. "Ease up, partner. We made it."

The window over the garage went dark.

"He saw us. He's coming down," Vasily said.

"Let's go." Nick reached to open the door.

"Just a minute," Vasily said, watching.

"Is he expecting you?"

"Maybe."

The rain had slowed to a drizzle, but the fog thickened by the moment.

"But he's not expecting us?"

"Probably just me."

"What gives?"

"It's complicated," Vasily said, turning to look at Nick.

"So, we're back to complicated again. Wait a minute, you mean? You and Bel Castro? You knew how to get here all along. You were stalling?"

"Marie's death left Don alone and isolated." Vasily began working the loose stitching on the steering wheel again. "My family were virtual prisoners. We both had Basil issues."

"So, shared miseries?" Nick reached over and yanked the loose thread from the steering wheel.

"We became close friends. Very close. But friends without benefits."

A lumbering figure with an umbrella appeared at the corner of the garage, strode through an opening in the hedge, and approached the passenger door. His right hand held the umbrella. Nick could not make out the objects in his left.

"Sometimes I've only got a few minutes," Vasily said. "If I don't go in right away, he comes out."

Nick shook his head and stared as Bel Castro's bear of a form filled his view.

"We're just friends," Vasily said.

"I told you, you don't have to justify anything to me. If it's not job related, I don't give a care."

Vasily lowered the passenger window. Bel Castro's left hand held a wine bottle and two stemmed glasses.

"Coming in?" Bel Castro leaned over, stopping short when he saw Nick. "It's been a long time." His recovery was instant. "Looks like we'll need another glass."

Nick and Vasily followed Bel Castro along the winding brick path toward the covered front porch. Evenly spaced solar lights shone like fireflies in the mist. The rain had nearly stopped, but the air was thick. They stepped onto the porch. Bel Castro dropped the umbrella and tried the door.

"Shit," he said. "Locked myself out again." Bel Castro handed Nick the wine bottle and glasses. He patted both pockets and sighed. "We'll go in the kitchen door." The brick path wound its way to a stone patio on the back side of the house. They entered the kitchen through an unlocked door.

"You leave your house unlocked?" Nick said.

"I lock it when I leave or go to bed. Not much happens here," Bel Castro said, shrugging. "I've locked myself out twice in the last two weeks. Besides, who gives a damn?"

Bel Castro led them through the kitchen and dining room, down a long hall, and into his library. The room was a study in taste and nostalgia. Two brown leather wing chairs faced a dark walnut desk flanked by a matching bar and a credenza littered with open scrapbooks. Nick took note of an "Eyes Only" CIA folder on top of the pile. Family pictures lined the wall. An oriental carpet covered all but a one-foot border of the bold-grained ash floor. Opposite the desk, a brick fireplace with a small fire separated two built-in bookcases stuffed with books, more family photos, kids' athletic trophies, and marine aviation memorabilia. The haze of happier times was as thick and palpable as the fog outside. Bel Castro paused at his desk and glanced down at a picture of his wife.

"I'm sorry about Marie." Nick placed his hand on Bel Castro's shoulder. "She was one of a kind."

Nick had spoken with her several times at joint Agency/Bureau family functions. He remembered her pointed question at their last encounter: "So why does someone with your academic chops waste their time with these adolescent testosterone games?"

So that's what's left? A picture on a desk? No, she raised a family. She made a difference. She was loved. She's two years gone but still remembered. Me? I'll just be gone.

"Thanks for that," Bel Castro said, sighing. "Marie liked you. She could never figure you out, but she liked you." He retrieved a third glass from the bar. "Take a load off." He gestured to the two wing chairs facing the desk. "What brings you gentlemen out on a night like this?"

Vasily cleared his throat. "Basil sent us to kill you."

"In that case, wine is out." Bel Castro removed the wine and stemware. "This requires something with gravitas." He placed a bottle of Dalmore single malt and three Glencairn glasses on the desk and turned to Nick. "Let's get to it then, shall we?"

"Fletcher wants you dead." Nick glanced at Vasily for backup.

"He knows you've compromised Marty," Vasily said. "And he knows from some inside source that you've got the goods on both of them."

"He also knows you're depressed about Marie," Nick said. "The bastard plans to dirty you up somehow and make it look like you were so down that you shot yourself with your service .45." Nick took a drink, enjoying the pleasant burn of the single malt.

"He got the dirty part wrong," Bel Castro said, "but he's not far off on the depression." He took a long pull on his scotch. "Besides, nobody lives forever."

"Basil would take issue with that statement." Vasily swished the whiskey in his glass.

Bel Castro picked up the brown CIA folder from the credenza.

"Well, you've seen this." He nodded at Vasily. "But let's bring Nick up to speed." He slid the folder across the desk to Nick. "It's like Basil has finally gone off his nut." Bel Castro refilled the glasses.

"Basil has transferred the bulk of his liquid assets to Belarus over the last six months," Nick said, commenting on what he read. "He dropped four million on a medical-research facility alone."

"Yeah," Bel Castro said, reading over Nick's shoulder. "He bought the whole damn hospital. Kicked the patients out and brought in a team of medical researchers."

"Bribing government officials." Nick thumbed through the first twenty pages. "Hiring and housing a team of neurobiologists and two experts on *Cnidaria*, whatever that is." Nick stopped to look at the last page. "And seven figures spread among four banks in the former Eastern Bloc. What's he up to?"

"An insurance policy," Vasily said. "Look at that cache of physical gold and silver."

"He sold the lodge and McLean offices to the Agency," Bel Castro added. "Possession in thirty days."

"He's moving fast," Nick said.

"And look who's handled the transfers," Bel Castro said, taking another drink.

"Rita," Nick said, scanning the last page. "I thought she wanted out."

"No," Vasily interjected. "She wants what Basil wants."

"And that is?" Nick asked, extending his glass in Bel Castro's direction.

"Agreeable, isn't it?" Bel Castro refilled Nick's glass. "Maybe this will help answer that question." He opened his desk drawer and removed a single sheet of paper on Agency letterhead. "I got this just yesterday. In the last six months, Basil has been invoiced nearly three hundred thousand by Carson Enterprises."

"The private intelligence agency. What's he looking for?"

"My niece and her mother's jellyfish notebook," Bel Castro said. "He's been conducting an off-the-books search for over a year. Finding her has now become an obsession." He nodded to Vasily. "Feel free to jump in." He moved to refill Vasily's glass.

"No more for me, thanks." Vasily covered his glass with his hand.

"*Cnidaria* is the phylum that jellyfish belong to," Vasily said. "Haven't you noticed Basil caressing that jellyfish globe he keeps on his desk?"

"So, his goal is to manufacture a neurotoxin for Belarus to sell to the Russians?" Nick asked. "I thought the Agency's science-and-tech boys said it wasn't worth the effort."

"No, not a neurotoxin," Bel Castro said. "He doesn't care about that."

"Then what does he want with your niece and the journal?" Nick asked.

"*Turritopsis dohrnii.*" Vasily glanced at Bel Castro. "The only creature in the world capable of immortality and eternal youth."

"What?" Nick said. "That's impossible."

"That's not the issue," Vasily said. "The issue is that Basil thinks it's possible, and he's willing to kill Chloe and anyone else who gets in his way. He won't stop until he has the notebook."

"Basil's too smart to believe in fairy tales. There must be another angle," Nick said. "It's all about money and power with him."

"Look, Nick, he's old and his health is failing," Vasily said. "This possible sighting of Chloe at the Marine Research Center has energized him."

"I thought she was dead," Nick said.

"No, that story was my doing," Bel Castro explained. "It didn't stop Basil completely, but it slowed him down by taking all official assets off the case."

"How does the journal figure into this?" Nick said.

"Money and power mean nothing if you're not around to exercise it." Bel Castro poured himself a third glass of scotch. "Personally, I can't see it." He took a sip. "You get your three score and ten, and you're out of here." He made an umpire-like gesture with his thumb. "Why stick around when everyone else you know is checking out?"

"It's different for you, Don." Vasily pointed to a picture of Bel Castro and his family. "You've had a life that means something. For Basil, it's all just dust in the wind. No friends, no family, no happy memories. I don't think he believes in an afterlife. And if he does, I'm sure he's in no hurry to get there."

"How about you, Nick? What's your take on immortality?" Bel Castro asked. "You look deep in thought."

Nick blinked and shook his head. "God help us. I'm just thinking about a world where people like Basil live forever."

"Would you want immortality?" Bel Castro moved to refill Nick's glass.

Nick pulled his glass away. "My problem with eternal life is motivation. Where's the incentive to do anything if you have forever to do it?" He looked at Vasily. "That said, given my present situation, I wouldn't mind a do-over to fix a few things."

"Your present situation?" Bel Castro said, looking at Nick.

"Lung cancer, advanced, no chance of cure." Nick fumbled with his glass. "Three months at most."

"I'm sorry, Nick," Bel Castro said.

"Nothing we can do about it," Nick said. "Let's deal with the problem at hand."

"Okay, enough philosophy. It's 9:45 and we're not immortal," Vasily said. "Fletcher wants Don dead. Basil wants Fletcher dead, and most probably"—he pointed to himself and then to Nick—"you and I are high on his to-do list."

"So, we go proactive," Nick said. "Fletcher is the linchpin. He has to go. Otherwise, he and Basil will off the three of us, and nothing changes. I want to help your niece. I feel responsible. It's the closest I'll get to a do-over."

"Well, let's get on with it then," Vasily said. "What's the method?"

"Wait," Bel Castro said, swaying from the effects of the scotch. He smiled at Vasily, raised his glass in a mock toast, walked to the bookshelf, and removed several tomes. He retrieved a small plastic case and returned to his chair. "You'll appreciate this." He opened the box and placed a small metallic disc on an elastic strap on the table.

"That looks familiar." Nick reached for the object. "Dearborn."

"A little different this time." Bel Castro pushed Nick's hand away. "That's 200 mg of a succinylcholine derivative." He downed the last of his scotch and slipped the device on his right hand with the disc in his palm. "Just a quick handshake," he continued. "But for God's sake, don't put it on backward." Bel Castro laughed. "He'll stop breathing in twenty seconds. It's virtually untraceable."

"Virtually?" Vasily asked. "We're dealing with the CIA. Is it traceable or not?"

"They have no incentive," Bel Castro said. "He's a couch potato with two heart attacks and a bypass who still smokes two packs a day. They're not going to look very hard. A basic Agency tox-screen and they'll call it quits." He waved his hand. "Nobody likes the bastard anyway."

"That's all fine. Now, we need to borrow your ring." Nick pointed to Bel Castro's left hand.

"My Corps ring?" Bel Castro placed his left hand over his right. "This ring never leaves my finger."

"Fletcher knows that." Nick said. "That's why he wants it as proof you're dead."

"And we need you to disappear for a week," Nick added. "Basil has to believe you're dead. Can you do that?"

"That's no problem," Bel Castro said. "People in our business disappear all the time." He placed his ring in Vasily's hand. "Bring this back tonight. I won't leave without it." He gripped Vasily's hand and made eye contact. "We can work out the details of my disappearance when you get back."

Bel Castro, legs wobbling, stood up and staggered to a far corner of the room. He knelt and pulled back the edge of the carpet to reveal a small floor safe. He punched a few numbers, opened the safe, and placed the "Eyes Only" folder inside. He returned to his desk and raised his glass. "Exceptional Scotch."

Nick looked at Vasily and raised his eyebrows

"Don, lock the door and keep your piece close," Vasily said.

"And try not to shoot yourself with it." Nick pocketed the succinylcholine dispenser. "We should be back a little after midnight."

Bel Castro's sigh emptied his lungs as he collapsed into his chair. "If you're still alive." He closed his eyes and waved them off.

63

ASAKAN

Tuesday, 20 April 2004—10:14 p.m.
A cave near Asakan, North Carolina

Tommie had spent hours sorting the precious few relics of his tribe. The Cape Fear Indians left few traces before vanishing from the North Carolina shores some two centuries before. By the mid-eighteenth century, they numbered scarcely two hundred souls scattered among five river villages near the coast. The villages consisted of hide-covered tents with grass-mat floors, easily moved to follow fishing and hunting migrations. The tribe's hunting and gathering kept them close to the water. Occasionally, they would range inland along the Cape Fear River before migrating back to the coast.

Each spring they would burn all the old corn and smash all the pottery to symbolize the beginning of new life. They would drink the "black drink," a tea made from the Yaupon holly leaf. Like the ancient Celts, the Cape Fear Indians regarded the holly as a tree of eternal life, gifted with powers of rejuvenation. Their culture revolved around the concepts of cleansing rebirth and immortality. This tea would induce vomiting and prepare them for the great feast of renewal, at which they would gorge themselves on the local shellfish. The shaman would add a few drops of a salty, pink-tinged jellyfish extract to the tea. This was said to impart a youthful vigor and restore health to those suffering from ailments or injuries. The effects were transient, waning well before the next spring feast when the shaman would again brew his dark potion.

Except for the reddish-brown sand pottery, very little remained of the Cape Fear Indians. Their language had been lost to antiquity. The name of a small North Carolina town is all that remained. *Asakan*, a curious combination of archaic eastern Siouan words: *a* meaning place of; *sa*, meaning red; and *kan*, meaning immortality.

Tommie removed several small, dark-brown apothecary bottles from a small leather pouch. The Cape Fear Indians did little trading with the early settlers. Their shaman, however, insisted that they procure these bottles for his most potent medicine. These few vials were all that remained of his most cherished potion. The bottles were stopped by pieces of natural sponge and sealed with large knobs of dark-yellow bee's wax. The shaman was a formidable figure. The Cape Fear Indians worshiped a deity known as "He Who Never Dies," and their shaman, whose great grandmother had been a priestess, claimed direct lineage to this spirit.

Tommie glanced up from the bottles. The yellow glow of the kerosene lamp illuminated a large two-panel painting on the cave wall. The cave's darkness and humidity had been kind to the fragile pigments. Tommie shook his head in wonder at the enduring brilliance of the blood-reds and sea-blues of the painting. The life-sized figures seemed to move in the shimmering light. On the first panel, several brown-skinned young men clad only in loincloths stood in a circle, their black hair tied in a knot and small tail at the nape. In the center of the circle stood a shaman; his wrists, ankles, and loincloth were accented with white oyster shells. His chest, thighs, and forehead were embellished with tattoos of an eight-tentacled jellyfish with a bright red center. Lying at his feet was a white-haired figure—naked, brown, and wrinkled.

The second panel contained the same figures, but now the young men kneeled with mouths open and arms above their heads, staring in wide-eyed awe. The wrinkled old man was gone. In his place, a young warrior sat cross-legged on the ground.

At the age of seven, Tommie's father, the tribal chief, had brought him to this cave to begin his education. "Your older brother will be chief," Tommie's father said, looking down at him and rubbing the top of his head. "Any donkey can be chief," he said, grinning. "But you," he continued, putting a small white feather into the knot of hair at the back of his son's head, "from this point forward, you will be White-feather, the tribal historian-in-training, the most important member of our tribe." He stared at the figures on the wall, frowning as he pointed to the tattooed figure. "The shaman tells me that you will be the most important tribal historian ever. The shaman says you will not just write history; you will make it. You will be the one to find and save the *Pahana*, the lost white brother." He'd looked into his son's eyes. "He says that your fate and his will be intertwined."

The image of his father gone, Tommie placed the bottles back in the pouch and picked up the knapsack and a worn spear from the cave floor. He looked up at the ceiling and closed his eyes.

All this time and no *Pahana*. Enough.

Another explosion of pinwheels and flashing lights brought him to his knees. The sensation faded. Tommie opened his eyes and picked up a small piece of broken pottery. Eyes closed, he held it close to his ear, rubbing the ragged edge with his thumb. As it had when he was a child, the surf-like grating sound relaxed him.

"You know the story." The voice in his ear was as soft as a leaf blowing in the wind. "The *Pahana* has lost his way." For a moment, there was only the raspy sound of his thumb on the pottery shard.

"Father?" Tommie said, continuing to rub the broken shard.

"Dig," the raspy whisper said. "Look beneath. Unearth the good." Tommie strained, but there was only the grinding of his fingers. He rubbed until the last remnant crumbled and fell to the floor.

Tommie stood, head down and eyes closed, for several minutes. He opened his eyes and placed the pouch containing the potion, a few of the shell tools, and a sand-pottery bowl into the knapsack. Tommie picked up the spear, snapped off the whelk-shell tip, and placed it with the other items. He stood at the entrance to the cave and panned the room, pausing on familiar objects as if taking a photograph. Sinking to his knees, he wiped his eyes on his sleeve, turned down the wick on the lamp, and savored the slow fade to inky darkness. Tommie crawled through the twisting cave opening, pushing the knapsack ahead of him, wondering as he always did if the grating murmur of his father's voice was real or imagined. He drew the hide over the opening, then arranged the branches and brush to hide the entrance. He took a few steps backward to examine the camouflage. Satisfied, he shouldered the knapsack and made the long hike back to his truck.

64

MUTATIS MUTANDIS

Tuesday, 20 April 2004—10:17 p.m.
U.S. Highway 1 northbound, Stafford, Virginia

Vasily eased the car into the northbound lane of U.S. 1. The rain had slowed. The thickening fog made the lights outside the shops into muted orbs of color.

"Jesus," Vasily said, looking left and right at the ugly landscape. "I can remember when all this was forest and farmland."

"Don't start," Nick said. "You're doing that 'old fart in the nursing home' thing again." Nick's cellphone buzzed. He checked the display: Restricted Number.

Nick pushed the talk button. "Fletcher?"

"Who else, history boy? Where are you?" Fletcher's speech was slow, his words slurred. "Did you make that dig for me? Did you get the artifact I asked for?"

"He's celebrating already." Nick mouthed to Vasily and keyed the speaker button. "Just leaving Stafford on our way to Reston." He gave his phone the finger. "Yeah, asshole, we did your errand and picked up the ring."

"Don't act so put out, Caedwallan. It's not your first prom, and you owed him big time," Fletcher said. "Anyway, that's why I called. I'm not in Reston. My wife's having a bridge party at the Reston house. I'm at the cabin on Abel Lake. Meet me here. Anyway, it's closer."

"I haven't been there for years," Nick said. "Those cow paths aren't in the nav unit."

"Tell that jughead driver of yours to put these coordinates in the GPS." Fletcher rattled off the numbers.

The trip took only eleven minutes. They met no vehicles after turning off U.S. 1.

"Park around the corner on the pavement," Nick said, slipping the injector onto his right hand and gesturing for Vasily to keep going and then turn right.

Fletcher opened the door before they could knock. He was barefoot and wearing khakis and a white oxford shirt, stained with whatever he was snacking on. He smelled of alcohol and aldehyde sweat. His thinning gray hair was plastered to his scalp. It was apparent he'd been drinking all evening.

"About damn time," he said as they walked in. "Let's see that fucking ring. Where's your car?" He peered around Vasily and Nick.

"Here's your trophy." Vasily handed him the ring. "And I'm not about to get the Benz stuck on that pig-path you call a driveway."

"And you owe me a pair of loafers." Nick pointed to his muddy shoes.

"Invoice Basil for it." Fletcher slipped Bel Castro's Marine Corps ring on his finger. "Would you boys like a drink?"

"No," Nick said. "We can't stay, but I thought about what you said—about doing me a favor. You know, the Bel Castro thing. It felt good. Thanks."

"That's more like it." Fletcher pointed to Bel Castro's ring. "Semper Fi, and all that shit." He held out his right hand.

"Yeah, and all that shit," Nick said, smiling broadly as he took Fletcher's hand and squeezed hard.

"Ow! God damn it!" Fletcher jerked away, noticing the device strapped to Nick's hand. His face contorted in fear. He opened his mouth to speak, but no sound came out. He clutched his chest and fell to the floor, face down.

Nick watched Fletcher convulse on the floor.

Better like this than drowning in your own blood.

"Christ," Vasily said, as he watched Fletcher twitch for twenty seconds and then lie still. "Is he dead?"

"Technically, no." Nick removed the injector and handed it strapfirst to Vasily. "But from his perspective, yes. His eyes are open. He can hear us. He's still thinking, but he knows he's dead."

Nick crossed the room to the small kitchenette and picked up a roll of paper towels. He tore one off and carefully picked up a partially filled highball glass from the counter. Returning to Fletcher, he poured the contents over his motionless hand. "Would you like to roll him over and watch him think about it?"

"God, no." Vasily averted his gaze. "He used to be one of us."

Nick leaned down beside Fletcher's body and rapped the glass briskly on the floor to break it. He picked up Fletcher's limp arm, made a swipe with the glass shard across his palm, then positioned the hand and glass on the floor.

"He was never one of us," Nick said. "Fletcher used the CIA as his personal cash machine and greasy pole to the top. He ordered the murder of Bel Castro to cover his crimes. He was a monster." He picked up Fletcher's left hand, retrieved Bel Castro's ring, and dropped it in the pocket of his jacket.

"So, what does that make us?" Vasily handed Nick the device and gave a head jerk toward Fletcher. "What's our place in this?"

"We are agents of change," Nick said, snapping the plastic case shut. "*Mutatis Mutandis*, we change that which needs to be changed and leave the rest alone." He placed the case in his pocket and wiped the small bits of mud from the floor. They stood next to the body without speaking, watching a small puddle of blood form under Fletcher's right hand. Nick checked his watch. "Fifteen minutes. It's done. Let's go."

Neither man spoke as they walked through the woods. They rode in silence through the thinning fog. As the mental and physical distance from the now-dead Fletcher lengthened, Nick's thoughts became increasingly analytical. He couldn't shake the feeling that he was missing something.

"Something's bothering me."

"Really? We just watched a man suffocate." Vasily gave Nick a sideways glance.

"It's not that," Nick said.

"What then?"

"It might be nothing," Nick said. "But the light above Don's garage was on when we pulled into the driveway."

"So?" Vasily asked.

"Then it went out."

"Yeah, and then Don appeared in the driveway with the wine," Vasily said. "So what?" A hint of anxiety crept into his voice.

"Don took us to the front door, then said he'd locked himself out again. If he came from above the garage—"

Vasily finished Nick's sentence. "He would never leave an 'Eyes Only' document on his library desk if he was working in the upstairs office." Vasily's speech came clipped and fast.

"Marty," they said simultaneously.

"Call Don Bel Castro." Vasily stabbed the 'talk' button on the Mercedes steering wheel and floored the accelerator. After five rings, the phone went to Bel Castro's voice mail. Two more attempts yielded the same result. They were in Bel Castro's driveway in under seven minutes. Nick pulled the ASP 9 from his shoulder holster, flicking the safety off as they ran for the kitchen door.

"Shit." Vasily slipped on the wet grass and fell into the shrubbery. He scrambled to his feet and passed Nick at a run.

The kitchen door was open.

Vasily ran through the kitchen and dining room, down the hall, toward the library.

"Vasily," Nick shouted. "Hold up." Vasily did not slow.

Vasily entered the library and stopped short. Nick ran into him, nearly knocking him down.

"Damn," Vasily said, looking down.

Bel Castro lay on the floor, face down, his service .45 by his right hand, a small puddle of blood by his head.

65

YOU'D BETTER MAKE ANOTHER POT OF COFFEE

Tuesday, 20 April 2004—10:57 p.m.
Lucy's farmhouse, rural Asakan, North Carolina

Tommie slowed the truck for the turn onto Lucy's driveway. The late spring night had been chilled by a fast-moving cold front and showers. The fresh air felt good. It was late, and the experience in the cave had been exhausting. He had known the time would come when he'd have to move on, but it never got any easier.

The driveway to the old farmhouse was a curving quarter-mile minefield of ruts, potholes, and loose rock. He had offered to fix it a dozen times. Lucy always refused.

"It's my low-tech alarm system," she would say, laughing. "I can tell someone's coming by the sound of car parts falling off."

Tommie hit the brakes for a particularly nasty pothole. He grabbed the cooler on the seat beside him as it slid forward. The cooler was packed with the cold fried chicken, potato salad, rolls, and desserts Noki had prepared for Lucy's trip to Richmond. Lucy had food allergies and hated road food. Tommie had gotten home at 10:30, tired and ready for bed, but Noki had insisted he deliver the food immediately.

"She's leaving at seven o'clock sharp tomorrow morning," Noki said, sliding the cooler across the table toward Tommie. "You'll miss her."

"If I do, she'll survive." Tommie slid the cooler back to Noki. "People have survived on fast food for fifty years now." He knew he would lose this game, but it was fun to play.

"No. She won't." Noki picked up the cooler and thrust it at Tommie's chest. "She'll come back with pimples and dandruff, all depressed, and pissed off."

"Fine." Tommie accepted the cooler in mock defeat. "But tomorrow I sleep in, and you open up."

As he rounded the curve in the driveway, Tommie could see the glow of light from several windows in the old farmhouse. He could just make out Lucy's silhouette sitting at the kitchen table. Her figure started as his headlights swept across the house.

Time to test Lucy's training again.

He shut off his engine, coasted the last fifty feet, and stopped behind the battered Land Rover. Lucy moved from the table, and the light went out.

So far, so good.

Tommie opened the truck door. The overhead dome light illuminated the interior of the truck.

Damn.

In a fraction of a second, his finger found the switch and killed the inside light. Within seconds, the interior and porch lights came on, and the front door opened. Lucy stood in the doorway, laughing.

"You're supposed to stay inside until you know who's here," Tommie said, walking toward the house.

"You're slipping," Lucy said. "You need a new muffler. I had you made when you slowed for the turn. Your engine still has that same miss. Besides, you left the lights on too long and swept the house." Lucy paused to catch her breath. "Plus, that stunt with the dome light was as good as a photograph."

Lucy led Tommie inside. The kitchen table was littered with Lucy's papers. The leather journal lay face down on the table, its tie undone. Two dark-green duffle bags were packed and ready by the front door.

"You finally finished packing?"

"I'll launder my dirties at the hotel on Thursday night, drive back Friday evening, and be good to go when you get here at midnight. Sit." Lucy pulled back a chair. "Coffee?"

"I shouldn't." He looked at his watch. "But okay."

Henry jumped to his feet and began howling piteously. "Good God." Tommie watched the dog shake its head back and forth for about thirty seconds before laying down as if nothing had happened. "What's wrong with him?"

"He's been doing that for the last two weeks." Lucy sighed, and her eyes moistened. "I took him to the vet. He said he has kidney failure. I know he's well over twenty."

"That's incredible for any dog, especially an Airedale. He looks like a two-year-old."

"He was my mom's dog." Lucy poured coffee and brought it to the table. "He's a miracle dog. Hit by a car. Shot last year with a bow and arrow." Lucy stopped and shook her head. "He always recovers. But now the vet says this kidney failure will kill him within a couple of weeks. He's too sick to go with us. Will Noki watch him?"

"Sure. He'll take good care of him. The next three days will be a good test run." Tommie cleared space for the coffee mug. A leather-bound journal fell to the floor, landing open and face up.

He reached for the journal. His breath caught in his throat. On the left page was a drawing of an eight-tentacled jellyfish with a red center with the heading, *Turritopsis dohrnii*. The right-facing page was a circular schematic of the organism's life cycle, indicating endless regeneration. Under the drawing was scrawled in pencil, "Applications?"

Tommie's heart pounded in his chest, "Lucy, what kind of work did your mom do?"

"She was a researcher. Marine biology. Her specialty was invertebrate genetics. Why?"

Tommie took a deep breath. "You know that story I said could wait 'til Friday?" He stared at the jellyfish drawing.

"Now?"

He glanced at Henry twitching in his sleep. "You'd better make another pot of coffee. We need to talk."

"So, you're telling me you know something about the jellyfish?" Lucy pointed to the bright red stomach in her mother's drawing. "This jellyfish?"

"Yes." Tommie stirred the near-empty cup.

"You've studied it?"

"No." He searched for the right words. "I've lived it."

Lucy shook her head. "I don't understand."

"I'm not sure where to start. You won't believe me."

"You're my best friend," Lucy said. "You've saved my life." Henry whimpered and twitched in his sleep. "There's nothing you can say that I won't believe."

"I'm immortal." He looked away. "I can't die."

He spoke in rapid bursts to get the gist of it out before she could interrupt. "I mean—I can die, but it's got to be catastrophic. Anything that doesn't obliterate me outright, my body can fix." He looked at her, hoping for a reaction.

"Well?" He swallowed hard. "Say something . . . anything."

Lucy leaned back, studying his face.

"Lucy!"

"Your eye?" She gestured toward his right eye. "Why is it blind?"

Tommie exhaled through pursed lips, relieved that she was asking questions. "A blunt trauma injury—Viet Nam. It became lazy over the years from nonuse. It no longer tracks."

"Okay," Lucy said. "So why didn't your body fix it?"

"Minor injuries and illnesses that aren't life-threatening, they don't trigger the effect." He studied her face for clues. There were none. "It has to be something that will kill me but is not instantly fatal."

"Hmm." Lucy nodded. "So, if a plane crashed on you?"

"Dead."

"Suppose a bear mauled you?" A smile lifted the corners of her mouth.

"As long as it doesn't eat me." Tommie returned the smile.

"Why are you telling me this now?"

"The journal." Tommie pointed to the drawing of the jellyfish and picked up the leather-bound notebook. "It's this they're after, Lucy." He placed the journal on the table and stretched the leather tie in the air. "To them, you're only a loose end needing to be tied up."

The coffeemaker gurgled and hissed. Tommie grabbed his cup and half-rose to his feet.

"I've got it." Lucy refilled both cups.

She placed a cup in front of Tommie and took a seat across from him. She leaned on her elbows with the steaming cup at her lips and took a cautious sip, then put the cup down. "I believe you," she said, dragging her fingers through her hair. "So, amuse and amaze me with the details."

"All right, close your eyes." He took a drink and set down his mug. "Except for my buddy Joe, you're the only person to hear this story." He took a deep breath. "For now, don't believe or disbelieve. Just listen." He studied her face as she sat there, eyes closed, like a child waiting for a bedtime story.

"To the best of my knowledge," Tommie said, "I was born in the village of Necoes on the Cape Fear River in 1711."

Lucy gasped and opened her eyes. "Sorry." She squeezed her eyes shut.

"The shaman of our tribe somehow discovered the secret of this jellyfish." Tommie stared at the illustrations in the journal. "The combination of that and Yaupon leaf tea had somehow made him immortal. No one knew how old he was. He had been with our tribe for as long as anyone could remember."

Tommie shifted in his chair and stared at Lucy's face. The world had changed so much since he was a child. Lucy was an anthropologist, but even so, how could he explain to the modern mind the power this man had held over his tribe? "From time to time, the shaman would do himself bodily harm to the point of near-death so that we could see him recover." Tommie's voice cracked. "He would inflict the same wound on another. That person would, of course, not recover."

Lucy sat, eyes closed, while Tommie described how he had cheated illness, trauma, and even old age for nearly three centuries.

"That's it," he said after talking for twenty minutes. "You can open your eyes now. We'll take a brief break from the Twilight Zone."

"But what about all the time since then? How many times have you—? What happens exactly? Is it just, bang, and you're thirty again? Can you pass it on? Do you have to take the serum every time?" Lucy fired questions like a machine gun.

"No." He gave a long sigh. "It's the gift that keeps on giving." Tommie rose to his feet just as the fireworks in his head erupted. He sat down hard, spilling the coffee across the table. "It never ends." He blinked and tried to focus on Lucy's face through the flashing lights. "Save the rest of those questions for our road trip. Right now," he said as he stood up, "we're going spelunking."

66

A DOZEN ACCOUNTS, A DOZEN NAMES, A DOZEN COUNTRIES

Wednesday, 21 April 2004—1:55 a.m.
Don Bel Castro's library, Stafford

Vasily knelt beside Bel Castro's motionless figure, palpated his neck, then placed his left ear against Bel Castro's back. "He's alive and breathing."

He examined Bel Castro's head for the source of bleeding. After a few seconds, Vasily exhaled. The relief in his voice was palpable. "It's just a scalp laceration, doesn't even need a stitch."

"Ow, what the hell? Get off me!" Bel Castro shook his head and attempted to rise on one arm. "Vasily," he said, smiling. He relaxed and sank to the floor again.

Nick picked up the empty liquor bottle and pointed to the blood on the edge of the desk.

"He either passed out and hit his head or someone clocked him from behind. My money is on the former."

"Someone obviously tossed the place," Vasily said, looking at the books strewn across the floor.

The shelves were mostly empty, their contents littered the floor. Pictures, trophies, and other mementos had been thrown about the room in a hasty search. The carpet was folded back, exposing the closed floor safe. Vasily examined the safe.

"He couldn't get in." Vasily ran his fingers over the scratches on the safe and gouges on the hardwood floor. "But he beat the hell out of it trying."

"It's on a time delay until noon." Bel Castro rubbed his head and rose to a sitting position. He touched his head and examined the blood on his fingers. "I must have hooked my foot on the carpet and hit my head on the corner of my desk."

"That fall probably saved your life." Nick threw the bar towel to Bel Castro. "Hold some pressure on it."

"Marty figured we'd made the hit," Vasily said. "He saw the blood and noticed the ring was gone."

"Typical slap-dash Marty," Nick said. "He didn't check the body and started tossing the place. No wonder Basil doesn't trust him to find the girl."

Vasily placed the broken picture frame containing the photo of Bel Castro and his wife on his desk and began putting books back on the shelf.

"Marty's incompetence is the only reason I'm still alive, but I'm sure he's been told to punch my ticket as soon as I find the girl," Nick said as he pulled Bel Castro's ring from his pocket. "Heads up, Sleeping Beauty." He tossed the ring.

The ring flew by Bel Castro's outstretched hand and struck him in the face.

Nick picked up a few books before turning to Vasily. "You, however, are of no further use to Basil. I know for a fact that you are on his immediate hit list."

Bel Castro mumbled and shifted his position from time to time but made no attempt to stand or join in the conversation.

"What makes you think so?" Vasily continued his book-shelving without turning to face Nick.

Nick set a stack of books on the desk. "I told Basil I wanted to take you along on the North Carolina job, and he said he had other plans for you." Nick tapped Vasily's shoulder. "Did he give you another assignment?"

"No." Vasily placed another stack of books on an end table. He plopped down in one of Bel Castro's wing chairs. "He told me to take a few days off and just hang out."

"Right. When did Basil ever tell anyone to just hang out?"

Bel Castro put on his ring and crawled to his desk chair. He struggled to follow the conversation, then picked up a pen and scrawled the same number on two pieces of paper from his desk pad. He pushed one in the general direction of each man.

"My encrypted satellite phone number. Call if I can help," he said. "I'm going to disappear for a few days. I would suggest the two of you do the same." He tapped the desk with his pen. "Nick, he's going to kill you as soon as you find Chloe."

"Or sooner if Marty beats me to her." Nick picked up the paper. "But I'm a dead man walking, remember? I'll take my shot at redemption in North Carolina." He turned to Vasily. "You, on the other hand, are very much alive and should endeavor to stay that way. You need to disappear permanently. You need to get out of the country tonight."

"He's right, Vas." Bel Castro stood and weaved toward the door. "If you gentlemen will excuse me, I'm going to sober up in a cold shower, shave, and get the hell out of Dodge. I'll start a pot of coffee. Help yourself." He shook both their hands, Vasily's first, and then Nick's. He held Nick's a little longer. "I'll see you again, Nick, maybe not here, but I'll see you again." He nodded to Vasily and left.

"No way." Vasily held up his hands in protest. "I won't let you do this by yourself. It's suicide."

"It's done, Vasily," Nick answered. "Please respect my wishes. I would do the same for you." He looked away. More than anything he would like to have Vasily with him. But he was not going to let Vasily die so that he could have companionship for one last mission.

Of all the ways to go. After all the times I should have died, I go out rotting from the inside.

"Let's go," Nick said. "We'll stop by your condo. You can pick up one of those fake passports you're so proud of. Then I'll drive you to Dulles. Do you need cash?"

"No," Vasily said. "Like you, I have a dozen accounts in a dozen names in a dozen countries."

They used Don's computer to search for flights. They checked BWI, DCA, and IAD, scanning both domestic and international flights in case anyone was monitoring Bel Castro's computer. They decided on a coach flight via Avianca Aerovias/LAN Airlines to Buenos Aires, departing Dulles at four-twenty a.m. With thirty-two seats remaining, there would no doubt be a seat available at the ticket counter. No need to leave an electronic trail by booking on the computer. To further obfuscate, Vasily booked a first-class ticket to Kiev on Air Canada departing BWI at two-twenty p.m. using his own name and credit card.

They drove by Nick's townhouse first. Nick picked up his car and followed Vasily to his apartment. The stop at Vasily's was brief. Like everyone in the profession, Vasily kept a bag packed. In less than ten minutes, they were on their way. They left the company Mercedes parked conspicuously in the condo lot.

67

YES, I AM OLD SCHOOL

Wednesday, 21 April 2004—1:52 a.m.
Main terminal, Dulles International Airport, Dulles, Virginia

Neither man spoke until they parked the car and entered the terminal at Dulles.

"So, what's the ID du jour?" Nick asked.

"Today I am Yuras Rybak, diplomatic attaché from the sovereign Republic of Belarus." Vasily's Belarusian accent was flawless. "I travel under diplomatic passport with all my goodies in an untouchable diplomatic pouch."

Nick accompanied Vasily to the ticket counter. Vasily charmed the clerk and purchased his ticket without incident. They prolonged the walk to security as long as possible.

Vasily stopped at security and turned to Nick. "Are you sure?"

Nick nodded, unable to speak.

"Well then, goodbye, Nick Caedwallan, CIA," he said, eyes glistening. "It has been a wild flight."

"Goodbye, Vasily Konovalov, Spetsnaz Alpha Group," Nick said. "We fly until we run out of fuel, or someone shoots us down."

Vasily placed his hand on Nick's shoulder. "At least we die on a first-name basis."

Nick watched as Vasily turned, flashed his credentials, and cleared security, remaining until his friend disappeared at the end of the long corridor. Then he walked back to the parking ramp and dropped hard into his car seat. He struck the dash with his fist, leaned forward, and wept unashamedly, partly for what he had lost, but mostly for what he'd never had. His sobbing was replaced by an uncontrollable bout of coughing. Nick climbed from the Lotus and stood, doubled over, his body racked by spasms. Gasping for air, he sank to his knees and vomited blood on the concrete. He glanced around, grateful for the empty parking deck. The thought of anyone, even a stranger, seeing him like this was too much to bear.

The fire in his lungs subsided, and the ragged breathing returned to normal. He cleaned his mouth and face with the wet wipes and paper towels he now carried in his car and drove home to get a few hours' sleep before leaving for North Carolina.

The tired Avianca Aerovias clerk looked up at the familiar face in front of her.

"Mr. Rybak, is something wrong?" She stared at the lines of worry in his face. "You look troubled."

"Dear lady." Vasily let his body droop forward. "My zonka, my beautiful wife." He wiped a tear from his eye. "She has been taken to Georgetown, to the emergency department. They want me there right away." He pretended to search for the right word. "I did not want to cause a *panika*, a panic, by not getting on the flight."

The attendant was visibly moved. "How thoughtful of you to think of others at a time like this. Would you like a refund?"

"No, kind lady." He forced a smile. "Just leave the ticket open. I hope to be going home in a few days."

Vasily maintained his troubled expression until he was in a stall in the men's room. There he packed away all traces of Yuras Rybak and pulled out a Canadian passport and driver's license along with a used Alaska Airlines ticket. He walked to the Hertz rental counter and plopped down his driver's license and credit card.

"You have a rental for Frederick Austin." He flattened his accent as much as possible.

"No, sir," the clerk said after searching through the reservation jackets on the wall and stabbing at his keyboard. "And we are all out of cars."

"Oh, no." Vasily brought the heel of his hand to his forehead. "My secretary strikes again. Do you know if any of the other agencies have cars?"

"Wait a moment." The clerk played his computer console like a piano. "We have one just back from an update."

"Thanks, you saved my secretary a kerfuffle."

"No problem, sir." The clerk smiled broadly and handed him the keys. "Would you like a complimentary GPS unit?" Vasily retrieved a sat phone from his bag, punched in Don Bel Castro's secure number, and waited while the encryption algorithm did its magic.

"No, thank you," Vasily said, returning the clerk's smile. "Do you have a North Carolina map?"

"Instead of a free GPS?" The clerk was shocked.

"Yes," Vasily said, taking the map. "I am old school."

68

I'VE LEFT ENOUGH MESSES BEHIND

Wednesday, 21 April 2004—8:03 a.m.
Garage, Nick's townhouse, Georgetown, Virginia

Nick tossed the battered leather duffle into the trunk of his old Elan. He could afford to drive whatever he wanted but preferred the raw edge of the little Lotus: British racing green with a simple black vinyl interior, no air conditioning, no radio, no windows, just plexiglass pull-up side curtains.

Nick bought the Lotus when he was finishing his doctoral dissertation at Leicester in 1983. He'd seen it sitting with a "for sale" sign on a weekend trip to Stratford-on-Avon and bought it on the spot.

As he tossed the duffle, Nick felt a stabbing pain in his right chest, followed by an irresistible urge to cough. He pulled a handkerchief from the pocket of his well-worn tweed jacket. It was already too warm for a coat, but he felt the need for the familiar comfort of his coat, duffle, and Lotus. He had learned in the last weeks to carry several handkerchiefs. Nick leaned against the car, unable to inhale as the relentless coughing turned his legs to rubber. His breath rattled in his throat. Head pounding, vision dimming, he slid to the floor. He forced an inhale and coughed hard into the handkerchief. He could breathe. He wasn't going to die. Not just yet. The cough subsided. The hammer in his head stopped, and he could see colors again. He remained seated, squeezing his eyes shut to deny what was happening. He opened his eyes and studied the bloody spot on his handkerchief. It was a small spot—not much bigger than an inch in diameter—no more than a teaspoon of liquid at most. Nick thought about the times he had water-boarded detainees for information. He remembered their panic as they struggled for air, the fear in their eyes wrought by a teaspoon of water. Now, he understood their terror.

So, this is what they felt, only I'm drowning in my own blood.

Nick sat with his back against the Lotus, taking comfort in the cool dampness of the concrete floor. He closed his eyes and revisited the day he bought the car. He just had to have it. It was like Stratford: calm, green, and anachronistic. He had purchased the roadster, the tweed sport coat, and the leather duffle that weekend: quite a splurge, his reward for finishing his degree. They fit the image he had for himself: understated, not bad looking, capricious, but competent. They didn't scream, "Look at me," but one couldn't help but notice. They fit the life he had envisioned for himself in those days, the eccentric professor of archaeology and ancient history with the quirky little right-hand-drive English car. He had successfully defended his dissertation and would receive his Ph.D. at the June graduation. He had been called back for a second interview at Princeton.

"I shouldn't be saying this," the secretary had said on the phone, "but the interview is just a formality. The chair said the job is yours for the asking."

Nick had been in a fog, babbling a few pointless questions.

"Yes," she said. "I'm sure you can have a parking space next to the archaeology building."

Nick had been ecstatic. He had never had a family, never belonged. At Princeton, he would be a part of something. What had happened to him? How did his life go off track? When did he make the transition from college professor to assassin?

Nick recalled the CIA's pitch.

"Two years in the Agency and you're debt-free and back to teaching. It's a once-in-a-lifetime opportunity."

So here he was, two decades and forty pack-years later, coughing up a lung in his garage. All that remained of the original Nick was the tatty Lotus, the worn tweed jacket, and the battered leather duffle. He threw the bloody handkerchief on the floor and rose to his feet.

What the hell? I won't be back.

On reflection, he picked up the handkerchief and stuffed it into his pocket.

No, I've left enough messes behind.

He leaned against the car until his head stopped spinning, punched the garage door opener, dropped behind the wheel, and pulled onto the tree-lined cobblestone street.

69

IT WOULD BE A HOT DAY IN THE LAND ROVER

Wednesday, 21 April 2004—9:58 a.m.
Just east of U.S. 301, rural North Carolina

Lucy drove west on the narrow two-lane blacktop, heading to Highway 301. From there, she would drive north to Richmond, spend the night at the Jefferson Hotel, and meet up with her Uncle Don on Wednesday.

Highway 301 ran parallel to I-95 for much of its length. Lucy preferred the slower pace to the eighty-mile-per-hour frenzy of the freeway. Her fellow drivers were in no hurry, preferring the steamy organic feel of windows down and forty-five miles per hour to the air-conditioned dryness of a sealed capsule rocketing along the interstate. The leisurely pace suited Lucy's ancient Land Rover. Even with overdrive, the former SAS four-wheel-drive diesel struggled to reach sixty, downhill, with a tailwind. The vague steering, leaf springs, and drum brakes conspired to make anything over fifty-five miles per hour the ultimate driving adventure. Highway 301 was mostly four-lane, allowing Lucy to pass the occasional slow-moving grain truck or dawdling tractor when not being overtaken by the rare hare-footed driver.

Lucy enjoyed the seagrass smells of the Albemarle Sound, which lay just a few miles behind her. Ten o'clock and eighty-four degrees. She could already feel the pleasant dampness of clean clothes sticking to a moist body. It would be a hot day in the Land Rover.

She reached for a bottle of water.

"Damn," she whispered, finding only an empty passenger seat where there should be a flat of bottled water. The usually organized Lucy had been so unsettled by Tommie's tale last night that she had forgotten to review her travel checklist and now wondered what else she might have forgotten.

She still struggled to comprehend his story. Tommie had no reason to lie, yet the tale and the cave paintings required a suspension of disbelief that was difficult to muster. She pushed the story to the back of her mind and made the turn north onto 301.

It was a rare treat to drive this nearly deserted four-lane highway. She could let her mind wander without fear of a head-on collision. Started in 1940 and completed during the construction frenzy following World War Two, U.S. 301 was a time capsule. The 1,099 miles of mostly forgotten three- and four-lane roadway stretching from Glasgow, Delaware, to its terminus in Sarasota, Florida, stood as a stark monument to the changing American lifestyle. Dating from a time of more conviviality and less pretense, the faded billboards beckoned travelers to visit establishments that had decades ago succumbed to the interstate bypass and sophisticated mass-marketing.

Lucy stared in wistful silence at the procession of long-abandoned mom-and-pop enterprises. A stucco castle surrounded by fairyland cottages, with most windows boarded or broken, sat forlornly while knee-high grass and thistles grew through the cracks in its parking lot. A washed-out marquee advertised Dinosaur Land. Next to the sign, a twenty-foot-tall brontosaurus, bereft of head, tried in vain to stare down an equally pitiful T-Rex that the sun had long ago bleached to the dull gray-white of concrete.

On the left side of the road, a peeling sign tempted southbound motorists: "Pedro says, only 78 miles to sombreros, tacos, and enchiladas. Pet live burros.'" It was a remnant of a naive time when a Mexican restaurant was a rarity, and the only Latino most North Carolinians had seen was the Cisco Kid.

Lucy imagined vacationers traveling this highway, kids begging to stop at the dinosaurs, and newlyweds posing for pictures in front of the fairy-land cottages. Traveling salesmen hawking everything from shoes to vacuum cleaners stayed at these motels or stopped to try a burrito or enchilada for the first time. Now the salesmen were gone, as were the companies they worked for. No one made anything anymore. The factories were all closed. The megamarts had long ago squeezed out their small competitors.

The families no longer came. They sped along the interstate to more-sophisticated vacation locales. In an age of thousand-dollar prom dresses, a visit to Dinosaur Land seemed tame indeed. Mother and father, in a family lucky enough to have both, each worked full-time. Kids were budding adults at thirteen, matured by an ever-more-explicit media. Families went their separate ways: a television for each room, a bathroom for each bedroom, a handheld computer game by grade school, a cellphone by middle school, and their own car by sixteen.

Lucy wondered why anyone would want to live forever. The changes in a single generation were significant enough. How could the human psyche possibly adapt to the technological and social changes of a century, much less eternity?

70

SUDDENLY SMALL AND DECIDEDLY SECOND-CLASS

Wednesday, 21 April 2004—10:06 a.m.
I-95 South, near Emporia, Virginia

Nick glanced at the Interstate sign:

Emporia 6

The growing circles of sweat in his armpits and the heavier-than-usual volume of truck traffic told him it was time for a break. He would pass this truck and exit at Emporia for air conditioning and a quick lunch.

He was almost even with the driver's door when he saw the truck's left-turn signal start to blink. Just ahead, his escape was blocked by two trucks side by side struggling up a long grade. Nick pressed the center of his steering wheel. The Elan's pitiful horn bleated like a sick sheep. The truck driver, unable to see the small sports car, continued to move into his lane. Nick checked his rearview mirror. An ancient Buick wagon with a rooftop cargo carrier was closing fast. Nick considered for a moment that he may not live long enough for the cancer to kill him.

Keeping his foot on the accelerator, he depressed the brake pedal and flicked the Lotus onto the apron just inches from the guardrail on his left and the truck on his right. It was a trail-braking technique

he'd learned at the Agency's defensive-driving school. The simultaneous application of brake and gas allowed the car to settle during violent
maneuvers. Once clear of the truck, he released the accelerator and
stabbed the brakes. The Elan came to a near-immediate stop on the left
shoulder. The station wagon shot by on his right.

Nick took a deep breath and jumped from the car. White-hot pain
seared his lungs. The first cough was explosive. Blood splattered across
the windshield. Nick fought a wave of panic as he found himself unable
to take a breath. His vision narrowed, his legs weakened, and he went
down on one knee. Moments passed before he was able to inhale. The
resulting spate of coughing left him starving for air. His heart pounding,
he used one of the brief respites to retrieve the roll of paper towels from
behind the seat. Thirty seconds seemed like thirty minutes. He gasped
for air—a drowning man adrift in a sea of bloody paper. He looked at
his hands. They were pale, blood-spattered, and shaking. Nick had seen
this much blood many times before. In fact, he had been the cause of
this much blood on way too many occasions. But this time, the blood
was his. He remembered asking the oncologist how it would end.

"Most likely, the tumor will erode a lobar artery. Then you'll drown
in your own blood." Seeing Nick's face, he had backed off. "Sorry," the
doctor said. "But you asked."

Nick climbed back into the Lotus and struggled to control his ragged breathing. He'd had enough interstate madness for one day; he'd
take the Emporia, follow 301 south, and then turn toward the coast.

Nick found a self-serve car wash at a nearby truck stop, hosed off
the Lotus, and paid eight bucks for the use of a truck-stop shower.
Buoyed by the change of clothes, he sat on a red vinyl stool at the lunch
counter, sipped a black coffee and teased a greasy burger and fries.

Nick placed a ten-dollar bill on the counter, walked to his car, and
folded down the top. He put three bottles of water on the passenger seat
and slid behind the wheel. He reread Rita's note from the night before.
It had been short on details:

Nick,

When you get to Asakan, see Tommie Whitefeather. You will find him at the café (the only one in town). You will have a private room at his hotel (the only one in town). Marty said to not let his appearance fool you. There's a lot more there than you see at first glance. He clearly knows the Spencer girl's whereabouts.

Happy hunting!

Rita

Asakan. Nick smiled at the meaning of the name. He would find Tommie Whitefeather, all right, and the Spencer girl, but he would also make sure Marty and Basil never bothered her again. He just needed to get to Asakan. The Lotus sprang to life on the first turn of the starter. He took a sip of water, and instinctively patted his shirt pocket for cigarettes that weren't there.

He glanced at the empty seat and wished Vasily were with him.

Nick wound the Elan to four grand, smiling at the satisfying snick of each gear change. He held his speed to a judicious fifty-nine miles per hour as he continued south on 301. Like everyone else, he believed that staying one mile per hour shy of ten over the limit conveyed some kind of magic speeding-ticket immunity. Meeting just three cars in over an hour, Nick had passed the time in a what-if daydream, an increasingly common exercise since his diagnosis. It was always filled with thoughts of being thirty again, teaching at a small-town college, living with a girl he couldn't put a face to but whose essence would elicit the lifetime love that had eluded him. Thinking of her, whomever she might be, got him to key in the Beatles' "I Will" on his media player. The daydream ended when he spotted a boxy British SUV, hood up, engine steaming, at an abandoned service station.

71

YOU CAN TRUST YOUR CAR TO THE
MAN WHO WEARS THE STAR

Wednesday, 21 April 2004—11:59 a.m.
U.S. 301 North, rural North Carolina

Lucy made her customary scan of the gauges, including the stick-on thermometer and clock attached to the windshield. Fuel okay. Engine temperature a little up but still in the normal range. Eleven fifty-nine a.m. Eighty-nine degrees. She would stop at the next convenience store, get some bottled water, and check the radiator. A loud pop and a cloud-like discharge from the front of the vehicle changed her plans. Lucy glanced in the mirror. Her view was completely obliterated by steam. She was, of course, in the middle of nowhere. A quick look at the instruments revealed the temperature gauge already pegged. Lucy shut down the engine and drifted onto the broken concrete of an abandoned service station. She stared up at the obsolete sign, "High Test, 69.9 cents per gallon." A smiling face in a service cap and dark-green coveralls beamed down at her from the billboard. The script in the bubble said, "You can trust your car to the man who wears the star."

Lucy opened the hood. The upper radiator hose had blown off. It could be fixed, but the clamp was gone. Steam continued to billow from under the hood. She followed the Rover's trail of antifreeze for about fifty feet. There on the ground was the missing hose clamp, a bit mangled, but serviceable.

Lucy put the clamp in her jeans pocket, walked back to the truck, and leaned against the door.

She looked north and south along Route 301. She was miles from anywhere with nothing in sight. She slid behind the wheel of the Rover and searched again for a bottle of water. No luck. A dot appeared on the horizon. Lucy watched through puffs of steam as the shimmering green smudge grew larger. Maybe they would stop.

72

CAN YOU DIG UP A WRENCH?

Wednesday, 21 April 2004—12:23 p.m.
U.S. Route 301, rural North Carolina

Nick saw the Land Rover sitting in an expanding puddle of antifreeze. He slowed as he passed to admire the vehicle's classic lines. The ex-military 88 was all stock, down to the jerry-can on the back and spare tire on the hood. Glancing at his watch, he calculated the distance to Asakan. It was a perfunctory exercise. He was already braking and signaling a left turn. He wasn't about to leave a kindred spirit caught out in the middle of nowhere. Nick made a U-turn, stopped a few feet behind the still-misting SUV, and switched off his engine and read the prominent bumper sticker:

Relax, I'm an Anthropologist

He sat for a moment, the silence broken only by the rhythmic ticking of the cooling Lotus and the diminishing hiss from the stricken vehicle.

Nick watched the breeze bend the weeds and thistles growing through the cracks in the concrete. He thought of his conversation with Bel Castro and Vasily about being young again. Right here, right now, among the broken windows, faded billboards, and shattered pavement of these modern ruins with only these anachronistic vehicles in sight, it almost seemed possible. He opened his door a crack but did not get out. Instead, he sat, right hand on the door latch and left hand on the wheel.

He decided that if offered the chance to go back and change things, he would take it. He softened on Basil a bit until he thought about motive. Nick wanted a chance to make things right; Basil just wanted to continue his greedy and malicious behavior forever. Nick dismissed the thought of rejuvenation as an old man's desperate pipe dream. Life had given him his chance, and he had wasted it.

Nick's melancholy was broken by the creak of the Rover's door. He looked up, expecting a guy, someone about his age. Instead, it was a young woman, late twenties, maybe thirty. His chest tightened. His pulse pounded in his ears. In an instant, subtext became text. His construct now had a face, at least what he could see of it: dark brown, short-cropped hair; oversize, rectangular, tortoise-shell sunglasses; a white shirt with long sleeves rolled to the elbows; faded jeans; and simple black flats. He stared at her five-foot-seven frame, tulip-shaped nose, and goofy smile. All in all, she was just about perfect.

He saw her mouth moving, but his ears were ringing too loud to hear. Nick shook his head, smiled his trademark crooked smile, and struggled back to reality. She looked half his age. She was young, with a life ahead of her. He was old and soon to be dead. She would be somebody's someone, but not his. The ringing in his ears subsided. He could hear her talking as she walked toward him.

"Excuse me." Miss Perfect flashed her too-wide smile. "Exactly who is rescuing who here?"

"Whom," Nick said, exiting the Lotus. "It's who is rescuing whom."

"Great. I need a mechanic, and I get an English professor."

"Ancient history, actually." Nick put on his best smile.

"Not for me." She spun on her heel and started back to the Rover.

"No, I mean me." Nick stammered, "I—I'm ancient history and archaeology."

His someone stopped midstride and turned to face him. She removed her sunglasses, chewed on the stem, and made an exaggerated show of examining him from head to toe. "You're not that far gone."

Nick could feel his face burning. She was spinning him like a top and enjoying every second of it.

"No, not me personally. I'm Nick. My degree is in archaeology," he said, struggling to make himself heard as a tractor pulling a hay wagon approached from the south.

"An archaeologist?" She stepped back and looked him up and down again. "Can you dig up a wrench?"

73

EASY DR. JONES

Tuesday, 20 April 2004—12:37pm
Abandoned Texaco station, rural North Carolina

The conversation was drowned out as the tractor, engine at full throttle, crept by. The driver, a nondescript, somewhat pudgy, thirty-something in jeans and T-shirt stopped in the road and throttled down the engine. He stared for a moment without speaking. The expression on his round, sunburnt face registered somewhere between a grin and a sneer. He shook his head in disgust at the foreign vehicles.

"Looks like you need help." He pointed first at the Rover and then the Lotus. "One tow truck or two?"

"We've got it." Nick gave a dismissive wave. "Asshole," he muttered under his breath as the tractor throttled up again.

The farmer must have been a lip reader. He throttled the tractor down again. "Suit yourself." He blipped the tractor's throttle for effect. "You and your granddaughter have a nice day." Satisfied that the insult hit home, he turned to gauge Lucy's reaction.

⌐

Lucy shot the farmer her best evil eye before turning to face Nick. He looked totally deflated, his shoulders slumped, his smile wilted, and the spark in his eyes she had seen when they bantered a few moments earlier was gone. The farmer's barb had obviously opened some deep wound. Lucy glanced at the farmer, then put both hands behind Nick's head, drew him closer, and kissed him full on the lips. After several seconds, she withdrew, her face inches from Nick's. She observed his perplexed expression.

"Play along," she whispered. "Don't give the bastard any satisfaction."

Lucy watched as the half-smile returned, and Nick's eyes brightened. The metamorphosis was astounding.

Nick slid his arm around Lucy's waist. His smile broadened. They turned to face the stunned farmer who sat eyes wide and mouth open. As Lucy waved, the farmer shook his head and increased the engine speed to its ear-splitting maximum. The tractor strained against the heavy wagon and moved away. When the driver looked back for a final glare, Nick pulled Lucy close and kissed her again.

Lucy felt a flood of conflicting emotions. This was her first kiss in over two years. She was at first passive, then yielding, but suddenly tense as she realized that she was kissing a total stranger at least twenty years her senior by the side of the road.

"Easy, Dr. Jones." She pushed him away and nodded toward the retreating tractor. "You can cease excavating. The dig's over."

"It's Nick," he said. "Nick—"

"Just leave it at Nick." She stopped him. "And I'm Lucy, just Lucy. I have a bit too much on my plate for anything more than that."

74

RC COLA AND A MOON PIE

Wednesday, 21 April 2004—12:42 p.m.
Abandoned Texaco station, rural North Carolina

"I couldn't agree more." Nick chided himself for mistaking a mercy kiss for genuine interest. He looked down as he walked to the Rover. "Let's get you back on the road," he said, confirming that the hose had blown loose from the radiator. The hose could be shortened and reattached, but the clamp was gone. He looked under the vehicle and then rummaged through the box of spare parts Lucy kept in the truck. "The hose is salvageable, but there's no clamp. You don't have another clamp, do you?"

Lucy put her hand in her pocket. She bit her lower lip and stared at Nick. "No." She smiled and shook her head. "I'm fresh out of hose clamps." She looked down and made small circles in the gravel with her foot. "I guess I'm just stranded."

Nick smiled, savoring the fact that fate was giving him a few more minutes with her. "That, Miss Lucy, was the worst attempt at feminine helplessness I have witnessed in decades."

"Did it work?" She lowered her sunglasses and looked up at him.

"What do you think?" Nick felt the eyes and smile drawing him in again. "Get in the car. I saw a convenience store and garage about three miles back." Nick followed her to the passenger side and opened the door for her. She hesitated but slipped into the seat. "They should have a hose clamp."

"And an RC Cola and a Moon Pie," Lucy said. "And you know—I'm not so weak that I can't open my own car door."

"What's a Moon Pie?" Nick asked. "And it's an indication of respect, not an implication of weakness."

"An RC Cola and a Moon Pie represent the epitome of the Southern traveling lunch," Lucy said, pronouncing the word as EP-ee-toam. "It has five times the minimum daily requirement of preservatives, fat, and sugar. It's wonderful," she said. "And I respect you, too, but I don't open the door for you."

"Point taken," Nick said. "Lunch, eh?" He glanced at her as they pulled onto the highway. "So, is this a date?"

"Of course." Lucy smiled and batted her eyes. "Every day's a date. Today is April twentieth."

About three miles later, Nick parked the car in front of the convenience store and took a few steps toward the nearby garage.

"We should get the hose clamp first and then—" He turned and saw that Lucy was still sitting in the car, looking at him expectantly. He walked back to the car and stood by her door.

"Waiting for something?" he asked.

"Aren't you going to open the door for me?" she said, her beaming face all teeth, as she looked up at him.

75

BAFFLE HIM WITH BUFFALO SHIT

Tuesday, 20 April 2004—1:31 p.m.
Service station and convenience store, U.S. 301 in North Carolina

Lucy sat on the curb in front of the Lotus arranging the bottled drinks and paper plates. She watched Nick as he approached carrying the hose clamp and a container of antifreeze in a clear plastic bag. Each time she looked at him, she thought less about the age difference and more about the instant chemistry between them. He acted half his age, but in a good way. His build and body movements said youth. The quick wit and quirky half-smile gave him a timeless quality. That said, something was not right. His face was lined, but not from age. The lines suggested worry or maybe fatigue. Maybe, like her, he was just tired. But tired of what?

"Yours looks tastier than mine." He held up the plastic bag. "And a tablecloth to boot." He pointed to the napkins.

"Curbside service. My treat." She handed him a cola and one of the confections. "I hope you don't mind. I took the liberty of ordering for you."

"Ouch. Damn." He tossed the cellophane-wrapped pie from hand to hand. "This thing is scalding hot."

"Well, of course," Lucy said. "You have to wave it for twenty seconds to make it gooey."

Lucy kept the conversation light and full of lies. She figured they would never cross paths again. In a week, she would either be dead or a thousand miles away. "I just spent the winter in Florida," Lucy said, "and now I'm on my way back to New Hampshire for graduate school." She figured she may as well make the story match the plates on the Rover.

"Oh, grad school. I'm a professor myself," he said. "What's your field?"

He looked down and to the left, eyes blinking rapidly. Lucy remembered what Tommie had said in survival school about eye movements and prevarication, before deciding that she was probably just doing a little psychological projecting.

"Well—I—political science." She pretended to choke on a bite of food.

"And what's your thesis topic?" Nick's follow-up question was instant.

Lucy struggled to say something intelligent.

Why hadn't I just said anthropology?

She asked herself what Tommie Whitefeather would do and was reminded of his revelation to her last night.

"Governmental Models of Lost Native American Tribes of the Coastal Southeast." She heaved a sigh of relief.

How's that for obscure and narrow?

"That's incredible." Nick put down his soft drink and grabbed Lucy's hand. "I mentioned the Cape Fear Indians in my dissertation at Leicester." He dropped her hand and vaulted to his feet. "What do you think of their judicial system?"

Lucy felt like a square peg being hammered into a round hole. She knew little about early Native American government and even less about the lost Cape Fear tribe. Still, Tommie had given her the cook's tour of the area around Asakan. And then there were those cave drawings. She decided if she couldn't dazzle him with brilliance, she'd baffle him with buffalo shit.

"Not much is known about the Cape Fear tribe, but they inter-acted a great deal with the Southeastern Siouan tribes. The difference between the Lakotan and Coastal Siouan systems indicates that the Cape Fear tribal system predated, and may have heavily influenced, the Coastal Sioux." Lucy looked up at Nick, wondering if he would buy it.

Nick's face was beaming. "Brilliant. I wish we could—" He stopped mid-sentence, the smile vanished, and he seemed to retreat to wherever the farmer's insult had taken him.

Sensing her opening, Lucy jumped to her feet.

"I have to go to the ladies' room, and then we should fix the Rover."

"Sure." The half-smile returned. "It would have been great to work with you on your thesis."

"We'll talk," she said and hurried off to the restroom.

76

ARE YOU OUT OF YOUR MIND? DEFINITELY

Wednesday, 21 April 2004—1:53 p.m.
Service station and convenience store, U.S. Route 301 in North Carolina

Lucy stared in the restroom mirror, wondering if she had stayed long enough to simulate a real trip to the ladies' room. She should just let him go. It was so wrong on so many levels. Nothing could come of it. She was just lonely. The age difference aside, it was wrong time, wrong place. Nothing could come of it. She was just lonely. Maybe she should just tell him the truth and let him decide. She flushed the toilet for effect, then turned on the faucet in case anyone was waiting outside. She looked in the mirror again, put on her best Audrey Hepburn smile, and considered how to best phrase this proposition. She wanted to hear how it sounded out loud.

"Look, Nick, we seem to have some chemistry. There is the age thing. We might overcome that, but, well, you see, the CIA is trying to kill me. I'm on my way to pick up a suitcase full of money, and then I'm on the run with a Native American friend of mine." The face in the mirror did not seem particularly convincing. "Would you like to come along? It could be fun."

The corners of Lucy's mouth sagged as she thought about her parents.

Or we could die in a hail of gunfire like Bonnie and Clyde.

She looked down at the rust-stained sink, turned off the water, and gave one last glance at her frowning reflection. When she unlocked the door, a girl of about seven stared up at her with wide eyes.

"I heard you practicing your lines," she said. "Are you an actress or something?"

"Or something." Lucy stood at the corner of the building and watched Nick deposit the wrappers and bottles in the trash and return to the Lotus. She ran for the car.

Maybe I should just leave the Rover and tell Nick the truth.

Nick looked up, saw her, and got out of the car. She slowed to a walk.

I must have sunstroke. When he hears the truth, he'll bolt. And, if not, they'll kill us both.

He walked around the car and opened the door for her.

Lucy said nothing but wiped her eyes with the back of her hand.

"Something wrong?" Nick pulled onto the highway.

"Paper-towel dust in my contacts." She turned away and pretended to take in the scenery as they drove back to the Rover. "I love this road. I feel safe on it. There's an innocence about it." She looked down. "I wish—"

Nick made a U-turn and stopped about ten feet behind Lucy's truck. "You'll be fine." He placed his hand on her shoulder. "It's getting hot out here." He picked up the bag containing the hose clamp and anti-freeze. "This should only take a few minutes."

Lucy stood by Nick's car while he worked on the Rover. She watched him as he leaned over the fender, his head and shoulders out of sight as he worked. He was very comforting to have around. Sort of like Tommie, only in a different way. She was aware of the impossibility of the situation. Reason told her to let it go. Her life was complicated—complicated and dangerous. She felt the old hose clamp in her pocket. She glanced at Nick. He was still buried under the Rover's hood.

"What the hell?" Lucy mumbled under her breath. "Go for it." She searched Nick's car for something to write on, plucking a scrap of paper from the floor. It had writing on one side. She opened the door and sat in the passenger seat. A quick check confirmed Nick was still working and swearing under his breath. She stuffed the scrap of paper in her shirt pocket and searched for a pen.

"How's it going?" she called out as she found a note pad and pencil in the door pocket.

"Nothing is easy on these—" The rest was unintelligible.

Satisfied that he was otherwise engaged, she reached in her pocket and retrieved the bent hose clamp. Forgetting about the scrap of paper, she scribbled "Call Me" and her carefully guarded cellphone number on a page from the pad. Then she paused.

You've been guarding your cellphone numbers for two years. Are you out of your mind?

She smiled.

Definitely.

She wrapped the paper around a bottle of water, secured it with the hose clamp, and stuffed it into Nick's door panel with the pad and pencil.

"What a mess," Nick said in an exasperated tone. Lucy turned to see him covered in grease, making his way to the car. "Even a British wristwatch leaks oil."

Lucy jumped from the car. "I can't thank you enough. I wish I had more time."

77

STAY HYDRATED

Tuesday, 20 April 2004—2:27 p.m.
Abandoned Texaco station, Rural North Carolina

Nick struggled to prolong the moment. "Yeah. Me, too. I would have enjoyed more time to talk about your thesis."

"Well, you never know," Lucy said, smiling. "Maybe another time."

"Sure," Nick said. "It was interesting."

"It was much more than that." She gave him a peck on the cheek and ran to the Rover. She paused and looked back before getting in. "It's a hot day. Be sure to stay hydrated." A quick wave and she was gone. She drove north on 301. The farther away she got, the bigger the hole in Nick became. He watched as the Rover became a speck and then a smudge, vanishing in the heat waves rising from the asphalt.

"Shit." He ran to the Lotus and punched the starter. He redlined every gear until he could just see the scintillating form of Lucy's truck. The impossibility of the situation struck him. Nick stood on the brakes, and the Lotus pitched forward, tires screaming in protest as it came to a halt facing east. Nick watched again as the Rover disappeared. She was going one way, and he was going another. In a week she would be dead to him, and he would, most likely, be dead to everyone. It was pretty clear he would never have his someone, but he could do his best to see that Chloe Spencer had hers.

He turned the car around to face south and pulled over to the shoulder. What he really wanted was a cigarette. This thought was followed by the urge to cough. He wiped the sweat from his forehead with his greasy shirtsleeve and remembered Lucy's hydration advice. Nick was about to reach into the rear packing shelf when he spotted a bottle of water in the door pocket. It was wrapped in paper secured by a hose clamp.

"What the—" Nick ignored the water but retrieved the burner phone he kept in the door pocket and dialed the number on the paper.

78

I DO MY BEST THINKING WHEN I DRIVE

Tuesday, 20 April 2004—3:01pm
Northbound, Highway 301 in North Carolina

Lucy smiled when her cellphone began to ring, but she didn't answer it. After the third call, she pulled to the sided of the road just long enough to send a text.

Later, professor. Let me have a little time to mull this over. I do my best thinking when I drive.

She pressed on to Richmond and the quiet luxury of the Jefferson Hotel. Once in her room, she stripped off her clothes and threw them in a to-be-laundered pile she'd deal with tomorrow. She took a long, hot shower before donning one of the hotel's legendary cotton robes and then ordered room service. She picked up her cellphone and started to dial Nick's number but punched the end button.

No. Let him marinate overnight.

79

LIKE BREAKDANCING, BUT WITHOUT THE MUSIC

Wednesday 21 April 2004—4:41 p.m.
Road to Asakan, North Carolina

The last twenty miles had been a slow procession of pickups, tractors, and elderly couples in nondescript GM sedans. Nick, in no hurry, had avoided passing. He'd waited patiently as, one by one, they peeled off on short gravel driveways to small farms with paint-deficient houses that hugged the road. Nick had never understood why someone with a hundred acres of farmland would choose to build their house within twenty feet of the road. Hereditary tobacco farmers, most of these folks had long since switched to growing corn to maintain their government subsidies.

The heat and boredom made it difficult to stay alert. Nick massaged the base of his skull as the stiffness in his neck became a dull ache. When he rested his hand back on the shift knob, he felt his little finger twitch. Nick watched with fascination and horror as it jerked as though it had a mind of its own. Though he willed it to stop, it continued to dance, its string pulled by some invisible puppeteer. Nick opened and closed his fist until the tremors stopped. He decided that the little maggot at Johns Hopkins had given him a pretty accurate prognosis.

Nick's third opinion visit to Johns Hopkins in Baltimore had been the first time he'd gotten any real insight into his future. The kid in the white lab coat with the stethoscope for a tie looked to be about twelve years old. Nick had thought he was a first-year medical student.

"Is the doctor coming?" He'd pulled out a pack of cigarettes and tapped them against his hand.

"I am the junior chief oncology resident. You can't do that here," Dr. Stethoscope said, pointing to Nick's cigarettes. "I would think with your diagnosis, you would—"

"So, about my diagnosis?" Nick returned the smokes to his pocket. "What should I expect?"

Dr. Stethoscope clicked the mouse next to his keyboard, and the wall monitor displayed a series of ever more ugly radiographic images.

"The CAT scan shows occipital lobe, cerebellar, and hepatic metastases." The news was presented as a canned speech. "Every case is different. You might be fortunate." His gaze never left the monitor. It was a studied exercise in avoidance, delivered without interest or empathy.

"I mean, what's going to happen to me?" Nick closed the distance between them.

"What do you think?" Stethoscope said, standing next to his desk. He tapped the keyboard, and the monitor winked out.

"What I think," Nick said, "is you just want to get me out of here." Nick reached out and grabbed the startled resident's chin, forcing him to make eye contact. "I'm not someone you want to bullshit." He accentuated each word. "The truth. Now." When Nick relaxed his grip, the doctor shook free and retreated behind the safety of his desk.

"Headaches at the back of your neck, an annoyance at first, but then exquisite. Pain like you've never felt before."

"See, that wasn't so hard? Was it?" Nick took a step toward the desk. "Now—the rest of it."

"Seizures." The doctor glanced at his telephone. "At first just a twitching in your fingers, but then—full blown." He slid his hand toward the phone. "Like break-dancing." He smiled. "But without the music."

"No need for that." Nick grabbed the phone and jerked the cord from the wall. "Just give me the happy ending to this fairytale."

"With pleasure." The doctor's voice was a scalpel. "The primary tumor will probably erode a lobar artery, and you will drown in your own blood." He smiled. "Or you might get lucky—the liver metastasis could make your ammonia levels rise—you could just go to sleep and never wake up."

The crunch of tires on the gravel shoulder brought Nick's focus back to the business of driving. Maybe he shouldn't have judged the kid. Nick, of all people, knew how important it was to view clients without emotion.

His thoughts shifted to the overheated Rover and the girl. He glanced from the temperature gauge to the fuel gauge to his little finger on the shift knob and, finally, back to the road. An enormous green shape loomed in his windshield.

"Shit." He gripped the wheel, braked hard, and swerved left to avoid the slow-moving tractor. The farmer, used to sleepy drivers and near misses, motioned him past. Nick overtook the creeping tractor, and gave a quick tap on the horn, a cheerio to the farmer's casual wave.

Nick shook his head to clear the cobwebs. The action turned the throb in his neck to a knifelike pain. White light filled his field of vision. He suppressed the urge to vomit. The pain subsided but was still a strong eight on a one-to-ten scale. He needed something for pain. Nick reached for the bottle of ibuprofen on the passenger seat. He had already taken six tablets twice today. As he fumbled to remove the safety cap, he remembered the smart-ass doctor's commercial-like caution.

"Ibuprofen is great for the pain. Anti-inflammatories reduce brain edema," he'd said, his jaw set in stone-faced condescension. "But keep the dose and frequency down or you'll find yourself in the operating room with a perforated ulcer."

Nick decided his initial assessment of the doctor as a narcissistic little prick had been spot-on.

"Safer to stick with narcotic intervention." Dr. Narcissus thrust his hands into the pockets of his lab coat. In a smooth motion, he produced a script pad and pen and looked at Nick, eyebrows raised, poised to write. "Hydrocodone?"

The action reminded Nick of the times he had drawn his weapon and then hesitated, extracting a last bit of information from a mark. "No," he said. "My profession requires a certain level of alertness."

"And just what is your profession?"

"Kind of like yours," Nick said, reaching inside his coat with his right hand. "Matters of life and death." The doctor's eyes widened, and his face drained of color. He dropped the script pad and pen. Nick withdrew a pack of cigarettes, tapped one loose, and pulled it free with his lips. "Last smoke." He half-smiled and extended the pack toward the doctor. "You?"

The pale resident shook his head. Nick turned and left the office with the steadfast determination that this would be his last visit to a doctor.

80

YOU HAVE REACHED YOUR DESTINATION

Wednesday 21, April 2004—5:27 p.m.
Approaching the Asakan turn-off, rural North Carolina

A green road sign flashed by on his right:

Asakan 6

Nick slowed the Lotus, kneaded his neck, and let out a long, slow sigh. *Weltschmerz*, he thought. World pain. That feeling you have when absolutely everything is wrong. The German psyche had a knack for summing up all-encompassing rotten situations in a single word. His impending death, the loss of Vasily, the too-late meeting with Lucy, and the gross unfairness of the Spencer girl's situation sucked on Nick's psyche like a black hole. He hit the accelerator and shifted gears, pushing the Lotus to just over ninety miles per hour. He watched the large trees streak by.

I could end it all in a second. A quick splat instead of a slow rot.

"No." Nick lifted his foot from the accelerator. He'd do his best to save the Spencer girl—an act that would, no doubt, result in his dying as surely as if he struck one of the passing trees at a hundred miles per hour. The GPS on Nick's dash chimed for the missed turn. The disembodied female voice announced the distance remaining from a set of coordinates preloaded into the device.

"What's this?" He'd asked Rita the night before as she slid the box across her desk.

"A GPS," she'd said, not looking up from her paperwork. "It's programmed to take you to Asakan."

"I don't need this." He pushed the box back.

"Just take it. It's easier than fighting with Basil. Besides," she said looking up, "he made the voice an English bird so you wouldn't get so lonely."

Nick reversed, turned left on the unlined tarmac, and shifted smartly through the gears.

"You are approaching your destination." The voice was like a BBC News broadcast—perfunctory and devoid of emotion. A one-lane wooden bow bridge spanned a small stream. The elevated bridge provided a clear look at the small town of Asakan. Nick stopped on the apex and shut off the engine to enjoy the spectacle. The GPS screen went dark. He stared at the box. It wasn't there to direct him anywhere. It was there to keep an eye on him. He knew that his cellphone could be tracked, but that would require a query to the phone company. With the GPS, Basil could simply bully one of his CIA contacts into following him real-time with a satellite. Nick spent a few moments listening to the birds and insects in the tall grass along the stream before turning the key and punching the starter button. The GPS came to life.

"You have reached your end point." The clipped accent carried an unpleasant air of finality.

"No." Nick plucked the GPS from the dash and tossed it into the stream. "Not quite yet."

81

LIKE A GHOST TIRED OF THE HAUNTING

Wednesday, 20 April 2004—4:49 p.m.
Whitefeather's Café, Asakan, North Carolina

Tommie wiped down the counter and looked around the café. He filled the last of the salt and pepper shakers and locked the front door. As he started to leave, it hit him hard: sparkling lights, a head full of fireworks, and the sensation that he was falling. Tommie stared through the jagged lines in his vision and stumbled toward a booth. The wooden seat groaned in protest as he half-fell, half-sat. He leaned forward, his hands covering his eyes.

"I'm not ready, not yet" he said to no one. But, then again, had he ever been ready?

A rattling sound brought Tommie back to the present.

"Mr. Whitefeather?" Someone shook the locked handle of the café's front door. "Tommie Whitefeather?"

Now, a tapping on the window next to his head. He lowered his hands and turned toward the sound. A thin man in khakis and a blue shirt, sleeves rolled to the elbow, walked toward a small green convertible. Tommie returned the rap on the window. The man glanced over his shoulder. He was a fit man, fiftyish, with a full head of brown hair. His face cracked into an engaging half-smile as he pivoted and strode toward Tommie. He stopped three feet short of the window and began an introduction that was only half-audible through the glass.

Tommie shook his head and tapped his ear.

"I'm Nick. Nick Caedwallan," he said, "team leader for the real-estate search." The man in the blue shirt moved closer, leaned over, and enunciated. "About the room?"

"Yeah. Sure," Tommie nodded and pointed toward the door. He hadn't expected an advance man; he'd assumed the whole crew would arrive tomorrow. The man's appearance surprised him. He'd expected a thug: Bobby Ray, the shooter, on steroids. Caedwallan looked more like the guy you sat next to at the Rotary Club.

Tommie placed both hands on the table and pushed himself to a standing position. His knees buckled and he grabbed the booth to keep from falling. His vision grayed at the edges, and cold sweat beaded on his forehead. His pulse was rapid and irregular. He was a boxer trying to stay on his feet in round fifteen. He took a deep breath. His vision brightened, but Tommie knew this reprieve was temporary. It was time to be thinking about where he wanted to be when the ball dropped. In a few weeks, the gray-outs would progress to a blackout, followed by twenty-four hours of helplessness as the process worked its way through his body.

He could just see Caedwallan out of the corner of his good eye. When Tommie stumbled, the Rotarian pretended not to notice. Instead, he returned to his car and began tugging at the convertible top. Tommie collected himself and wobbled toward the door, watching the man's fingers worry the same spot on the convertible top. At the clack of the deadbolt, Caedwallan ceased fumbling, raised the top in one fluid motion, and retrieved a leather duffle from the seat. The gambit was confirmed. Tommie wondered what kind of hired gun would go to such lengths to spare the feelings of his opposition.

"I hope I didn't cause too much trouble coming a day early." Nick extended his hand. He looked tired and a bit pale.

"No sweat," Tommie said. The man's grip was firm, but his hand was cold despite the warm day. Tommie gave a single pump but maintained his grasp for a few seconds to sense Nick's body language and study his face. Like an experienced emergency-room doctor who can diagnose a patient by his walk, three centuries of living made for a pretty accurate first impression. He felt Nick tense slightly as if he knew he was being read. The broad smile faded, replaced by a more genuine half-grin as Nick's hand relaxed.

Nick's gaze lingered briefly on Tommie's bad eye, then soft-focused, seeming to look both at and through him at the same time. Tommie sensed fatigue and regret, but something else—resolve. It was as if his new acquaintance had one foot in this world and one in the next, like a ghost tired of the haunting but with business to finish before he moved on. This was a man on a mission. It wasn't real estate, and Tommie hoped it wasn't to kill Lucy. One last squeeze and Tommie let go.

"Sorry I took so long to get to the door. Come on in," Tommie patted his right knee. "Arthritis."

"I didn't notice." Nick followed Tommie inside. The look in his eyes said he'd been there and done that. Tommie considered that there might be a personal reason for his empathy.

Nick coughed and cleared his throat. He looked down and cleared his throat again. After a series of small coughs, he pulled a handkerchief from his pocket and covered his mouth as a nonstop coughing frenzy began. After each deep rattling hack, he would suck in a shallow breath that sounded like someone draining the last of his milkshake through a straw. His knees buckled; his face turned purple from the effort of coughing. As the spell waned, he perched on a stool and leaned back against the counter, his white-knuckled hand still clenching the duffle.

Tommie stepped forward and grabbed the leather bag. He had to shake the handle a few times before Nick relaxed his grip. "Let me take that," he said, relieving Nick of the bag and placing it on the floor.

Nick shook his head but was too weak to resist. His neck veins stood out as he wiped the sweat from his forehead.

"Do you need to see the doc?" Tommie said.

"No," Nick said through the handkerchief. "I'm okay now." He wiped his mouth and stood up. "Damn spring bronchitis." He took several deep breaths. "Same time, every year." Nick gasped for air. "Too many cigarettes, not enough water."

"I can help with that." Tommie poured a glass and set it in front of Nick, trying not to stare at the tinge of red on the handkerchief. Nick followed Tommie's gaze to the stained cloth.

"Thanks." Nick stuffed the handkerchief in his pocket. "How about you point me toward my motel room?" He bent over and picked up the duffle. "I'll freshen up, then buy you a beer."

"Forget the motel," Tommie said, as he watched Nick's color return. "I have a spare room at my house." Nick looked approachable—not exactly the cold-blooded assassin he had been expecting. "It's much more comfortable. You can take your meals with my nephew and me at the house." If he could eat and drink with the man, Tommie reasoned, he might glean some insight into his plans for Lucy.

"I wouldn't want to impose."

"It's a done deal," Tommie said, grinning as he reached for Nick's bag. "I'm sure we have a lot to talk about."

"Oh?" Nick moved the bag just out of Tommie's reach.

"You know, the thrill of the chase." Tommie gave a dismissive wave of his hand. "Searches, acquisitions, closure, exploiting your fellow human beings."

"I don't know what you mean." Nick sucked in a deep breath.

"Real estate." Tommie smiled broadly. "Isn't that why you're here?"

"Real estate." The words came out like leaves in a breeze as Nick released the breath he'd been holding. His half-smile returned. "My secretary told me there was more to you than met the eye. These should be interesting negotiations."

"My lodge is about six miles out on a gravel road." Tommie locked the café door. "Ride with me. We'll get your car later."

"I can just follow you."

"This isn't the city," Tommie said. "Your car's safe here. Besides, it won't do your bronchitis any good to follow me on the dusty roads." Tommie reached for the duffle. "Would you like me to throw that bag in the back?"

Nick gave a quick shake of his head, opened the door, and climbed into the truck.

"I thought not." Tommie laughed and slid behind the wheel. "What you got in there, gold?" He looked over his left shoulder as he backed the truck into the street. "It weighs a ton, and you hold it like a Brinks guard."

82

SECRETS AND SOFT SPOTS

Wednesday, 21 April 2004—5:33 p.m.
Tommie Whitefeather's truck, rural Asakan, North Carolina

"You have a lodge?" Nick was anxious to steer the conversation away from his duffle. "I'm impressed."

"Figure of speech." Tommie waved to a man on the street. "You know, a man's home is his castle."

Several miles out of town, the road entered a forest of towering pines. The temperature dropped at least ten degrees, and the trees' scent filled the cab. Nick took a deep breath and closed his eyes. What was it like to live in a place like this and know everyone in town?

"Do you mind a little music?" Tommie glanced at Nick, who shook his head. Tommie pushed in the CD and Linda Ronstadt belted out the lyrics to "Blue Bayou."

I'll never be blue; my dreams come true.

Nick sang along in his head. It was incredible how a Ronstadt song could uplift and depress at the same time.

"She's one of my favorites," Nick said.

"Mine, too." Tommie nodded. His duck-lip grin told Nick his stock had just risen a few points.

The next fifteen minutes passed without conversation as Gordon

Lightfoot, Cusco, and Iron Horse blared from the radio. Tommie turned onto a gravel road. Dust billowed behind the truck. When Tommie slowed for a turn, a small cloud wafted through Nick's open window. Tommie turned on the A/C and started to raise his window.

"No," Nick said, "leave it."

"Your bronchitis?" Tommie toggled the switch to lower the window.

"Forget it." Nick stuck his head out the window. "The breeze feels great, and the dust is just seasoning. I hate air conditioning."

"Me, too," Tommie said.

Nick released his grip on the duffle and placed it on the floor. He opened and closed his hand to ease the cramping.

"Finally." Tommie glanced at him and gave him a thumbs-up.

"You must think I'm a real tight-ass." Nick rubbed the aching spot on the back of his neck.

"No. Just a man on a mission burdened with something heavy and important." Tommie nodded toward the duffle.

The gravel road twisted through the tall pines. Tommie stopped the truck at a barely visible driveway barred by a bent and rusting iron farm gate.

Nick stared at Tommie's lined face and chiseled nose. "Can I ask you a personal question?"

"Hold that thought." Tommie held up his index finger and got out to unlock the gate. He returned to his seat, pulled through, closed the gate, and reset the padlock. Back in the truck, he shot Nick a quick grin. "You might not get an answer, but you can ask."

"What's your tribe?"

Tommie focused on the lane. For a full thirty seconds, there was only the crunch of gravel and the low crooning on the radio. "My tribe's been gone a long time." He sighed. "Why?"

"Can you tell me anything about the Cape Fear tribe?" Nick said.

Tommie's face blanched. The truck popped into a clearing.

"We're here," Tommie said, stopping in front of a large two-story log building with a wrap-around porch. He jumped from the truck, ran around to the passenger side, opened Nick's door, and gestured toward the lodge. Tommie reached for Nick's duffle.

"Sorry, I didn't mean to pry." Nick surrendered his bag without resistance and the pair started for the porch. "It's my background in archaeology and ancient history. I have a soft spot for things that are lost. I'm trained to dig."

"Trained to dig?" Tommie's muttered words were just audible as he dropped the bag and seemed to lock up.

"What's wrong?" Nick veered left to keep from running into him.

"Arthritis." He picked up the bag and resumed his trek to the porch. "Come on in," he said. "It's *Miller* time."

A barefoot teenager wearing jeans and a white T-shirt appeared in the lodge doorway. His skin was copper-brown like Tommie's but without the wrinkles. He stepped onto the porch as they approached.

"I'm starved," the boy said.

"You're always starved." Tommie handed him Nick's bag. "This is Nick Caedwallan. He wants me to show him some real estate."

"Pleased to meet you, Mr. Caedwallan." Noki shook Nick's hand and shouldered the duffle.

"Can we show him some dinner first?"

"Forget the mister. Just call me Nick."

"Put that bag in the guest room, take some steaks out of the fridge, and light the charcoal," Tommie called to the retreating figure. He turned to Nick. "My adopted son—the perfect eating machine."

Nick followed Tommie inside. The gray slate floors, rough-hewn log walls, and soaring pine-paneled cathedral ceiling of the lodge's great room were impressive in their simplicity. To the right, a stainless-steel kitchen covered the end wall. To the left, a walk-in fireplace seemed to grow out of the rock wall. Several blackened logs emitted wisps of smoke. An island with a stone countertop, surrounded by chairs, separated the kitchen from the rest of the room. A well-worn, overstuffed leather sofa and two matching chairs hugged a large tree-trunk coffee table. A floor-to-ceiling window afforded a panoramic forest view to the rear of the lodge. Hallways at either end of the room led to what Nick supposed must be bedrooms. Nick sniffed. The air was sweet and smoky.

"Hickory," Tommie said, smiling. "Nothing beats a hickory fire." He retrieved two beers from the refrigerator.

"About the Cape Fear thing…" He twisted the tops from the bottles. "We all have our soft spots; we all have our secrets." He handed Nick a beer. "Right now, let's wash down the road dust and get this beef on the grill."

"Sounds great," Nick said.

"Tonight," Tommie said, "we'll drink until we don't care. Then we'll talk secrets and soft spots."

83

COMPLIMENTARY—NOTHING IS FREE

Wednesday, 21 April 2004—5:27 p.m.
Virginia Museum of Fine Arts, Richmond, Virginia

Lucy left the Jefferson Hotel in Richmond just after breakfast. Her uncle, Don Bel Castro, who had reserved the room for her, provided a list of four very public potential meeting places throughout the city. The understanding was that if the location were secure, he would appear, a copy of the *Washington Post* under his arm. If there was no paper, she was to ignore him and make her way to the next location. As each event passed without his appearance, Lucy became more concerned. The final scheduled meeting place was the visiting Van Gogh exhibit at the Museum of Fine Arts. Lucy arrived at the museum at the appointed time, but Bel Castro was nowhere to be seen. She spent several hours perusing the museum, passing by the exhibit every fifteen minutes. When closing time came, and her godfather had not appeared, she started for the door.

"Miss?"

Lucy ignored the voice. She felt a touch on her shoulder and turned. A tall, sixty-something man with thinning gray hair held out what looked like a business card. She gave him the ten-second White-feather once-over: white shirt, red tie, gray trousers, and a navy-blue blazer with a Museum of Fine Arts patch on the pocket. He looked legitimate.

"What's this?" Lucy took the card but kept her eyes on the man.

"Best latté in Richmond," he said.

She glanced at the card.

CARYTOWN CUP OF JOE
"Escape from the usual grind."
West Main near Fresh Market

Scrawled on the bottom was "one complimentary latté."

"Please, take it." He glanced around. "We're not supposed to do this, but security guards don't make much." He scanned the room again and pushed the card toward her. "Please. I get paid to hand these out, but only if they're used."

"I don't know." Lucy's feet hurt from walking the hard museum floors. She just wanted to go back to her room and lay down.

"Please," he said again. "I need the money, and you need this latté." He smiled. "It's not far."

"Okay." She nodded as she took the card. "A free latté sounds pretty good right now."

"Complimentary," he said.

"Pardon?"

"Nothing is free." The guard smiled and turned away.

Lucy made her way down North Boulevard and turned right onto West Main. The coffee shop was in a small faux-stone building with three cars in the parking lot. It was easy to see why they solicited business at the museum. She started to drive by but remembered the security guard's plea and turned into the lot. The day had gone gray. Large droplets tapped the Rover's roof. Lucy parked and grabbed her umbrella. The rain and wind assaulted her as she hurried toward the coffee shop's door.

The place was nearly deserted. Lucy ordered a latté and carried it to a corner table with a single chair. She leaned her dripping umbrella in the corner and sat down. Lucy took her time savoring the warm liquid, then slipped into the restroom to wash her face. The bell over the front door tinkled as she returned to her corner table. She glanced up to see a man scurry out into the rain. A handful of patrons held hushed conversations over cradled mugs. A section of the *Washington Post* lay on the table next to hers. It hadn't been there before. Lucy watched the barista work his way around the shop, wiping tables and picking up used napkins.

"Are you reading this?" He gestured toward the newspaper.

"No." Lucy shook her head. "That guy, or someone, must've left it here."

The barista glanced at the retreating figure. "He could have recycled instead of using my place for a trash can." He picked the paper up and shook it. "Didn't even buy a joe, just threw this on the table and left." He thrust the paper toward her.

An article below the fold was circled with a red marker. "I'll take it." She pulled the paper from his hand. "Something to kill time." She glanced up at him and smiled.

"Whatever," the barista said. "Just make sure it finds the trash can or take it with you when you leave." He shook his head and went back to the bar.

The circled article was a short piece about the CIA, discussing the turmoil at the Agency following the sudden heart attack and death of Deputy Director Robert Fletcher. Written next to it in pencil was the note, "See page five." Lucy glanced around the coffee shop. The other patrons had left, and the barista was flipping the OPEN sign on the door.

"Take your time," he said when he saw her looking. "I have to clean up yet." He stepped behind the counter and turned his attention to the espresso machine.

Lucy watched him work for a moment and then turned to page five. At the bottom of the page was another penciled note: "Brown Saab in the parking lot."

Lucy squinted at the lot through the rain-streaked window. She could make out a greasy smear of brown parked next to her Rover in the otherwise empty lot. She rolled up the newspaper, stuffed it in her pocket, and threw her cup in the trash. The bell sounded as she opened the door. Before stepping out, she glanced back at the barista, who stood with his back to her, still fumbling with the steamer on the espresso maker. Lucy thrust the umbrella into the storm, but it provided little protection against the horizontal rainfall. She made her way to the brown Saab. The driver's window lowered about four inches as she approached. A man in his mid-fifties wearing a rag-wool sweater sat behind the wheel. His close-cropped hair was mostly gray. He removed his steel wire-rimmed glasses and wiped away the spray blowing in the open window.

"Well, get in."

She hesitated—

"Lucy," he added.

Surprised, Lucy didn't move.

"Bel Castro sent this for you," he said, tapping a fat manila envelope on the passenger seat.

At the mention of her uncle's name, she walked around the car. She glanced at the coffee-shop window where the barista stood watching.

The driver lowered the passenger window a few inches. "Get in, now," the man said. Lucy noticed a slight accent. Eastern European. Russian? He closed the window.

Lucy opened the door and retracted her umbrella. She pushed the envelope aside, sat down, and pulled the door shut. Shivering, she dropped the wet umbrella to the floor and looked at the driver. "Where's Don?"

Classical music was just audible in the background. The driver wiped his face and glasses again. "Relax, Lucy. If I wanted you dead . . ." He jerked his head toward the just-visible figure in the coffee shop window. "Hector would have offed you in the bathroom."

Lucy saw the figure in the window give a quick wave and move out of sight.

"I thought he was going to have to say, 'Here, read this.'" The driver laughed and put his glasses on. "Let's not sit here too long." His smile faded as he picked up the envelope and placed it on her lap. "Your uncle wanted me to give you this."

"What is it?" Lucy looked at the package without touching it.

"Cash from your uncle." He retrieved a bag from the floor. "Here's a burner, a disposable—"

"I know what a burner is."

He smiled and tossed the cellphone in her lap. "No outgoing calls. Keep it charged." He put one hand on the wheel and peered through the rapidly fogging windshield. "After you're called, take the battery out and throw the phone in the water."

"Where is he?" Lucy looked from the man to the package in her lap.

The driver's expression softened. "He's alive, but certain parties must believe otherwise until a few things play out." He stuck something other than a key into the ignition and twisted. The car engine started, and warm air began to clear small circles on the windshield. He leaned forward and watched a black-and-white troll by, then stop at the intersection, its brake lights glaring on the wet pavement. "Don will call you on this phone as soon as he can." The driver pushed up his sleeve and glanced at his watch. "You need to go now." He took a deep breath and focused on the idling police car. Its brake lights blazed a few seconds longer, then winked out as the car pulled away from the traffic light. "And I should be dropping off this car."

Lucy stared at the screwdriver hanging out of the ignition. "You stole it?"

"Such a harsh word," he said, watching the black-and-white disappear into the developing fog. "Let's call it a temporary appropriation."

"Who are you?"

"All in good time." He reached across her and pushed open the door. "Go back to the hotel, get your things, and get out."

Lucy slipped the phone into her pocket, tucked the envelope under her jacket, and hurried back to the Rover without raising her umbrella.

She slid into the driver's seat, keyed the glow-plug, and counted to ten. The brown car remained immobile. She pressed the starter. At the sound of the diesel clatter, the Saab driver flicked her a two-finger salute, pulled onto Patterson, and melted into the storm.

84

WE BOTH KNOW YOU'RE NOT HERE FOR REAL ESTATE

Wednesday, 21 April 2004—7:30 p.m.
Tommie's lodge, rural Asakan

Nick kept the dinner conversation light, sticking to general questions about Asakan and Cape Fear Indians. Noki brought up the Chippewa legend of the Dream Catcher.

"That's what I need." Nick stared out the window at the darkening landscape. "A web to catch everything bad with a small hole in the middle to let the good through."

"We all have a Dream Catcher," Noki said. "Maybe your net just needs a little tightening."

Tommie spoke little, studying the interaction between Noki and Nick. He tested the water by asking Nick how long he'd been in real estate. Nick countered by asking Tommie if he was born in Asakan. After several hours of pointed questions answered by half-truths, Noki began to clear the dishes from the table.

"I'm off to my room now," Noki said. "It's my turn to open the café. Six comes early." He gestured toward Tommie with his thumb. "And my boss is a stickler for punctuality. Nice to meet you, Nick."

"If you didn't play video games until one, six wouldn't seem so early." Tommie grinned.

"Where else can I drive a Jag and a Lotus?" Noki said.

Nick smiled. "You're a Lotus fan?"

"Yeah." Noki made a steering gesture with his right hand and shifted gears with his left. "Just last night I drove a '64 Elan S1 at Brand's Hatch." He interlocked his fingers and took first place." He buffed his nails on his T-shirt. "The second place E-type was four seconds behind me."

"Nick drives a Lotus." Tommie glanced at Nick. His expression said, "Wait for it."

"You're kidding," Noki said. "What model? What color? Right-hand drive?"

"A '64 S1, British racing green," Nick said. "And yes, it's right-hand drive."

"Can I have a ride?"

"I think we can do better than that." Nick glanced at his host.

Tommie answered with a nod.

"How would you like to drive it?" Nick said.

"But only if you go to bed now," Tommie added.

"No problem." Noki spun 180 degrees and made for his bedroom. His right hand clutched an imaginary steering wheel, his left executed flawless gear changes, all accompanied by running commentary. "And it looks like the brilliant rookie, Noki Whitefeather, driving for Team Lotus, is on his way to another win here at Brand's Hatch." At this point, the voiceover was interrupted by Noki's rendition of engine and crowd noises. "Whitefeather, the first Native American to compete on the European circuit . . ." The door to Noki's bedroom banged shut, and the announcer's voice faded, replaced by howling tire sounds as Noki braked hard before throwing himself on his bed. Tommie and Nick exchanged glances.

"I assume you're well-insured," Tommie said, grinning.

They stood and moved to the picture window to enjoy the dying light of a spectacular sunset.

"It'll be fine. Do you remember being that young?" Nick stared at the faint glow in the darkening sky.

"Time for secrets and soft spots." Tommie retrieved a bottle of bourbon from a side cabinet, poured two glasses, and gave one to Nick.

Nick raised his glass. "To Noki's racing career."

"That's a frightening thought."

"Well, then . . . to youth, health, and a dignified death."

Tommie returned the toast. "To a dignified death— but only after a meaningful life."

Nick took a sip and choked. A violent coughing spell doubled him over. He set his glass on the table and stepped back, turning away from Tommie. After several minutes, Nick wiped his mouth with a handkerchief and returned to the table.

Tommie sat down across from his guest. "You know," he leaned back in his chair, "you don't strike me as a real-estate broker, and that sounds like more than bronchitis."

"And I suspect there's more to you than flipping burgers." Nick downed his bourbon. "As for the bronchitis—" He set his glass on the table and made his way to the porch. "I need some air."

Nick dropped to a porch step and sat, hunched over, like a comma in an unfinished sentence. Tommie grabbed two fresh glasses and a bottle of Knob Creek and went outside to play therapist.

Nick twitched but didn't turn at the sound of the squeaking screen door. Tommie sat down and placed the glasses and bottle between them. A comforting blanket of darkness had crept in on all sides. The occasional plaintive cry of a nighthawk interrupted a continuous chorus of cicadas. Nick looked tired. His breathing was heavy. He swiped his mouth one more time and balled up the bloody handkerchief. Nick ground the heel of his shoe in the gravel at the bottom of the porch step. The grinding was rhythmic, keeping time with the unceasing song of the cicadas.

"Why do they do it?" Nick asked.

"Who?"

"The cicadas." Nick sat still. "Why do they scream like that?

"Sometimes to warn of danger." Tommie poured bourbon into

both glasses and handed one to Nick. "But mostly, it's a cry for companionship." He took a sip. "To attract a mate."

"Why bother?" Nick picked up his glass and gestured toward the chorus-filled forest. "They'll be dead in six weeks." He looked down. "And everyone will forget they were even here."

"They make a difference. They sacrifice themselves to warn others away and perpetuate their kind."

"But their lives are so short."

"We all have problems of one kind or another, I guess." Tommie tipped his head toward the bloody handkerchief. "What's yours?"

"My problem is I'm dying," Nick said.

"Ironic." Tommie made a clucking sound. "My problem is I'm not."

Nick looked up. "What does that mean?"

"You show me yours, and I'll show you mine."

"By all means."

"You go first." Tommie said as he took another sip. "We both know you're not here for real estate."

"What the hell, time is short." Nick stared into the darkness. "My whole life has been not telling people who or what I really am." Tentatively at first, he told Tommie about his illness and dismal prognosis. Then, his thoughts tumbled out. The revelations grew to a cathartic torrent: grad school, how the CIA recruited him and then made his university job disappear, poor choices, and a hint of a slow slide into something worse, much worse.

"Don't beat yourself up so much," Tommie said. "Sounds like you were shanghaied."

"No, I jumped in the water willingly. The Agency just pulled up the pool ladder so I couldn't get out."

"You're only human."

"You better reserve judgment on that."

"Go on."

"It starts bad and gets worse." Nick stared down as he confessed his failure to intervene when Basil had Chloe Spencer's parents murdered.

He turned to face Tommie. "I did nothing. I didn't listen when my partner told me that we needed to help them." Nick put his hand over his glass as Tommie moved to refill it. "I knew something was wrong, but I did nothing."

"There was no way you could know for sure."

"Not true. I'm as guilty as if I shot them myself." Nick jumped up. He staggered and would have fallen if Tommie hadn't helped him back to a sitting position. "All that's needed is for good men to…" His voice trailed off.

"It could be worse."

"It is." Nick turned to face Tommie. "That got us all booted from the Agency." He leaned against the porch rail and reached into his pocket for a nonexistent pack of cigarettes. "I could have taken my lumps and started over, but I didn't." Nick described his final chapter in his slide from academic to assassin. "Instead, I became the fixer for the man who ordered the hit, his personal bitch for seven figures a year, ignoring the truth and convincing myself that I was doing the world a favor, that the people I neutralized somehow had it coming." He stopped. "Enough?"

"For me, yes," Tommie said. "But I think you need to keep going."

"Okay. Here's the part you won't be able to swallow." Nick tried to stand but gave up. He leaned back against a post. "I'm not here to acquire real estate."

"No revelation there."

"I was sent to find Chloe Spencer, a leather journal, and a dog." Nick noticed that the cicadas had stopped. For now, there was only the ringing in his ears.

"You were sent to bring back the girl and the journal?" Tommie prodded. "Is that it?"

"No." Nick looked away. "Not the girl, just the journal. I was told to make it look like she was a traitor whose past caught up with her." Nick looked up at Tommie. "Isolate, humiliate, eliminate. Tie up all the loose ends."

"But you haven't done that, and you aren't going to," Tommie said.

"I said all the loose ends, remember?" Nick coughed. "There's more."

"I already feel like I'm dodging cars on the interstate."

"Well, here comes the Mack truck. After killing the Spencer girl and securing the journal . . ." He searched for words. "My orders were to kill you and Noki." Nick bowed his head and closed his eyes. A chorus of crickets had taken over for the cicadas.

Nick looked up. Tommie said nothing. Nick nodded his head, set his glass on the porch step, and rose to his feet. He stood, swaying, his feet planted wide apart. "I'll get my stuff together." He turned toward the door. "Maybe you could give me a lift back to town."

"Sit." Tommie blocked his path. "You're in no shape to go anywhere." He shook his head. "What is it with white guys and alcohol?"

Nick sat down on the step with a thud.

"It took a lot for you to say all that, but there's not much there I hadn't already guessed," Tommie said. "Now, let's have the rest."

"What do you mean?"

"Why did you come here? What do you really want?"

"I don't know, maybe a shot at redemption." Nick took a deep breath. "I just put my good friend—my only friend—on a plane out of the country."

Tommie nodded. "A lot has happened today. Why don't we pack it in for tonight? We'll make plans over breakfast."

"And then on the way down here," Nick said, ignoring Tommie's suggestion. "I stopped to help this girl, Lucy, in a broken-down Land Rover."

85

EVOLVING, BUT NOT IN A POSITIVE WAY

Wednesday, 21 April 2004—7:35 p.m.
Jefferson Hotel, Richmond

Lucy returned to the Jefferson Hotel and examined the contents of the envelope the car thief had given her. Besides the bundled cash, there was a cryptic handwritten note from her Uncle Don explaining why he couldn't be there himself. The note referenced two associates: Nick Caedwallan and Vasily Konovalov. "They will help you. I have explicit faith in Vasily. Nick, on the other hand, is evolving. I believe he is now one of the good guys, but I'm not entirely sure."

Lucy assumed the Slavic-accented driver of the Saab was Vasily Konovalov.

Her uncle also included a note from her mother that had been written to him but he thought would be of interest to her. Lucy smiled at her mother's familiar handwriting, but her expression sobered when she saw the mention of the name Chloe, a name that was no longer hers. The note began by offering condolences to Bel Castro for the loss of his wife, Marie. It went on to mention several outings that she had taken with her daughter. She described conversations she had with Chloe about life while sitting on a bench next to the von Steuben statue in Lafayette Park in D.C.

"We discussed death as a new beginning." Lucy's mother continued. "I have come to regard death not necessarily as an end but as a new beginning. The passing of a person may be thought of in the context of a sailing ship crossing a sea from west to east. Those who are left behind on the western shore as the sails pass from sight say, 'It is gone.' Those in the new world on the other shore look east and say, 'Here it comes.' When you lose something, do not look to the west where the sun sets, look to the east where it rises for a new day. Don, please share this with Chloe should she suffer such a loss—if I am gone. Some things are KEY to understanding life."

Lucy was puzzled. She had never been to Lafayette Park with her mother, and only once with her Uncle Don. The cryptic metaphors, the word "key" in all caps. Lucy reached for the key she wore on a chain around her neck. The answer must be in D.C., somewhere east of Lafayette Park.

Lucy began to pack. She saw the small pile of dirty clothes in the corner of the room and decided to wash and dry one load, have a bite to eat, and then leave. She picked up the shirt worn the day before. The scrap of paper from Nick's car fell to the floor.

Nick. Lucy's heart pounded as she made the connection between her Nick and the Nick in her uncle's note. If the man in the Saab was Vasily, then might not the stranger she'd met on the road be the "evolving" Nick? She wondered why he hadn't introduced himself, then remembered.

He tried and I cut him off. But still—

If he had known it was her—one look at her reflection in the wall mirror answered that question. There was no way he could have recognized her. She hardly recognized herself. Lucy pulled her private cellphone from her backpack. She would call him right away. She would tell him who she was. Maybe he would jump in the green sports car and meet her in D.C.

Lucy opened the crumpled paper. It was from someone named Rita. She read the note. Her knees buckled. She slid to the floor, leaned against the wall, and reread the note. It was her Nick, and he was indeed evolving, but not in a positive way. And she'd given him her private phone number. Lucy walked to the bathroom and removed the lid from the toilet tank. She separated the battery from the phone, dropped both into the reservoir, and replaced the cover. She stuffed the dirty clothes into her canvas bag and left for D.C.

86

OPEN YOUR EYES AND I'LL SHOW YOU MINE

Wednesday, 21 April 2004—11:15 p.m.
Tommie's lodge, rural Asakan

"Lucy?"

"You know her?" Nick's eyes narrowed.

"Maybe," Tommie said. "Go on."

Nick revealed the intense feelings Lucy had stirred. The impossibility of it all—his age, health, and past. "But it gave me a glimpse of what might have been—of what should be—for Chloe Spencer."

Tommie listened, seeking clarification of Nick's intentions.

"When I met Lucy . . ." Nick paused. "I knew that I needed to protect Chloe Spencer from Basil and his crew. I need to go out on the right side of things."

Tommie sighed in relief, but he sensed that Nick, even in his inebriated state, might be getting close to connecting the dots. He decided to change the subject.

"Okay," Tommie said. "You showed me yours. Now I'll show you mine." He rose to his feet. "Let's go."

"Sure," Nick said. "Where to?"

"A short drive and a long hike." Tommie pulled Nick to his feet.

Nick swayed but remained standing, stutter-stepping his way to the truck. They rode in silence. Nick slumped in the seat; eyes closed, his head bouncing gently against the doorframe. When Tommie stopped the truck, Nick's eyes opened and he sat up.

Tommie walked around the truck, opened the passenger door, retrieved a flashlight from the glove box, and gestured for Nick to follow. Nick's breathing was labored as they trudged up a long hill, weaving through trees and brush.

"How are you with caves?" Tommie paused to let Nick catch his breath.

"Fine, unless there are bats. I hate bats."

"No bats in this cave." Tommie smiled. "But you know, their guano makes good fertilizer."

"My whole life since grad school has been fertilizer." Nick looked around. "Why did you bring me here?"

"To see a Cape Fear Indian."

"That's impossible." Nick put his hand on Tommie's shoulder. "They're long dead."

"Patience," Tommie said. "You showed me yours."

They followed the flashlight beam through a small clearing of knee-high grass. Tommie stopped next to a stone outcropping and cleared away rocks and branches to reveal a narrow tunnel.

"Wait here." Tommie handed Nick the flashlight and dropped to his belly, crawling in total darkness through the winding tunnel to the mouth of the cave. He felt for the kerosene lamp and matches that he kept on a ledge next to the cave opening. He lit the lamp but kept the wick turned low.

"Are you sure there aren't any bats?" Nick called out.

"Yes. Come on through."

Tommie watched the flashlight beam dance off the tunnel walls and listened to Nick's labored breathing as he struggled through the narrow passage. When Nick reached the opening, he told him to turn off the flashlight. Tommie leaned down and put his hand on Nick's shoulder to stop his forward progress.

"Close your eyes." He guided Nick into the cave and turned the lamp wick up, illuminating the cave with a golden glow. "Keep 'em closed." Tommie helped Nick to his feet and turned him toward the paintings. "Open your eyes," he whispered, "and I'll show you mine."

87

SAFE, SECURE . . . YOU HOLD THE KEY

Thursday, 22 April 2004—1:01 a.m.
Street-side, Willard Hotel, Washington, D.C.

Even at one in the morning, every parking space was filled. Due to the hotel's proximity to the White House, police patrols were frequent. Lucy trolled the streets that formed the park's boundary in search of an empty spot. A heavy mist reduced the illumination of the streetlamps to haloed moons over dark sidewalks. The pale yellow of the ancient Rover's headlights did little to pierce the thickening fog. Lucy widened her search to 14th Street. As she crept past Pennsylvania Avenue, the soft glow of the Willard Hotel entrance caught her eye. There were several empty spaces near the main entrance. She checked for traffic and made a slow turn onto Pennsylvania Avenue.

She inched past the uniformed concierge and parked in an open space about 30 feet from the main entrance. Ahead of her, at the outer limits of her feeble headlights, an apparition appeared: a thin gray shape of indeterminate gender bent low over a battered shopping cart. As the figure stepped from the curb, the Rover's small circle of light revealed a middle-aged woman: shoeless, wearing soggy mismatched socks, baggy pants, and a trash-bag slicker. Her shopping cart contained a few wet paper sacks. A tall floor lamp, bereft of cord or shade, protruded over the specter's shoulder. The sound of the idling diesel reflected by the heavy air and facade of the hotel vibrated like the bass drone of a bagpipe. The mist ruffled like a curtain in pale stage lights. The marcher paused and turned to face her. She nodded as if to say, "We are the same," before resuming her dirge. Lucy watched as the phantom piper turned and marched into the mist, the idling British vehicle thrumming in sympathy.

"Is that me?" Lucy squeezed the wheel. "Is that where I'm going?"

A pleasant Jamaican accent followed a gentle tapping on her window. "Can I help you, ma'am?"

Lucy slid the Rover's window open. "Did you see her?"

"See who, ma'am?" The round black face was creased in genuine concern. "Are you all right?"

"The woman with the shopping cart…"

"Didn't see her, ma'am." He peered into the mist. "We have some homeless. They move from park to park." He glanced at the empty street and then turned back to face Lucy. "They got nowhere to go. Live in boxes. Anyway, can I help you?"

"Do you know where I could park for a couple of hours?" Lucy read the name tag on his doorman's uniform. "Satchel?" she added, doing her best to look pitiful.

"A couple of hours?" He raised his eyebrows. "What can you do at this time of night?" His face wrinkled into a smile. "And it's Satch. Ain't nobody called me Satchel but my mum, and that's been thirty years."

"I'm just passing through town." She paused, searching for the right words. "I don't have much time." She didn't want to lie to this man. "I want to see the park where my mother took me when I was a child." Lucy touched a tissue to the corner of one eye.

"You lived here when you was a child?" Satch waved to a passing D.C. police cruiser. Lucy took note of the number on the front fender: 9033.

"My mother is dead," Lucy said, hoping this would stop the probing questions. She blotted her eyes again, where real tears had appeared.

"It's not safe to go to the park now." He looked down the street. "Not in the dark. How about you park your car here in the loading area for a bit. It's light here. You can wait in our lobby until daylight." A horn sounded, and Satch held up his index finger to a limo that had just pulled up at the entrance. "I got to go now." He nodded and started for the limo. "See you inside."

"Thanks," Lucy said to the retreating figure. "Inside."

She contemplated her options, grabbed her windbreaker, and waited until Satch and guests disappeared into the lobby. After a final glance at the Willard's entrance, she set off toward Lafayette Park amidst the light drizzle. By the time she reached the von Steuben statue, her clothes were soaked. Lucy thought about the woman with the shopping cart sleeping outside with a piece of cardboard for a roof. She shivered and stared east across the park, searching for a bank building. Although the streetlights illuminated the entire area to near-daylight, the view across Madison Place revealed only the Federal Claims Court. Evidently "look to the east" meant she would have to do some walking.

A police car slowed as she reached the northeast corner of the park. Lucy watched from behind the statue of General Kościuszko as the cruiser came to a stop. Before the blinding spotlight came on, she saw the last two numbers on the front fender: 33. Lucy lay on her stomach as the beam played across the statue and surrounding area. A long minute passed, the light was extinguished, and the cruiser moved on. Lucy stood up and ran her fingers over her muddy clothes. A combination of fear and hopelessness washed over her. The only difference between her and the homeless woman was her old Land Rover and the cash from Don. She wondered how long that would last. She had no home, family, profession, or identity. She was officially dead.

Lucy made her way east on H Street and crossed New York Avenue. She saw only one vehicle as she walked: a nondescript tan pickup truck that slowed and tooted its horn as it passed. After walking a few more blocks, she saw a small time-and-temperature sign hanging over the sidewalk. It flashed: 2:44 AM, then 49° F. Lucy drew her wet windbreaker tighter around her and walked toward the sign. It was a small independent bank. The windows contained a wide variety of hand-lettered advertisements. One caught her eye:

Long-Term Safe-Deposit Boxes
10-Year Rates
Safe, Secure
You Hold the Key

Lucy's breath caught in her throat. Below the script was a gold-leaf icon. She reached for the key she wore on a chain around her neck. Her fingers closed around the cool metallic object. She held it up for comparison. The logo on the window matched that on her key. Her heart beat faster.

Maybe she could avoid pushing a rusty shopping cart.

The posted opening time was nine o'clock. Lucy stared at her reflection in the window. If she wanted to get into that safe-deposit box, she would have to get some sleep and find someplace to clean up before the bank opened.

The rain and wind picked up. Lucy shivered and stared at the headlights of an approaching vehicle. When it was a block away, she recognized it as the same pickup truck that blew its horn earlier. Lucy turned and began the trek back to the Willard. It was nearly ten blocks, and she wasn't sure which cross-street would get her there. The truck pulled even and then crept along, keeping pace with her. Facing forward, Lucy watched out of the corner of her eye. The vehicle's window lowered, and a glowing cigarette arced like a bottle rocket toward the curb, exploding near her feet. Lucy jerked but kept walking. She heard a twitter of laughter, muffled conversation, and the thumping of music from within the vehicle.

"Cold out there?" A man's voice, not young but not old. His speech was slurred but intelligible. She increased her pace and stared straight ahead.

"Warm in here." The voice sounded hopeful. "We got beer." There was a long pause. "And money, if that's what it takes." Lucy fought the urge to break into a run. She saw an alley on the left and considered ducking in. But what if it was blind? She remembered Tommie's instructions:

Always leave yourself an escape route.

She mentally replayed the basic self-defense tactics he'd taught her. She spread her keys between her fingers and wished for the 9mm hidden under the Rover's front seat.

"Forget it," another male voice chimed in from the passenger side. "Let's go."

"Screw you, bitch!" The driver tossed a beer bottle. Shards of glass hit her legs—not hard enough to cut, but hard enough to sting.

The truck's tires spun on the wet pavement as it accelerated.

Thank God.

Lucy relaxed her grip on the keys and slowed her pace. But then the driver slammed on the truck's brakes and stopped a block away. The backup lights came on, and the truck started to move toward her. Lucy froze. The alley was looking like her only alternative when another vehicle turned onto H from New York Avenue. The pickup truck stopped, and the backup lights winked off. The driver's window went up, and the truck drove past the oncoming car. Blue lights began to flash as the cruiser stopped next to her. Lucy looked at the number on the front fender—9033.

"Crap," Lucy said under her breath.

The officer stepped out of the cruiser and stood between his open door and the car.

"Was the driver of that vehicle threatening or harassing you, ma'am?" His voice was calm as he shined the flashlight up and down her torso, pausing at her feet before shutting off the light.

"No, they were just asking directions." Lucy hated to give the perverts a free ride, but the thought of police reports and possible discovery trumped civic duty.

"And they thanked you with a beer bottle?"

"No," Lucy said. "That was already here." She felt the noose tightening. She conducted Tommie's ten-second assessment: mid-twenties, African American, very polite, but with a policeman's skepticism.

"You have glass fragments in your shoelaces." He clicked the flashlight on and illuminated her feet. The pieces of glass sparkled in the glow of the flashlight beam.

"I must have kicked them while I was walking," she said.

"I grew up in the hood, ma'am." He smiled for the first time. "You can say, 'I don't want to get involved.'" The smile faded. "Just don't bullshit me."

"Okay," Lucy said. "I don't want to get involved. Besides, I didn't see a face. I can't identify them." She sighed and let her shoulders sag. "I'm tired. I'm wet. I'm cold, and I just want to get back to my car."

And where's your car?" He was suddenly all business again. A cold blast of wind nearly lifted Lucy from her feet.

"Look." Lucy's temper got the better of her. "You know exactly who I am and where my car is." She could hear her voice cracking. "The doorman probably called you when I didn't come to the lobby. You probably ran my plates and came looking for me." She stopped and smiled. "And God, I'm glad you did. I was terrified. I got disoriented when I left the park."

"Yeah." He smiled, "Must have been that mud bath by the statue."

"I—"

"Get in." He slid behind the wheel. "I'll give you a ride back to the Willard."

She climbed in.

He made a U-turn and headed west. "You had my friend Satch worried sick."

He cranked the heater to max, but Lucy was still shaking when they reached the Willard. "That's a classic," he said as the cruiser stopped next to the Rover. "New Hampshire, eh?" He nodded toward her plates. "On your way home?"

"Yeah." Lucy was ready for the trap this time. "Been visiting family down south." She looked around for the doorman. "Where's Satch?"

"Probably settling guests."

"Tell him I said good-bye." She extended her hand. "And thanks to both of you."

"Good luck." He shook her hand. "Are you sure there's nothing else?"

"No." She managed a closed-mouth smile. "I'm fine. Just tired and cold." She climbed out of the warm cruiser.

"Drive carefully then," he said through the open window before turning back toward the Willard. Lucy wished she could tell him everything. She started the Rover and made a U-turn. The rain had stopped, and stars were visible through the broken clouds. She glanced at her watch: three thirty-seven. Five and a half hours until the bank opened. She brushed a few flakes of dried mud from her windbreaker. Her immediate needs were food, sleep, and a low-profile place to clean up. She turned south on U.S. 1 and crossed the Rochambeau Bridge into Arlington, Virginia. Still shivering, she felt the beginnings of warmth from the Rover's anemic heater. She wished she could walk into the police station and tell her story. She just wanted to get on with her life. But without proof in hand, she could trust no one in government.

Just as the heater began to produce a breath of warmth, Lucy found what she was looking for, a twenty-four-hour doughnut shop. Another casualty of an aging population and rising property taxes, the once homey exterior sported a crackling green neon marquee:

Our Baker Never Sleeps
Watch Waldo Work

Lucy scanned the parking lot for a spot where she could catch a few winks shielded from the road. She eschewed the perfect dark space behind the building because it was near an open dumpster. She parked in the back, next to what she assumed was an employee's car, a rusty Toyota sporting an "Eat More Donuts" bumper sticker. A large tree minimized the light from the overhead pole lamps. Lucy noticed the sign on the side of the building:

No Overnight Parking
Cars Towed

Lucy locked the truck and headed for the front door of the donut shop. She glanced back at the Rover and hoped it would pass for an employee vehicle. The truck was mostly invisible, but the headlights of a turning car illuminated the reflective surface of the New Hampshire plates. She may as well have a sign stating, "Not from around here." Lucy contemplated moving the car but decided against it. She was too tired, too cold, and too hungry. She held the front door open for the slow-moving elderly couple who had just pulled into the lot. She followed them in and waited while they marveled at the automated doughnut assembly line.

Behind a glass wall, a robotic apparatus dropped life-preserver shaped globs of raw dough into a tank of hot oil. Small oars hurried the fried doughnuts to a channel where a metal spike whisked them from the oil and passed under a shower of sugary glaze before dropping them onto wax paper.

"Do you mind if I cut in?" Lucy asked the elderly man who was mesmerized by the doughnut-making machine. He waved to her to pass.

"Better than a TV in a waiting room." The tattooed, stick-thin girl said to Lucy, nodding toward the elderly couple. "What'll it be?"

"Two glazed and a coffee with milk," Lucy said. "Tough shift?"

The clerk slid the tray toward Lucy. "Hard on the feet, but it pays the tuition. That's two thirty-seven." She tore the receipt from the cash register.

"What are you studying?" Lucy pushed a five-dollar bill across the counter. "I'm Lucy."

"I'm Caren, with a C," the girl said. "Cosmetology, if you can believe it." She patted her pink-dyed hair and laughed. "I graduate in two weeks." She raised her chin. "Renting a chair in an established shop."

"Congrats, you must be—"

"Excuse me, miss." The elderly man leaned across the counter. "If you're finished, we'd like to order now." Caren with a C shot him an icy stare.

"Two weeks." Lucy shook her head and smiled.

"Yeah. Two weeks." Caren returned the smile and slid Lucy's change across the counter.

Lucy slid it back. "Keep it. Consider it a scholarship."

"Thanks." Caren turned to the older man. "Yes?"

Lucy picked up her tray and headed for a booth.

"Did you see the size of that tip?" The old guy complained to his wife. "No wonder they're always complaining about the minimum wage. That's more than I made…"

Lucy chose a booth in the far corner. She was going to sit facing the wall to avoid any conversation but remembered Tommie's instructions: "Always face the door and never let anyone get between you and the exit." She picked up her tray, slid into the front booth, and faced the parking lot. Lucy finished the doughnuts and coffee, dumped her trash, and took the tray to the counter. She could hear Caren moving around in the back. She wanted to ask how strict they were with the overnight parking. Five minutes passed; no customers and no Caren. Lucy decided to take her chances. It was still chilly, but the wind had died, and she'd dried off in the restaurant. She set her phone alarm for six-thirty, covered herself with her sleeping bag, and was out in less than a minute.

88

PERHAPS SHE'S IN THE WITNESS PROTECTION PROGRAM

Thursday, 22 April 2004—8:51 a.m.
Parking ramp, Washington, D.C.

Parking was going to be a problem. Seven-thirty on a weekday morning was not the best time to enter the nation's capital. Even at ten dollars per hour, every parking lot was full. After searching for over an hour, Lucy was desperate. She glanced at her reflection in the mirror. She looked tired. In the last two and a half days, she'd slept less than six hours and driven over three hundred miles in a military vehicle designed for off-road use at speeds under thirty-five miles per hour. Thank God Caren with a C had offered the use of the doughnut shop's shower. In desperation, she pulled up to one of the kiosks of a multilevel ramp five blocks from the bank.

"We're full," the attendant shouted over the cacophony. "Contract and reservation only." He leaned out the window of the kiosk. "You have reservation?" He spoke in broken English. Lucy tried to place the accent—Greek, she thought. His name tag said "Andreas."

"Can I get a reservation now?" Lucy jumped as the driver of the black Mercedes behind her sounded an unending blast on his horn. When Lucy looked back, he was waving both middle fingers in the air.

"*Malaka*, asshole." Andreas jumped out of the kiosk. He raised his hands in the air. "Why you no go 'round?"

"You're Greek," Lucy said, hoping to establish a connection.

"No Greek—Turk, from Cyprus," he said, smiling. "My father had a sense of humor with names."

Lucy smiled.

"It takes two days to get a parking reservation." Andreas pulled a dirty business card from his pocket. "Call this number."

"If I'm not at the bank by nine-thirty, they're going to take my house." Lucy felt terrible for the lie, but she was desperate. "Please, isn't there, someplace?"

"Okay." Andreas put his hand over his mouth. "I help you." He retrieved an orange road cone from the kiosk. "Wait." He placed the cone behind the Rover and held up his middle finger to the departing Mercedes driver.

"Thank you," Lucy said. "I don't know how to—"

"Don't be so quick to thank. Two hundred fifty dollars and you have a spot until noon." He glanced around. "It is a contract spot. If you there when other driver come," he said, making a hand-washing gesture, "they tow your car for five hundred dollars, and I do not know you."

"Two hundred and fifty dollars," Lucy said. "That's—"

"Yes, it's robbery." He shrugged and smiled. "Goodbye."

"No, wait." Lucy pulled money from her bag. "Here."

"A pleasure," he said, taking the money. "Spot number thirty, level three, the sign says Jenkins. "I get off at six." He smiled as he raised the bar for her to pass.

"Right. In your dreams." She drove by him.

"It's a date then, at six." He laughed and lowered the gate.

Lucy pulled into the parking space at five past nine and half-ran the five blocks to the bank. Pausing a half-block away, she readjusted the scarf tied at her chin and straightened her sunglasses. She had purposely dressed in Capri pants, white blouse, and flats to make the scarf and sunglasses disguise believable.

Lucy pushed open the massive ten-foot-tall door and entered the bank. She paused to survey her surroundings while the air conditioning chilled her nervous sweat.

The interior was a dingy anachronism of twenty-foot-high painted tin ceilings, cracked plaster walls, in contrast to the six strategically placed surveillance cameras.

Five of the six teller windows were shuttered, with the only open one unoccupied. In the back were two offices with candy-store type windows. A man sat behind a desk in one, while the other had an open door and no furniture. A three-foot-high oak wall with a low swinging gate formed a ten-by-ten cubicle in one of the front corners. Inside were two well-worn side chairs and a large wooden desk. Hunched over the desk, transfixed by the screensaver on his computer monitor, sat the motionless embodiment of Ebenezer Scrooge, replete with green see-through visor and black sleeve garters on his frayed white dress shirt. The swinging gate screeched like an owl when Lucy entered the cubicle. She took a step toward him and nearly fell when her shoe caught on a hole in the worn carpet.

"Good morning." She wondered if the clerk might have succumbed sometime earlier and his demise not yet discovered. She would not have been surprised to see cobwebs attaching him to his desk. She would have enjoyed the comedy of the situation if not for the urgency of getting the contents of the box and retrieving her Rover before Jenkins had it towed.

"Yes." He delivered the reply with no discernible body movement.

"I would like to access my family's safe-deposit box." There was no response. "Please." She lowered her sunglasses for just a moment.

"Box number?" the clerk asked in a monotone.

"I'm sorry," Lucy said. "I've forgotten it."

"Really." The clerk seemed on the verge of waking up. "Box owner?" The ancient fingers made a couple of taps on the computer keyboard.

"Karen Spencer." Lucy willed her voice to remain steady. She wanted to run.

"ID, please."

"Actually," Lucy said, "that's my mother." Lucy began to tear up. "She's deceased."

"Are you a signatory?" he peered over the top of half-rimmed glasses.

"No." She blotted her eyes.

"I'm sorry then." His tone softened just a bit. "I can't let you in." He pushed back his chair and regarded her for the first time. Lucy thought she saw the hint of a smile.

"My mother died in an accident." Genuine tears streamed down her cheeks.

The clerk gave a deep sigh. The phone on his desk rang. He picked up the receiver and turned his head to look at the man in the back office. Lucy suspected he had been listening to their conversation.

"Yes, sir," he said, returning the receiver to its cradle. "One moment." He held up an index finger and rolled his chair to an adjacent desk. "Let me check something." He tapped away at another keyboard. "Well," he said, sliding back to his original computer, "it has come to my attention that there is a written provision for a daughter named Chloe Spencer to access the box with proper identification." He arched his eyebrows. "Are you Chloe Spencer?"

"Yes." Lucy waited for the next question.

"And do you have proper identification?" he said, adjusting his glasses.

Lucy pulled out her Chloe Spencer college ID.

"Proper ID, in this case, means two documents." He leaned forward. "Do you have a second ID?"

"Not on me."

"I suspected as much." He looked down and shook his head.

"It's in my car," she said, frowning. Lucy never carried her Chloe Spencer driver's license. She kept it in a smuggler's box that Tommie had installed in the raised platform that supported the driver's seat.

"Well?" He held out his hands.

Lucy said nothing.

"For God's sake, child, go get it. This isn't a career move. We close at noon sharp."

"I'll be back in less than thirty minutes." She jumped up and hurried for the door. Her sunglasses fell off. When she leaned over to retrieve them, the silk scarf came undone and slid to the floor. Flustered, she grabbed the scarf and, as she stood, she looked up at the camera. "Damn." She glanced at the clerk who was now on the phone and staring at the manager's office. She ran out of the door and made her way to the parking garage. As Lucy passed the kiosk, Andreas smiled, held up his left arm and tapped his watch. She retrieved her driver's license and sprinted back to the bank.

The bank clock lashed out its warning—11:08.

"Chloe Spencer," the clerk said. "This face looks like you, but I'm not sure we can use these documents." He picked up the receiver and punched a button on the phone.

Lucy squirmed in her seat as the phone buzzed in the back office. "Double confirmation required, please." He smiled at her.

She bit her lip and checked the time—11:20.

He seemed invigorated by her discomfort. A short, balding man in a gray pinstripe suit appeared in the doorway of the back office and sauntered to the front.

"I'm Oscar Stedman, the bank manager." He flashed Lucy a toothy smile. "Let's see if we can clear this up." He looked first at the computer screen, then at Lucy, then at the two IDs, and finally back to Lucy. "I can reconcile the weight change, but both of these documents have expired."

"I live in town and no longer drive." Lucy crossed her fingers in her lap. "And I graduated two years ago."

"You should get a valid ID," the bank manager said.

"Perhaps she's in the witness protection program." The clerk rolled his eyes.

"These will be adequate," Stedman said. "Show her to the vault." The bank manager handed Lucy her IDs. "I have some calls to make."

The clerk led Lucy to the vault holding the safe-deposit boxes. He stood on a stepladder, retrieved a medium-size box, and placed it on the table in the center of the room.

"Thank you," Lucy said, "I'm sorry to—"

"It's okay. Insert your key here, please." He pointed to one of the two locks on the side of the box, placed his key in the second lock, turned it, and stepped back.

Lucy turned her key. There was a satisfying "click" and the lid popped open an inch. Lucy lifted the lid and pulled out a thick, blue, three-ring binder and a manila envelope. She heard a shuffling and glanced up.

"Will there be anything else?" The ancient clerk had stepped forward and was staring down at the binder and envelope.

"No." Lucy put the items back in the box and partially closed the lid. "That will be all."

The clerk edged sideways until he stood in the doorway. "Very well, then." He backed out, pulling the heavy door shut behind him.

Alone in the vault, Lucy opened the lid and removed the binder and manila envelope. A plain white envelope lay on the bottom of the box. She saw her mother's handwriting scrawled across the small white envelope. It read, "Chloe, open this first."

Lucy broke the seal, unfolded the single page, and started to read.

My dearest Chloe,

Her eyes filled with tears and the ten-foot ceiling seemed to hang just above her head.

If you are reading this, your father and I are likely dead. The contents of the manila envelope will tell you why and who was responsible. It will tell you what happened and explain my research in lay terms. The blue binder contains my in-depth research notes. Do not try to read it now. Leave the bank immediately and go to a private place. Take care that you are not followed. If Don Bel Castro is still alive, he may be able to help you. If not, you will have to decide whom you can trust. We love you.

Despite her mother's instructions, Lucy opened the envelope and flipped through the pages. The pages started with notes about their trip to North Carolina. As she scanned the pages, three things appeared over and over: *Turritopsis dohrnii*, the word *immortality*, and the name Basil Orlov.

She stole a quick peek at her watch—11:42.

Oh, God. The parking ramp.

She had an immediate vision of being stranded in D.C. with no money and no transportation. She stuffed the envelopes and the binder into her backpack, closed the safe-deposit box, and took her key. Stedman and the clerk were standing by the desk in the alcove. The bank manager was talking on the phone.

"Miss Spencer," the clerk said as she passed by. "We need some more information in case we have to contact you." He stepped forward.

"I'm in-between addresses right now." She increased her pace. "I'll call you." Lucy exited the bank and walked west, away from, instead of toward, the parking ramp. After one block, she stopped and looked back. The clerk stood outside the bank, watching her. Lucy continued west for several more blocks. Satisfied she was not being followed, she changed course and walked north on Tenth Street, turning east after a half block to blend with the upscale shoppers trolling along Palmer Alley. Lucy paused long enough to buy chocolate and a floppy hat. Hands shaking, she ate the chocolate and replaced her scarf with the hat. She looked at her watch: 12:03.

At the end of the shopping district, Lucy walked north on Ninth Street and then doubled back on I Street to reach the parking lot. Andreas spotted her as she entered the parking garage.

"You totally screwed." He smiled and pointed at his watch.

"I'll make it."

"No." He patted the cash drawer. "You paid two-hundred-fifty dollar for thirty-dollar worth of parking. You screwed big time, either way." Several car horns sounded, and he jerked his head toward the street where a delivery truck was blocking the entrance ramp. He ran to the curb to confront the driver.

Lucy watched until he began his shouting match with the driver then stepped into the kiosk and opened the cash drawer. She glanced at Andreas, reached into the drawer, and withdrew two hundred twenty dollars, leaving thirty behind to cover the parking. As Andreas turned back, she stuffed the cash into her pocket, waved, and ran up the stairs. The Rover was still in the stall and no Jenkins. She jumped in, turned the key, and waited for the glow-plug to go out. She had just started the Rover when a horn sounded behind her. Lucy looked in the rearview mirror. A middle-aged man in a white BMW had his arm out the window, pointing to the name "Jenkins" stenciled on the wall.

Lucy jumped from her car and ran to his door. *"Oh non, je pensais que cela était le niveau quatre."* She placed one hand over her mouth and pointed to the huge level-three sign with the other. "That's okay," he said. "It happens." He looked at the New Hampshire plates and back at her.

"Quebecois?" His accent was terrible.

Lucy nodded enthusiastically and flashed her toothy smile.

"You don't speak English, do you?" he said, reversing his car to let her out.

"Merci." She gave an animated wave as she backed out.

Andreas blocked her path as she approached the exit ramp. Lucy briefly considered running him down but braked to a stop. She held her breath as he approached her open window.

"Don't rush off." He flashed his unctuous smile.

Lucy exhaled. He hadn't spotted the cash shortage yet. "Gotta go." She blipped the accelerator.

"I thought I might take you somewhere nice for dinner." He patted the cash in his shirt pocket.

"You can't afford it." She popped the clutch and accelerated onto I Street.

Lucy followed the blue signs, reaching the I-395 entrance ramp in less than five minutes. She traversed the maze of interstate highways that would get her out of D.C. and back to the more familiar U.S. 301. The traffic thinned as she made her way east on Suitland Parkway.

She found it difficult to concentrate on driving. When she wasn't watching the rearview mirror, she was glancing at the backpack containing the contents of the safe-deposit box. She was desperate to read what was in the manila envelope. A pounding headache and rumbling stomach told her she was well past hungry. Each exit beckoned with fast-food restaurants. She could have something to eat and read a few pages. What could it hurt? But her mother had said to go to a private place.

Tommie would agree with her mother.

She was about to give in when she spotted a Maryland trooper in her rearview mirror. She held her speed at fifty-five, hoping he would pass. After three miles, he signaled a lane change and moved into the left lane. He drew even with her door, and she waited for him to pass. She could sense he was watching her, his front fender just visible out of the corner of her eye. A long thirty seconds later, he blipped the siren.

Lucy glanced toward the officer. He nodded at the Rover, flashed a thumbs-up, and accelerated away. Shaking with relief, she turned south on MD-5. In several miles, she reached 301 and made her way to Waldorf, where she stopped at a fast-food restaurant. She took the backpack with her but resisted the temptation to remove the envelope. She forced a few French fries, confident that there was a pimple in every delicious bite.

89

WE'RE APPROACHING THE END GAME

Thursday, 22 April 2004—1:13 p.m.
Basil's office, McLean, Virginia

"Jerry Harwood on line three for you." Rita sounded tired. The seven-hour time difference between D.C. and Minsk made her job nearly impossible. She'd been making last-minute fund transfers and negotiating with recalcitrant Belarus politicians through translators for eleven straight hours.

"Who the hell is Jerry Harwood?" Basil had been working the phones, trying to convince the CIA to accelerate the purchase date of his McLean office. Fletcher's death had opened an internal audit of all pending contracts and put the sale in doubt. He made a mental note that going forward, he would keep the principals alive until the deals closed.

"Don Bel Castro's assistant . . . something about Chloe Spencer."

"Put him through." Basil sprang to his feet—his aches, pains, and fatigue forgotten. With Bel Castro out of the picture, Harwood was privy to every document that crossed Bel Castro's desk. "Jerry!" Basil put on his friendliest voice. "What have you got for me?"

"Good news, Mr. Orlov. A bank manager in D.C. made a positive ID of Chloe Spencer when she accessed a safe-deposit box." Harwood was excited, speaking so fast that Basil could only catch random phrases. "Expired ID . . . thirty pounds lighter . . . left with a binder and an envelope."

"When?" Basil looked at his watch.

"Just before noon." Harwood paused and sucked in a breath. "The bank security officer called."

"Noon?" Basil shouted. "It's after one!"

"It went from bank manager to security, to local LEO, to FBI, to Bel Castro's office. I'm sending you the bank's security-camera shot by fax now." Harwood's voice trembled. "I've only had it for ten minutes."

"Ten minutes. A Russian sub could drop a nuke in my lap in seven. Let's have the rest of it."

Basil listened while Harwood told him what he already surmised: the FBI and local LEO would be gearing up. In short order, a BOLO on Chloe Spencer would go active, and Basil would have competition. And that competition would have unlimited assets and resources. Basil hung up and buzzed Rita.

Rita entered Basil's office and approached his desk, frowning as she stared at the paper in her hand. "You're not going to believe this." She dropped the faxed photo on his desk.

"Get Schwartz on the line." Basil's energy had ebbed. He dropped into his desk chair and reached for the proof. He studied the shocked face that stared back at him: brown eyes, short dark brown hair, and well-defined jawline. Basil opened a desk drawer and retrieved a file photo of the Spencer girl at the beach with her parents in 2000. No wonder she hadn't been ID'd from the grainy Marine Science security image. The girl in the beach photo had shoulder-length hair, round soft facial features, and an air of puppy-dog innocence.

Basil tapped the flashing button on his desk phone.

"Mr. Orlov?" Marty's voice was deferential, but also hungry and hopeful, like a junkyard dog waiting to be unchained and pointed toward its target. Nick had been like that once, a point-and-shoot assassin. Marty wasn't exactly point-and-shoot, but his total lack of morals was a definite asset.

"We're approaching the end game, Marty." Basil leaned back in his chair, phone in one hand and jellyfish orb in the other. "Chloe Spencer has been positively sighted in D.C." He placed the globe on its stand.

"The command center is up and running," Marty said with confidence. "It's all under control."

"Really?" Basil slammed his fist on the desk hard enough to make the jellyfish globe jump from its base. "We have less than forty-eight hours until local law enforcement, the FBI, and God-knows-who get involved." He tried to shake off the ache in his hand as he watched the jellyfish globe do a slow-motion roll. "Vasily got away and Bel Castro's body hasn't been found. Are you damn sure he's dead?" Basil grabbed the globe before it dropped from the desk. His hand and elbow rewarded him with another jolt of pain.

"Sir." Marty's voice took on a comfortable, authoritarian bent. "Konovalov has fled the country and is not a player. Bel Castro called his administrative assistant, Jerry Harwood, early in the evening and said he needed a few days to clear his head. Harwood said he was clearly intoxicated. He took an LOA through Monday. It will be even more convincing when they find his bloated corpse in a puddle of blood next to his service revolver. He smelled like a distillery." He paused for effect. "We have it covered."

"Okay, okay." Basil put the orb back on its base and sighed. "Just locate the Spencer girl and that journal. Call this Harwood guy and get all the information you can." He rubbed his hand over his face. "The Spencer girl could be anywhere by now, but my money is still on North Carolina. I want you to take a larger role in this."

"What about Caedwallan?" Marty said.

"He's on his way out." Basil hung up.

"Yes?" Rita answered Basil's page.

"Call Dr. Stills." Basil cradled the phone with his shoulder and massaged his wrist. "Tell him—I think I broke my hand."

90

NEKULTURNY

Thursday, 21 April 2004—1:07 p.m.
Tommie's Café, Asakan

Nick probed the bowl of cold chili with his spoon. He had spent the better part of an hour trying to break down the last of Tommie White-feather's resistance. He knew time was growing short on all fronts. The bloody cough—hemoptysis, the medical prick had called it—had become more frequent and progressed to a rusty-nail taste that eliminated any desire to eat or drink. His new fellow travelers, double vision and vertigo, told him he was off peak and fading fast. Diplomacy gave way to direct action. "Look," he said, watching the spoon stand unassisted in the bowl of chili. "I know that you and Chloe Spencer are friends. And you need my help."

"I've done okay for over a year," Tommie said.

"This is different." Nick watched the small finger of his left hand begin to tap out its Morse code message to no one. "And I need to help."

"Let me think about it." Tommie watched the last of the lunch customers file out. "Take a ride around town," he said. "I need a few minutes to finish working this out."

"Time is short." Nick stuffed his twitching hand into his pocket. "And growing shorter."

"One hour." Tommie walked Nick to the door.

Nick stepped onto the sidewalk. The bell tinkled as the door shut behind him. He glanced up. A freshening breeze pushed a few fluffy, white cotton balls across a field of blue. A barely perceptible rumble of thunder drew his attention to the southwest, where a line of dark clouds piled up on the horizon. A storm was coming, but there was still time for a top-down reconnoiter. Nick ignored a car horn somewhere behind him and began to lower the top. When the horn gave another sustained blast, he turned toward the sound. A dusty pickup truck and two black SUVs were parked at the motel adjacent to the café. Marty stood next to the pickup. His right arm reached through the open truck window and pumped the horn while his left hand clawed at the sky in an attempt to summon Nick. People walking by on the street stared and shook their heads.

The horn began to blow nonstop. Marty grinned and bobbed his head at a frowning pedestrian.

Nekulturny, Nick thought. Uncivilized. Vasily's one-word assessment of Marty was spot on.

"Hell, Marty." Nick pulled Marty's arm from the truck. "Do you always have to be such an ass?"

"Screw the locals," snarled Marty. "Mornin', ma'am," he added, saluting a woman passerby. "There've been developments." He looked around as if expecting an eavesdropper. "Come inside where we can talk." He pulled on Nick's arm. The small motel room paneled in a rust-brown wood contained two double beds with nightstands and a small desk. Colorful hooked cotton rugs adorned the heart-pine floor. Watercolor paintings depicting local scenes hung on the walls. The motel phone sat disconnected on one of the nightstands. A black phone-fax combination unit sat in its place on the small wooden desk.

"It has a bug detector," Marty said, smiling. "It beeps if we're being tapped." A large whiteboard leaned against the wall. Nick noted the words scrawled in red marker:

Leather Journal—Intact
Spencer Dog—Intact
Chloe Spencer—Disposal
Indians—Use and Lose

"Use and lose?" Nick jerked his head toward the board. "This isn't some third-world shit-hole where you just have your way with people and then off them." He searched for something that would slow Marty down. "I don't think Basil would appreciate the publicity associated with kidnapping and murder in a small town."

"The Spencer girl was sighted in DC," Marty said, grinning. "In forty-eight hours, the Fibbies and local LEO will be all over this case."

Nick's eyebrows shot up.

"Surprised that I got the news first?" Marty pointed at Nick with both hands shaped liked guns. "Basil plans to have what he needs and be out of the country before that happens." He flashed his thin-lipped grin. "I'm going to pick up Cochise and Tonto and sweat them. Bad publicity is not an issue."

"We'll see." Nick pulled out his phone and punched in his boss's number. Nick played the voice of reason. "Basil, I think you need to rein in the pit bull on this Whitefeather thing." Five seconds passed before Basil spoke.

"He's enthusiastic, Nick." Basil's voice was flat. "You could use a little of that."

"Listen," Nick said. "I have Whitefeather's confidence." The silence spoke volumes. "He won't respond to torture." Still no response from Basil. "I can take care of the girl if she's here and secure the journal in forty-eight hours—"

"Oh, she's there all right," Basil broke in. "Twenty-four hours—then the leash comes off."

Nick glanced at Marty. "Call Fido and tell him." Nick pushed the end-call button and stepped onto the porch.

Marty started to follow Nick outside but paused when the phone rang inside the room.

"Your master calls." Nick gestured toward the door. Marty pushed the door partially closed. Nick took a step toward the door and watched Marty through the narrow opening.

"Yes, sir." Marty's shoulders slumped. His voice was a combination of deference and disappointment. "I will play it any way you want, sir." There was a long pause. Marty turned toward the door and grinned. "Are you sure you want him to have that?" The fax machine squealed and began to print. "Okay." Marty hung up, pulled the sheet from the fax, and folded it in half.

Nick nudged the door open. "Well?"

"We play it your way for now." Marty handed Nick the folded paper.

"What's this?" Nick took the paper without looking at it.

"A picture of Chloe Spencer from the bank's surveillance video."

"I already know what she looks like." Nick turned and strode toward his car. "Basil has a dozen old photos from the Spencer house."

"She's changed." Marty wiggled his hand in a crude gesture. "She's lost weight and got hot."

Nick opened his mouth and raised a finger, but decided Schwartz wasn't worth it and started for his car, unfolding the fax as he walked.

"Go on, professor." Marty trotted backward alongside Nick. "School me, but check it out." He gestured toward the fax.

Nick unfolded the paper and glanced down at the image.

Thunder rumbled in the background.

91

THIS COULD TAKE SOME TIME

Thursday, 22 April 2004—1:39 p.m.
Tommie's Café, Asakan

"Can I go hiking with Jamie now?" Noki slipped his apron over his head and draped it across the swinging door to the kitchen. "The lunch rush is over, and I've wiped all the tables."

"First, the dishes." Tommie stood up and headed for the kitchen. "You wash. I'll rinse."

"Can't we do it later?"

"You know what a mess it is when stuff dries." The café door banged hard against the stops. Nick stood in the doorway, holding a piece of paper. The square stance and jaw set told him it was not good news.

"Someone hit your Lotus?" Tommie half-sat on one the stools.

"I suppose you could say I was rear-ended pretty hard." Nick smacked the photo on the counter.

"Oh," Tommie said when he saw Lucy's face looking up at him.

Noki peered over Tommie's shoulder, then glanced back at Nick's scowl. "I think I'll do the dishes now." He pushed through the swinging door to the kitchen.

"No, they can wait. Go hiking." Tommie picked up the photo, dragged himself to the door, and reversed the "Open" sign.

"What about the dried on . . .?"

"Jamie's waiting. Just go." Tommie moved toward a corner table and motioned for Nick to follow. Noki paused. *"Now."* Tommie pointed to the door. Noki shrugged, slipped out the door, and crossed the street to where a thin, sandy-haired teenager in jeans and T-shirt waited.

Tommie pulled out a chair for Nick and sat down.

"I drank with you." Nick sat down, his posture rigid. "I told you everything—things I haven't told anyone. And you stiffed me."

"I showed you the cave." Tommie looked at Nick's face and decided that, yes, Nick had probably told him everything. "I can tell you the rest now."

"And Chloe, Lucy, or whatever she calls herself?" Nick tapped the photo.

"Okay. You're in," Tommie said. "Where and when was this taken?"

"This morning in D.C., just after she accessed a safe-deposit box."

"Implications?" Tommie sighed. Things were going pear-shaped. He had survival skills, but Nick knew the system.

"The FBI and local LEOs will have this in forty-eight hours. She won't last that long without my help."

"I said you're in." Tommie stood and began to pace. "What more do you want? Let's hear your plan."

Nick took a deep breath and leaned back. The angry scowl melted as his shoulders fell. "Sit down. Relax. Marty's manageable. It's the exit strategy we need to work on." He looked down at the photo. "First, where is she?"

"She's safe for the moment. She'll be back Friday at midnight. What's your exit plan?"

"Later." Nick flashed the half-smile. "Right now, I want the story on those cave paintings."

Tommie glanced at the wall clock: 2:07. He pushed back the chair and stood. "This could take some time." He padded toward the kitchen. "Coffee or beer?"

"Let's save the coffee for this evening's planning session. It could be a long one."

"Noki and I will cook dinner here." Tommie returned with two beers in hand and two in an ice bucket. "Right now—"

"It's story time."

"First, just listen." Tommie uncapped two beers, handed one to Nick and recounted the same story he'd told Lucy two days before.

At the conclusion, Nick asked the same questions: What about your eye? What does it take to kill you? Does it just go on and on forever?

Tommie answered as he had with Lucy. He looked up at the clock: 2:38. It had taken less time than he thought.

"Satisfied?" Knowing the answer before he asked the question, he retrieved the two remaining beers from the bucket and twisted off the tops.

"You're kidding, right?" The PhD in archaeology and ancient history leaned back in his chair, grinned, and made a "come forward" motion with his hands.

"I thought not." Tommie sighed and pushed one of the beers across the table. Despite the cold beer and the air conditioning, he could feel himself beginning to sweat. Three hundred years—the physical wound was long gone, but the guilt remained.

"The shaman had planned it well." Tommie began. "He was entertaining my mother and father in his tent when two of his conspirators burst in." Tommie could feel the heat rise in his face. "One carried me in his arms. The other threw down a rifle and reported that a white man had shot me with it."

"Were you conscious?" Nick took a sip of his beer.

"I was awake but couldn't speak." Tommie felt like he was giving a deposition. "I had no breath. I moved my mouth, but no sound came out. Each breath was like a hot poker."

Nick nodded.

"I could hear my mother screaming, begging the shaman to save me. The shaman looked down at me with a knowing smile. He held one of the brown bottles over my wound and kept telling my mother to have patience. I was barely conscious. Everything was black."

Tommie jumped up from his chair and began pacing back and forth.

"Go on," Nick said, insisting.

"He jammed the bottle into my wound. I started shivering. My heart was skipping all over the place."

Nick sat on the edge of his chair, mesmerized at hearing ancient history from a live witness.

"The shaking became more violent, then it stopped. I was awake but I couldn't move."

Nick muttered something unintelligible about Dearborn and seizures.

"I heard the shaman say that Roger Moore—"

"Roger Moore?" Nick interrupted. "The owner of the Orton Plantation? The one who burned Necoes in reprisal for his daughter's death?"

"I'm getting to that." Tommie sat down and continued. "The shaman had promised a few braves immortality in exchange for their treachery. They raided the plantation, killed Moore's daughter, and stole a rifle and a sword. It was all part of his plan to get what he wanted."

"He wanted a massacre?"

"He wanted to be chief," Tommie said. "And he wanted my mother." He took a sip of his beer. "The massacre was a means to an end. He told my father to take the rifle, go to Moore, and tell him a white man had shot me. The shaman pretended to be the voice of reason, counseling my father that only a personal meeting with Moore could avoid all-out war."

"I have read what little history exists a dozen times." Nick tapped the empty beer bottle. "No one could explain why the Cape Fear Indians burned Orton and killed Moore's daughter."

"The shaman told my father that he and a few braves would take me and my mother and brother to a small village upstream and wait for him.

Tommie clenched and unclenched his fist. "I could have stopped it."

"No, he had it all worked out. The shaman was sending your father to certain death." Nick's face reddened. "Basil!" He spat out the name. "Same MO, different century."

"When I came to, we were in a hut somewhere upriver. It was late the next day. I touched the gunshot wound." Tommie stopped talking and pushed on a spot between his chest and abdomen. "There was nothing—no pain, no scar, not a trace of the wound that should have killed me. My mother was there. She was weeping. A brave had just told her that my father was dead. Moore had seen him with the rifle and assumed he was the leader of the raid who burned his plantation and murdered his daughter. He killed my father and the members of the peace delegation at first sight. In a fit of rage, he—"

"Burned Necoes to the ground and killed every inhabitant of the village." Nick finished the sentence for him. "That much is in the history books."

"Yes, the traitors the shaman had promised to make immortal died with them." Tommie turned up his bottle and drank the last sip of now-warm beer. Its bitter aftertaste matched the story.

"Brilliant treachery." Nick said. "What happened to the rest of the tribe?"

Tommie held up a finger. "I told my brother what had happened and said we should kill the shaman."

"But if the shaman was immortal?"

Tommie continued. "He said we would do it together. He . . . he said he would wait."

"But he didn't."

"No, he didn't want me involved." Tommie shook his head again. "Later that night, I woke to the sounds of screaming." He stared straight ahead, his good eye losing focus. "I ran toward the angry voices and muscled my way through the mob forming around the shaman's hut."

The scene that Tommie described was horrific. His brother, Red Feather, stood in the corner; his blood-covered body held by two braves. On the mat in front of him, smeared with red, was the shaman's treasured saber. The tent was filled with the feral smell of the hunt. The braves were struggling to stand in a rapidly congealing puddle of blood and the shaman's corpse lay on the grass mat, still oozing.

"Several feet away, his severed head stared at . . . my brother, Red Feather, in sightless indictment.

"This time, there would be no resurrection."

"What happened to your brother?"

"The judgment of the tribal elders had been swift but deliberate. There was no proof of the shaman's treachery, only the half-conscious observations of a young boy. Red Feather was put to death."

Tommie stood again and paced as he recounted how he and his mother were exiled to save the tribe from the anger of the shaman's spirit.

Tommie stared at the clock: 3:51.

He stood, placed the bottles and caps in the ice bucket, and placed it behind the counter.

"Okay, let's wrap this up." Tommie took a seat facing Nick, his back to the door. "My mother and I became nomads, accepting the hospitality of other tribes, only to be cast out when our story became known. Through the bitter winter of 1718, we kept moving, spending time first with the Peedees to the south and then the Catawba, who, even with their known penchant for absorbing outsiders, could not overcome their fear of the bad medicine associated with harboring us. Our last hope was the Waccamaw. Not only were they a Siouan tribe, but my great-grandfather had been the youngest son of a Waccamaw chief. The Cape Fear tribe had purchased him for twenty ponies when their chief died with no heir, leaving them without a leader. The Waccamaw refused to take us in but provided supplies and an introduction to a visiting Cherokee trader who would guide us further west to search for a tribe who would accept us. My mother died when a three-day blizzard surprised us in the mountains of the western Carolinas. I was granted the hospitality of the Cherokee for several years but continued west. At the age of fifteen, I found a home with the Anasazi in Colo—"

"Tommie." Nick's face went pale. He nodded toward the front door, jumped from his chair as the door banged against the stops again.

"Need a hand here," Dan Parker called out, trying to carry Noki's, blood-soaked body.

92

YOU GOT THE BAD NEWS PART RIGHT

Thursday, 22 April 2004—4:03 p.m.
Tommie's Café, Asakan

"I was driving out by the Strand," Dan said, guiding Noki to a booth just inside the front door. "He staggered out of the pines and stepped right in front of me. I could have killed him."

"And just who are you?" Nick moved toward the corpulent man with the rapidly expanding sweat stains under his arms who looked as if he would pass out at any second.

"Dan—Dan Parker." The man offered a quivering hand.

"A friend." Tommie extended his arm to slow Nick's advance.

Tommie wiped the dried blood from Noki's face with a damp kitchen towel and began a primary field evaluation.

Noki winced as Tommie touched the blue-black swelling around his left eye.

"The eye is swollen, but the orbital ridges are intact and there's no neck tenderness. I would guess a couple of cracked ribs. No bruising belly or flanks. He's lucky."

"You sound like a doctor giving report," Nick said.

"Another story for another time." Tommie replaced the warm cloth with one filled with ice. "Where was Jamie all this time?"

"He said it was too hot to hike," Noki said. "We hung out in town for a while, then he went home, and I went up the trail alone. I was in the pines, near the small waterfall, when a guy came up behind me." Noki paused to wiggle one of his front teeth. "That bad-news guy, you know, Billy Ray, he—"

"His real name is Marty," Nick said. "But you got the bad news part right."

"He had a gun. He told me to lie on the ground, face up." Noki grimaced as Tommie placed the cold towel to his eye." Noki explained Marty had bound his wrists and ankles with duct tape, then spent the next hour alternating between beatings and questions. "Then he got a phone call and said a lot of yes-sirs and no-sirs."

"Basil," Nick said.

"After the call, he let out a string of profanity, smacked me in the face with his gun, and left."

"What did you tell him?" Tommie handed Noki a glass of ice water.

"Like your escape and evasion lecture. I told him what he already knew." Noki took a sip. "He shoved that picture of Lucy in my face." Noki smiled and looked at Nick. "I acted surprised, and he went back to beating me. He doesn't know where she is, where she lives, or what she drives. He still thinks her name is Chloe."

"How did you get loose?" Nick was impressed by Noki's coolness under Marty's brutal interrogation.

"I did like Tommie taught me." Noki looked at Tommie and managed a weak smile. "I held my arms close together while he taped my wrists. After he left, I got up, put my arms above my head with my elbows touching—"

"And you brought your arms down as hard and fast as you could." Nick finished the sentence for him.

"The tape split on the first try—just pulled off some skin." Noki held his wrists up. "I used a piece of shell to saw through the tape on my ankles. I was kind of stunned. Some of his punches were hard. I ran through the trees and onto the road. Dan saw me." He looked toward his still-puffing rescuer.

"I'm going for the sheriff." Dan heaved himself from the booth.

"No!" Tommie stepped between Dan and the door. "This is about Lucy. No police."

"The land sale?" Dan said.

"Still good to go." Tommie said. "Just keep this quiet. I'll take care of it."

"Let me." Nick grabbed Tommie's arm.

"Lucy and Noki are my responsibility," Tommie said.

"Schwartz has a dozen men over there." Nick tipped his head toward the motel. "That guy will torture you until he gets what he can; and then he'll kill you."

"But I can't just . . .." Tommie looked at Noki.

"You said I was in." Nick released his grip on Tommie's arm. "If you're gone, Lucy has no one to trust. She doesn't know me, not really." He thought of what Marty would do to Lucy if he found her. He stepped into the afternoon heat, pulled the door shut, and suppressed an urge to cough.

93

TELL THEM YOU FELL—IT'LL SAVE FACE

Thursday, 22 April 2004—4:27 p.m.
Motel parking lot, Asakan

The dusty pickup truck was parked in the corner of the motel lot with the windows down and the sound system cranked to maximum volume. Marty leaned against the door; his Stetson tilted forward over his eyes.

Nick heard Johnny Cash's prophetic lament:

I shot a man in Reno, just to watch him die.

"Sooie," Marty yelled along with the singer. He pointed an imaginary gun at Nick, popped his wrist in recoil, and blew on his fingertip. "The rest of the crew has gone off to some beaner restaurant." He tossed his hat through the truck's open window and gave Nick his flat grin. "Shall we?"

Nick grabbed Marty's right wrist with his left hand and pulled the arm into full extension. He rotated the arm externally, then struck just medial to the shoulder joint with the heel of his right hand. He was rewarded with a sound like a foot being pulled from wet cement.

"God damn!" Marty screamed as Nick doubled him over with a knee to the groin.

Nick spun Marty until he was facing the truck, placed his left hand behind Marty's head, and drove his face into the B-pillar. The sickening crunch and explosion of blood told Nick the nose was broken.

"Shit!" Marty spat blood and a tooth fragment on the parking lot. "You broke my arm." He rolled to a sitting position and leaned against the truck, cradling his right arm in his left.

Nick flashed his half-smile. "No, your arm is only dislocated. It's your nose that's broken." He retrieved Marty's Stetson from the truck and placed it on his head, tipped slightly forward. "There, you look better," Nick said, tilting his head from side to side. "Stay away from the Whitefeathers. You'll live longer."

"I take my orders from Basil." Marty wiped his bloody face on his shirt sleeve. "I would have killed the little shit if Basil hadn't stopped me."

This squared with Noki's account of Marty's phone call in the woods. Basil had no intention of giving Nick twenty-four hours. "I'd get to the hospital if I were you." Nick turned to walk away. "That nose needs attention. Tell them you fell—it'll save face."

"I can't drive like this."

Nick walked back to where Marty sat leaning against the truck. He grabbed Marty's arm, put his foot in his armpit, and pulled while rotating the arm back and forth.

Marty screamed. "You're ripping my arm off."

"No, I'm putting it back." Nick released his wrist. "But next time…"

94

AND YOU KNOW WHAT WE DO WITH LIABILITIES

Thursday, 22 April 2004—6:33 p.m.
Basil's office, McLean, Virginia

"Rita," Basil called through the open office door. "Did you get through to that idiot Schwartz yet?"

"No." Rita's face appeared in the opening. "I've tried three times."

"Damn." Basil stared at the Spencer girl's faxed photo. "By Saturday morning she'll be in the wind, and that little shithole will be crawling with all manner of law enforcement and reporters."

Rita's face disappeared from the doorway.

Basil studied the cast that ran from the tip of his fingers to his right elbow and remembered the orthopedic visit. That slam on the desk fractured his fifth metacarpal, and he'd have to wear the cast for six weeks.

"Marty on the secure line," Rita called out. "Something's wrong with him."

"That's for damn sure." Basil swore under his breath. Marty's interrogation of the Indian kid had been brutal but worthless. He wondered if Marty was up to the task. Two years of meticulous planning had brought Basil to the brink of his goal. To be sure, there had been problems—the Spencers, Strenke, Officer Fine, Fletcher, Bel Castro, and Vasily. But those were just speed bumps. Except for Vasily, who'd run to

South America, they were all dead. And as far as Basil was concerned, Vasily was nothing without Nick to back him up. The one thing he had not planned for was Nick's cancer. If not for the crisis of conscience suffered by his go-to guy, Chloe would be dead now and the journal would be his. But then, Nick had been on a slow burn ever since the Spencer hit.

Basil heard Marty mumble "yes, sir" as he picked up the receiver. "Where have you been?" Basil struggled to hear over a loud hissing on the encrypted phone. "And what's wrong with your voice? You sound like Marlon Brando in *The Godfather*."

Basil covered the mouthpiece with his hand. "Rita," he yelled. "What's wrong with this phone? It's hissing like a goddamn snake."

"I don't know," Rita answered without appearing in the doorway. "I was on the other line with an Agency lawyer. They're offering to settle the office contract tomorrow at noon for seventy-five percent of the agreed price."

"Opportunistic shits." Basil hesitated. "Tell them yes."

"I already have." Rita's voice was calm and confident. "Shall I get a tech up here for the sat phone?"

"Screw it." Basil watched the steady green glow of the sat phone's safety indicator. "We'll be gone before they could fix it." He marveled at Rita's transformation. In a scant eighteen months, she had gone from timid to terrible. She had negotiated most of the Belarus setup, dealing directly with crime bosses, corrupt politicians, and even the science types. He remembered how she had shrunk when she first learned the modus operandi of Basil's company. Rita had a dramatic change in attitude after Nick solved the problem with her ex. She now negotiated contract hits with dispassion, dropping them on Basil's desk for final approval. There was no doubt that Rita had the skill and temperament to manage a Fortune 500 company if she so desired. But she didn't because he promised a fringe benefit no other company could offer. Rita had conquered all her demons, save the one she shared with Basil.

". . . and he dislocated my arm."

Basil had been half-listening to Marty's garbled speech while he spoke with Rita.

"I lost two teeth and have a hairline fracture in my jaw."

"Forget Caedwallan for now." Basil couldn't care less about how many teeth Marty lost. "We need to convince Whitefeather to give up the girl."

"But how?" Marty sounded like he was gargling. He cleared his throat and spat. "I roughed up the kid like you said. I should have taken him out."

Basil wished there was someone to take Marty's place, but things were moving too fast. "Just show him we're serious."

"How?"

"I don't know." It was like dealing with a child. "Use that expensive truck I bought you. Hit and run, but don't kill him, just brush him. Then we'll sweat the old guy."

"What about Caedwallan?" Marty explained how Nick had told him to stay away from the Whitefeathers, or else. "He's turned."

"I'm afraid the good doctor's terminal lung cancer and sudden onset of scruples have moved him from the asset to the liability column." Basil let out a long sigh. "And you know what we do with liabilities."

"Sir?"

"We take them off the books."

"Huh?"

"I'm just saying," Basil expressed his thought aloud. "Things will go a lot smoother once Nick is out of the picture."

"Roger that," Marty said, his voice suddenly clear.

"And remember, don't kill him," Basil said.

"Who?" Marty sounded confused.

"The Indian, dumb ass. Just knock him down."

"Got it."

The sat phone clicked twice, and the hissing stopped. Basil stared at the glowing green light for a moment, then half-dropped the receiver in the cradle with his left hand. He wondered if his secretary thought he didn't know that she listened in to his phone calls.

"Rita." Basil walked to the door. "How about something to eat? I'm starved."

95

EXIT, STAGE LEFT

Thursday, 22 April 2004—8:17 p.m.
Tommie's Café, Asakan

"Looks like we're going to get the storm they promised." Nick slid closer to the café's street-side window, which rumbled with every clap of thunder as the storm clouds closed ranks.

Noki cleared the dinner dishes, then reached over Nick's shoulder to flip the switch to light the wall sconces. "Can I get you guys anything else?"

"No, thanks," Tommie said. "It's time to do your homework. Nick and I will take care of the wash and dry." Tommie waited until Noki disappeared into the kitchen. "I'm concerned for Lucy's safety. Now that your boss knows she's in the area, and with a BOLO coming out any minute, I don't see how we pull this off."

"I'm not worried about the short term," Nick said. "I can make us disappear. It's the long haul for Lucy that concerns me. You'll be rebooted as Tommie Whitefeather 2.0, and me, I'll exit, stage left. But Lucy—" Thunder rattled the windows. "I plan to slip away before it gets too bad. But if it should happen before then—promise me . . . card in my wallet." Nick fell silent as Noki approached.

The youth set two perspiring bottles of beer on the table. A flash of lightning illuminated Nick's Lotus, top down, parked across the street. "Your car!"

"I'll be right back," Nick said, as a few large drops of rain appeared on the sidewalk.

"I could pull it under the carport behind the café and put the top up for you." Noki sounded hopeful. "With your cough, you shouldn't go out in the rain."

"Yeah, my cough." Nick forced a smile. He reached into his pocket, pulled out the keys, and slid them across the table toward Noki.

"Really?" Noki said, grinning.

Another flash of lightning was followed by a clap of thunder and wind-driven rain splattering on the window.

"Go, before the car fills up."

Noki bolted through the front door.

"He'll need those." Tommie laughed and pointed at the car keys still laying on the table. Nick grabbed the keys and headed after him before Tommie could protest. Tommie watched the comedy of errors from his dry vantage point. Nick paused on the sidewalk, one hand held to his forehead to deflect the rain. Noki stood next to the Lotus patting his pockets. Realizing he had no keys; he threw up his hands and turned to face the café. Noki shrugged when he saw Nick dangling the car keys above his head. Nick glanced at something down the street. Tommie leaned closer to the window for a better look. The street was deserted except for a single truck parked a half-block away, vapors rising from its exhaust. A flash of lightning illuminated the vehicle.

"Marty!" Tommie yelled and ran toward the door. He watched in horror as Noki, unaware of Marty's truck, started to cross the street. Tommie could hear the truck's engine revving.

"No!" Nick was waving his arms above his head.

Noki smiled and jogged toward Nick.

Nick jabbed at the air, pointing toward Marty's truck.

Noki turned, saw the accelerating truck, and froze.

Nick sprinted into the street and hit Noki at full stride, arms extended. The force of the blow sent Noki tumbling to safety in front of the Lotus just as Marty's right front fender struck Nick. His arms and legs splayed, he spun and fell to the pavement. Tommie reached the curb just as Noki got to his feet and started toward Nick. Dazed and bleeding from his nose and mouth, Nick rose to his knees and held out a hand to motion Noki back. Marty had stopped the truck and was reversing for another strike.

Tommie drew his pistol and brought it up to fire as the truck's bumper knocked Nick to the tarmac. The tires rolled onto the crumpled form. The truck hung there for a moment then lurched forward. A boom of thunder masked the report of Tommie's pistol as the truck's rear window disintegrated. Marty sped off in the driving rain.

Tommie and Noki ran to Nick's side. He lay on his back, eyes blinking, his left hand moving toward his hip. His lips moved, but no words came out. His chest heaved as he gasped for breath.

Tommie's first thoughts were to dial 911. He retrieved his cellphone and flipped the cover open.

Nick shook his head. His left hand pawed at his hip pocket.

"Okay. Okay." Tommie snapped his phone shut. He retrieved Nick's wallet and placed it on his chest. "I get it. Exit, stage left."

Nick stopped struggling and managed a weak version of his half-smile. He exhaled hard, his eyes closed, and his body went slack. Tommie felt his neck. There were several thready beats, and then nothing.

"I'll call 911." Noki started to stand.

"No." Tommie grabbed Noki's arm. "Call Carlton Smith."

"The undertaker?" Noki stared at him.

"Just do it." Tommie stuffed Nick's wallet in his pocket, pulled Nick's lifeless form to its feet, and carried him to the café.

PART FOUR

ALL THINGS MUST PASS

96

BUT ONLY AFTER A DIGNIFIED LIFE

Thursday, 22 April 2004—8:35 p.m.
Sleeping room off kitchen, Tommie's Café, Asakan

"Let's get him on the cot," Tommie said. They lowered the motionless body to the bed in the small sleeping room off the kitchen.

Nick's right arm slipped from his side and dangled, fingertips just touching the floor. His skin had assumed a bluish hue. Noki knelt, placed Nick's arm on the cot, and wiped at the rapidly crusting blood around his mouth and nose.

"Do something," Noki pleaded, shaking. "You have to do something." He jumped to his feet. "I'm calling 911."

"No." Tommie undid Nick's pants and pulled at his shirt, popping the buttons. Nick's abdomen and pelvis were distended. The overlying skin was one continuous blue-black bruise.

"Get my crash bag." Tommie nodded toward the closet where he kept his field-medic pack. His fingers probed Nick's neck for a pulse. He thought he felt a weak beat, but it was gone in an instant. Noki dropped the bag by his side. Tommie retrieved a pocket doppler and a polished stainless-steel mirror from the pack. He held the mirror to Nick's mouth and nose, hoping for the telltale signs of breathing, but there was nothing. The pocket doppler screeched as Tommie turned the volume to max. He slathered conduction gel on the probe. The doppler squealed and moaned as Tommie scanned Nick's carotid artery. The pulse tapped faintly for three or four beats, faded, returned for two beats, and was gone. Tommie looked at his watch. He would have to decide soon.

"He's alive." Noki dragged his arm across his face to clear the tears and wipe his nose. "Call for help."

"He won't make it." Tommie put his hand on Nick's bruised and bloated abdomen. "He's bleeding internally."

"Blood, fluids, surgery." Noki clawed through the field-medic pack and produced a bag of saline. "Like in your survival course."

"The closest hospital is an hour away, and they have no surgeon." Tommie gently took the bag of fluid from Noki and placed it back in the case. He shifted items around until he found what he was looking for: a long cardiac needle on a 50cc syringe. He'd made his decision. The problem was implementation—that, and time.

"The helicopter!" Noki was shouting now. "Charlotte. Twenty minutes tops."

"Not in this weather." Tommie hurried to the phone. Noki bent over Nick and was crying.

"So, we just let him die?" Noki's tone was a mixture of grief and accusation.

"Yes," Tommie said. "That's exactly what we do. He pulled Nick's wallet from his pocket and removed the DNR card. "Here," he said, handing the card to Noki.

"DNR?" Noki stared at the card.

"He deserves a dignified death." Tommie recalled the second half of his toast. "But only after a dignified life." He punched in Carlton Smith's number.

"Carlton." Tommie hesitated. "I need your help right now on something delicate."

"Anything, Tommie. You know that." Carlton had a long memory when it came to returning favors, and he owed Tommie a big one.

"I need a death certificate right now." Carlton didn't ask why. Tommie could see the street through the café's glass-paneled front door. A pickup trolled by with its lights off. Even in the rain and darkness, Tommie could tell that it was Marty's truck.

"How soon is now?" The statement was an obtuse request for more time. "I'm just loading Mrs. Simpson's casket into the hearse now."

"Charlotte Simpson?" French toast, butter, pepper, no powdered sugar. Tommie thought of the older woman with the infectious smile who often ate breakfast alone in the café.

"She died yesterday," Carlton said. "She was eighty-one and still active in every charity in town. Drove herself to Richmond to visit her family. Damn shame. She'll be remembered. The family wants me to bring up her casket for the chapel services and then transport her ashes back here for burial in the family plot." The funeral director paused, clearly soliciting more information.

Tommie glanced at Nick and then back to the street where Marty's truck was making another pass. He placed his hand over the mouthpiece and gestured for Noki to come over. "Run to the truck and get that green canvas knapsack." He removed his hand from the mouthpiece. "Better yet," Tommie said to Carlton as the side door banged and Noki reappeared. "Back the hearse down the alley and stop next to the side entrance. Open the hearse's load door and bring in the casket."

The red dust from the cave puffed a small cloud as Noki dropped the knapsack at Tommie's feet.

97

UNTIL NOW

Thursday, 22 April 2004—8:39 p.m.
River's Edge Motel, Port Royal, Virginia

"So, Beverly, I mean Miss Sheldon." The scruffy twenty-something male clerk glanced first at the photo on the New Hampshire driver's license and then at the girl who presented it. "How long will we have the pleasure of your company?"

"I've been driving all night and need some sleep. I'd like a room on the back where it's quiet." Lucy yawned as she pushed the pre-paid credit card across the counter. "And can I have the room until six p.m. tomorrow?"

"Check-out time is noon." The young man's tone was apologetic. "There's a twelve-dollar day-fee for late departures." He shoved his sweat-stained glasses up on his nose.

"Well, that's okay if you have to." Lucy tilted her head, forced a smile, and pointed at the clerk's faded and stained James Madison University T-shirt. "Do you go to JMU?"

"I got bounced out after a semester." He smiled and bobbed his head. "Too much fun, substance unknown." He pushed her license across the counter. "Are you a student there?"

"Took a couple of courses as an undergrad." She lied. "Same story as yours. Better living through chemistry."

"What the hell?" The clerk shrugged. "Forget the day-charge. Call it professional courtesy." He handed Lucy her credit card. "Room fourteen on the backside. More private." He winked. "Better for business."

Lucy started to protest but instead gave a weak smile, pushed through the door, and made her way to the Rover. She was backing out of the parking space when the kid ran out of the office waving his arms. For a moment she thought she'd been made.

"Not much to eat around here." He appeared to be angling toward something. "There's an okay pizza place that delivers, or"—he looked away—"I could drive you somewhere for something better."

"That's a tempting offer." Lucy inched the Rover backward, "but I'm shot. Maybe next time."

"Yeah, next time." He gave a weak wave and turned toward the office.

Lucy pulled the Rover behind the motel's second row of rooms and parked in front of room fourteen. The room was in the center of the strip, making her car invisible from the road.

The River's Edge Motel met Lucy's criteria. It was cheap, had cable television, the air conditioning was cold, there was parking in the rear, and the place looked empty. The clerk didn't even run her credit card—he just slid it through a vintage seventies imprint machine to be submitted later. Very discreet—though she suspected there would be an increase in short-term business once the sun went down.

She entered her room through a windowless steel door and breathed a sigh of relief as it clicked shut behind her. The window air conditioner was turned off, but there were no strange smells. The black-and-white checkerboard linoleum floor seemed clean. The walls were faux-wood paneling, with identical landscape scenes hung on three of the walls. The bedspread was a bright yellow cotton chenille rather than the silver ironing-board type usually found in this sort of motel. A punch on the air-conditioner start button produced a loud grumble and a refreshing blast of cold air. Lucy turned on the TV and flipped through the channels, pausing briefly on an ancient rerun of *America's Most Wanted*. After cycling through twice without seeing her picture on a news alert, she pressed the mute button but left the picture on for periodic monitoring.

Lucy pulled her mother's papers from her backpack and spread them on the blond laminate desk, then decided to take a nap before diving in. She was hungry, but food could wait. She set the alarm on her phone for ten p.m. and took a long, hot shower before stretching out on the bed.

The alarm jarred her awake. The temperature in the room was frigid, and her empty stomach rumbled with hunger. A pizza-delivery flyer on the phone stand caught her eye.

"Twenty minutes guaranteed," the clerk said. "Address?"

Lucy gave the name of the motel. After a brief silence, the clerk requested credit-card payment in advance and a five-dollar delivery fee for the one-mile round trip. She gave her number, hung up, and took another quick shower to fully wake up. Thirty minutes later, the clerk knocked on the door, handed her a pizza box, and waited for a tip.

"You wish," Lucy said, closing the door. She ate half of the cold pizza and retrieved her mother's letter from the manila envelope.

Chloe,

I purposely kept my leather-bound journal separate from my other papers. I will get it to you by hook or crook in the hope that you can, in some way, share my fascination with this marvelous and unique creature. As I'm sure you've noted, the journal alone reveals nothing. It is, by design, all flash and no substance, a shameless solicitation of research dollars containing the what, but not the how of the jelly-fish research—all wrapped up in an evocative leather cover. I have carried this journal everywhere, and most people, including Basil Orlov, are convinced it contains "the jellyfish secret."

The envelope contains a brief synopsis of my research and findings that goes into more detail and is intended as a "tease" for the more scientifically astute. This document is the "hook."

The title says it all.

Potential Mammalian Applications of
Turritopsis dohrnii Research

I suggest you start (and finish) with the synopsis, as the two hundred and six pages in the blue binder would put a cell biologist to sleep. After you read the synopsis, you will understand why the blue binder must never fall into the wrong hands. The binder is both the proof and the "how-to" for mammalian transdifferentiation. The findings are simultaneously wonderful and terrible. I know I should destroy it, but my scientific ego will not let me. You are grounded in anthropology and will fully understand the social, cultural, and political implications of this research. I sincerely hope you never have to read this letter; if you do, it means you have become the custodian of the most significant agent of change since the discovery of nuclear fission.

Mom

Lucy picked up a slice of cold pizza and began reading the synopsis.

Until now, it has been established science that mammalian cells are only able to replicate a limited number of times before dying.

She reread the first two words:
Until now—

98

DON'T KILL THE UNDERTAKER

Thursday, 22 April 2004—9:13 p.m.
The rear seat of Basil's chauffeur-driven car, Washington, D.C.

Basil opened the seat-mounted minibar just as the limo's secure phone began to chirp. The safety light flashed green.

Rita glanced at the ID as the phone chirped a second time. "It's Marty. Aren't you going to take it?"

"See what he wants." Basil noticed that Rita was trembling, staring wide-eyed at the phone. "Are you expecting trouble?" He toggled the switch to close the privacy window. The phone chirped a third time. "Quick now, he has a short attention span."

He knew Rita despised Marty, but he didn't think she was afraid of him. Basil punched the talk button and handed her the phone. Marty's excited speech began before Rita could put the phone to her ear.

"Nick," Rita said, her voice little more than a whisper. Her face drained of color, she raised her fist to her mouth, handed Basil the phone, and turned toward the passenger window.

"I'm saying he's gone." Marty was chattering nonstop. "Your Caedwallan problems are over."

"What the hell, Marty? I said scare the Indian."

"That's what I was doing. I was about to graze the kid with my truck when Caedwallan tried to play the hero. He made a dive and pushed the kid out of the way, and I clipped him with the truck."

"And that killed him?" Basil relaxed a bit. He covered the mic with his hand, leaned over, and touched Rita's knee. "He's high on something, sounds like he just grazed him." She shrank from his touch, still staring out the window. Basil removed his hand from the mouthpiece. "Sounds like maybe you just injured him."

"Hell no, man. I remembered what you said about things being better when he was gone. I can read between the lines. After I knocked him down, I backed over him, then pulled forward." Marty giggled. "Rolled him like a fucking log."

"I don't need the details," Basil said, shocked at his feeling of loss.

"Fuckin' Indian tried to kill me. Shot out my window." Marty's speech was racing again.

"Witnesses?" Basil said, trying to formulate a plan.

"What? No." Marty's speech slowed. "Rain, thunder, lightning. The streets were rolled up." His speech accelerated again.

"Are you on blow?" Basil said.

"Just one hit each side to stop the bleeding and help me breathe," Marty said. "The bastard really fucked up my nose." Marty spoke in short machine-gun bursts. "But he's the one who's fucked up now."

"Did you see the body?"

"See it?" Marty sounded incredulous. "I told you, man, I rolled him twice."

Rita had turned and was now staring at him, her eyes puffy and red.

"It's Caedwallan," Basil said to Marty, lowering his voice and turning away from Rita. "We need eyes-on confirmation. Where are you?"

"I'm parked across the street and down a bit from the café. It's raining like a pissing cow." Marty snorted a few times. "Should I go in and check? I might have to make a mess."

"Get a grip on yourself. Go inside, visualize the body, get the location of the girl, and finish the Indians." Basil found himself again wishing for the old Nick.

"Wait," Marty said, whooping so loud Basil's earpiece shut down for a moment. "There's a hearse backing down the alley. How's that for fucking confirmation?" He whooped again. "Gotcha, motherfucker."

When Marty quieted down, Basil continued. "Listen carefully. Leave two crews to watch the exits at the café. If anyone comes out, they are to follow them, but not engage. Do you understand?"

"Yes, sir." Marty's speech slowed. "And what should I do?"

"What do you see?"

"Whoa!" Marty's voice roared in Basil's ear. "They're bringing out a god-damned coffin. Should we raid this shithole and finish things now?"

"No. This changes everything." Basil pinched the bridge of his nose and shook his head. For some reason, the thought of Nick in that casket troubled him. "The Indians may lead us to the girl. Take a man and follow the hearse." Basil glanced at Rita, who sat head down, hands in her lap.

"When the hearse stops, pry the lid off the box and eyeball Caedwallan. Then call me." He sighed. "But Marty?"

"Yes, sir?"

"Don't kill the undertaker." Basil tapped the end button.

"You told Marty you wanted Nick dead," Rita said, pulling a pack of cigarettes from her purse.

"I did not." Basil flicked his lighter and leaned in.

"You implied it." Rita brushed his hand away and lit up with her own lighter. "You had to know Marty would run with it. He hates Nick."

"I didn't think he would do it." Basil thought of the tacit command he had given Marty. "I only meant he was difficult. You know I liked Nick." Basil felt the pang of loss again. "But he was uncontrollable."

"He was your Becket!" She blew out a cloud of smoke. "And, like Henry II, you'll miss him."

"I already do," Basil said, pouring a drink from the decanter.

99

JUST MAKE SURE IT'S A TALL ONE

Thursday, 22 April 2004—9:13 p.m.
Sleeping room, Tommie's Café, Asakan

"Watch for Carlton," Tommie said as Noki, still holding Nick's advanced directive card, trudged toward the kitchen. "When he backs down the alley, unlock the side door and show him in."

Tommie stared at the cork-stoppered brown bottle in his hand. He had made his decision but was still conflicted. Nick's instructions had been for no extraordinary lifesaving measures, and what Tommie had in mind was unquestionably extraordinary. On the other hand, Nick still had unfinished business with Lucy.

Tommie considered what his own life had been like: the changes, the lost friends and loved ones, the sheer otherness of his existence. Would Nick want this? Would it even work? He shook his head and drew the contents of the vial into the syringe. The bottom line was that he needed Nick to save Lucy.

"Sorry, buddy." Tommie located a spot just below the tip of Nick's sternum, then pushed the cardiac needle in at a forty-five-degree angle. "If you don't like it, you can always jump off a building." He kept back pressure on the syringe and advanced the needle until blood flashed back. "Just make sure it's a tall one." He injected the contents into the left ventricle of Nick's heart. Tommie knew Marty was still outside, trolling like a shark. It was only a matter of time until he and his crew came in, guns blazing.

Tommie also knew his one chance to prevent a confrontation with Marty lay with Carlton Smith. His instructions to Carlton had been clear. It was a long shot, and not without risk. But Carlton would do it. He owed Tommie. Two years earlier, Tommie had retrieved Carlton's runaway fifteen-year-old daughter from a pimp in Charlotte. When the pimp came looking for the girl, Tommie solved that problem as well. "Yeah," Tommie thought aloud, "Carlton will do whatever it takes."

Tommie withdrew the needle and began compressions on Nick's chest. When Noki and Carlton came in, he stopped pumping and switched on the doppler. The machine squealed. Tommie maxed the volume so Noki and Carlton would hear. He moved the moaning probe over Nick for nearly a minute without picking up a beat. He put down the doppler, made eye contact with Noki, and shook his head. Carlton put his arm around Noki's shoulder and mumbled something that funeral directors reserve for these occasions.

Tommie turned to Carlton. "Have your attendant bring in the coffin. You may as well load and go."

Carlton and the attendant took their time sliding the casket and its transport mechanism into the hearse. The attendant handed Tommie the death certificate, gave a somber wave, and dashed through the downpour to take his seat behind the wheel.

"The kid's taking it pretty hard." Carlton gestured to where Noki stood in the side doorway, staring at the rain-covered casket. Tommie and Carlton stood behind the long black vehicle.

"I think he'll be okay." Tommie pushed the loading door shut and followed Carlton to the passenger door. "Remember," he said through the open window. "No heroics. Just drive to Richmond like you were planning."

Carlton nodded without speaking and began to raise the window.

"If they stop you—let them look in the box. It'll be fine."

The hearse rolled down the alley, turned the corner, and disappeared. Somewhere out of sight, an engine started.

Marty's truck rolled by.

100

ZOMBIE CELLS, PITUITARY GLANDS, AND DEATH HORMONES

Thursday, 22 April 2004—11:40 p.m.
Lucy's room, River's Edge Motel, Port Royal, Virginia

Lucy sat cross-legged on the bed, trying to make sense of the material in the blue binder. For the past several hours, the headboard of the neighboring street-side room had banged hard against her wall. By her count, the energetic tenant of the room had entertained four clients with only a ten-minute intermission between audiences. At least she didn't have to worry about the blue binder putting her to sleep, although hearing, "Oh! You're so big," for the fourth time had become a bit tedious. A door slammed, and moments later a diesel engine groaned as a semi pulled onto 301 and headed south. Lucy figured she would use the next ten minutes of silence to cross reference the synopsis and her mother's journal.

The drawings and notes in the leather journal made for fascinating reading but were woefully short on mechanics. They titillated and inspired but were simple arithmetic to the blue binder's complex differential calculus.

Lucy took a bite of cold pizza and picked up the synopsis. She soon realized that the synopsis, while only a few pages, covered not only the "how" but also the equally important "when" of successful utilization.

Potential Mammalian Applications of Turritopsis Research
Mechanism of Cell Death

Until now, it has been established science that mammalian cells are only able to replicate a limited number of times before dying. This is because the ends of the chromosomes contain a protective, but nonfunctional extension known as telomeres. Each time the chromosomes replicate, the telomeres shorten, and a small part of the protective coating is lost. Eventually, after twenty to fifty replications, depending on cell type, the protective layer is lost, and chromosomes are damaged to the point of being unable to replicate. Essential cell activities shut down and the sodium channels cease to function. Cell membrane permeability increases and the now hyper-osmotic cell becomes bloated with water. Lysosomes, the cell's garbage bags, begin leaking waste into the extracellular environment. This attracts killer t-cells, which hasten cell death. Also attracted are macrophages, which ingest and clear away the remnants of the now-dead cell. The loss of function is, at this point, limited to the loss of that cell.

As an ever-increasing percentage of cells succumb to either outright death or senescence, the organ systems deteriorate and the entire organism ages. When the totality of lost function is great enough, the organ systems fail, followed shortly by the death of the organism itself.

Zombie Cells

Not all damaged cells rupture and draw the attention of t-cells. Some become senescent husks, alive, but only as nonreproducing and minimally functional placeholders. These zombie cells exist as shriveled shadows of their youthful selves, filled with the toxic, deteriorating remnants of their particular cell type. This material further compromises the functioning of the cells. The deteriorating cells develop small nodules that communicate with the cell's exterior.

These nodules constantly leak minute amounts of this waste into the interstitial space in which the cells lie. While this amount is below the threshold needed to summon the t-cells and macro-phages, it is sufficient to compromise the immune system, weaken the surrounding cells, and stimulate the pituitary gland to secrete the DECO (DECreasing Oxygenation) or DEATH Hormone.

The DECO Hormone

It appears that the rise of these toxic substances and the related decrease in oxygen consumption stimulate the pituitary gland to produce ever-increasing quantities of DECO, a hormone that further suppresses a cell's function, hastening its demise.

At the moment of an individual's death, whether from lethal trauma or senescence, an overwhelming number of cells rupture and release their toxic load, the pituitary gland secretes a massive "burst" of DECO, the purpose apparently being to hasten dying and induce mild narcolepsy to ease the process.

Turritopsis dohrnii

Turritopsis dohrnii, the dime-sized jellyfish with the bright red stomach thought to have originated in the Mediterranean Sea but now found in most temperate areas including the coastal waters of the Southeastern United States, has solved this problem and claimed for itself the mantle of biologic immortality.

When faced with starvation, trauma—short of total oblitera-tion—or simple senescence, this small invertebrate has the unique ability to affect a repair of all damaged tissue and emerge a healthy youthful version of itself. Most amazing is that the organism can perform this function a seemingly unlimited number of times. For this feat, I have given it the well-earned nickname of Immortal Red.

Transdifferentiation

Turritopsis does this by transdifferentiation, a process by which one mature cell type becomes a different mature cell type.

The closest mammalian equivalent is the pluripotent fetal

stem cell, which undergoes a one-time differentiation into a pre-programmed cell type, whereas the metaplasia perfected by the Turritopsis *allows any cell to immediately assume the genotype and phenotype of any adjacent dying cell.*

Mammalian Possibilities

The question becomes: Could a serum be made from the Turritopsis that would affect mammalian cells? While it is a fact that a jellyfish, even one as accomplished as Immortal Red, is many orders removed from an organism as complex as a mammal, it is also a fact that the basic building block of all life is the single cell. It is also true that the cell death described above is universal to all organisms. My research with amphibians, mice, and an accidental experiment with "man's best friend" suggests that there may well be mammalian applications of a jellyfish serum. With that in mind, I present my preliminary postulate of the mechanism of action.

The jellyfish serum enters the cell through the hyper-permeable membrane while at the same time inducing a similar hyper-permeable state in adjacent healthy cells regardless of cell type. The chromosomal material of the dying cell is absorbed into the healthy cell where, boosted by the effects of the serum, it becomes the dominant genetic material. This cloning continues until the organ, be it liver, muscle, bone, or skin, is fully repaired. These changes take place throughout the entire organism until every organ system is mature but flawless. At this point, aging begins again, and the process will not repeat itself until the organism again comes to the moment of demise.

This immediate activation of all traumatized and senescent cells results in the process moving to completion in several hours. Because there is some secondary attraction to healthy nerve cells, the patient will exhibit some initial motor seizures and a profound bradycardia as slow as three to four weak, but effective, beats per minute. These effects are transitory, the seizure activity lasting less than two to three minutes, and the bradycardia resolving in thirty minutes to an hour. Although the subject's outward appearance is that of full restoration to mature youthfulness in several hours, the actual recovery requires three to five days to be complete. The subject will experience periods of confusion for six to twelve hours and may sleep for up to twenty-four hours.

That which does not kill you makes you stronger or, Timing is everything

The jellyfish serum has a strong affinity for electrical activity. In an individual on the cusp of death, this results in the mild seizures and cardiac rhythm irregularities previously mentioned. In the absence of the DECO hormone, the seizures and cardiac effects are rapidly fatal.

Without DECO, the serum's stimulating effects that revive the senescent or traumatized cells tremendously overstimulate the healthy nerve cells resulting in violent seizures and cardiac dysrhythmias—and resulting in death (as observed in early primate trials and the ill-advised administration to the single human subject).

The way the DECO hormone interacts with the jellyfish extract to initiate the transdifferentiation cascade instead of a fatal response requires further research. Also of interest is the fact that the minimal data available on the Cape Fear Indians' "Spring Renewal" rituals suggest that there is something in the Yaupon Holly leaf that partially mimics the DECO hormone.

This synopsis is, of course, a dramatic oversimplification of the process. Discussion of the chemical reactions/interactions of DECO hormone, Turritopsis extract, and Yaupon lie beyond the scope of this simple monograph and are dealt with in detail in my research notes. My notes also document my observations to date.

"Open up ma'am." The voice was authoritative. "Virginia State Police."

Lucy stood on her bed and put her ear to the wall. She heard the door open and the sounds of excited, but unintelligible conversation. "Illegal activity . . . solicitation for money." And finally, " . . . under arrest and the right to remain silent." The door slammed shut, and the room was quiet. Lucy put the pizza box in the trash and placed the blue binder and the personal notes from her mother in her backpack. She kept the synopsis, her mother's journal, and a few other general explanation papers separate. Lucy clicked off the television, turned off the bedside lamp, and thought about the girl in the next room being carted away by the authorities. She did not judge her but thought about her own troubles and wondered what circumstances had driven the girl to that lifestyle. Her last thoughts before falling asleep were that the research notes had to be preserved but hidden. She knew just the spot.

101

ASSETS HAVE A FINITE SHELF LIFE

Thursday, 22 April 2004—11:58 p.m.
Basil's townhouse, Washington, D.C.

"The hearse is still idling in front of the funeral home." Marty still sounded edgy but had obviously come down considerably from his earlier cocaine-induced mania. "Maybe we should go in."

"Sit there and wait," Basil instructed. "Your job is to follow the casket, not the undertaker." Basil hung up, picked up the townhouse master-control unit, and punched a few buttons. Downstairs, all lights, except those blazing in the kitchen, were extinguished. It was the beginning of a sequence that would last until dawn. The system would periodically illuminate and extinguish selected lights to simulate some insomniac moving throughout the house. From time to time, the television or sound system would come on, the intermittent music or flickering screen light giving the illusion of activity. As the security system entered overnight mode, outside lights winked out, and myriad infrared cameras went from motion activation to permanent on. The eight well-placed cameras sent a real-time stream to a small room at Basil's McLean headquarters, where two men monitored the images until morning, when Basil returned the system to daytime mode.

Basil stretched out on the bed and tried to go back to sleep. He could only manage three to four hours on a good night. The older he got, the less he slept—not that he needed less. Awake by six, he was exhausted by noon and struggled to make it through the rest of the day. He could feel his body failing, his organ systems weakening one by one. He needed to get that journal and some answers soon.

The stress of the past few days hadn't helped. He couldn't shake the sense of loss he felt over Nick. "Just fear of change," he told himself. Nick was an asset, and assets have a finite shelf life. "A matter of adaptation."

Then there was Rita. She had denied monitoring his phone calls, but he knew she was lying. It didn't matter. She had been useful and would continue to be—until he closed the real-estate transaction, acquired the research journal, and made his way to Belarus. She had been an interesting distraction, filling long-forgotten needs. He knew she was increasingly disgusted by his physical limitations. For the last few nights, after their brief sojourns in bed, she had wanted to go back to her apartment rather than sleep in his guest room. But she would stay with him. Rita wanted what he had promised. She would never get it, of course. Rita would not be a part of his new world. He wondered if she ever suspected.

The ringing phone jolted him awake from the beginning moments of sleep. "Damn," Basil said angrily in the dark as he knocked the phone to the floor with his casted hand. He glanced at the digital bedside clock—3:47 a.m.

"What?" Basil yelled at the receiver as he retrieved it from the floor.

"I've been following the hearse for three hours. It's still raining and so foggy I can hardly see the taillights. We just turned north onto Route 301. How long do I keep following them?" Marty mumbled something unintelligible to his partner, Tanner.

"Until they stop, genius. And don't call me again until they do." Basil dragged the receiver across the nightstand several times before locating its cradle. "Shit."

Three hours to get to sleep and that idiot woke me to say he was still driving.

He had already decided that Marty, like Rita, would go when he reached Belarus. There were many ex-KGB guys who were more capable—and stable. Did Marty even have an inkling that his days were numbered? "Not that dumbass," Basil told himself.

The phone rang again. This time Basil turned on the light. "For Christ's sake, Schwartz. It's been five minutes. What's so important that—"

"They've stopped." Marty whispered to his partner. "Tanner, go stand next to the hearse."

"You're at a funeral home?"

"No." Marty's voice was a hiss. "In the parking lot of an abandoned restaurant. It's bat-shit creepy. There's a cement dinosaur with its fucking head broke off."

"Just go check the casket," Basil said. "And try not to kill anyone. Leave your phone on." Basil could hear muffled conversation, then the sound of a creaking hinge followed by what he assumed was the rattling of the casket's transport mechanism. More tapping and scraping followed.

"Shit!" Marty's shouted epithet was clearly audible.

"Marty." Basil tried to get his henchman's attention while struggling to hear the conversation with the undertaker. "Marty."

"It's empty, boss. He said he was just at the café to sign a death certificate."

"Then why did they take the casket inside, and where are they going now?"

There was more unintelligible conversation as Marty questioned the undertaker.

"He says the casket was on board for pick-up of cremated ashes in Richmond. He was confused and thought Whitefeather wanted the body transported to the crematorium."

"And why didn't that happen?"

"He says a hearse is on its way from Georgetown to pick up Caedwallan. He swears he's dead. Says he saw the body." The rapid speech indicated Marty was on edge again. "Sounds like bullshit to me. Should I—"

"No," Basil interrupted. "Just let them go. Get back to the café. Tell the other crews to resume canvassing for the girl. You and Tanner watch the café. Nobody in, nobody out. And that includes another hearse for Caedwallan."

Basil hung up the phone and looked at the clock—4:09. He may as well get dressed. There would be no sleep this night.

102

MATURITY AND YOUTH, SENTIENCE, AND INNOCENCE

Thursday, 22 April 2004—11:59 p.m.
Side alley, Tommie's Café, Asakan

Tommie took one last look down the alley and went inside. He touched Noki's shoulder as he passed and gestured for him to follow. Noki shadowed him through the kitchen. When they reached the sleeping room, he pointed to where Nick still lay on the cot.

"I don't understand." The boy stared at the lifeless body.

"Sit down." Tommie pulled two chairs close to the low bed. "I have something to tell you." Noki listened as Tommie revealed for the third time in as many days the secret he had kept from everyone but Joe for nearly three centuries.

From time to time, Tommie would pause. Each time, Noki would shake his head and say, "And then?"

Tommie completed his explanation and waited. The kid just wiped his eyes and stared at Nick's motionless body.

"You don't seem surprised," Tommie said.

"Joe said you were special," Noki said. "He didn't say how, just that I'd find out." He glanced at Nick and then at Tommie. "He's alive, isn't he?"

"Maybe."

"What do we need to do for him?"

"Nothing," Tommie said. "It's all taken care of."

"How long until…" A long, low moan interrupted him.

"It's starting." Tommie retrieved a stethoscope from his medic bag and listened to Nick's chest as his limbs began to rhythmically spasm and relax.

"What's happening?" Noki watched as the activity increased and Nick's mouth foamed. "Is that normal?"

"Tonic-clonic seizures. "I wouldn't call it normal," Tommie said. "But it's part of the process."

"Did you do this?" Noki stared at Tommie. "Will you do this?"

"I wasn't awake for it." Tommie watched Nick's seizures trail off and stop, "but people told me I did."

"There are people around who saw you do this?"

"Not anymore." Tommie placed the stethoscope on Nick's chest again and held up a finger to silence Noki. He looked at his watch for thirty seconds, counted twenty beats, and doubled it. He retrieved a blood-pressure cuff from the bag. He pumped the gauge to one hundred millimeters, then started a slow release. The tapping began at seventy and faded around thirty-six. "Heart rate of forty and blood pressure of seventy over thirty-six. He's stabilizing."

Nick's dusky blue color had given way to a pale white.

"Is he going to be alright?"

"Should be, this is uncharted territory, and this serum is three hundred years old."

"And so, are you?" Noki stared at his adopted uncle.

"Actually, two hundred ninety-three." Tommie stood up and headed for the kitchen. Noki followed. Tommie opened the refrigerator, retrieved a bottle of beer, and reached for a soda for Noki.

"Can you tell me what's going on with him?"

Tommie handed Noki the soda, and the pair returned to Nick's side. "Some time ago," Tommie paused, "a long time ago—I went to college and then grad school to learn as much as I could about what was happening to me."

"Were you . . . are you a PhD?"

"Another story, another time." Tommie took a sip of beer. "We didn't have the expertise or equipment then that we have now, but I learned as much as I could about jellyfish, genetics, and aging."

Tommie looked at Noki's broad smile and suspected he was trying to wrap his head around the concept of him as Dr. Whitefeather.

"Special," Noki muttered and fell silent.

Tommie watched Nick's color continue to improve. "Take his pulse and blood pressure like I taught you in survival school." He handed the stethoscope and cuff to Noki.

"Fifty and eighty-over-forty," Noki said. "What's happening to him?"

"I'll tell you what I know based upon my own experience and now-outdated education," Tommie said. "At this point, all of Nick's DNA is essentially unlocked. His cells, somehow aided by the Shaman's jellyfish serum, are repairing the wear and tear of age, trauma, and disease."

Tommie explained how Nick would be comatose for the next four to six hours, during which time his wounds would completely disappear and all his organ systems: skin, cardiovascular . . . even his diseased lungs will revert to a mature but biologically perfect state.

Tommie took a breath and looked at Noki before continuing. "The brain and nervous system will be the next target, followed by his senses—vision, hearing, taste, smell, and touch. While the external changes will be the most visible, the changes in his brain will be even more impressive."

"Will he still be Nick?" Noki asked. "I mean his memories. Will he still have his memories?"

"I don't know how to explain it other than to say that what remains will be the best of Nick." Tommie then explained that while Nick has been unconscious, his brain has been undergoing a complete "house-cleaning," not just a rejuvenation. The process was one of changing only what must be changed to affect a healthy mental state. "The brain," Tommie explained, "has the inherent capacity to differentiate good from bad, that is, benign memories from those that are harmful. Memories of past actions that may cause distress are ameliorated. They are retained, but like witnessed events rather than personal experiences. They become information to be evaluated without guilt or remorse."

Noki opened his mouth to speak, then closed it, nodding for Tommie to continue.

"Over the next four to six hours, Nick will revert to an age of approximately thirty years old, the perfect blend of maturity and youth, sentience and innocence. Although his intellect will be preserved, he will wake up confused from an amnesia that will clear over the next twenty-four hours or so, depending on received stimuli. When the process is completed, all body functions will be normal, and Nick will age as before. The difference is that senescence, life-threatening trauma, or starvation will again set in motion the forces of rejuvenation."

"You mean he can't die?" Noki asked.

"No. Nick has not become indestructible," Tommie said. "But short of trauma sufficient to kill instantly, he is, well, immortal."

Noki stood and walked around the cot, examining Nick from every angle. In the nearly four hours since receiving the serum, his appearance had changed. The physical signs of his attack had disappeared. But there was something else.

"He looks younger," Noki said, his brow furrowed. "A lot younger. Is that going to happen to you?"

"Everything will be okay," Tommie told Noki. "I need you and Henry to stay with Dan while I get things sorted out."

"But I could help."

"Don't fight me on this. It will be all right."

"And then you'll tell me the rest of the stories?"

"It's a deal." Tommie went to the phone and dialed Dan's number.

Nick moaned again and began to mumble.

103

YOU ARE HALAL

Friday, 23 April 2004—4:14 am
Sleeping room, Tommie's Café
Asakan, North Carolina

Nick's first conscious sensation after Marty's attack was the perception of white-hot pain from his knees to his chest. He was vaguely aware of conversation:

"So, we have to let him die . . . Yes, that's exactly what we have to do."

"No," Nick wanted to tell them. "I'm not finished yet." He could sense Tommie struggling with a decision. "Do it," he thought as hard he could. Even though his eyes were closed, Nick could feel a cold darkness pressing in around him. He was dying. "I'm sorry, Lucy."

"Sorry, Buddy." Tommie's voice seemed far away.

Nick felt the cold creeping in and struggled to focus on the small point of light just visible in the distance.

"You can always jump off a building . . . just make sure it's a tall one." The point of light grew brighter. A pleasant burn started in his chest and spread throughout his body, replacing the cold. The conversation stopped. Nick was aware only of himself. He could feel his body changing. Nick had a qualitative but not quantitative sensation of the passing of time. He was aware that something was happening. Fear crept in until he heard a calm, familiar voice describing how the metamorphosis would unfold. Like a patient teacher, this narrator explained that he, himself, had experienced this transformation many times.

"While the exact mechanics are beyond my understanding," the narrator explained, "the effects were empiric, and as such, describable." The soothing voice grew distant, a pleasant white noise. The point of light grew brighter and closer. A figure silhouetted against the brightness moved toward him. As the figure closed, he could sense more than see who it was.

"Kasra?"

"*Doostam.*" Kasra stopped at what seemed like inches away. "You have made it. The good Nick has won. You are *Halal.*"

"It's all right, Nicholas," another familiar voice reassured him.

"Sister Hildegard." Nick could see her habited silhouette standing next to Kasra.

"You're where you're supposed to be. Now you can do the right thing."

The light dimmed, and the silhouettes faded.

"No." Nick tried to motion them back.

The narrator's voice began again. "Short of trauma sufficient to kill instantly . . . he is immortal."

"Tommie." Nick recognized the voice as he drifted off again.

104

NO WAY . . . THAT GUY'S HALF NICK'S AGE

Friday, 23 April 2004—8:14 p.m.
Dining room, Tommie's Café, Asakan

"When can we talk to him?" Noki said, staring at Nick.

"Another hour or so." Tommie racked the slide on his P10, checked the safety, and tucked it into his waistband at the small of his back. "He can understand you now, but speech is one of the last things to return."

Nick had been awake for about three hours. Although his level of alertness seemed to be increasing, he had not spoken. Tommie had removed Nick's bloody and torn clothing. Noki had rummaged through the dresser in the sleeping room and found a white T-shirt and pair of khaki chinos.

"He looks like any other dopey twenty-something," Noki said. He glanced at Nick, who seemed content to sit on the chair and sip water from the glass Tommie had put in his hand.

"Thirty-something." Tommie gave Nick another glass of water. "He looks thirty-something."

After the third glass of water, Tommie led Nick to the toilet. He brought him back with a wet patch from his groin to his knee.

"He's on a steep learning curve," Tommie said when he saw Noki staring at Nick's pants. "He just needs a little time to reboot."

"Yeah, well, I hope his processor's waterproof."

"Sit down, Nick." Tommie guided him to the chair. Nick sat down, picked up the glass of water, and took another sip. Tommie took the glass of water from Nick and turned to Noki.

"This is what we're going to do. You will hide in the attic until Dan arrives. The only access is in the ceiling of the utility closet in the women's restroom. Once you're in the attic, I'll replace the access door and stack boxes on the shelf below to hide the opening. When Dan arrives, he'll remove the boxes and let you out. You must not move until you hear Dan call your name."

Tommie picked up a box of snack crackers and a bottle of water for Noki to take with him.

"I could help you babysit." Noki watched Nick pat his pockets and chest as if looking for something.

"This is settled territory. He won't need a babysitter much longer. Will you, Nick?"

Tommie tossed a bottle of water toward Nick, who raised his right hand and caught the bottle. Nick smiled, struggled with the cap for a moment, then took a sip.

"There's something about the process that makes you thirsty," Tommie said. He picked up another bottle of water. "Let's get you tucked in."

Nick trailed after them, bottle in hand, as they made their way to the restroom. There, Nick watched Tommie button Noki into the attic.

"Okay." Tommie checked his watch, "it's nine-fifteen and as dark as it's going to get. There's a bit of a moon, but we'll make the best of it."

Nick didn't speak, but something in the set of his jaw told Tommie Nick's level of comprehension had increased. In any event, they were running out of time and had to go for it.

"This is going to be dangerous," Tommie said. "You hang back in the kitchen until I see if Schwartz is out there."

The frown on Nick's face made it clear that he recognized the name.

Tommie considered giving Nick his gun but decided he was as likely to shoot himself as anyone else.

Nick followed Tommie to the kitchen but hung back as directed.

Tommie picked up his knapsack, opened the door, and stepped into the alley. The rain had stopped. A full moon darted in and out of the fast-moving clouds as the front moved offshore.

"That's far enough, Cochise. Drop the bag." Marty and his partner, guns in hand, stepped into the small circle of light emitted by the bare bulb over the kitchen door. Tommie moved to a position between the pair and Nick. "Where have you stashed Caedwallan?"

"He's died." Tommie used his right arm to push Nick back into the shadows. He stepped back and gave a head jerk toward the door. "See for yourselves. He's in the sleeping room behind the kitchen."

"Lead the way."

Tommie held Marty's gaze and slid his hand toward the pistol in his belt.

"Gun!" Marty's partner shouted.

Marty smacked the side of Tommie's head with his pistol, knocking him to the ground.

"Stay down." Marty stomped hard across Tommie's back, pinning him to the alley tarmac. "You, Tonto." He pointed the gun at Nick. "Step into the light so I can see you."

Nick stepped into the dim glow of the overhead fixture. A car turned into the alley, its high beams magnified by the wet pavement. Tommie craned his neck and saw Marty and his partner raise their forearms to shield their eyes.

"Find out who that is, Tanner." Marty turned to face Nick. Tommie watched Marty's expression transition from thin-lipped grin to slack-jawed recognition. "Caedwallan."

The car door swung open. The driver crouched behind in a shooter's stance, the barrel of his rifle visible through the open window. A near-continuous muzzle flash and the unmistakable sound of an AK-47 firing over their heads brought Marty and his partner to kneeling positions. Marty ground his knee into Tommie's back. Nick dashed past the pair. Tanner fired.

"Got him." Tanner drew a bead for a second shot. "This one should do it."

"Stop." Marty jumped to his feet and pushed Tanner's arms upward, causing his shot to go wild. "That's Caedwallan, you idiot."

"No way." Tanner raised his weapon again. "That guy's half Nick's age."

Tommie saw his opportunity when another burst of automatic-weapon fire distracted the pair. He reached for the P-10. His right hand closed around the grip. He flipped off the safety as he brought the weapon from behind his back and started to rise.

His movement caught Marty's attention. "Fucking blanket-ass," Tommie heard his intended target shout just before Marty's roach kicker struck him in the temple and everything went black.

105

JUST PUT THEM ON A PIECE OF RUSTY SHEET METAL

Friday, 23 April 2004—9:03 p.m.
Chez Marseille Restaurant, Washington, D.C.

Basil hated Chez Marseille. The decorative white metal chairs were hard on the ass, and the silver-dollar-sized, glass-top tables were so close together that private conversation was impossible. This did not, however, deter the owner from charging forty-five dollars for five steamed barnacles, which he referred to as *Percebes* for purposes of price enhancement. Rita had ordered without consulting Basil. Two plates arrived accompanied by a teaspoon of cold mashed potatoes that sprouted sprigs of parsley and julienned carrots. A miniature baguette and a dish of olive oil rounded out this culinary disaster. Basil watched Rita peel the brown leathery skin, grasp the walnut-sized crustacean's dinosaur-like foot, and plop the ugly dollop of pink-gray flesh into her mouth.

Basil was contemplating the *chutzpah* needed to charge ten dollars apiece for something scraped off the side of a derelict boat when his phone buzzed. He pulled it from his pocket and glanced at the caller ID:

Schwartz/Urgent

The surrounding patrons glared at him before returning to their conversations.

"Yes?" Basil glanced at the elbow-to-elbow diners and hoped Marty would give his report with a minimum of prompting.

"Caedwallan's alive," Marty said. "And—"

"As I suspected. And his physical condition?" Basil asked. "You said he was dead."

"Nick?" Rita said, her tone far too enthusiastic for Basil's liking.

Basil held up a finger to silence her. Her stone-faced look of contempt was something Basil had not seen before. The thought was lost as Marty continued.

"That's what I'm trying to tell you." Marty tripped over his words as he described Nick's appearance.

"Jesus Christ!" At Basil's shouted ejaculation, the hum of conversation ceased, and a half dozen diners stared. "Was it a heart attack?" he added, trying to tone it down. The patrons nodded their artificial concern and returned to their private chatter.

"Heart attack?" Marty seemed confused but continued. He told Basil about the shooting and how he had tracked Nick to an area of marsh near the ocean known as the Strand. He had lost him there, but the crew was conducting a close-walk search of the area.

"You said someone fired at you with an automatic weapon?"

"Yeah," Marty casually replied. "Maybe a deputy."

"Small-town deputies don't generally use automatic weapons." A thought formed, but Basil dismissed it. He put his head down, cupped the phone in his hand, and whispered. "Shoot to wound if you have to. But, Marty . . ."

"Yes?"

"I want him alive."

"*Garçon.*" Basil summoned the waiter to his table. "An emergency has spared me the trauma of eating these."

"*Et donc?*" The waiter pointed to the crustaceans on Basil's plate.

"Why don't you just put them on a piece of rusty sheet metal, so they'll feel at home."

106

10-66 ON THAT SUSPECT

Friday, 23 April 2004—9:45 p.m.
Side alley, Tommie's Café, Asakan

"Whitefeather." The voice was a faint whisper in a roar of noise. "Tommie Whitefeather."

Tommie shook his head and was immediately rewarded with crushing pain.

"He's coming around." Tommie recognized the voice of Sheriff Doug Watkins, one of his closest friends. He was speaking to someone. "How many fingers do you see?"

Tommie opened his eyes. Watkins and Dan moved in and out of focus above him.

"Where's—?" Dan said.

"Later." Tommie cut him off. He touched the side of his head. It was warm and sticky. He tried to sit up.

"Easy." Watkins eased him back into a supine position. "What the hell happened here?"

"Robbery." Tommie shook off the sheriff's hand and sat up.

"Robbery?" Watkins shook his head. "And that's the perp?" His chin jerked toward a figure lying at the outermost reaches of the porch light's glow.

The body lay splayed in a rather sizable pool of congealing blood. Tommie took in the Bruno Magli shoes, beige linen slacks, yellow polo shirt, and shaved head. It was the man Marty had called Tanner. He was relieved that it wasn't Nick but disappointed that it wasn't Marty.

"I suppose." Tommie stared at the corpse. "It was dark." Tanner's hand still gripped his pistol; his sightless right eye still in search of a target. The left side of his head was mostly gone.

"He was alone?" Watkins asked, still looking at the body.

Tommie nodded.

"And you shot him with this?" He turned to study Tommie and the P-10.

"Yes." Tommie knew he was stepping in it but had nowhere else to go.

"Excellent." Watkins hit the magazine release and caught the clip as it fell. "So that leaves a couple of issues." He glanced at the body and made a show of tilting his head. "From this angle, he looks a lot like one of those guys staying in your motel."

"Can I have that?" Tommie reached for his sidearm.

"Your clip is still full." Watkins ignored the request but popped the magazine back in the weapon. "This guy was shot three times with a high-power round; the other end of the alley is littered with 7.62 shell casings. So, if you killed him," Watkins started to ask as he jerked his head toward Tanner, "who clocked you in the head?"

"Sheriff," the patrol car's radio blared. Watkins reached in the window and grabbed the mic.

"Yeah?"

"Report of possible gunfire out on the Strand." The dispatcher's voice sounded bored.

"Don't suppose you'd know anything about that." Watkins stared at Tommie.

"We go back a long way Doug . . ." Tommie said.

"This wouldn't have anything to do with Lucy, would it?"

"I need two hours."

Watkins keyed the mic. "Probably just those Packett kids blowin' up coffee cans again. I'll check it out."

"What's up with you?" the dispatcher said.

"10-53A with a 10-72." The sheriff gave the code for a robbery with shooting.

"Are you requesting a squad?" The dispatcher was no longer bored.

"Negative." The sheriff glanced at Dan, who stood over the body. "10-66 on that suspect. Send transport."

"Roger that. Out."

"You sure you got this?" Watkins handed Tommie his gun.

"Yeah." Tommie stuck the gun in his waistband and rose to his feet.

"You better say a few words to Dan," Watkins said.

Tommie walked over to Tanner's body, stepping around the ooze.

"Dan," he said.

"What the hell, Tommie?" Dan looked stunned.

Tommie pulled Dan away. He retrieved his knapsack, and the two walked to Tommie's truck. "Noki's still in the attic. Take him out the front way so he doesn't see this. I'll call when I can." Tommie got into the truck and started the engine.

Dan nodded. "What the hell," he said again.

107

THAT QUICK

Friday, 23 April 2004—11:09 p.m.
The Strand near Beach Road, two miles east of Town Center
Asakan, North Carolina

Searcher moved through the knee-to-chest-high brush and vines grow-ing in the area the locals referred to as "the Strand." He had grown up on the strip in Myrtle Beach, South Carolina, where the word meant something altogether different. Marty Schwartz had placed his team members at roughly one-hundred-foot intervals in a line stretching from the narrow beach road across the marsh to the slim strip of sand between the scrub and the ocean. Where the line neared the elevated roadway, it hooked forward, allowing the landward players to survey the road and lessen the chance of their wounded quarry darting across and into the near-limitless pine forest beyond.

Searcher was lucky—he was number two in the hook, just forty yards behind the point man. He and Point walked mostly on the high ground next to the road. The passing front and the shifting wind had brought a fresh ocean breeze, which helped with the biting insects. Vis-ibility improved as the moon sailed in and out of the thinning clouds. The occasional flashes and dark sky in the west signaled the approach of round two.

Searcher's line meant trudging through ankle-deep sand and chest-high sea-oats, maneuvering around the scattered Yaupon bushes, and tripping over the clumps of hair grass that populated the area, but it beat the hell out of being down in the soggy salt marsh.

There would be no such relief for the ten searchers slogging through the area known as the bowl. The bowl was salt marsh—a sunken mass of Virginia Creeper, poisonous snakes, knee-deep salt-water ponds, and sand that tried to suck the boots from your feet. There was no breeze, and the sandflies, undeterred by insect repellant, were voracious.

The land sloped gently next to the road, falling little more than four feet for the first thirty yards. From there it fell rapidly, dropping ten feet in a little more than ten yards. It remained that way until it was about fifty feet from the ocean where it again jinked upward to meet the thirty-foot-wide beach that formed the Strand. The effect was a four-mile-long, thousand-foot-wide, elongated football-shaped bowl that paralleled the beach road until reaching the southern tip of the football where the land sloped gradually upward. It was there that Marty Schwartz would be waiting with his SUV to take the prey. That was also where the road made a near ninety-degree turn inland and disappeared into the pine forest. If they hadn't found their quarry by the time they beat their way to that turn, the object of their search would be in the wind, and Basil Orlov would have their asses.

Their prey, they were told, had been wounded, possibly twice. Each man carried an H&K MP-5 with a tool-less release silencer. On the rail of each weapon was high-powered krypton light, allowing them to see at least shapes and motion out to sixty yards. They didn't know who they were tracking, but it was someone important. Their instructions were clear. No shots above the knee—shoot to disable, not to kill. This meant that shot placement was critical. To this end, the three-thirty round mags each man carried were loaded with eighty-five-grain full copper jacket, round-nose bullets. The low grain-load made for a subsonic round that dissipated a significant portion of its energy at sixty yards. The round nose would create a slightly smaller wound cavity, possibly passing through the limb without tumbling. The full metal jacket would limit fragmentation, also diminishing tissue damage.

They were to swing their high-powered flashlights in forty-five-degree, barely intersecting arcs, while constantly moving forward. Every three to five minutes, they were to fire a round into the sand where the light met the darkness. The muffled pop of the silencer and clicking of the bolt would have the effect of driving their quarry toward Marty's funnel. If a round should find its mark in the darkness, all the better. They would deliver the immobilized package to Schwartz, and then it would be Miller Time.

The beam of Searcher's light caught Point just as he completed the landward sweep of his arc. Point's hand shot up. He gestured toward the beach road and killed his light. Searcher did the same. Two slow-moving vehicles made their way south along the narrow tarmac. The pale-yellow headlights of the lead vehicle did little to illuminate the road, while the lights of the trailing vehicle, although misaligned, were of normal brightness. He observed to see if either vehicle stopped, perhaps to assist a wounded man. The lead vehicle slowed, and the trailing vehicle closed to three car lengths but did not stop. As they passed his position, the taillights of the slow vehicle were two scarcely visible red-pink dots in the darkness. Searcher heard a slight exhaust note as the trailing car overhauled the slower vehicle. He followed the bright taillights of the new lead vehicle to the turn. When the driver applied his brakes for the turn, the bright red light flooded Searcher's vision.

"Shit," he cursed his carelessness. His night vision compromised, he searched for the glowworm taillights of the slower vehicle. Nothing. "Shit," he said again. Had the second vehicle made the turn too or did they stop? He looked toward Point. His fellow searcher turned to face him and shrugged, then gestured that they move closer to the road. Searcher set up about forty yards behind Point, and they angled toward the road. They had been moving forward for about ten minutes when Point's hand shot up again, signaling him to stop. Point disappeared into the brush along the road. Searcher heard a starter cranking.

"Over there, a jeep, or something." Point's voice sounded like he was running.

Searcher slipped on one tactical glove and removed the tool-less silencer. He slipped it into the side pocket of his cargo pants and ran toward the sound. He cleared the brush and entered the road about forty yards behind where Point was leaning through the window of an old four-wheel-drive vehicle. There were two loud pops and Point slumped to the ground. Searcher raised his H&K to firing position. The bright, halogen beam illuminated the scene. A figure in camo pants and brown T-shirt, hand raised, stood by the road.

"No, it can't be." Searcher rubbed his right eye and re-aimed. By the time he fired, the man, rifle in hand, had disappeared in front of the SUV. His shot hit the vehicle's metal top. The vehicle started to move forward. He squeezed off one more ineffective round as the man dashed into the woods. By now the SUV was several hundred yards away and nearing the turn. Several other searchers joined him in the road, firing at the departing vehicle, which rounded the turn and disappeared into the woods. Searcher ran to where Point had fallen. A quick pulse check told him what he already knew. Just last night they had been drinking beer and chatting up girls. "That quick," he said, stripping off his T-shirt and covering Point's head. He walked to where he'd first seen the shooter and picked up a shell-casing. He ran his fingers over the distinctive markings on the hand-reloaded casing and dropped the shell in his pocket. He glanced at the turn and then at the spot where the shooter had vanished into the woods.

The vehicle was unfamiliar, but there was no question who had run into the woods.

108

RC COLA AND A MOON PIE—AGAIN

Friday, 23 April 2004—11:31 p.m.
Roadside pull-off, rural Asakan, North Carolina

Lucy's heart pounded in her chest. Her hands shook. She was euphoric, riding an adrenaline high. She had cheated death and escaped the bad guys in a hail of gunfire. "Wait—" She looked at the shattered mirror and remembering the rounds striking the rear of the Rover. Lucy guided the Rover to the side of the road and killed the lights but left the engine running. She set the emergency brake and leaned over the seat to check on her passenger who was curled up in a ball near the load gate.

"Hey . . ." Lucy shook her head as she considered what to call him. "You there in the back seat." The figure remained motionless and silent.

She grabbed her flashlight, opened the door, and scanned the darkness. There were no headlights, nor would she expect any on this road. Lucy opened the rear cargo door and braced herself against the now-snoring passenger to keep him from rolling onto the pavement. She repositioned him and pointed her flashlight at his gunshot wound. The injured site was nothing more than a red circle.

Was I imagining his wound?

She looked at the copious blood drying on his clothing.

I didn't imagine that.

She pushed him toward the front of the load space and tucked a blanket around his shoulders.

He moaned, but his eyes remained closed.

As the thrill of the escape faded, Lucy's euphoria turned to anxiety. There was no way she was going to leave an unconscious man on the doorstep of a closed service station. If the people hunting him were willing to put a small army in that marsh to look for him, chances are they would find him at the service station before anyone else did. And if the Saab thief from the coffee shop was in the area, that could only mean one thing. She could be on the menu as well. "I'll bring him to the farm." Lucy closed the load door and checked the latch. "Tommie will know what to do."

One last stop before the farm.

Lucy retrieved the knapsack containing the blue binder and the papers she had separated from the manila envelope from the passenger footwell. She peered over her shoulder at the road. It remained dark, but she couldn't shake the feeling that she was being followed.

She released the brake, turned on the headlights, and pulled onto the tarmac.

Not far up the road, Lucy pulled the Rover into the trees just off the short stub of an abandoned driveway near Tommie's cave and doused the lights. This time she silenced the motor and listened. A glance over the seat assured her that her passenger was still out. "Feel free to leave while I'm gone." She grabbed the knapsack and made her way to the cave.

Returning to the Rover, she pushed on to her primitive driveway where the moon glistened on the familiar rain-filled potholes. She swiped her eyes as she realized this might be the last time she would see the farm. The house lights were off, but Tommie's truck was parked next to the back door. The snoring figure in the load area stirred and mumbled when she parked and turned off the ignition. Lucy jumped from the truck and hurried toward the front porch.

Tommie appeared at the door, holding two cups of coffee.

"You made it." He handed her a cup.

"Barely," Lucy said. She hadn't noticed how much she was shaking until she took the cup. "I hit a man with the Rover—out on the Strand, by the marsh. I put him in the back."

"Did you—is he dead?"

"No, but he should be," Lucy said, following Tommie. "He flew across my hood and bounced off the windshield. There was blood everywhere." She cradled the cup in both hands. "I thought I saw gunshot wounds, but then—. She stammered as the words tumbled out. "I would have been shot if not for the car thief from the coffee shop."

"What? Car thief?" Tommie kept walking. "Someone shot at you?"

"I was just incidental fodder; they were shooting at him." Lucy paused. "I don't understand. He had wounds. I put Bloodstopper on his wounds."

Tommie paused and took Lucy by the shoulders. "They? You're not making any sense. Focus."

"There was a small army out there—sweeping with flashlights and firing silenced weapons. It looked like he had been shot—twice." Lucy described the gaping wounds, pumping, and large enough to admit her finger. "When I went to use the Bloodstopper, the wounds were just—gone."

Tommie released her shoulders, set his mug on the porch railing, and sprinted to the rear of the Rover.

Lucy followed, standing back as Tommie threw open the cargo door.

Her passenger was awake and sitting up. "Tommie," he said, half-smiling.

"You know him?" Lucy thought she knew most of Tommie's friends. She didn't recognize this guy, but there was something familiar about his lop-sided smile.

"Yes, and so do you." Tommie helped the man pivot so that, although he remained seated, his feet touched the ground.

A crunch of gravel caught Lucy's attention. "Are you expecting someone?" Lucy asked as a car, headlights extinguished, made its way down the driveway, stopping less than twenty feet from them. The driver held his empty hands out the open window.

"Don't move." Tommie pulled his pistol from his belt. He and Lucy approached the car.

"Empty hands." The driver wiggled his fingers. "No threat."

"Get out slow." Tommie motioned with his pistol.

The driver opened the door using the outside latch. He stepped out, keeping his hands above his head.

"You." Lucy recognized the close-cropped gray-blonde hair, camo pants, and brown T-shirt immediately. "How did you find me?"

"I gifted you with a bug at the coffee shop," the man with no name said, staring at something behind Lucy.

Lucy heard the Rover creak behind her. She glanced back to see her passenger stand and take tentative steps toward them. She turned to look at coffee-shop man.

"Vasily," the voice behind her said.

"Nick?" The man in camo squinted through the darkness. "What the hell?"

"Nick?" Lucy echoed as she whirled to face her passenger. "My . . . ?" Lucy remembered Rita's note. "I mean, Nick who helped me with my overheating radiator?" She looked from Nick to Tommie. "Did he? Did you?" Lucy stammered as a dozen questions competed to get out. She took a step closer to Nick and placed her face inches from his, then jerked back. "Oh, my God! It is you, isn't it?"

"Of course, it's me," Nick said. "RC Cola and a Moon Pie—again."

Vasily stepped closer to examine Nick's face. "Yeah, it's you, but have you looked in a mirror?"

"I don't need a mirror," Nick said, covering his mouth with his hand and forcing a cough. He examined his bloodless palm and looked at Tommie. "Did you do this?

Tommie stared at the three questioning faces. "Let's take this inside."

PART FIVE

LIVE LET DIE

109

OUR DEAD ARE NEVER REALLY DEAD . . .

Saturday, 24 April 2004—12:05 a.m.
Kiffin Field, forty miles northwest of Asakan

"Touchdown in twelve minutes, Mr. Orlov." The turn, like the pilot's voice, was buttery smooth, the Gulfstream II's transition from crosswind to final approach marked only by the changing angle of the amber-tinged liquid in Basil's lowball glass. A double click on the pilot's mic triggered the runway lights that illuminated the concrete landing strip.

The numbers 21 and 30 adorned opposite ends of the garish slash of light in the otherwise black twenty-seven-hundred-acre preserve. The engines warbled as the pilot adjusted the throttle to compensate for the windy remnants of the previous evening's storm. The field, over an hour's drive from Asakan, was the only secure facility with a strip long enough to accommodate Basil's jet. The plane could be set down in as little as thirty-two hundred feet, but tomorrow, the fully fueled jet would require a fifty-seven-hundred-foot rollout for its final departure from the United States.

The first leg of the trip would be a thirty-one-hundred-mile pull to Reykjavik, where the plane would refuel. This would be followed by an eighteen-hundred-mile jump to a military airbase near Babruysk,

Belarus, where the local authorities would welcome Basil with open arms.

Basil stared at Rita's sleeping form, watching the rhythmic rise and fall of her chest. There was no denying her beauty and intelligence. She had been an asset. But even the best asset had a finite lifespan. He held the encrypted sat phone to his ear and listened as Marty Schwartz attempted to excuse the evening's string of failures.

"I interrogated one of the search crew." Marty droned on. "He thought he saw Vasily."

It was circumstantial, but Basil knew it meant Konovalov was here.

Basil drained the last of his eighteen-year-old Jameson and rattled the melting cubes.

"You assured me that Konovalov had run scared to South America." Basil felt the soft thump of the landing gear locking into place. "My sources tell me that your partner, Tanner, was killed in your clown show at Whitefeather's Café."

"Yes, sir," Marty said. "I…"

"That was probably Konovalov's handiwork as well." Basil waited for a response. When there was none, he continued. "What else have you screwed up? Is Bel Castro going to show up, too?"

"No, sir," Marty said. "I know he's dead."

"Just like you knew Konovalov was out of the picture. I will be on the ground shortly, and you better have some answers."

Basil disconnected and stared out the window where the flashes of lightning outlining distant clouds warned of another approaching storm.

"Schwartz." Basil shook his head.

"He's one of a kind!" Rita awakened, rubbed her eyes, and reached for Basil's empty glass.

"I'll get it." Basil stood and crossed to the bar. There was another bump, and the sound of disturbed air rushed over the now quartered flaps. The abrupt decrease in speed caused him to pitch forward. He instinctively tried to steady himself with his fractured right hand and was rewarded with a shot of pain. He cursed softly, then smiled at the thought that in a few hours his aches and pains would be a thing of the past.

"Forget about that idiot." He dropped to his seat. "Tomorrow at this time, we will be on our way to Belarus and a new life." The hydraulics whined as the pilot went to half-flaps. "And I do mean new."

The Gulfstream shuddered and bounced as it slowed and descended into the ground turbulence. Lightning outlined the storm clouds on the starboard side.

"And no Marty."

The sat phone rang just as Rita was about to speak.

The ID revealed it was one of Basil's Agency contacts. He held up one finger and mouthed, "Wait."

The North Carolina humidity was overcoming the Gulfstream's air conditioning as they descended. The plane slowed for landing, and the air rushing over the fully extended flaps became a roar. Basil cursed his failing hearing and put a finger over his open ear.

"Make it fast."

"Konovalov cleared security," said the voice on the other end, "but never got on the plane. He went back to the Avian Aerovias ticket counter and kept his ticket open to avoid suspicion." Basil's contact explained that a Canadian businessman matching Vasily's general description had rented a car that night, refused a GPS unit, but asked for a North Carolina map. A check with RCMP Security, the Canadian version of the FBI, revealed that the passport used for ID at the car-rental desk was still valid. However, a quick online search revealed that the subject had died in 2003."

"So, Vasily's in-country, and we're twisting in the breeze?" Basil said.

A loud thump and the chirping of tires announced the landing.

"Maybe not." The voice sounded hopeful. "I'm checking on one more thing. I should have a call-back from the rental company's purchasing department momentarily." The contact did not elaborate. "I'll call you."

"The airstairs are down, sir," the pilot said, placing a hand on Basil's shoulder. An attendant opened the cabin door and Basil stepped through to the near one-hundred-percent humidity. Sweat beaded on his forehead, his vision clouded and blackened at the edges.

He looked down the stairway where two men stood waiting. One was Marty. The other was a thin man with sandy hair who appeared vaguely familiar.

"Nick." Basil's knees buckled. His vision cleared, and he realized that the young man wasn't Nick. He was Jason Stearns, the liaison from Carson Enterprises.

"I don't give a damn who you have to wake up," Marty yelled, making sure Basil heard his rant. "Mr. Orlov wants to know if Vasily Konovalov is in-country or not."

A somewhat bedraggled Marty stood a few feet behind the per-fectly groomed Stearns, who held at parade rest as he waited for Basil to step onto the pavement. Stearns was doing his best to ignore Marty, who waved one arm in the air while swearing into his cellphone.

Basil had been to Kiffin Field the year before with Nick, when they had been helping the House of Saud deal with an errant prince whose decadent lifestyle had placed him at odds with his elders. That conflict had been solved when the prince's Maserati, side-swiped by a hit-and-run vehicle, crashed through a section of "defective" guardrail in the Alps and plunged eleven hundred feet.

"Mr. Orlov." Stearns stepped forward to meet Basil, leaving Marty to continue his loud cellphone conversation several feet back on the tarmac. "Mr. Carson sends his warmest regards. He also thought that you might need my assistance." Stearns gave a nearly imperceptible head tilt toward the source of the noisy conversation.

"That's very thoughtful, Stearns," Basil said, "but I can take it from here."

Marty snapped his phone shut and stepped in front of Stearns.

Basil's phone rang. "Okay," he said, listening to the caller's brief message. "Excellent." Basil pushed past and addressed Jason Stearns. "I will need a helicopter on standby immediately."

"Yes, sir." Stearns showed no emotion.

"And a car waiting when we reach our destination," Basil said.

"And the destination?" Stearns produced a pad and pen.

"To be determined en route. It's a bit of a logistical challenge."

"We can handle it." Stearns remained stoic.

Basil continued to pepper Stearns with requests as they walked along a row of six meticulously maintained C-141 Starlifters on loan from Military Air Command. On paper, MAC had already decommissioned these transports and sent them to the Boneyard, the aircraft graveyard in the dry Arizona desert. In actuality, these still-serviceable, sixty-thousand-pound capacity workhorses formed the backbone of Carson Enterprise's Middle East operations.

"A sleeping room, meals for my pilots, and the Gulfstream serviced and fueled for an afternoon departure." Basil continued. "Can you make it happen?"

"At once, sir." Stearns shot Marty an almost imperceptible smirk, turned on his heel, and trotted toward the terminal's small command post.

"Why can't you do that, Schwartz?" Basil asked rhetorically before turning to Rita. "Coffee?" He offered Rita his arm, as much for his own support as chivalry.

Rita nodded. Her eyes were on a nameplate by one of the planes: Kiffin Rockwell.

"Weird first name," she said.

"Caedwallan idolized the guy," Basil said.

The last time they were here, Caedwallan, ever the historian, had insisted on giving Basil a dissertation on the history of the airfield: Rockwell, a North Carolina boy, held several distinctions in the War to End All Wars. He was the first American to see service in France, the first to be added to the American Escadrille (soon renamed the Lafayette Escadrille to reinforce America's neutrality), and the first American pilot to shoot down a German aircraft. On 23 September 1916, he established another less-fortunate distinction when he became the second American pilot to die in combat when a German bullet pierced his heart. This won him the Croix de Guerre, burial with full military honors, and an airfield named in his honor.

The base was neglected until 1939 when the Army Corps of Engineers lengthened the runway to its present seventy-two-hundred feet to train bomber pilots. The facility, little-used post–World War II, was abandoned as derelict by the U.S. Air Force in 1977. With a generous contribution from the agency's black-ops funding, Carson added ten inches of reinforced concrete to the runway, fenced the perimeter, and established one of the most sophisticated paramilitary training and staging centers in the world.

It wasn't really Basil's area of interest, but Nick had been on fire with it, and that was a little contagious. In hindsight, Basil knew Nick had had regrets even then.

"Kiffin Rockwell's not really dead," Nick had said.

"Oh, I promise you he is," Basil had replied.

"George Eliot said our dead are never really dead to us until we have forgotten them." Nick had used that condescending tone that academics use to express their contempt for the less educated.

"Who is he?" Basil had replied.

"She." Nick had corrected him. "*She* was an author."

Basil thought about mistaking Stearns for Nick earlier. Caedwallan was living in his head, rent-free.

"What's the plan, sir?" Marty ran a few steps ahead and stopped.

"See if the aircrew needs help with the bags." Basil gave the command without looking at Marty. Rita took his arm, and they strolled toward the terminal.

110

NOT REALLY ALIVE, BUT NOT QUITE DEAD

Saturday, 24 April 2004—12:57 am
Lucy's rental farmhouse, rural Asakan

The fair weather proved to be short-lived. What light had been provided by the moon disappeared behind wind-swept clouds.

Tommie put his hand on Vasily's shoulder. "Sir, why don't you and Nick help yourself to coffee? We'll be right in." He gestured toward the porch where a single yellow bulb glowed.

Vasily tensed. "Secrets?" he asked.

"No." Tommie noted the sharp tone and reminded himself that the man with the gray eyes was a spy. He probably stayed alive by being suspicious. Paranoid or not, he'd just saved Lucy's life. "A lot has gone down. I thought you might want a moment with Nick."

"Of course. Thanks." Vasily's face softened. He gestured toward Nick. "This is a lot to take in." He started for the porch but turned back to face Tommie. "My enemies call me sir." He grabbed Tommie's right hand and pumped it twice. "My friends call me Vasily."

Tommie nodded once. "Mind the loose porch step." He was silent until Vasily and Nick entered the house. When the kitchen light came on, he turned to face Lucy. "I hope that stunt with the safe-deposit box was worth it. I don't know whether to be angry or relieved. You could have been killed. They've got your picture now, you know. Soon it will be out there—everywhere." He swept the air with his hand, then hugged her. "What was in the bank box?"

Lucy looked away and took a half-step back. "Just some personal papers and a draft of a speech about the jellyfish serum," she said. "Why did you give him the serum?" She pointed to the light in the kitchen window. "He's part of the group that killed my parents. He's here to kill me."

"No," Tommie said. "He came here to help you." A wind-driven mist signaled the arrival of another storm front. "It's going to pour buckets any minute. We should head inside."

Lucy ignored his observation and continued. "I found a note in his car from someone named Rita." Lucy wiped droplets of rain and tears from her face.

"Nick knew nothing about the plan to kill your parents," Tommie said, guiding Lucy toward the porch. "His only sin was not intervening on a hunch. Their murders were a turning point for him even before the lung cancer."

"Nick has cancer?" Lucy squeezed her eyes shut. "Damn."

Tommie raised his eyebrows, surprised at her reaction. "No, that's gone." He led her onto the porch. "Look, I don't know what happened when you met on the road, but he cares a lot about you. He told me—."

"No." Lucy backed away and waved him off. "My parents! I can't . . ."

"We'll talk later." Tommie could tell she was still processing Nick's change. "Let's just go inside and figure out an exit plan."

"What's to figure? I thought it was just you, me, and the Rover." Lucy opened the door and they stepped inside. "You know—kick the tires, light the fires, and brief on guard."

Tommie thought about the impending BOLO and Basil's crew out on the Strand. He latched the door against the gathering storm. Through the kitchen doorway, he saw Nick and Vasily, coffee in hand, at the kitchen table, laughing and talking.

Vasily turned his head at the sound of the door closing. His smile faded.

"It's raining," Tommie announced as they entered the kitchen.

Lucy and Nick eyed each other. Vasily caught Tommie's eye and silently mouthed, "Now what?"

Tommie poured two mugs of coffee and handed one to Lucy. He pulled out a chair at the table for her, but she continued to lean against the worn butcher-block countertop. Tommie pulled out a chair for himself and sat at the table with Vasily and Nick.

Tommie explained Nick's transformation to Vasily as best he could. He paused from time to time, hoping Lucy would jump in. She just stared at Nick and said nothing.

Tommie wrapped up his explanation and reached for Vasily's mug. "More coffee?"

"How can this be?" Vasily held out his cup. "I saw this serum kill a man in Dearborn." He looked at Nick and shook his head.

"It appears that it's all about timing," Tommie said, turning to Lucy. "Does that square with your mother's research?"

"Don't ask me." Lucy looked down at the floor. "All I have is a journal with some drawings and scribbles and a copy of a fundraising speech." Her face reddened. "Why don't you ask the lab rat?" She jerked her head toward Nick. "He's the one who gets to come back from the dead. My parents didn't get that option."

"That was my decision," Tommie stood up. "He didn't ask for it."

Lucy remained silent.

Nick sat, head down, clenching his coffee mug.

Tommie liked Nick and Nick had saved Noki's life, but Nick had also made a big deal of showing him the do-not-resuscitate card. In the final analysis, it had been a selfish act of desperation that had made Tommie's decision to give Nick the serum. "Well," said Tommie, considering how to phrase his next statement, "the situation has changed. We need his help."

Lucy slammed her mug onto the counter. "So, you and Nick are partners now?"

Nick looked at Lucy but said nothing.

"You were at my parents' house the morning they were killed. You just left them?"

"I ignored my gut. I should have listened to Vasily."

"We turned around," Vasily said, attempting to share the blame. "But it was too late."

"Why didn't you give me your full name when we met on the road?" Lucy's cross-examination continued.

"I tried, remember? You wouldn't let me."

"You could have come right out and told me that you kill people for a living." Lucy's face was flushed.

Tommie considered intervening but knew that Lucy had to vent before dealing with the more immediate problem of an escape plan. He suspected that Lucy had held something back when she dismissed his question about the contents of the safe-deposit box. He was surprised when she didn't ask for details about Nick's rejuvenation. Her response to one of Vasily's questions reinforced his suspicions that the box contained something she was reluctant to share.

"What were you doing in the woods for so long after our little adventure on the highway?" Vasily asked.

"Call of nature." Lucy started for the doorway. "Speaking of which."

"That's quite the call, nearly twenty minutes—and the backpack?" Vasily kept his eyes on Lucy.

"Privacy and toilet paper," Lucy said.

"You left your backpack in the woods."

"Is the inquisition over?" Lucy shot Vasily a cold stare and headed toward the powder room. "Thanks for the help," she said as she passed Nick.

"You told me you could take care of yourself," Nick said to her retreating figure.

Tommie ignored the tense exchange and began the planning session in earnest. "Five days ago," he said, "it was just Lucy and me. No one knew she was here. Now, Basil has confirmation that Lucy is alive. He has her photo. In a matter of hours, so will every law-enforcement agency."

"Basil is obsessed with the concept of immortality," Vasily said.

"Yeah. Remember the jellyfish globe that Basil keeps on his desk? He'll never quit looking for Lucy and the research notes," Nick said.

Lucy returned, refilled her mug, and leaned against the counter.

"From the looks of that little beach party tonight, we are all in danger," Vasily said. "Schwartz is Basil's rabid bloodhound." Vasily looked at Nick. "Don't forget that Marty shot his partner."

"I went to see her in the hospital," Lucy said. "I sat with her for two hours."

"At St. Martha's in Barringer?" Nick's face became animated. "So did I. Right after . . ." His words caught in his throat. He looked at Lucy and then down at the mug gripped in both hands. "It was—"

"A life-changing experience," Lucy said, completing Nick's thought. She set her cup on the counter and stared at Nick.

"Yeah," Nick said, as he stared at the floor, "a reorienting of priorities."

Tommie was relieved that Lucy was taking part in the conversation.

"It must be terrible to be like that," Lucy said, still staring at Nick. "In a coma. Not really alive, but not quite dead."

"If only she could talk." Vasily joined Lucy at the counter.

"Maybe she can," Tommie said.

111

WHILE THE DEMIGODS HAVE THEIR ADVENTURE

Saturday, 24 April 2004—3:51 a.m.
Northbound on Secondary Road, rural North Carolina

"What are the odds that Blair can survive the serum?" Lucy said, glancing in her rearview mirror. She could just see the headlights of the rental sedan Vasily and Nick were in ten car lengths back. The continuous storms of the past few days and the humid air made for thick fog through which the Rover's pale-yellow headlights carved a cone-shaped path.

"Maybe fifty-fifty, if it's done right." Tommie retrieved a wad of paper towels from the seat and rubbed the condensation from the windshield.

"Only fifty-fifty?" Lucy glanced at Tommie. "But Nick—"

"Nick was dead. Fifty-fifty was better than zero," Tommie said. "It was a hard decision. I had no time to think about it."

Lucy said nothing. She knew she would have made the same choice.

"I don't think Vasily appreciated that it was me who helped Nick and not him," Tommie said.

"They've been partners for a long time. You have to appreciate their special relationship," Lucy said.

"Like your special relationship with Nick?"

"I have no relationship with Nick." Lucy leaned forward, her face almost touching the fogged windshield. "I can't see." She turned the wipers on and then off again, wishing for the modern de-mister and bright lights of Tommie's truck. She had been almost convinced to take his truck until Vasily confirmed her suspicions that a factory-installed GPS, whether switched on or off, could be used to track a car.

"That's not the way Nick told it. It seems you made quite an impression on him while he was fixing your car." Tommie laughed. "He told me he met this girl—well, that was before he knew that girl was you—and . . ."

Lucy could feel Tommie's gaze as he watched for her reaction. She could see him out of the corner of her eye. They had played this game before. He was baiting her and then reading her facial expressions.

"What was it he said? Oh, yeah, you were his someone. That once-in-a-lifetime soulmate." He paused and looked at Lucy. "But then, that was how he felt before the transformation."

"And now?" Lucy bit her lip and she realized she had been sucked in.

"You'll have to ask him yourself. I thought you weren't interested?"

"It's more the fact that I could be dead in twenty-four hours." Lucy looked straight at Tommie. "That fact and also what he is."

"You mean what he used to be."

"I mean the immortality thing as well as his past." Lucy shook her head and checked the mirror. "Before, I could handle the age difference, but this?" The silver sedan had fallen further behind, but she could see it more clearly. The fog was thinning, but the gap between her and Nick seemed wide.

"Think of this life, not the next one." Tommie picked up Lucy's North Carolina atlas and looked at the green spot representing the national forest. "How do you know the Uwharrie?"

"My parents loved the unspoiled setting. We camped there every year until the—" Lucy paused. She couldn't say murders again. "I stayed there after I visited Blair. It's remote, but it's only twenty minutes from Barringer and St. Martha's."

"You and Vasily will be safe there until we get back," Tommie said, nodding.

"Yeah," Lucy said. "I suppose we mere mortals will just have to console each other while the demigods have their adventure."

112

SUIT YOURSELF. I'M JUST THE BABYSITTER.

Saturday, 24 April 2004—5:47 a.m.
Vasily's rental car, Northbound on Secondary Road Near Uwharrie
National Forest, rural North Carolina

"Twenty years we're together and you pick some guy you've known for two days for the most important mission we've ever had." Vasily's eyes never left the road.

"I didn't pick him." Nick searched for some way to lessen the sting. "He just pointed out—"

"Since when do amateurs call the shots?" Vasily made no effort to mask his disappointment.

"He's the closest thing we have to an expert. That's the only reason I gave him the nod." Nick stared at Vasily and tried not to second-guess his decision. In the two decades that they'd been partners, each had saved the other's life too many times to count. Under normal circumstances, Nick would pick Vasily without hesitation. But this was not a normal day or circumstance. On a normal mission, the mark died and stayed dead. Today's target, Blair Underwood, would also die, but then live and, in the process, if the timing was perfect, restore Lucy's life.

"Shit." Vasily pointed to the Rover. "Forty-eight miles per hour, fog or not."

"Relax." Nick gestured toward the east, where the first light of dawn was tinting the sky pink. "We're in no hurry."

"Easy for you to say," Vasily said. "You and your new partner have all the time in the world."

Nick was pitched forward as Vasily braked hard to avoid hitting the Rover as it slowed and veered onto an unmarked trail. The narrow gravel lane was more path than lane and more mud than gravel. They rose steadily, twisting left and right through a mixture of conifer and deciduous trees, until Lucy angled off the trail at a small hand-painted sign:

Primitive Site #22

A short stub led to a clearing about a hundred feet in diameter. The entire clearing, save for a small break in the south, was surrounded by tall white pines, the tops of which rustled and swayed with the breeze. The drizzle had stopped, and the fog thinned to reveal a dull gray ceiling at about a thousand feet. The Rover stopped. Lucy and Tommie climbed out, stretched, and stood next to their vehicle. Lucy pointed toward a break in the trees on the southern edge of the clearing. Nick and Vasily parked and got out of the rental sedan.

"Well. Here we are," Tommie said to the pair as they approached the Rover.

Vasily passed without acknowledgment and headed for the break.

Nick and Tommie followed Lucy to the edge of the clearing. What looked like an opening to another clearing was the rock-encrusted precipice of a sheer cliff. Granite outcroppings, some as high as four feet, formed a broken wall along the grassy edge. Less than ten feet short of the edge was a small fire pit surrounded by stones large enough to sit on.

Lucy walked to the edge where Vasily stood, arms crossed, staring down. "I wouldn't get too close," she said. "The ground is soft, and it's a good forty-foot drop to the first shelf. If you miss that one, it's a sixty-foot drop to the next, and then another hundred to the bottom. Not much other than bushes and a few scrub pines to slow you down."

"Who'd notice?" Vasily's reply was little more than an unintelligible grunt. Lucy shrugged and crossed to the fire pit where Tommie waited. She stared at the collection of wet wood and hugged her shoulders against the chill. "How about a fire?"

"Looks pretty wet." Tommie examined the small pile of kindling left by the last camper. "Do you remember the wilderness course?"

"I have a bag of corn chips in my go bag." Lucy hurried toward the Rover. "You can make a rock burn with those."

"It's nearly six-thirty." Nick glanced from his watch to Tommie. "We better go."

He turned to Vasily. "Do you mind if we take the rental car?"

"Suit yourself. Keys are in the ignition." Vasily glanced at the cliff. "I'm just the babysitter."

"Vasily—" Nick wanted to say something that would make his partner understand.

"I'm more used to the Rover." Tommie grabbed Nick's arm and pulled him away.

"I wish he could understand," Nick said as they walked to the Rover.

"Put yourself in his place," Tommie said in a lowered voice. "First, his partner of twenty years tells him he's dying in six months. Now, you're half his age and you tell him you're immortal. What do you expect?"

"Wait." Lucy grabbed a bag of corn chips from the Rover and closed the door. Then she ran to the rear of the vehicle, opened the cargo door, and retrieved a small, green oilcloth pack. "Reading material," she said, looking back toward Vasily and the fire pit. "Here's the key."

"Let me." Nick reached for the key. "I can drive English."

Lucy withdrew the key until Nick made eye contact. "Be careful." She pulled at a strand of hair. "Don't let a plane fall on you."

"A plane?" Nick edged backward. He slid into the driver's seat and turned the key to "on" without hitting the starter. Nick executed this entire maneuver without averting his gaze from Lucy.

"I'll explain later," Tommie said from the passenger seat. "Start the car."

"Waiting for the glow," Nick said, looking away from Lucy for the first time.

"I'd say you've got the glow. Start the car."

Nick and Lucy exchanged glances as the Rover inched backwards toward the main trail. Lucy gave a final wave and angled toward the fire pit.

Tommie tapped Nick on the shoulder and pointed as Lucy paused and gave a last look over her shoulder. "Chemistry." Tommie nodded toward her retreating figure.

"More like alchemy in this case." Nick put the SUV in first gear and headed to the highway.

113

IF I WERE YOU, I'D ASK FOR A DO-OVER

Saturday, 24 April 2004—7:17 a.m.
St. Martha's Convalescent Center, Barringer, North Carolina

Tommie looked at Nick and then at his watch. It had been less than ten hours since the injection and Nick's physical transformation was complete. His mental faculties were almost normal, but the psychological adjustment could take a couple of go-rounds. Even then, in light of what they were about to undertake, Tommie reasoned that a test of Nick's recall and cognitive abilities was not unreasonable.

"I've lived in Asakan for nearly thirty years," Tommie said. "Noki and I have camped in Uwharrie a few times, but I've never heard of St. Martha's or Barringer."

"Barringer isn't that big, but it's got some history. The town is named for Brigadier General Rufus Barringer, a hero of the national unpleasantries of the early eighteen-sixties." Nick paused and turned to smile at Tommie. "He was born here in rural Cabarrus County."

"What about St. Martha's?" Tommie said, digging. "The buckle of the Bible Belt seems like a strange place for nuns."

"That's the real history," Nick said. "Barringer was wounded at the Battle of Brandy Station. He was especially impressed by a group of nuns he saw giving aid to soldiers on both sides during the height of the engagement. He watched the nuns scurry about in full habit . . ."

Nick went into full professorial mode.

Tommie, satisfied that his friend's mental faculties were adequate to today's task, gazed out the window while Nick explained that Barringer crossed paths with the nuns again during the Bristoe Campaign and while he was a prisoner of war at Fort Delaware. He met Lincoln shortly after his capture in April of 1865 and was impressed by the president's concern for the soon-to-be vanquished Southerners. He was deeply affected by Lincoln's death.

"He was so moved," Nick continued, "that he gave the Little Sisters of Hope land and money to establish a convent and hospital in Cabarrus County." He finished the tale as they turned into the parking lot of St. Martha's. "He was already a war hero. The hospital was just icing on the cake." Nick shut off the Rover and turned to Tommie. "The locals overlooked the fact that he had imported a pack of papists and named the town after him."

"All right then." Tommie looked at Nick and shook his head. "You're on."

They climbed the dozen or so stone steps to a small piazza surrounded by a low wall. The abbey was made up of three structures. Straight ahead was the century-old kirk made of rough-cut gray stone with a large arched wooden door secured by black iron-strap hinges. The roof was steeply pitched and constructed of well-aged standing-seam copper. A narrow bell tower topped by a white cross rose forty feet above the piazza. To the right was the residence hall, and to the left lay the original hospital, now a clinic and convalescent center. Like the abbey, it was constructed entirely of stone, with a steep-pitched roof of new copper.

"I feel like I'm in the old sod." Tommie leaned back to take in the height of the bell tower.

"That's the idea," Nick said, returning the smile of a nun who had exited the chapel and was making her way to the clinic. "Sister." Nick hailed the nun as she passed by. "We were passing through the area and wondered if we might sit with Blair Underwood and offer a few prayers."

"That should be fine." She looked them up and down. "Are you family?"

"Friends," Nick replied, falling into step with the nun's brisk stride. He opened the clinic door for the sister. "I used to work with Blair."

The entry room contained a desk with a large computer monitor, several chairs, and a low table. In the corner was a table containing religious pamphlets and a dozen or so plastic rosaries. On the wall were pictures of the pope, the local bishop, and an older woman in full habit. Tommie assumed she must be the Mother Superior.

"Let me just bring up Blair's visitor log." The nun tapped at the keyboard for a moment. "Over a year and no one." Her smile faded, and she shook her head.

"I will need to see some ID. Sorry." She shrugged. "State requirement."

"Of course." Tommie fished out his driver's license and handed it to her. The sister examined the photo, entered his name in the log, and returned the license.

Nick glanced at Tommie and shook his head. He shuffled through several of the cards in his wallet, selected his grainy community college instructor ID, and handed it to the nun. He noted that her nametag said Sister Ann.

Sister Ann looked first at Nick, then at the ID, and then back to Nick. "I have to say," she said, typing Nick's name in the log. "This picture does not do you justice."

"I was sick that day."

"If it were me, I'd ask for a do-over." She handed him the ID.

"I'm in the process of getting one now." Nick gave her his half-grin.

114

PICTURES OF MATCHSTICK MEN

Saturday, 24 April 2004—7:23 a.m.
Primitive Campsite 22, Uwharrie National Forest, rural North Carolina

Lucy and Vasily swapped wet-weather survival tips as they collected firewood.

"I hope your friend can pull this off." Vasily threw another piece of wood on the fire. "It's a pretty tall order for a restaurateur."

"Tommie's a lot more than that," Lucy said, coughing. The wet wood made more smoke than heat, but at least it looked warm. "He's probably the only person who could do this."

"Well, he sure convinced my ex-partner." Vasily poked at the coals with a small branch.

"Nick thinks he's the second coming."

"Shhh." Vasily put his finger to his lips and stood to look south.

Lucy didn't hear or see anything. The sky was still a seamless gray canopy.

"There." Vasily pointed south.

Lucy heard a choppy vibration, the faint sound of rotors beating, and then the whine of a turbine. Finally, the helicopter, dark blue with a red stripe, popped from the clouds and passed almost overhead before disappearing to the north.

"Do you think they're looking for us?" Lucy hugged the oilcloth folio.

Vasily waited until the last vibration had ceased before speaking. "Probably not." He sat down again next to the fire. "Two thousand feet, one hundred knots, and no course deviation or change in speed." He poked at the smoking fire. "Probably a medevac scud running."

"Scud running?" Lucy said.

"Flying below the clouds instead of using instruments—risky business if the ceiling starts pushing you down." He pulled a flask from his pocket, unscrewed the cap, and passed it to Lucy. "Antifreeze?"

She thought about saying no, but in the interest of stimulating conversation, she put the flask to her lips and had a small sip. It was like drinking gasoline. "Smooth," she said, coughing as she handed it back. "What is it?"

"Johnny Walker Black." Vasily tilted the flask and took a drink.

"I thought it was a fuel additive," Lucy said, smiling.

"I think there is some magic between you and my lost partner," Vasily said.

"Not going there." Lucy kicked at the dirt.

"If it's about your parents—" Vasily tucked the flask back in his pocket. "He didn't—"

"Partly that," she said. "But it's more the same thing that's eating you."

"And what would that be?"

"The gap," Lucy said, jumping to her feet. "Tommie and Nick are immortal, bigger than life. Next to them, we're just pictures of matchstick men."

"Where are you going?" he called after her.

"Nature calls, remember?" She started walking toward the woods. "I'll be back."

115

FROM DEAD TO ALIVE IN A HALF-HOUR. NOT BAD

Saturday, 24 April 2004—7:27 a.m.
St. Martha's Convalescent Center, Barringer, North Carolina

Nick picked up two of the plastic rosaries from the table. "May we?" he asked Sister Ann.

"Of course." She smiled and tilted her head toward the hallway. "Follow me."

They passed a half dozen patient rooms. The polished concrete floor, stone accents, and religious pictures on the wall reminded Nick of St. Joseph's in Milwaukee. Most doors were open; the occupants read, watched television, or chatted with the staff. Sister Ann stopped at the end of the hall, in front of the only closed door.

"Stay as long as you like." She opened the door and ushered them in. "You're the first visitors since her friend from New Hampshire over a year ago." She closed the door. Tommie walked to the bedside and began pushing buttons on the various monitoring devices attached to Blair.

Nick was lost in the sound of the retreating nun's footsteps. A soft hiss turned his attention to Blair. Nick walked around the bed and stood opposite Tommie.

"Automatic air mattress," Tommie said. "Prevents pressure ulcers."

He rummaged through the drawer on the side table. "Excellent." He held up a syringe in a labeled wrapper:

20cc / 22 ga-1 inch

Blair looked pretty much the same as she had at the Spencer home the day Marty put a bullet in her head. Her hair was still honey-blond, but her skin was pale, and she looked thin—not emaciated, but thin. A bag of intravenous fluid hung from a post at the head of the bed. Nick read the label on the bag.

1000ml NS/10KCl

The line ran from the IV bag to a box with an LED readout; from there it ran under the blanket near Blair's left shoulder. The screen read: 40ml/hr.

"She already has a PICC line," Tommie said.

"What's that?"

"It stands for peripherally inserted central catheter." Tommie grinned. "It means I won't have to stick her in the heart like I did you."

"You stuck me in the heart?" Nick's eyes widened. The cuff on Blair's left arm made a whooshing sound as it filled with air. Nick traced the tube to a large monitor by the bed with a variety of readouts. The monitor clicked several times as the cuff slowly deflated and displayed a new set of numbers.

BP 102/68

"Push the mute button on that monitor and push the interval button next to the BP readout until it changes from thirty minutes to two hours," Tommie instructed.

A plastic tube covered the tip of Blair's left index finger. A wire ran from the tube to the side of the large monitor.

"Pulse oximetry." Tommie pointed to the monitor. "See the two numbers in the lower left?"

O2 SAT 98%

Pulse 68

"These?" Nick said, touching the numbers on the screen.

"They're going to tank once we get started." Tommie removed a small brown vial from the pack he wore around his waist. "Tap that glowing green button marked *mute*."

Nick pushed the button, and the color changed to red.

"It doesn't like it when you silence the alarm," Tommie said.

"How do you know all this?" Nick had taken the Agency's field medic training, but this was way above his skill level.

"Internal Medicine was my profession." Tommie said. "Way before all these gizmos, but I still keep up my reading." He silenced yet another instrument where a sine wave snaked up and down in response to Blair's inspirations and expirations. The machine updated her per-minute rate with each breath and displayed it below the waveform.

Respiratory Rate

12—14—12—12

"One more to go." Tommie nodded toward the cardiac monitor where the QRS—a multispiked wave, indicating cardiac electrical activity—danced across the screen, only to be replaced by another just like it. Below the image, the monitor flashed:

Normal Sinus Rhythm

Rate 68

"Hit the mute button for that, and we're ready to start." Tommie removed the wax-covered cork from the vial and drew the contents into the syringe. He held the syringe needle up, pushed the plunger until a few drops exited the needle, tapped the side, and evacuated a few more drops. "Air bubbles." He grinned at Nick. "Bad medicine."

Nick muted the cardiac monitor. He felt bad about hurting Vasily's feelings, but the last few minutes left no doubt that he had made the right decision.

"Now, the hard part." Tommie lifted Blair's head and removed the pillow. "I'll do this." He lifted the pillow and held out the capped syringe to Nick. "When I tell you to push, be quick about it."

"No." Nick thought about Vasily begging him to go back to the Spencer home. "I'm part of the reason she's here. I'll do it."

"Okay." Tommie handed him the pillow.

"Are you sure we have to do this?" Nick squeezed the pillow.

"Unless you want her to die and stay dead."

"Wait." Nick looked down at Blair. "Do you think it's right?"

"Right?" Tommie asked.

"To do it without her permission?" Nick looked at Tommie. "She may not want to live forever."

"I didn't ask you."

"You didn't have to kill me," Nick said. "I was already dead."

"And essentially, so is she." Tommie glanced at Blair. "Fed through a tube, all these monitors, trapped in that bed for the rest of her existence. She deserves a chance for a normal life, and so does Lucy."

"Okay, but we don't tell her about the rebirths."

"Agreed." Tommie eyed the door. "We'd better get on with this before someone pays us a visit." He punched a button on the cardiac monitor. A new display lit up.

Code Time 00:00:01

Nick took a last look at Blair and put the pillow over her face. Nothing. In spite of Blair's condition, he had somehow expected a writhing body, flailing limbs, and fingers clawing at his arms. This wasn't at all like the last time.

The last time? Nick struggled to remember.

Had I done this before?

Yes, he recalled, six months after the Spencer murders. A banker. He pulled the information from someplace deep and dark. In Cape

Town, the man was a pedophile, a large corpulent hulk of a man who trafficked in kidnapped children. If anyone deserved to die—at least that's what Basil had told him. Nick had suffocated the man with his two-hundred-dollar pillow while his wife slept in the next room. The pervert had fought for his life, his nails plowing bloody furrows in Nick's arms. But in the end, he had died, choking to death on his vomit.

Later, Nick had discovered the truth. The man was not a child-slaver. He was just a banker who had developed a conscience and refused to finance a weapons deal for one of Basil's clients. But the dossier had been so damning. All of the dossiers over the years had been damning. Nick had begun digging. How many targets had been lies? A lot, it turned out—most, actually. A few months later, Nick had received his death sentence.

It's just data—I'm not that person anymore.

He pushed the information back to the dark place where it was stored and relaxed his hands.

"Keep the pillow tight on her face." Tommie's voice jarred him back to the present.

"I can't do this." Nick took his hands off the pillow. "It's not who I am now. I can't kill her."

"No, you're right, you can't kill her. She's already dead." Tommie placed his hands over Nick's and pressed down. "Now push. You can have your existential crisis later."

Nick pushed down hard, bringing both sides of the pillow into contact with the bed. One by one, their alarms silenced, the monitors began to click in a futile attempt to summon assistance. Nick glanced at the read-outs:

Code Timer: 00:05:23

Respiratory Rate 0/0/0/0

Pulse Ox 81%

Sinus Tachycardia / Rate 132

B.P. 100/66

He could feel himself starting to sweat in spite of the air conditioning. "Those monitors—they can't see this at the desk, can they?" Nick relaxed the pressure on the pillow.

"No. The monitors were not hooked up, and the telemetry antennae were still in boxes at the end of the hall." Tommie scanned the monitors. "Stay focused." He nodded toward the pillow.

Nick increased the pressure. The monitors played drumbeats in varying tempos.

Code Timer: 00:10:03
Respiratory Rate 0/0/0/0
Pulse Ox 61%
Ventricular Tachycardia / Rate 182
B.P. 52/28

Nick looked down at Blair's unmoving limbs. Her skin was pale, her nail beds blue. The monitors clucked like angry chickens. He kept pressing for what seemed like hours.

"Now?" Nick said.

Tommie shook his head.

"She's dying," Nick said, nodding toward Blair's dusky extremities. "So, she can live."

Code Timer: 00:15:39
Respiratory Rate 0/0/0/0
Pulse Ox 34%
Ventricular Fibrillation / Rate ???
B.P. 0/0

"For God's sake." Nick removed one hand from the pillow and gestured toward the chattering monitors.

"Soon," Tommie said, looking at the pillow.

Nick put both hands on the pillow and pushed hard. He would not ask again.

Code Timer: 00:21:55
Respiratory Rate 0/0/0/0
Pulse Ox 22%
Asystole / Rate 00
B.P. 0/0

"Now." Tommie took the pillow from Nick's hands and tossed it onto a nearby chair. He uncapped the syringe, stuck the needle into a port on the IV line, and depressed the plunger.

"Thumb that IV Rate up to 1000 ml/hr.," Tommie instructed.

Nick increased the IV rate and stepped back from the bed.

"Start compressions," Tommie said.

"How fast?" Nick stepped back to Blair's side.

"'1812 Overture.'"

Nick began pumping Blair's chest at a rate of one-hundred compressions per minute. He continued for several minutes until Blair gave a forceful gasp and began a rhythmic jerking of her arms and legs. Nick jumped back from the bed and stared at the monitors.

Code Timer: 24:32:01
Respiratory Rate 20
Pulse Ox 85%
Sinus Tachycardia / Rate 122
B.P. 68/40

Blair's seizures stopped. Her skin and nail beds were pink. She gave an occasional soft moan.

"She's young," Tommie said. "This won't take long. "She'll be awake and minimally sentient before long."

Blair's eyes opened. Tommie moved his hand back and forth in front of her face. She blinked but did not track.

"How long until she—

"Thinks and talks?" Tommie capped the needle and put the syringe in his pocket. Blair's eyes darted from side to side, and she pulled at the sheets with her hands. Tommie tapped the monitor screen. "From dead to alive in a half-hour. Not bad."

Code Monitor 00:29:16
Respiratory Rate 16
Pulse Ox 99%
Normal Sinus Rhythm / Rate 68
B.P. 92/64

"We better get busy." Tommie reset the code monitor to zero and turned it off. "Now we turn all the alarms back on, and all hell, pardon the expression, breaks loose. Even though her vitals are normal, they're all going to begin to chime. Are you ready?"

"Do it." Nick pulled the pair of rosary beads from his pocket. He grasped one set of beads in his left hand and gave the other to Tommie.

"You're on in, three, two, one—" Tommie smiled, pointed at Nick and began punching buttons. The various alarms began chirping, beeping, and making gong-like tones. Blair raised her head from the pillow and lowered it again.

"Sister! It's a miracle." Nick ran into the hall and toward the desk clutching the beads. Sister Ann, reacting to the shouts, bells, and whistles, stopped just short of a collision. "We were praying." Nick did his best to appear breathless. "She opened her eyes, and all the alarms went off." He and Tommie started down the hall. "Sister," he called to the retreating figure. "Can we use your phone to call home? We have no cell service." Nick knew that even with Basil's connections, the hardline would buy several hours of anonymity.

"Main desk. Line one and dial nine for outside." Sister Ann gestured toward the entrance and dashed into Blair's room.

Nick waited until the entire staff was either in Blair's room or standing outside her door, then he punched in the secure sat phone number Bel Castro had given him what seemed like a lifetime ago.

"Don." Nick waited a moment while Bel Castro fired off a half-dozen questions. "Lucy or Chloe—your niece, is fine." He ignored another barrage of queries. "We're going to get her now. No worries. She's with Vasily at a secure location."

"You're calling from St. Martha's." Bel Castro's speech was still so rapid as to be almost unintelligible. "Is Blair . . .? Did Marty?"

"Right now, just listen. Basil's jellyfish pipe dream is real. Blair is back in the land of the living. She'll be communicating soon," Nick explained to an obviously incredulous Bel Castro. "And you know what that means."

"She can clear Chloe." Bel Castro used Lucy's given name. "And you and Vasily can come back to the Agency."

"Well," Nick said, examining his reflection in the computer monitor. "You're half right. Marty and his crew, and by now, the old man himself, are in the area."

"What do you need?" Bel Castro slowed down.

"Protection for Blair."

"One minute," Don said and stopped talking. Nick could hear clicking in the background and then muffled speech as Bel Castro spoke with someone on another phone.

Nick looked at his watch. "Don?" He was eager to get away before he had to start answering questions for Sister Ann.

"Okay. I'm back," Don said. "Barringer has a five-person police force. Three of them are on their way." Nick could hear a siren approaching. A half-dozen State Police and County guys will be there in less than fifteen minutes to cordon off the clinic. Nobody in. Nobody out."

"Great, we're going to collect Lucy and Vasily."

"We?" Bel Castro seemed confused.

"Long story," Nick said, looking at Tommie. "I'll call you in an hour."

Nick and Tommie met the Barringer Police on the Piazza. "We're—" Nick started to explain.

"We know." The sergeant waved him off. "We've got it."

Additional sirens wailed in the distance as they pulled onto the road to Uwharrie. Nick turned to Tommie as a state police cruiser, blue lights blinking, flashed by. "It's just a matter of time now," he said.

"When Blair tells her story, Marty and Basil will be toast, and Lucy will have her life back."

"And you?" Tommie said.

"I can't go back to my old life," Nick said.

"Would you want to?" Tommie studied his expression.

Nick was silent. "I'd like to go back to my *other* old life," he said. "You know, the one with possibilities. The path not taken, and all that."

"You will find that you have plenty of time to figure that out," Tommie said. "Right now, let's give Lucy and your partner the good news."

116

NOW WHAT?

Saturday, 24 April 2004—11:37 am
Primitive Campsite 22
Uwharrie National Forest, rural North Carolina

"Now remember," Tommie said as they pulled into the clearing. "You're his best friend. He's glad you're alive."

Nick shut off the Rover.

Tommie grabbed Nick's arm before he could get out. "But you are now a constant reminder of his mortality. That's why I never tell anyone." Tommie released his grip and opened the door. "That, and I have no desire to become some government science-fair project."

Lucy and Vasily were not in the clearing. "Maybe a bathroom break?" Nick said.

Nick and Tommie made their way across the clearing. Nick noticed a few embers glowed in the fire pit. The air was still chilly, but the sun was streaming through broken clouds. A fresh breeze blew, and the trees whispered to one another in that gentle language that only pines can speak. It had the makings of a pretty good day. He was anxious to spread the day's good news and make amends to his partner.

"Lucy! Vasily!" Nick called out as they walked toward the fire and the cliff. The only answer to Nick's call was the wind in the pines.

"They'll be along," Tommie said as they admired the forty-mile view from the cliff.

"Hands where we can see them, girls." The voice came from behind them. "Turn around, slow-like."

"Marty." Nick turned.

Lucy and Vasily walked in front. Basil and Marty followed with pistols drawn. Rita trailed behind, hugging Lucy's canvas folio in her left arm. Her right hand was stuffed in her pocket. Basil held his gun in his left hand. A cast was on his right.

"You two snakes are tough to kill." Marty shifted his gaze from Nick to Tommie. "But I have a solution." He pushed Vasily aside and moved his pistol back and forth between Nick and Tommie. "I'll treat you like any other snake." He pointed his gun at Tommie's face. "A headshot followed by a damn big rock."

"You have to forgive Marty." Basil gestured for his henchman to lower his weapon. "The events of the past few days have left him, well, somewhat frustrated. But we're all together at last. Speaking of which—I do want you all where I can see you." Basil pushed Lucy forward. "Vasily, you and the young lady stand over there." He motioned with his pistol toward the rocky cliff. "Vasily, stand on one of those rocks. Yes, that's right. The tall one." He looked at Tommie and smiled. "And do stand near the back. You, Lucy or Chloe, whatever you call yourself. It's so hard to keep track." He motioned again with his pistol. "Stand on the ground there in front of him."

"How did you find us?" Nick asked.

"Sorry, Nick," Vasily said. "My fault. Apparently, the rental company had just installed theft recovery trackers in their newest cars."

"Yeah," Marty said. "Tracked you from a helicopter. Our car's just down the road."

"Shut up, Marty," Basil said. "But seriously, Nick, you look fantastic." He turned to Tommie and shook his head. "But you, Brownfeather, look well past your expiration date. When do you turn into a handsome young brave again?"

"And you, Rita, you're with these two?" Nick asked.

"You know why, Nick."

"I could talk all day," Basil said, "But Mother Russia beckons, and we have a plane waiting. We have the papers we need, but it seems that you and the happy warrior have some serum. I'll have that, and then we'll be on our way."

Tommie pulled a brown vial from his waist pack.

"I read the brief," Basil said. "For some reason, it requires the cusp of death for this shit to work." He pointed the gun at Lucy. "Is that true?"

"Yes," Nick said. "You've got the serum and the papers, now let us go."

"Sorry, Nick. But I need proof." Basil fired twice, hitting Lucy in the chest and abdomen. She fell without speaking and lay motionless on the ground. "Show me."

Nick and Tommie ran to Lucy. Vasily started to step down from the rock. Basil nodded to Marty, who fired twice. Vasily fell over the cliff. Nick could hear him striking objects as he fell. There was the muffled thud of Vasily's body landing on the shelf forty feet below, followed by the sound of more branches cracking and rocks falling.

Tommie pulled a syringe from his waist pack. He drew up the contents of the vial, turned Lucy's neck to the left, and palpated landmarks. He stuck the needle where the internal jugular should be and depressed the plunger. He rolled Lucy onto her back and began cardiac compressions. Basil and Rita moved closer. With his pistol, Marty motioned to Nick to move away from Lucy. Two minutes later, Tommie stopped compressions and put his ear to Lucy's chest.

Nick saw the trace of a smile on his lips. Lucy gasped, had thirty seconds of tonic-clonic seizure activities, and then moaned softly.

"Let me see her wounds." Basil pressed his pistol against Tommie's temple. Lucy's gunshot wounds were no longer bleeding but looked like raw meat. One of the pistol rounds was lying on the wound surface. The other had fallen to the dirt.

"Incredible." Basil lowered his weapon. "As advertised." He looked at Tommie and raised the gun again. "The serum," he ordered.

Tommie reached into the pack and produced a single vial. "This is the last of it."

"Shit," Basil said. "You're lying."

Tommie took the pack off and turned it inside out. A syringe fell to the ground. "See for yourself." Tommie pointed to the pack and its contents. "I had a few vials of the serum, but no way or desire to make more. The formula used by the shaman died with him. I know it's from the jellyfish, but I have no idea how to make it."

"That's okay," Basil said. "One will do for now." He turned to Nick. "Do you want to come with me, like old times? You can even bring your new squeeze."

"I'd rather die," Nick said. "Permanently," he added.

"Your choice." Basil turned to Marty. "Take these two into the woods, shoot them between the eyes, then pound their heads into hamburger."

"And the girl?" Marty's voice sounded hungry.

"Bring her along." Basil shrugged.

"For what?" Rita's voice had a sharp edge.

"For Marty." Basil grinned at Nick. "A diversion."

Nick thought of Lucy at the mercy of Marty. He had to think fast. Something in Rita's tone gave him an idea.

"Who gets the remaining serum?" He looked at Rita. The expression on her face told him he was mining the right vein.

"That's not your concern," Basil answered. "Take them, Marty."

"No. Wait," Rita said. "Who *does* get this vial?"

"I do, of course," Basil said. "I'm the oldest. I need it now. You can wait until we make more serum."

"This batch was three hundred years old," Nick said, looking at Rita. "What if it can't be duplicated?" Nick was counting on Basil's ego and arrogance to help him out.

"Yes." Rita's right hand was back in her pocket. "What then?"

"Well, then you're shit out of luck." Basil turned toward Rita but kept his gun pointed at Nick. "Now, shut up and—"

Rita's right hand, now out of her pocket held the Walther PPK Nick had given her for personal protection. It was pointed at Basil's forehead. Nick prayed the safety was off.

"No, not the head." Basil brought his weapon around and fired. The pistol was an unfamiliar weight in his left hand. His premature shot went wide, missing its mark.

Rita's did not. Blood, bone, and gray matter spattered Marty. Basil sank to his knees, fell forward, and dropped.

"Think about it, Marty," Rita said. Before Marty could react, Rita had rotated and fixed her pistol on him. "Basil's gone. You killed your wife, your mother-in-law, and your dog."

Nick took a step toward Basil's gun.

"Forget it, Nick," she said. "If I don't shoot you, dumbass here will." She put her foot on Basil's hand, which still gripped his pistol. "Marty," she continued. "I'm taking over for Basil. Carson is onboard with the idea. You can do for me what you did for Basil, except I won't treat you like shit if you do your job." She paused for him to think about it. "Well?"

Marty nodded, wiped Basil's blood and brain tissue from his face, and put his pistol back in his shoulder holster.

"Nick." Rita picked up the brown bottle. "Do you want to go along on this ride? I think I'll be turning thirty in a few days."

Nick said nothing but glanced at Lucy.

"Is that your type now?" Rita said.

"I think maybe that was always my type."

"I see," Rita said. "More than your age has changed. You're not the same guy."

"And you're definitely not the same girl." Nick tilted his head toward Basil's crumpled form.

She picked up Basil's gun and threw it over the cliff. She tossed her head. Her long red hair spilled across her shoulders. "I'll need the keys to that rental car. I have a plane to catch."

"They're in it," Nick said.

"They better be." Rita made her left hand into the shape of a gun and pointed her finger at Nick. "Until next time then." Her finger recoiled. "Is there any chance that saving your life could buy me a couple of hours?"

Nick nodded. Eyeing Marty, "Do you know what you've got there?" Marty sat on a rock, unholstering, twirling, and then reholstering his weapon.

"Definitely," Rita said. "Heel." She pointed to a spot near her leg. Marty flashed Nick a rude gesture and fell in step beside her. "Last chance," she said, looking over her shoulder.

Nick shook his head.

"Your loss," Rita said.

Nick hurried to where Tommie knelt beside Lucy. "How is she?" Lucy lay flat and motionless, but her eyes were open. When she saw Nick, she gave a weak smile.

Tommie nodded at Nick. "Vasily?" Tommie said, looking toward the precipice.

Nick walked to the edge of the cliff and looked down. He could visualize about half of the second ledge but could not see Vasily. He had no idea if his partner was on the ledge or had fallen through the dense brush another hundred feet down. The near-vertical face and lack of objects to hold onto made it impossible for Nick to descend.

"Vasily," Nick called out. The chasm echoed his partner's name, each reply quieter and more distant than the last. Nick turned from the cliff, punched in Bel Castro's number, and put the phone to his ear. He watched Marty and Rita's shrinking forms cross the field and vanish into the woods. Car doors slammed; an engine started and the sound of tires crunching on gravel faded to nothing as the last vestige of Nick's old life picked its way down the rocky mountain lane.

Now what?

117

SORRY, BUT I NEED TO THINK

Saturday, 24 April 2004—7:28 p.m.
Primitive campsite
Uwharrie National Forest, Rural North Carolina

Lucy affected a complete recovery from her gunshot wound in a little less than four hours. She stood with Nick by the cliffs while he stared at the horizon, waiting for the search team to arrive. It was well after dark when Nick felt rather than heard the beating rotors of the approaching rescue helicopter.

Two members of a Coast Guard SAR team, the search and rescue unit sent by the Agency, secured lines to the boulders and rappelled as far as the first ledge while the helo hovered just south of the meadow, its searchlight playing up and down the cliffs.

"It's Vasily," Lucy said, taking Nick's hand. "He's the Spetsnaz superman. If anyone can survive . . ." One of the searchers appeared at the grassy lip of the cliff.

"There's no one on the ledge." He looked at Nick. "There was some blood on the rocks, and the brush looks like someone went over. We're going to drop down to the next ledge. It's going to take some time."

"I should be down there," Nick said. "We're partners."

"Let's get some coffee." Lucy pulled him away from the edge.

Nick went willingly, not for the coffee, but for the alone time with Lucy. When they arrived at the car, Lucy pulled him past the cooler with the sandwiches and drinks and into the woods.

She turned toward him and took his hand.

"What happens to us now?" The grip on his hand tightened.

"What do you want to happen?" He pulled her closer.

"I'm cold." She dodged the question but looked up at him, eyes wide, and lips slightly parted.

Nick put his arms around her and kissed her, half expecting one of her coy push-aways and a slap. Instead, she returned the kiss and pressed against him. Nick pulled her closer and moved his arms to the small of her back.

"They're coming up." Tommie pushed through the brush, stopping short when he saw them. "Sorry, I just thought . . . anyway." He backed away. "They're coming up." He turned and hustled away through the brush.

Lucy's smile faded almost as quickly as it had appeared.

"I should . . ." Nick wanted to check on Vasily but was afraid to let the moment go.

"Go on." Lucy pressed a finger to his lips, gave him a quick peck on the cheek and disappeared into the woods.

Nick made his way to the cliffs where two sailors were showing Tommie an article of clothing.

"Is this Mr. Konovalov's jacket, sir?" The look on the younger man's face told Nick he already knew the answer. The jacket was shredded and covered in blood.

Nick gave a single nod.

"We found it near the lower ledge." The sailor looked away while he talked. Nick could tell there was more.

"No body?" Nick wasn't sure he wanted an answer.

"No, sir. But it's a long drop, and . . ." The sailor paused and looked at Tommie.

"And?"

"Nothing sir, we'll keep searching."

Nick nodded. The two searchers hooked up their lines and disappeared over the edge.

"Buy you a drink?" Tommie asked.

They crossed the field to where several members of the search team and Lucy stood talking by the cooler.

"I need to leave for Red Lake ASAP," Tommie said. "Your buddy Bel Castro pulled some strings and got me on a red eye out of Raleigh-Durham at eleven thirty tonight. I just need a ride to the nearest rental—

"We'll drive you." Lucy interjected.

"I'll be fine." Tommie glanced from Lucy to Nick. "Besides, you two have some unfinished business to attend to."

"No." Lucy glanced from Tommie to Nick and back. "I—we—insist."

11:53 p.m.

"Northwest flight 1480 to Minneapolis–Saint Paul. Gate closing in fifteen minutes," the disembodied airport voice proclaimed.

"That's me." Tommie stood up. "I'd better go. I have to clear security."

"I hate goodbyes," Lucy said. "Even short ones." She stood and gave Tommie a quick hug. "I'll finish my coffee while Nick walks you to security."

They passed the five-minute walk without speaking.

"I wonder about Rita and Marty." Nick broke the awkward silence. "How long will it be until one of the Odd Couple kills the other."

Tommie grinned, dropped his bag, and shook Nick's hand.

"I wouldn't go," Tommie said, picking up his bag. "But Joe's not well. I want to see him one last time, and I want to be at the reservation when—you know—when *it* happens."

Nick walked with him to the security entrance. "Go," Nick said. "You'll miss your flight."

"I'll call you in a couple of weeks," Tommie said.

Nick watched his friend clear security and stop to put on his belt and shoes. Tommie picked up his bag, gave a final wave, and disappeared around a corner, just as Vasily had. A wave of depression swept over him. Nick didn't feel immortal. All around him, relatives and friends hugged or shook hands with arriving or departing passengers.

Nick Caedwallan had ceased to exist when Marty Schwartz ran him down outside a café in Asakan, North Carolina.

He had no friends; no one knew him, not even Lucy, but he had time to change that, plenty of time. He half-walked, half-jogged back to the restaurant.

Nick found a half-filled coffee cup and partially eaten scone, but no Lucy.

He was about to sit when a frowning waitress approached.

"She's gone," the waitress said.

"Gone?"

"She said to give you this." The waitress pulled a folded napkin from her apron pocket and handed it to Nick.

Nick unfolded the napkin and read the short sentence.

Sorry, but I need to think.

EPILOGUE

Monday, 03 January 2005—4:52 p.m.
Westbound on Highway 160, Piedra, Colorado

Nick cursed his impulsiveness as he double-clutched the ancient SUV and shifted down to second gear. The combination of the 3/1 grade and eighty-four-hundred-foot altitude had reduced the forward progress of the normally aspirated diesel to little more than walking speed. His lecture at the community college was at seven thirty. He had promised to meet Tommie in Durango for dinner at six. At this rate, it would be close. The Rover crawled past the green road sign:

Durango 17 mi

Snow pattered against the windshield but did not stick. There were two reasons for this: the heater defroster was minimally functional and these were not the wet, sticky giant snowflakes of the East Coast. These were the gritty, sand-like flakes that formed the powder prized by the skiers who flocked to the Rockies. The Rover had been not so much an impulse purchase as an attempt to channel Lucy. Nick had given his Lotus to Noki and spent weeks looking for a replacement. One sleepless morning at 4:00 a.m., he punched up Coys auction house, and there it was, not quite Lucy's ex-SAS Land Rover, but it was damn close, a 1969

Series IIA 88 right-hand drive French blue diesel. He had called the London-based auction house, secured a proxy bidder, and told them to spend what it took to win the vehicle. Nine thousand three hundred pounds and three weeks later, Nick took delivery of the car at the Port of Norfolk, Virginia, and drove it three thousand miles cross-country to his new teaching job in Colorado, all the while casting forlorn glances at the empty passenger seat. The appointment was courtesy of Don Bel Castro. Thanks to Don's Agency contacts, Nick had the contents of his bank accounts, a new name, and a freshly minted PhD. True, his last name was now that of another, albeit more benign Welsh Catholic saint, Llewellyn, but at least his first name was still Nicholas. Don had used his CIA connections to get Nick the new doctorate from his alma mater, Leicester University. The honor had to be of the distance-learning, research type to preserve Nick's cover, but it was still a PhD, and best of all, it was in ancient history and archaeology.

There had been no sign of Lucy or Vasily since that day in the Uwharrie National Forest.

The bucking of the Rover brought Nick back to the present. He tried to downshift, but the unsynchronized first gear refused to cooperate. The 88 gave a final lurch and stalled. Nick turned the key off and counted to twenty while horns sounded behind him. The engine started on the first try. Nick slipped the transmission into first and pulled off the road to allow the three cars behind him to pass before continuing.

Nick pulled into the restaurant parking lot at 5:59. He parked next to a dark gray Chevy Suburban and ran inside, nearly colliding with a dark-haired man in a leather jacket standing just inside the door.

"Sorry." Nick sidestepped and stood peering into the dining room.

"Nick." The man he had nearly knocked to the floor called his name. The voice was familiar, but—Nick turned to face him.

The voice was Tommie's, but it was filled with an infectious vigor and enthusiasm. Tommie had called numerous times over the last eight months, mostly to inquire if Nick had heard from Lucy or to give news of Noki and the Lotus. Last week, the call had been different. "Joe passed."

"I'm sorry."

"Don't be, he was ready to go," Tommie said. "He was surrounded by friends who gave him a hell of a send-off." Tommie continued, telling Nick that eight months on the reservation had given him a lot of time to think. "I thought I might fly into Denver, rent a car, and drive down." He said he had come up with an idea he wanted to discuss with Nick.

"Let me guess—a peanut butter and jellyfish sandwich franchise."

"Just as intriguing, but more dangerous."

"Come to my lecture in Durango," Nick suggested. "I have a theory of what may have happened to the Mesa Verde Indians."

"I've never had anyone I could share the past with." Tommie laughed. "I'll listen to your lecture, then I'll tell you what really happened to those cliff dwellers."

Seeing him here, in person, "Look at you" was all Nick could manage. He knew it was Tommie, but only because he knew it was Tommie. Had his own transformation been this striking?

The smiling figure before him returned his gaze without speaking. Shiny, coal-black hair poured over his ears and shirt collar. His eyes were dark brown and clear, his face smooth and unlined. The battered leather jacket, untucked plaid flannel shirt, gray woolen sweater, faded jeans, and black Doc Martens with bumblebee laces were an update of classic Tommie Whitefeather, but the change was overwhelming.

"Was I this . . ."

"Yes," Tommie said, guiding him to a table. "But you were asleep while we stared at you."

Dinner was pizza and beer. Nick watched the clock to be sure he would make it to the lecture on time.

"Do you think Lucy had more research notes?" Nick said.

"I suspect she did."

"What did she do with them?"

"I have a pretty good idea."

"Aren't you concerned?" Nick asked.

"She called me last week."

"And you didn't call me?" Nick felt slightly betrayed.

"She made me promise not to."

"Where is she?"

"I don't know," Tommie said. "She told me she'd be in touch."

Nick was crushed. He'd always thought that Lucy was out there, "doing her best thinking when she drove," and would show up on his doorstep any day. Nick thought about their encounter in the woods. Had it been just another "mercy" kiss?

Nick paid for dinner, and they walked outside. The snow was accumulating at a prodigious rate; an icy gust blew Nick backward a step. The tiny crystals felt like wind-driven razors. The display on the bank next door flashed the time and temperature.

Temp 19 F

Time 7:03 p.m.

Tommie retrieved a key fob from his pocket, pushed a button. And the shiny gray Chevrolet Suburban started up.

"Nice ride." Tommie nodded toward the Rover. "Channeling your inner Lucy?"

"It was a mistake," Nick said, deflecting Tommie's question about the Rover. "On a more positive note, what's this venture you have in mind for us?" Nick searched for a change of subject.

"Let's talk after the lecture." Tommie gestured toward the bank display. "You're short on time."

"Okay." Nick noticed that Tommie's Suburban had already cleared the windshield. "Should I ride with you?"

"I'll meet you there." Tommie looked away. "I have a quick errand to run."

The weather and road conditions worsened. Nick pulled over for the third time to rub at the inside of the windshield with his gloved hand. He was about to pull back onto the highway when his cellphone rang. He noted the caller ID:

Bel Castro

The snow was piling up on the Rover's hood. The hard tatting against the windshield had given way to a soft rustling as the wind arranged the snow in hillocks and valleys on the road. The phone chimed a second time. Nick considered letting the phone go to voice mail but decided that Bel Castro's calls, while not rare, were infrequent enough that the content might be important. He slipped off his glove to take the call.

"Don," Nick said, striving to be upbeat. "What's happening?"

"Just called to say *bon chance* before the big event." The hard edge in Bel Castro's voice made it clear that there was much more.

"So, let's have it."

"Have what?" Bel Castro's feigned ignorance was thin.

"You didn't call to wish me luck."

"Harsh," Don said, "but there have been a few developments in Belarus you need to know about."

"I'm out of the Agency."

"One is in the Agency for life." Don hesitated, then chuckled. "Which for you is—anyway, there are two items of importance. Your friend Marty is dead—professional hit, garroted at a whorehouse in Minsk. No suspects."

"And?" Nick looked at his watch; he needed to get going. The wipers were icing up, and his breath was freezing on the windshield.

"Rita's in-country, or at least that's what the facial recognition software tells us."

"Have you seen the pictures?" Nick knew where this was going.

"Looking at them now." Bel Castro said. "New name, Belarusian passport. It's her but . . ."

"I know, she doesn't look a day over thirty." Nick finished the sentence.

"So at least we know who got the last vial, but that's not why I called."

"I'm running late, Don." Nick used an ice scraper to clear the inside of the window.

"Did Lucy hold back any of Karen's research material?"

"Possibly, probably." Nick remembered Lucy's evasive answers when questioned about her trip to the woods and her missing backpack. "Why?"

Don went on to explain that Rita's image had also turned up on the security camera at the Almost a Bank, where the Spencers had their safety deposit box. Rita and two robust acquaintances had demanded to see the Spencer box. When the bank manager threatened to call the local authorities, they left. That night, however, the bank was the site of a very stealthy break-in. The security cameras were disabled, and the safety deposit vault room breached. "And if they didn't find what they wanted there . . ."

"You need me to find her." Nick said.

"You're highly motivated," Don said.

"Okay, I'm in. But I need to go now." Nick watched his breath frost the windshield.

"Sure," Bel Castro said. "But there's one last thing."

"Jesus Christ, Don," Nick said. "I'm freezing to death, and I'm late."

"It's Blair." He sighed. "Something's happened. She won't say what—only that she talks to you, or she goes looking for answers."

"Put her off for a couple of days," Nick said.

"Done. We'll talk tomorrow." The display went blank.

Nick pulled back onto the road. By directing the Rover's meager heat output to the windscreen and freezing his feet, Nick was able to maintain an ice-free area the size of a dinner plate directly in front of his face.

He had reached the access road to the community college when he spotted the ice-covered vehicle by the road. Nick rubbed at the mostly clear spot in his windshield. It was a Land Rover, 88. Its two tiny taillights blinked like dying pink fireflies. A small cloud of condensation billowed from its tailpipe.

Nick parked behind the idling Rover and read the bumper sticker:

RELAX, I'M AN ANTHROPOLOGIST

Made in the USA
Monee, IL
06 December 2023

48420863R00277